A Machen Omnibus

The Great God Pan
&
The Hill of Dreams
&
The Angels of Mons

Arthur Machen

Introduction by Catherine Mntz

Published by the Copper Penny Press 2008
Reissued by Copper Publishing 2015

Cover, interior art, and introduction
Copyright 2015 by Catherine Mintz

ISBN 978-0-6152-3578-3

Library of Congress Control Number: 2008923992

Table of Contents

Introduction

Arthur Machen is the pen name of Arthur Llewelyn Jones. He was born in 1863 in Caerleon, Monmouthshire, Wales, an area rich in atmosphere, scenery and antiquities, all of which appear in his works. His father, a clergyman, added the boy's mother's maiden name to his own in order to receive an inheritance, becoming Jones-Machen. Machen is pronounced as if it were spelled "MacHen" and more or less rhymes with "blacken."

From age eleven, the boy received an excellent classical education at Hereford Cathedral School, but family finances ruled out university—his father was an Oxford man—and the young man failed at an attempt to enter medical school. Given the shape of his life and the attitudes displayed in his writing, one wonders just how well he knew himself to consider a life as a doctor.

Machen stayed in London, working in the daytime—as journalist, publisher's clerk, and tutor—while trying to write at night. He took long walks through every part of the city, gathering material that would later appear in his works. The atmosphere and many details of *The Hill of Dreams* are based on Machen's life up to this point. He was a pensive young man who had, as yet, not achieved anything like his hopes.

Unlike the hero of *The Hill of Dreams*, he did have the support of his family in seeking a literary career. He had already shown promise, having written one long poem on the Eleusinian Mysteries. These are best known to us as the myth of Demeter and her daughter Persephone, who was seized by Hades, the god of death and the underworld, with the consent of her father, Zeus.

In this public version, the Eleusinian Mysteries are a personified version of the growth and death cycle of the year, but the two thousand year old cult had secret rituals that we can only guess at. Open to anyone, man or woman, free or slave, who spoke Greek, it greatly influenced Greek and Roman history, weaving an invisible web through societies.

Its influence dyed Arthur Machen's view of the world and may have made him more receptive to membership in the Hermetic Order of the Golden Dawn, which had similar open membership policies and gathered and spread the kind of information used in modern day pagan religions. However, what amounted in his case to a flirtation was to come later in his life and after his best-known works had been completed.

In the early 1880's, and despite the experiences that he reworked into *The Hill of Dreams*, Machen moved to London permanently, where he worked at various poorly paid jobs associated with publishing and writing, including as a translator and as a magazine editor. His translations, including the *Memoirs* of Casanova, were fluently written and accepted as standard editions for many years.

The deaths of sundry Scottish relatives provided Machen with a modest competence, and he became free to spend more time writing. His work began appearing in literary magazines, and in 1894 his first major success, "The Great God Pan," appeared. It was denounced for its horrific and sexual content, and the book it appeared in went into a second edition.

However, the connections that had aided him were also to prove a problem, for, following the Oscar Wilde scandal, the literary decadence movement Machen had been a part of fell from public favor. Indeed, it was actively campaigned against. He continued to write fiction but there was less of a market for his works.

Machen married in 1887, when he was twenty-four. His wife, Amy Hogg, was an independent woman, a music teacher interested in the theater, who had friends in London's Bohemian circles. She provided an entree that would prove helpful to her husband's career and help nurture the growth of the circle of people that sustained him throughout his life.

In 1899 Machen's wife died of cancer, then a painful, lingering disease that was almost untreatable. Disconsolate, he grieved for over a year, supported by his friends, most notably A. E. Waite. Waite encouraged him to join the Hermetic Order of the Golden Dawn, an organization that numbered about one hundred people interested in mysticism and similar subjects. Among them were major literary figures, like William Butler Yeats.

It seems likely that the major appeal of the Golden Dawn to Machen lay in its revival of pagan traditions celebrating sensuality, passion, and beauty, something that had attracted him as a boy and as a young man. Eventually the group was riven by internal politics, and after that scandal. Long before then, Machen, deeply rooted in Christianity from his childhood—his father was a vicar—had moved on.

Indeed, the rites and mysteries of the Golden Dawn do not seem to have played as important a role in Machen's life as a change of occupation did. In 1901 he became one of a company of traveling players, and he made a second marriage, to the actress Dorothy Purefoy Hudleston, in 1903.

After his first wife's death, his becoming an actor, and his second marriage, Machen's personality changed from that of a rather retiring man to one more worldly and outgoing. The tone of his writing changed also and his later works, less aesthetic and more solidly commercial, are noticeably different from those completed earlier in his career but not published at the time they were written.

Machen became interested in grail legends, and further developed his theory that the goal of great literature is to convey ecstasy. It was during this time that *The Hill of Dreams*, which contains so much of his own experience as a younger man, was finally published. Many consider it his masterpiece. It had been written about ten years before, although it seems likely that he revised it before publication.

Some of Machen's works are marred for us by pointed references to then-contemporary affairs not familiar to later generations. His story, "The Bowmen," which inspired the legend of the angels of Mons, was uplifting fiction intended to inspire the British during the darker days of WWI.

Printed in a newspaper with no indication it was fiction, "The Bowmen" found a public eager to believe fiction was fact. Machen came to dislike it as not up to his standards and not even lucrative. The paper he worked for owned the rights and it was much reprinted before he issued that story, and others he thought better, as a book, *The Angels of Mons.*

He makes his opinion abundantly clear in his comments before and after *The Angels of Mons* and they, and the comments by his friend "The Londoner," are included in this omnibus edition. It is interesting to see Machen, who spent a so much of his life working as a journalist, analyzing the development of a story into a rumor and then a legend. He is in the end perhaps a little wistful that the wonderful tale had no hard evidence for its existence: he was a man who would have welcomed marvels.

Although he continued to be a member of literary circles, Machen's standard of living began to fall as his inheritances were exhausted. He found earning his living as a journalist disagreeable—he particularly disliked being at anyone's beck and call and subject to an editor—but he did well enough to buy a bigger house that became the meeting-place of his literary friends and their friends.

He was in demand as an essay writer, but it was not until the 1920's that his more literary fiction saw revival and reprinting, aided by various connections and admirers. By no means a bestseller, he was central to the web of genre development, influencing people like H. P. Lovecraft, James Branch Cabell, and Robert Howard. His reputation seems to have been much greater in the US than in the UK. In his homeland, his work was viewed as more a collection of curiosities than substantive literature.

Machen became relatively obscure, a figure from the past. By 1927 he was reduced to reading manuscripts for the publisher Ernest Benn. His margin for living was so thin that, despite his receiving a Civil List pension of a hundred pounds a year, the loss of work from Benn in 1933 was a major blow.

Seeking financial stability, Machen had moved away from London, to Amersham in Buckinghamshire, but that was not enough and problems continued until, in 1943, an appeal for his eightieth birthday moved a number of distinguished men of letters to provide him with an income until his death in 1947, shortly after that of his wife.

Among people who cite his influence, some of who have built upon his creations, are T. E. D. Klein, Peter Straub, Jorge Luis Borges, and Sylvia Townsend Warner, his great-niece. His great-granddaughter, contemporary artist Tessa Farmer, was surprised to discover there were parallels between her works and those of her great-grand-father. She has since explored his oeuvre and acknowledges his impact upon her own subsequent creations. At second and third-hand, there is almost no genre writer today who has not been touched by Arthur Machen's influence.

Catherine Mintz
Philadelphia, 2008

The Great God Pan

Arthur Machen

I: THE EXPERIMENT

"**I** am glad you came, Clarke; very glad indeed. I was not sure you could spare the time."

"I was able to make arrangements for a few days; things are not very lively just now. But have you no misgivings, Raymond? Is it absolutely safe?"

The two men were slowly pacing the terrace in front of Dr. Raymond's house. The sun still hung above the western mountain-line, but it shone with a dull red glow that cast no shadows, and all the air was quiet; a sweet breath came from the great wood on the hillside above, and with it, at intervals, the soft murmuring call of the wild doves. Below, in the long lovely valley, the river wound in and out between the lonely hills, and, as the sun hovered and vanished into the west, a faint mist, pure white, began to rise from the hills. Dr. Raymond turned sharply to his friend.

"Safe? Of course it is. In itself the operation is a perfectly simple one; any surgeon could do it."

"And there is no danger at any other stage?"

"None; absolutely no physical danger whatsoever, I give you my word. You are always timid, Clarke, always; but you know my history. I have devoted myself to transcendental medicine for the last twenty years. I have heard myself called quack and charlatan and impostor, but all the while I knew I was on the right path. Five years ago I reached the goal, and since then every day has been a preparation for what we shall do tonight."

"I should like to believe it is all true." Clarke knit his brows, and looked doubtfully at Dr. Raymond. "Are you perfectly sure, Raymond, that your theory is not a phantasmagoria—a splendid vision, certainly, but a mere vision after all?"

Dr. Raymond stopped in his walk and turned sharply. He was a middle-aged man, gaunt and thin, of a pale yellow complexion, but as he answered Clarke and faced him, there was a flush on his cheek.

"Look about you, Clarke. You see the mountain, and hill following after hill, as wave on wave, you see the woods and orchard, the fields of ripe corn, and the meadows reaching to the reed-beds by the river. You see me standing here beside you, and hear my voice; but I tell you that all these things— yes, from that star that has just shone out in the sky to the solid ground beneath our feet—I say that all these are but dreams and shadows; the shadows that hide the real world from our eyes. There is a real world, but it is beyond this glamour and this vision, beyond these 'chases in Arras, dreams in a career,' beyond them all as beyond a veil. I do not know whether any human being has ever lifted that veil; but I do know, Clarke, that you and I shall see it lifted this very night from before another's eyes. You may think this all strange nonsense; it may be strange, but it is true, and the ancients knew what lifting the veil means. They called it seeing the god Pan."

Clarke shivered; the white mist gathering over the river was chilly.

"It is wonderful indeed," he said. "We are

standing on the brink of a strange world, Raymond, if what you say is true. I suppose the knife is absolutely necessary?"

"Yes; a slight lesion in the grey matter, that is all; a trifling rearrangement of certain cells, a microscopical alteration that would escape the attention of ninety-nine brain specialists out of a hundred. I don't want to bother you with 'shop,' Clarke; I might give you a mass of technical detail which would sound very imposing, and would leave you as enlightened as you are now. But I suppose you have read, casually, in out-of-the-way corners of your paper, that immense strides have been made recently in the physiology of the brain. I saw a paragraph the other day about Digby's theory, and Browne Faber's discoveries. Theories and discoveries! Where they are standing now, I stood fifteen years ago, and I need not tell you that I have not been standing still for the last fifteen years. It will be enough if I say that five years ago I made the discovery that I alluded to when I said that ten years ago I reached the goal. After years of labor, after years of toiling and groping in the dark, after days and nights of disappointments and sometimes of despair, in which I used now and then to tremble and grow cold with the thought that perhaps there were others seeking for what I sought, at last, after so long, a pang of sudden joy thrilled my soul, and I knew the long journey was at an end. By what seemed then and still seems a chance, the suggestion of a moment's idle thought followed up upon familiar lines and paths that I had tracked a hundred times already, the great truth burst upon me, and I saw, mapped out in lines of sight, a whole world, a sphere unknown; continents and islands, and great oceans in which no ship has sailed (to my belief) since a Man first lifted up his eyes and beheld the sun, and the stars of heaven, and the quiet earth beneath. You will think this all high-flown language, Clarke, but it is hard to be literal. And yet; I do not know whether what I am hinting at cannot be set forth in plain and lonely terms. For instance, this world of ours is pretty well girded now with the telegraph wires and cables; thought, with something less than the speed of thought, flashes from sunrise to sunset, from north to south, across the floods and the desert places. Suppose that an electrician of today were suddenly to perceive that he and his friends have merely been playing with pebbles and mistaking them for the foundations of the world; suppose that such a man saw uttermost space lie open before the current, and words of men flash forth to the sun and beyond the sun into the systems beyond, and the voice of articulate-speaking men echo in the waste void that bounds our thought. As analogies go, that is a pretty good analogy of what I have done; you can understand now a little of what I felt as I stood here one evening; it was a summer evening, and the valley looked much as it does now; I stood here, and saw before me the unutterable, the unthinkable gulf that yawns profound between two worlds, the world of matter and the world of spirit; I saw the great empty deep stretch dim before me, and in that instant a bridge of light leapt from the earth to the unknown shore, and the abyss was spanned. You may look in Browne Faber's book, if you like, and you will find that to the present day men of science are unable to account for the presence, or to specify the functions of a certain group of nerve cells in the brain. That group is, as it were, land to let, a mere waste place for fanciful theories. I am not in the position of Browne Faber and the specialists, I am perfectly instructed as to the possible functions of those nerve centers in the scheme of things. With a touch I can bring them into play, with a touch, I say, I can set free the current, with a touch I can complete the communication between this world of sense and—we shall be able to finish the sentence later on. Yes, the knife is necessary; but think what that knife will effect. It will level utterly the solid wall of sense, and probably, for the first time since man was made, a spirit will gaze on a spirit-world. Clarke, Mary will see the god Pan!"

"But you remember what you wrote to me? I thought it would be requisite that she—"

He whispered the rest into the doctor's ear.

"Not at all, not at all. That is nonsense. I assure you. Indeed, it is better as it is; I am quite certain of that."

"Consider the matter well, Raymond. It's a great responsibility. Something might go wrong; you would be a miserable man for the rest of your days."

"No, I think not, even if the worst happened. As you know, I rescued Mary from the gutter, and from almost certain starvation, when she was a child; I think her life is mine, to use as I see fit.

Come, it's getting late; we had better go in."

Dr. Raymond led the way into the house, through the hall, and down a long dark passage. He took a key from his pocket and opened a heavy door, and motioned Clarke into his laboratory. It had once been a billiard-room, and was lighted by a glass dome in the centre of the ceiling, whence there still shone a sad grey light on the figure of the doctor as he lit a lamp with a heavy shade and placed it on a table in the middle of the room.

Clarke looked about him. Scarcely a foot of wall remained bare; there were shelves all around laden with bottles and phials of all shapes and colors, and at one end stood a little Chippendale bookcase. Raymond pointed to this.

"You see that parchment Oswald Crollius? He was one of the first to show me the way, though I don't think he ever found it himself. That is a strange saying of his: 'In every grain of wheat there lies hidden the soul of a star.'"

There was not much furniture in the laboratory. The table in the centre, a stone slab with a drain in one corner, the two armchairs on which Raymond and Clarke were sitting; that was all, except an odd-looking chair at the furthest end of the room. Clarke looked at it, and raised his eyebrows.

"Yes, that is the chair," said Raymond. "We may as well place it in position." He got up and wheeled the chair to the light, and began raising and lowering it, letting down the seat, setting the back at various angles, and adjusting the footrest. It looked comfortable enough, and Clarke passed his hand over the soft green velvet, as the doctor manipulated the levers.

"Now, Clarke, make yourself quite comfortable. I have a couple hours' work before me; I was obliged to leave certain matters to the last."

Raymond went to the stone slab, and Clarke watched him drearily as he bent over a row of phials and lit the flame under the crucible. The doctor had a small hand-lamp, shaded as the larger one, on a ledge above his apparatus, and Clarke, who sat in the shadows, looked down at the great shadowy room, wondering at the bizarre effects of brilliant light and undefined darkness contrasting with one another. Soon he became conscious of an odd odor, at first the merest suggestion of odor, in the room, and as it grew more decided he felt surprised that he was not reminded of the chemist's shop or the surgery. Clarke found himself idly endeavoring to analyze the sensation, and half conscious, he began to think of a day, fifteen years ago, that he had spent roaming through the woods and meadows near his own home. It was a burning day at the beginning of August, the heat had dimmed the outlines of all things and all distances with a faint mist, and people who observed the thermometer spoke of an abnormal register, of a temperature that was almost tropical. Strangely that wonderful hot day of the fifties rose up again in Clarke's imagination; the sense of dazzling all-pervading sunlight seemed to blot out the shadows and the lights of the laboratory, and he felt again the heated air beating in gusts about his face, saw the shimmer rising from the turf, and heard the myriad murmur of the summer.

"I hope the smell doesn't annoy you, Clarke; there's nothing unwholesome about it. It may make you a bit sleepy, that's all."

Clarke heard the words quite distinctly, and knew that Raymond was speaking to him, but for the life of him he could not rouse himself from his lethargy. He could only think of the lonely walk he had taken fifteen years ago; it was his last look at the fields and woods he had known since he was a child, and now it all stood out in brilliant light, as a picture, before him. Above all there came to his nostrils the scent of summer, the smell of flowers mingled, and the odor of the woods, of cool shaded places, deep in the green depths, drawn forth by the sun's heat; and the scent of the good earth, lying as it were with arms stretched forth, and smiling lips, overpowered all. His fancies made him wander, as he had wandered long ago, from the fields into the wood, tracking a little path between the shining undergrowth of beech-trees; and the trickle of water dropping from the limestone rock sounded as a clear melody in the dream. Thoughts began to go astray and to mingle with other thoughts; the beech alley was transformed to a path between ilex-trees, and here and there a vine climbed from bough to bough, and sent up waving tendrils and drooped with purple grapes, and the sparse grey-green leaves of a wild olive-tree stood out against the dark shadows of the ilex. Clarke, in the deep folds of dream, was conscious that the path from his father's house had led him into an undiscovered country, and he was wondering at the strangeness of it all, when suddenly, in place of the hum and murmur of the summer, an infinite silence seemed to fall on all things, and the wood was hushed, and for a moment in time he stood face to face there with a presence, that was neither man nor beast, neither the living nor the dead, but all things mingled, the form of all things but devoid of all form. And in that moment, the sacrament of body and soul was dissolved, and a voice seemed to cry "Let us go hence," and then the darkness of darkness beyond the stars, the darkness of everlasting.

When Clarke woke up with a start he saw Raymond pouring a few drops of some oily fluid into a green phial, which he stoppered tightly.

"You have been dozing," he said; "the journey must have tired you out. It is done now. I am going to fetch Mary; I shall be back in ten minutes."

Clarke lay back in his chair and wondered. It seemed as if he had but passed from one dream into another. He half expected to see the walls of the laboratory melt and disappear, and to awake in London, shuddering at his own sleeping fancies. But at last the door opened, and the doctor returned, and behind him came a girl of about seventeen, dressed all in white. She was so beautiful that Clarke did not wonder at what the doctor had written to him. She was blushing now over face and neck and arms, but Raymond seemed unmoved.

"Mary," he said, "the time has come. You are quite free. Are you willing to trust yourself to me entirely?"

"Yes, dear."

"Do you hear that, Clarke? You are my witness.

Here is the chair, Mary. It is quite easy. Just sit in it and lean back. Are you ready?"

"Yes, dear, quite ready. Give me a kiss before you begin."

The doctor stooped and kissed her mouth, kindly enough. "Now shut your eyes," he said. The girl closed her eyelids, as if she were tired, and longed for sleep, and Raymond placed the green phial to her nostrils. Her face grew white, whiter than her dress; she struggled faintly, and then with the feeling of submission strong within her, crossed her arms upon her breast as a little child about to say her prayers. The bright light of the lamp fell full upon her, and Clarke watched changes fleeting over her face as the changes of the hills when the summer clouds float across the sun. And then she lay all white and still, and the doctor turned up one of her eyelids. She was quite unconscious. Raymond pressed hard on one of the levers and the chair instantly sank back. Clarke saw him cutting away a circle, like a tonsure, from her hair, and the lamp was moved nearer. Raymond took a small glittering instrument from a little case, and Clarke turned away shudderingly. When he looked again the doctor was binding up the wound he had made.

"She will awake in five minutes." Raymond was still perfectly cool. "There is nothing more to be done; we can only wait."

The minutes passed slowly; they could hear a slow, heavy, ticking. There was an old clock in the passage. Clarke felt sick and faint; his knees shook beneath him, he could hardly stand.

Suddenly, as they watched, they heard a long-drawn sigh, and suddenly did the color that had vanished return to the girl's cheeks, and suddenly her eyes opened. Clarke quailed before them. They shone with an awful light, looking far away, and a great wonder fell upon her face, and her hands stretched out as if to touch what was invisible; but in an instant the wonder faded, and gave place to the most awful terror. The muscles of her face were hideously convulsed, she shook from head to foot; the soul seemed struggling and shuddering within the house of flesh. It was a horrible sight, and Clarke rushed forward, as she fell shrieking to the floor.

Three days later Raymond took Clarke to Mary's bedside. She was lying wide-awake, rolling her head from side to side, and grinning vacantly.

"Yes," said the doctor, still quite cool, "it is a great pity; she is a hopeless idiot. However, it could not be helped; and, after all, she has seen the Great God Pan."

II: MR. CLARKE'S MEMOIRS

Mr. Clarke, the gentleman chosen by Dr. Raymond to witness the strange experiment of the god Pan, was a person in whose character caution and curiosity were oddly mingled; in his sober moments he thought of the unusual and eccentric with undisguised aversion, and yet, deep in his heart, there was a wide-eyed inquisitiveness with respect to all the more recondite and esoteric elements in the nature of men. The latter tendency had prevailed when he accepted Raymond's invitation, for though his considered judgment had always repudiated the doctor's theories as the wildest nonsense, yet he secretly hugged a belief in fantasy, and would have rejoiced to see that belief confirmed. The horrors that he witnessed in the dreary laboratory were to a certain extent salutary; he was conscious of being involved in an affair not altogether reputable, and for many years afterwards he clung bravely to the commonplace, and rejected all occasions of occult investigation. Indeed, on some homeopathic principle, he for some time attended the séances of distinguished mediums, hoping that the clumsy tricks of these gentlemen would make him altogether disgusted with mysticism of every kind, but the remedy, though caustic, was not efficacious. Clarke knew that he still pined for the unseen, and little by little, the old passion began to reassert itself, as the face of Mary, shuddering and convulsed with an unknown terror, faded slowly from his memory. Occupied all day in pursuits both serious and lucrative, the temptation to relax in the evening was too great, especially in the winter months, when the fire cast a warm glow over his snug bachelor apartment, and a bottle of some choice claret stood ready by his elbow. His dinner digested, he would make a brief pretence of reading the evening paper, but the mere catalogue of news soon palled upon him, and Clarke would find himself casting glances of warm desire in the direction of an old Japanese bureau, which stood at a pleasant distance from the hearth. Like a boy before a jam-closet, for a few minutes he would hover indecisive, but lust always prevailed, and Clarke ended by drawing up his chair, lighting a candle, and sitting down before the bureau. Its pigeonholes and drawers teemed with documents on the most morbid subjects, and in the well reposed a large manuscript volume, in which he had painfully entered he gems of his collection. Clarke had a fine contempt for published literature; the most ghostly story ceased to interest him if it happened to be printed; his sole pleasure was in the reading, compiling, and rearranging what he called his "Memoirs to prove the Existence of the Devil," and engaged in this pursuit the evening seemed to fly and the night appeared too short.

On one particular evening, an ugly December night, black with fog, and raw with frost, Clarke hurried over his dinner, and scarcely deigned to observe his customary ritual of taking up the paper and laying it down again. He paced two or three times up and down the room, and opened the bureau, stood still a moment, and sat down. He leant back, absorbed in one of those dreams to which he was subject, and at length drew out his book, and opened it at the last entry. There were three or four pages densely covered with Clarke's round, set penmanship, and at the beginning he had written in a somewhat larger hand:

Singular Narrative told me by my Friend, Dr. Phillips. He assures me that all the facts related therein are strictly and wholly True, but refuses to give either the Surnames of the Persons Concerned, or the Place where these Extraordinary Events occurred.

Mr. Clarke began to read over the account for the tenth time, glancing now and then at the pencil notes he had made when it was told him by his friend. It was one of his humors to pride himself on a certain literary ability; he thought well of his style, and took pains in arranging the circumstances in dramatic order. He read the following story:

The persons concerned in this statement are Helen V., who, if she is still alive, must now be a woman of twenty-three, Rachel M., since deceased, who was a year younger than the above, and Trevor W., an imbecile, aged eighteen. These persons were at the period of the story inhabitants of a village on the borders of Wales, a place of some importance in the time of the Roman occupation, but now a scattered hamlet, of not more than five hundred souls. It is situated on rising ground, about six miles from the sea, and is sheltered by a large and picturesque forest.

Some eleven years ago, Helen V. came to the

village under rather peculiar circumstances. It is understood that she, being an orphan, was adopted in her infancy by a distant relative, who brought her up in his own house until she was twelve years old. Thinking, however, that it would be better for the child to have playmates of her own age, he advertised in several local papers for a good home in a comfortable farmhouse for a girl of twelve, and this advertisement was answered by Mr. R., a well-to-do farmer in the above-mentioned village. His references proving satisfactory, the gentleman sent his adopted daughter to Mr. R., with a letter, in which he stipulated that the girl should have a room to herself, and stated that her guardians need be at no trouble in the matter of education, as she was already sufficiently educated for the position in life which she would occupy. In fact, Mr. R. was given to understand that the girl be allowed to find her own occupations and to spend her time almost as she liked. Mr. R. duly met her at the nearest station, a town seven miles away from his house, and seems to have remarked nothing extraordinary about the child except that she was reticent as to her former life and her adopted father. She was, however, of a very different type from the inhabitants of the village; her skin was a pale, clear olive, and her features were strongly marked, and of a somewhat foreign character. She appears to have settled down easily enough into farmhouse life, and became a favorite with the children, who sometimes went with her on her rambles in the forest, for this was her amusement. Mr. R. states that he has known her to go out by herself directly after their early breakfast, and not return till after dusk, and that, feeling uneasy at a young girl being out alone for so many hours, he communicated with her adopted father, who replied in a brief note that Helen must do as she chose. In the winter, when the forest paths are impassable, she spent most of her time in her bedroom, where she slept alone, according to the instructions of her relative. It was on one of these expeditions to the forest that the first of the singular incidents with which this girl is connected occurred, the date being about a year after her arrival at the village. The preceding winter had been remarkably severe, the snow drifting to a great depth, and the frost continuing for an unexampled period, and the summer following was as noteworthy for its extreme heat. On one of the very hottest days in this summer, Helen V. left the farmhouse for one of her long rambles in the forest, taking with her, as usual, some bread and meat for lunch. She was seen by some men in the fields making for the old Roman Road, a green causeway which traverses the highest part of the wood, and they were astonished to observe that the girl had taken off her hat, though the heat of the sun was already tropical. As it happened, a laborer, Joseph W. by name, was working in the forest near the Roman Road, and at twelve o'clock his little son, Trevor, brought the man his dinner of bread and cheese. After the meal, the boy, who was about seven years old at the time, left his father at work, and, as he said, went to look for flowers in the wood, and the man, who could hear him shouting with delight at his discoveries, felt no uneasiness. Suddenly, however, he was horrified at hearing the most dreadful screams, evidently the result of great terror, proceeding from the direction in which his son had gone, and he hastily threw down his tools and ran to see what had happened. Tracing his path by the sound, he met the little boy, who was running headlong, and was evidently terribly frightened, and on questioning him the man elicited that after picking a posy of flowers he felt tired, and lay down on the grass and fell asleep. He was suddenly awakened, as he stated, by a peculiar noise, a sort of singing he called it, and on peeping through the branches he saw Helen V. playing on the grass with a "strange naked man," who he seemed unable to describe more fully. He said he felt dreadfully frightened and ran away crying for his father. Joseph W. proceeded in the direction indicated by his son, and found Helen V. sitting on the grass in the middle of a glade or open space left by charcoal burners. He angrily charged her with frightening his little boy, but she entirely denied the accusation and laughed at the child's story of a "strange man," to which he himself did not attach much credence. Joseph W. came to the conclusion that the boy had woke up with a sudden fright, as children sometimes do, but Trevor persisted in his story, and continued in such evident distress that at last his father took him home, hoping that his mother would be able to soothe him. For many weeks, however, the boy gave his parents much anxiety; he became nervous and strange in his manner, refusing to leave the cottage by himself, and constantly alarming the household by waking in the night with cries of "The man in the wood! Father! Father!"

In course of time, however, the impression seemed to have worn off, and about three months later he accompanied his father to the home of a gentleman in the neighborhood, for whom Joseph W. occasionally did work. The man was shown into the study, and the little boy was left sitting in the hall, and a few minutes later, while the gentleman was giving W. his instructions, they were both horrified by a piercing shriek and the sound of a fall, and rushing out they found the child lying senseless on the floor, his face contorted with terror. The doctor was immediately summoned, and after some examination he pronounced the child to be suffering form a kind of fit, apparently produced by a sudden shock. The boy was taken to one of the bedrooms, and after some time recovered consciousness, but only to pass into a condition described by the medical man as one of violent hysteria. The doctor exhibited a strong sedative, and in the course of two hours pronounced him fit to walk home, but in passing through the hall the paroxysms of fright returned and with additional violence. The father perceived that the child was pointing at some object, and heard the old cry, "The man in the wood," and looking in the direction indicated saw a stone head of grotesque appearance, which had been built into the wall above one of the doors. It seems the owner of the house had recently made alterations in his premises, and on digging the foundations for some offices, the men had found a curious head, evidently of the Roman period, which had been placed in the manner described. The head is pronounced by the most experienced archaeologists of the district to be that of a faun or satyr. [Dr. Phillips tells me that he has seen the head in question, and assures me that he has never received such a vivid presentment of intense evil.]

From whatever cause arising, this second shock seemed too severe for the boy Trevor, and at the present date he suffers from a weakness of intellect, which gives but little promise of amending. The matter caused a good deal of sensation at the time, and the girl Helen was closely questioned by Mr. R., but to no purpose, she steadfastly denying that she had frightened or in any way molested Trevor.

The second event with which this girl's name is connected took place about six years ago, and is of a still more extraordinary character.

At the beginning of the summer of 1882, Helen contracted a friendship of a peculiarly intimate character with Rachel M., the daughter of a prosperous farmer in the neighborhood. This girl, who was a year younger than Helen, was considered by most people to be the prettier of the two, though Helen's features had to a great extent softened as she became older. The two girls, who were together on every available opportunity, presented a singular contrast, the one with her clear, olive skin and almost Italian appearance, and the other of the proverbial red and white of our rural districts. It must be stated that the payments made to Mr. R. for the maintenance of Helen were known in the village for their excessive liberality, and the impression was general that she would one day inherit a large sum of money from her relative. The parents of Rachel were therefore not averse from their daughter's friendship with the girl, and even encouraged the intimacy, though they now bitterly regret having done so. Helen still retained her extraordinary fondness for the forest, and on several occasions Rachel accompanied her, the two friends setting out early in the morning, and remaining in the wood until dusk. Once or twice after these excursions Mrs. M. thought her daughter's manner rather peculiar; she seemed languid and dreamy, and as it has been expressed, "different from herself," but these peculiarities seem to have been thought too trifling for remark. One evening, however, after Rachel had come home, her mother heard a noise which sounded like suppressed weeping in the girl's room, and on going in found her lying, half undressed, upon the bed, evidently in the greatest distress. As soon as she saw her mother, she exclaimed, "Ah, mother, mother, why did you let me go to the forest with Helen?" Mrs. M. was astonished at so strange a question, and proceeded to make inquiries. Rachel told her a wild story. She said—

Clarke closed the book with a snap, and turned his chair towards the fire. When his friend sat one evening in that very chair, and told his story, Clarke had interrupted him at a point a little subsequent to this, had cut short his words in a paroxysm of horror. "My God!" he had exclaimed, "think, think what you are saying. It is too incredible, too monstrous; such things can never be in this quiet world, where men and women live and die, and struggle, and conquer, or maybe fail, and fall down under sorrow, and grieve and suffer strange fortunes for many a year; but not this, Phillips, not such things as this. There must be some explanation, some way out of the terror. Why, man, if such a case were possible, our earth would be a nightmare."

But Phillips had told his story to the end, concluding:

"Her flight remains a mystery to this day; she vanished in broad sunlight; they saw her walking in a meadow, and a few moments later she was not there."

Clarke tried to conceive the thing again, as he sat by the fire, and again his mind shuddered and shrank back, appalled before the sight of such awful, unspeakable elements enthroned as it were, and triumphant in human flesh. Before him stretched the long dim vista of the green causeway in the forest, as his friend had described it; he saw the swaying leaves and the quivering shadows on the grass, he saw the sunlight and the flowers, and far away, far in the long distance, the two figures moved toward him. One was Rachel, but the other?

Clarke had tried his best to disbelieve it all, but at the end of the account, as he had written it in his book, he had placed the inscription:

**ET DIABOLUS INCARNATE EST.
ET HOMO FACTUS EST.**

III: The City of Resurrections

"**H**erbert! Good God! Is it possible?"

"Yes, my name's Herbert. I think I know your face, too, but I don't remember your name. My memory is very queer."

"Don't you recollect Villiers of Wadham?"

"So it is, so it is. I beg your pardon, Villiers, I didn't think I was begging of an old college friend. Goodnight."

"My dear fellow, this haste is unnecessary. My rooms are close by, but we won't go there just yet. Suppose we walk up Shaftesbury Avenue a little way? But how in heaven's name have you come to this pass, Herbert?"

"It's a long story, Villiers, and a strange one too, but you can hear it if you like."

"Come on, then. Take my arm, you don't seem very strong."

The ill-assorted pair moved slowly up Rupert Street; the one in dirty, evil-looking rags, and the other attired in the regulation uniform of a man about town, trim, glossy, and eminently well to do. Villiers had emerged from his restaurant after an excellent dinner of many courses, assisted by an ingratiating little flask of Chianti, and, in that frame of mind which was with him almost chronic, had delayed a moment by the door, peering round in the dimly-lighted street in search of those mysterious incidents and persons with which the streets of London teem in every quarter and every hour. Villiers prided himself as a practiced explorer of such obscure mazes and byways of London life, and in this unprofitable pursuit he displayed an assiduity which was worthy of more serious employment. Thus he stood by the lamp-post surveying the passersby with undisguised curiosity, and with that gravity known only to the systematic diner, had just enunciated in his mind the formula: "London has been called the city of encounters; it is more than that, it is the city of Resurrections," when these reflections were suddenly interrupted by a piteous whine at his elbow, and a deplorable appeal for alms. He looked around in some irritation, and with a sudden shock found himself confronted with the embodied proof of his somewhat stilted fancies. There, close beside him, his face altered and disfigured by poverty and disgrace, his body barely covered by greasy ill-fitting rags, stood his old friend Charles Herbert, who had matriculated on the same day as himself, with whom he had been merry and wise for twelve revolving terms. Different occupations and varying interests had interrupted the friendship, and it was six years since Villiers had seen Herbert; and now he looked upon this wreck of a man with grief and dismay, mingled with a certain inquisitiveness as to what dreary chain of circumstances had dragged him down to such a doleful pass. Villiers felt together with compassion all the relish of the amateur in mysteries, and congratulated himself on his leisurely speculations outside the restaurant.

They walked on in silence for some time, and more than one passer-by stared in astonishment at the unaccustomed spectacle of a well-dressed man with an unmistakable beggar hanging on to his arm, and, observing this, Villiers led the way to an obscure street in Soho. Here he repeated his question.

"How on earth has it happened, Herbert? I always understood you would succeed to an excellent position in Dorsetshire. Did your father disinherit you? Surely not?"

"No, Villiers; I came into all the property at my poor father's death; he died a year after I left Oxford. He was a very good father to me, and I mourned his death sincerely enough. But you know what young men are; a few months later I came up to town and went a good deal into society. Of course I had excellent introductions, and I managed to enjoy myself very much in a harmless sort of way. I played a little, certainly, but never for heavy stakes, and the few bets I made on races brought me in money—only a few pounds, you know, but enough to pay for cigars and such petty pleasures. It was in my second season that the tide turned. Of course you have heard of my marriage?"

"No, I never heard anything about it."

"Yes, I married, Villiers. I met a girl, a girl of the most wonderful and most strange beauty, at the house of some people whom I knew. I cannot tell you her age; I never knew it, but, so far as I can guess, I should think she must have been about nineteen when I made her acquaintance. My friends had come to know her at Florence; she told them she was an orphan, the child of an English father and an Italian mother, and she charmed them as she charmed me. The first time I saw her was at an evening party. I was standing by the door talking to a friend, when suddenly above the hum and babble of conversation I heard a voice which seemed to thrill to my heart. She was singing an Italian song. I was introduced to her that evening, and in three months I married Helen. Villiers, that woman, if I can call her woman, corrupted my soul. The night of the wedding I found myself sitting in her bedroom in the hotel, listening to her talk. She was sitting up in bed, and I listened to her as she spoke in her beautiful voice, spoke of things which even now I would not dare whisper in the blackest night, though I stood in the midst of a wilderness. You, Villiers, you may think you know life, and London, and what goes on day and night in this dreadful city; for all I can say you may have heard the talk of the vilest, but I tell you you can have no conception of what I know, not in your most fantastic, hideous dreams can you have imaged forth the faintest shadow of what I have heard—and seen. Yes, seen. I have seen the incredible, such horrors that even I myself sometimes stop in the middle of the street and ask whether it is possible for a man to behold such things and live. In a year, Villiers, I was a ruined man, in body and soul—in body and soul."

"But your property, Herbert? You had land in Dorset."

"I sold it all; the fields and woods, the dear old house—everything."

"And the money?"

"She took it all from me."

"And then left you?"

"Yes; she disappeared one night. I don't know where she went, but I am sure if I saw her again it would kill me. The rest of my story is of no interest; sordid misery, that is all. You may think, Villiers, that I have exaggerated and talked for effect; but I have not told you half. I could tell you certain things which would convince you, but you would never know a happy day again. You would pass the rest of your life, as I pass mine, a haunted man, a man who has seen hell."

Villiers took the unfortunate man to his rooms, and gave him a meal. Herbert could eat little, and scarcely touched the glass of wine set before him. He sat moody and silent by the fire, and seemed relieved when Villiers sent him away with a small present of money.

"By the way, Herbert," said Villiers, as they parted at the door, "what was your wife's name? You said Helen, I think? Helen what?"

"The name she passed under when I met her was Helen Vaughan, but what her real name was I can't say. I don't think she had a name. No, no, not in that sense. Only human beings have names, Villiers; I can't say anymore. Good-bye; yes, I will not fail to call if I see any way in which you can help me. Goodnight."

The man went out into the bitter night, and Villiers returned to his fireside. There was something about Herbert which shocked him inexpressibly; not his poor rags nor the marks which poverty had set upon his face, but rather an indefinite terror which hung about him like a mist. He had acknowledged that he himself was not devoid of blame; the woman, he had avowed, had corrupted him body and soul, and Villiers felt that this man, once his friend, had been an actor in scenes evil beyond the power of words. His story needed no confirmation: he himself was the embodied proof of it. Villiers mused curiously over the story he had heard, and wondered whether he had heard both the first and the last of it. "No," he thought, "certainly not the last, probably only the beginning. A case like this is like a nest of Chinese boxes; you open one after the other and find a quainter workmanship in every box. Most likely poor Herbert is merely one of the outside boxes; there are stranger ones to follow."

Villiers could not take his mind away from Herbert and his story, which seemed to grow wilder as the night wore on. The fire seemed to burn low, and the chilly air of the morning crept into the room; Villiers got up with a glance over his shoulder, and, shivering slightly, went to bed.

A few days later he saw at his club a gentleman of his acquaintance, named Austin, who was famous for his intimate knowledge of London life, both in its tenebrous and luminous phases. Villiers, still full of his encounter in Soho and its cons-quences, thought Austin might possibly be able to shed some light on Herbert's history, and so after some casual talk he suddenly put the question:

"Do you happen to know anything of a man named Herbert—Charles Herbert?"

Austin turned round sharply and stared at

Villiers with some astonishment.

"Charles Herbert? Weren't you in town three years ago? No; then you have not heard of the Paul Street case? It caused a good deal of sensation at the time."

"What was the case?"

"Well, a gentleman, a man of very good position, was found dead, stark dead, in the area of a certain house in Paul Street, off Tottenham Court Road. Of course the police did not make the discovery; if you happen to be sitting up all night and have a light in your window, the constable will ring the bell, but if you happen to be lying dead in somebody's area, you will be left alone. In this instance, as in many others, the alarm was raised by some kind of vagabond; I don't mean a common tramp, or a public-house loafer, but a gentleman, whose business or pleasure, or both, made him a spectator of the London streets at five o'clock in the morning. This individual was, as he said, 'going home,' it did not appear whence or whither, and had occasion to pass through Paul Street between four and five a.m. Something or other caught his eye at Number 20; he said, absurdly enough, that the house had the most unpleasant physiognomy he had ever observed, but, at any rate, he glanced down the area and was a good deal astonished to see a man lying on the stones, his limbs all huddled together, and his face turned up. Our gentleman thought his face looked peculiarly ghastly, and so set off at a run in search of the nearest policeman. The constable was at first inclined to treat the matter lightly, suspecting common drunkenness; however, he came, and after looking at the man's face, changed his tone, quickly enough. The early bird, who had picked up this fine worm, was sent off for a doctor, and the policeman rang and knocked at the door till a slatternly servant girl came down looking more than half asleep. The constable pointed out the contents of the area to the maid, who screamed loudly enough to wake up the street, but she knew nothing of the man; had never seen him at the house, and so forth. Meanwhile, the original discoverer had come back with a medical man, and the next thing was to get into the area. The gate was open, so the whole quartet stumped down the steps. The doctor hardly needed a moment's examination; he said the poor fellow had been dead for several hours, and it was then the case began to get interesting. The dead man had not been robbed, and in one of his pockets were papers identifying him as—well, as a man of good family and means, a favorite in society, and nobody's enemy, as far as could be known. I don't give his name, Villiers, because it has nothing to do with the story, and because it's no good raking up these affairs about the dead when there are no relations living. The next curious point was that the medical men couldn't agree as to how he met his death. There were some slight bruises on his shoulders, but they were so slight that it looked as if he had been pushed roughly out of the kitchen door, and not thrown over the railings from the street or even dragged down the steps. But there were positively no other marks of violence about him, certainly none that would account for his death; and when they came to the autopsy there wasn't a trace of poison of any kind. Of course the police wanted to know all about the people at Number 20, and here again, so I have heard from private sources, one or two other very curious points came out. It appears that the occupants of the house were a Mr. and Mrs. Charles Herbert; he was said to be a landed proprietor, though it struck most people that Paul Street was not exactly the place to look for country gentry. As for Mrs. Herbert, nobody seemed to know who or what she was, and, between ourselves, I fancy the divers after her history found themselves in rather strange waters. Of course they both denied knowing anything about the deceased, and in default of any evidence against them they were discharged. But some very odd things came out about them. Though it was between five and six in the morning when the dead man was removed, a large crowd had collected, and several of the neighbors ran to see what was going on. They were pretty free with their comments, by all accounts, and from these it appeared that Number 20 was in very bad odor in Paul Street. The detectives tried to trace down these rumors to some solid foundation of fact, but could not get hold of anything. People shook their heads and raised their eyebrows and thought the Herberts rather 'queer,' 'would rather not be seen going into their house,' and so on, but there was nothing tangible. The authorities were morally certain the man met his death in some way or another in the house and was thrown out by the kitchen door, but they couldn't prove it, and the absence of any indications of violence or poisoning left them helpless. An odd case, wasn't it? But curiously enough, there's something more that I haven't told you. I happened to know one of the doctors who was consulted as to the cause of death, and some time after the inquest I met him, and asked him about it. 'Do you really mean to tell me,' I said, 'that you were baffled by the case, that you actually don't know what the man died of?' 'Pardon me,' he replied, 'I know perfectly well what caused death. Blank died of fright, of sheer, awful terror; I never saw features so hideously contorted in the entire course of my practice, and I have seen the faces of a whole host of dead.' The doctor was usually a cool customer enough, and a certain vehemence in his manner struck me, but I couldn't get anything more out of him. I suppose the Treasury didn't see their way to prosecuting the Herberts for frightening a man to death; at any rate, nothing was done, and the case dropped out of men's minds. Do you happen to know anything of Herbert?"

"Well," replied Villiers, "he was an old college friend of mine."

"You don't say so? Have you ever seen his wife?"

"No, I haven't. I have lost sight of Herbert for many years."

"It's queer, isn't it, parting with a man at the college gate or at Paddington, seeing nothing of him for years, and then finding him pop up his head in such an odd place. But I should like to have seen Mrs. Herbert; people said extraordinary things about her."

"What sort of things?"

"Well, I hardly know how to tell you. Everyone who saw her at the police court said she was at once the most beautiful woman and the most repulsive they had ever set eyes on. I have spoken to a man who saw her, and I assure you he positively shuddered as he tried to describe the woman, but he couldn't tell why. She seems to have been a sort of enigma; and I expect if that one dead man could have told tales, he would have told some uncommonly queer ones. And there you are again in another puzzle; what could a respectable country gentleman like Mr. Blank (we'll call him that if you don't mind) want in such a very queer house as Number 20? It's altogether a very odd case, isn't it?"

"It is indeed, Austin; an extraordinary case. I didn't think, when I asked you about my old friend, I should strike on such strange metal. Well, I must be off; good-day."

Villiers went away, thinking of his own conceit of the Chinese boxes; here was quaint workmanship indeed.

IV: THE DISCOVERY IN PAUL STREET

A few months after Villiers' meeting with Herbert, Mr. Clarke was sitting, as usual, by his after-dinner hearth, resolutely guarding his fancies from wandering in the direction of the bureau. For more than a week he had succeeded in keeping away from the "Memoirs," and he cherished hopes of a complete self-reformation; but, in spite of his endeavors, he could not hush the wonder and the strange curiosity that the last case he had written down had excited within him. He had put the case, or rather the outline of it, conjecturally to a scientific friend, who shook his head, and thought Clarke getting queer, and on this particular evening Clarke was making an effort to rationalize the story, when a sudden knock at the door roused him from his meditations.

"Mr. Villiers to see you sir."

"Dear me, Villiers, it is very kind of you to look me up; I have not seen you for many months; I should think nearly a year. Come in, come in. And how are you, Villiers? Want any advice about investments?"

"No, thanks, I fancy everything I have in that way is pretty safe. No, Clarke, I have really come to consult you about a rather curious matter that has been brought under my notice of late. I am afraid you will think it all rather absurd when I tell my tale. I sometimes think so myself, and that's just what I made up my mind to come to you, as I know you're a practical man."

Mr. Villiers was ignorant of the "Memoirs to prove the Existence of the Devil."

"Well, Villiers, I shall be happy to give you my advice, to the best of my ability. What is the nature of the case?"

"It's an extraordinary thing altogether. You know my ways; I always keep my eyes open in the streets, and in my time I have chanced upon some queer customers, and queer cases too, but this, I think, beats all. I was coming out of a restaurant one nasty winter night about three months ago; I had had a capital dinner and a good bottle of Chianti, and I stood for a moment on the pavement, thinking what a mystery there is about London streets and the companies that pass along them. A bottle of red wine encourages these fancies, Clarke, and I dare say I should have thought a page of small type, but I was cut short by a beggar who had come behind me, and was making the usual appeals. Of course I looked round, and this beggar turned out to be what was left of an old friend of mine, a man named Herbert. I asked him how he had come to such a wretched pass, and he told me. We walked up and down one of those long and dark Soho streets, and there I listened to his story. He said he had married a beautiful girl, some years younger than himself, and, as he put it, she had corrupted him body and soul. He wouldn't go into details; he said he dare not, that what he had seen and heard haunted him by night and day, and when I looked in his face I knew he was speaking the truth. There was something about the man that made me shiver. I don't know why, but it was there. I gave him a little money and sent him away, and I assure you that when he was gone I gasped for breath. His presence seemed to chill one's blood."

"Isn't this all just a little fanciful, Villiers? I suppose the poor fellow had made an imprudent marriage, and, in plain English, gone to the bad."

"Well, listen to this." Villiers told Clarke the story he had heard from Austin.

"You see," he concluded, "there can be but little doubt that this Mr. Blank, whoever he was, died of sheer terror; he saw something so awful, so terrible, that it cut short his life. And what he saw, he most certainly saw in that house, which, somehow or other, had got a bad name in the neighborhood. I had the curiosity to go and look at the place for myself. It's a saddening kind of street; the houses are old enough to be mean and dreary, but not old enough to be quaint. As far as I could see most of them are let in lodgings, furnished and unfurnished, and almost every door has three bells to it. Here and there the ground floors have been made into shops of the commonest kind; it's a dismal street in every way. I found Number 20 was to let, and I went to the agent's and got the key. Of course I should have heard nothing of the Herberts in that quarter, but I asked the man, fair and square, how long they had left the house and whether there had been other tenants in the meanwhile. He looked at me queerly for a minute, and told me the Herberts had left immediately after the unpleasantness, as he called it, and since then the house had been empty."

Mr. Villiers paused for a moment.

"I have always been rather fond of going over empty houses; there's a sort of fascination about the desolate empty rooms, with the nails sticking in the walls, and the dust thick upon the window-sills. But I didn't enjoy going over Number 20, Paul Street. I had hardly put my foot inside the passage when I noticed a queer, heavy feeling about the air of the house. Of course all empty houses are stuffy, and so forth, but this was something quite different; I can't describe it to you, but it seemed to stop the breath. I went into the front room and the back room, and the kitchens downstairs; they were all dirty and dusty enough, as you would expect, but there was something strange about them all. I couldn't define it to you, I only know I felt queer. It was one of the rooms on the first floor, though, that was the worst. It was a largish room, and once on a time the paper must have been cheerful enough, but when I saw it, paint, paper, and everything were most doleful. But the room was full of horror; I felt my teeth grinding as I put my hand on the door, and when I went in, I thought I should have fallen fainting to the floor. However, I pulled myself together, and stood against the end wall, wondering what on earth there could be about the room to make my limbs tremble, and my heart beat as if I were at the hour of death. In one corner there was a pile of newspapers littered on the floor, and I began looking at them; they were papers of three or four years ago, some of them half torn, and some crumpled as if they had been used for packing. I turned the whole pile over, and amongst them I found a curious drawing; I will show it to you presently. But I couldn't stay in the room; I felt it was overpowering me. I was thankful to come out, safe and sound, into the open air. People stared at me as I walked along the street, and one man said I was drunk. I was staggering about from one side of the pavement to the other, and it was as much as I could do to take the key back to the agent and get home. I was in bed for a week, suffering from what my doctor called nervous shock and exhaustion. One of those days I was reading the evening paper, and happened to notice a paragraph headed: 'Starved to Death.' It was the usual style of thing; a model lodging-house in Marylebone, a door locked for several days, and a dead man in his chair when they broke in. 'The deceased,' said the paragraph, 'was known as Charles Herbert, and is believed to have been once a prosperous country gentleman. His name was familiar to the public three years ago in connection with the mysterious death in Paul Street, Tottenham Court Road, the deceased being the tenant of the house Number 20, in the area of which a gentleman of good position was found dead under circumstances not devoid of suspicion.' A tragic ending, wasn't it? But after all, if what he told me were true, which I am sure it was, the man's life was all a tragedy, and a tragedy of a stranger sort than they put on the boards."

"And that is the story, is it?" said Clarke musingly.

"Yes, that is the story."

"Well, really, Villiers, I scarcely know what to say about it. There are, no doubt, circumstances in the case which seem peculiar, the finding of the dead man in the area of Herbert's house, for instance, and the extraordinary opinion of the physician as to the cause of death; but, after all, it is conceivable that the facts may be explained in a straightforward manner. As to your own sensations, when you went to see the house, I would suggest that they were due to a vivid imagination; you must have been brooding, in a semi-conscious way, over what you had heard. I don't exactly see what more can be said or done in the matter; you evidently think there is a mystery of some kind, but Herbert is dead; where then do you propose to look?"

"I propose to look for the woman; the woman whom he married. She is the mystery."

The two men sat silent by the fireside; Clarke secretly congratulating himself on having successfully kept up the character of advocate of the commonplace, and Villiers wrapped in his gloomy fancies.

"I think I will have a cigarette," he said at last, and put his hand in his pocket to feel for the cigarette case.

"Ah!" he said, starting slightly, "I forgot I had something to show you. You remember my saying that I had found a rather curious sketch amongst the pile of old newspapers at the house in Paul Street? Here it is."

Villiers drew out a small thin parcel from his pocket. It was covered with brown paper, and secured with string, and the knots were troublesome. In spite of himself Clarke felt inquisitive; he bent forward on his chair as Villiers painfully undid the string, and unfolded the outer covering.

Inside was a second wrapping of tissue, and Villiers took it off and handed the small piece of paper to Clarke without a word.

There was dead silence in the room for five minutes or more; the two men sat so still that they could hear the ticking of the tall old-fashioned clock that stood outside in the hall, and in the mind of one of them the slow monotony of sound woke up a far, far memory. He was looking intently at the small pen-and-ink sketch of the woman's head; it had evidently been drawn with great care, and by a true artist, for the woman's soul looked out of the eyes, and the lips were parted with a strange smile. Clarke gazed still at the face; it brought to his memory one summer evening, long ago; he saw again the long lovely valley, the river winding between the hills, the meadows and the cornfields, the dull red sun, and the cold white mist rising from the water. He heard a voice speaking to him across the waves of many years, and saying "Clarke, Mary will see the god Pan!" and then he was standing in the grim room beside the doctor, listening to the heavy ticking of the clock, waiting and watching, watching the figure lying on the green char beneath the lamplight. Mary rose up, and he looked into her eyes, and his heart grew cold within him.

"Who is this woman?" he said at last. His voice was dry and hoarse.

"That is the woman who Herbert married."

Clarke looked again at the sketch; it was not Mary after all. There certainly was Mary's face, but there was something else, something he had not seen on Mary's features when the white-clad girl entered the laboratory with the doctor, nor at her terrible awakening, nor when she lay grinning on the bed. Whatever it was, the glance that came from those eyes, the smile on the full lips, or the expression of the whole face, Clarke shuddered before it at his inmost soul, and thought, unconsciously, of Dr. Phillip's words, "the most vivid presentment of evil I have ever seen." He turned the paper over mechanically in his hand and glanced at the back.

"Good God! Clarke, what is the matter? You are as white as death."

Villiers had started wildly from his chair, as Clarke fell back with a groan, and let the paper drop from his hands.

"I don't feel very well, Villiers, I am subject to these attacks. Pour me out a little wine; thanks, that will do. I shall feel better in a few minutes."

Villiers picked up the fallen sketch and turned it over as Clarke had done.

"You saw that?" he said. "That's how I identified it as being a portrait of Herbert's wife, or I should say his widow. How do you feel now?"

"Better, thanks, it was only a passing faintness. I don't think I quite catch your meaning. What did you say enabled you to identify the picture?"

"This word—'Helen'—was written on the back. Didn't I tell you her name was Helen? Yes; Helen Vaughan."

Clarke groaned; there could be no shadow of doubt.

"Now, don't you agree with me," said Villiers,

"that in the story I have told you to-night, and in the part this woman plays in it, there are some very strange points?"

"Yes, Villiers," Clarke muttered, "it is a strange story indeed; a strange story indeed. You must give me time to think it over; I may be able to help you or I may not. Must you be going now? Well, goodnight, Villiers, goodnight. Come and see me in the course of a week."

V: THE LETTER OF ADVICE

"**D**o you know, Austin," said Villiers, as the two friends were pacing sedately along Piccadilly one pleasant morning in May, "do you know I am convinced that what you told me about Paul Street and the Herberts is a mere episode in an extraordinary history? I may as well confess to you that when I asked you about Herbert a few months ago I had just seen him."

"You had seen him? Where?"

"He begged of me in the street one night. He was in the most pitiable plight, but I recognized the man, and I got him to tell me his history, or at least the outline of it. In brief, it amounted to this—he had been ruined by his wife."

"In what manner?"

"He would not tell me; he would only say that she had destroyed him, body and soul. The man is dead now."

"And what has become of his wife?"

"Ah, that's what I should like to know, and I mean to find her sooner or later. I know a man named Clarke, a dry fellow, in fact a man of business, but shrewd enough. You understand my meaning; not shrewd in the mere business sense of the word, but a man who really knows something about men and life. Well, I laid the case before him, and he was evidently impressed. He said it needed consideration, and asked me to come again in the course of a week. A few days later I received this extraordinary letter."

Austin took the envelope, drew out the letter, and read it curiously. It ran as follows:

"My Dear Villiers, I have thought over the matter on which you consulted me the other night, and my advice to you is this. Throw the portrait into the fire, blot out the story from your mind. Never give it another thought, Villiers, or you will be sorry. You will think, no doubt, that I am in possession of some secret information, and to a certain extent that is the case. But I only know a little; I am like a traveler who has peered over an abyss, and has drawn back in terror. What I know is strange enough and horrible enough, but beyond my knowledge there are depths and horrors more frightful still, more incredible than any tale told of winter nights about the fire. I have resolved, and nothing shall shake that resolve, to explore no whit farther, and if you value your happiness you will make the same determination.

"Come and see me by all means; but we will talk on more cheerful topics than this."

Austin folded the letter methodically, and returned it to Villiers.

"It is certainly an extraordinary letter," he said, "what does he mean by the portrait?"

"Ah! I forgot to tell you I have been to Paul Street and have made a discovery."

Villiers told his story as he had told it to Clarke, and Austin listened in silence. He seemed puzzled.

"How very curious that you should experience such an unpleasant sensation in that room!" he said at length. "I hardly gather that it was a mere matter of the imagination; a feeling of repulsion, in short."

"No, it was more physical than mental. It was as if I were inhaling at every breath some deadly fume, which seemed to penetrate to every nerve and bone and sinew of my body. I felt racked from head to foot, my eyes began to grow dim; it was like the entrance of death."

"Yes, yes, very strange certainly. You see, your friend confesses that there is some very black story connected with this woman. Did you notice any particular emotion in him when you were telling your tale?"

"Yes, I did. He became very faint, but he assured me that it was a mere passing attack to which he was subject."

"Did you believe him?"

"I did at the time, but I don't now. He heard what I had to say with a good deal of indifference, till I showed him the portrait. It was then that he was seized with the attack of which I spoke. He looked ghastly, I assure you."

"Then he must have seen the woman before. But there might be another explanation; it might have been the name, and not the face, which was familiar to him. What do you think?"

"I couldn't say. To the best of my belief it was after turning the portrait in his hands that he nearly dropped from the chair. The name, you know, was written on the back."

"Quite so. After all, it is impossible to come to any resolution in a case like this. I hate melodrama, and nothing strikes me as more commonplace and tedious than the ordinary ghost story of commerce; but really, Villiers, it looks as if there were something very queer at the bottom of all this."

The two men had, without noticing it, turned up Ashley Street, leading northward from Piccadilly. It was a long street, and rather a gloomy one, but here and there a brighter taste had illuminated the dark houses with flowers, and gay curtains, and a cheerful paint on the doors. Villiers glanced up as Austin stopped speaking, and looked at one of these houses; geraniums, red and white, drooped from every sill, and daffodil-colored curtains were draped back from each window.

"It looks cheerful, doesn't it?" he said.

"Yes, and the inside is still more cheery. One of the pleasantest houses of the season, so I have heard. I haven't been there myself, but I've met several men who have, and they tell me it's uncommonly jovial."

"Whose house is it?"

"A Mrs. Beaumont's."

"And who is she?"

"I couldn't tell you. I have heard she comes from South America, but after all, who she is is of little consequence. She is a very wealthy woman, there's no doubt of that, and some of the best people have taken her up. I hear she has some wonderful claret, really marvelous wine, which must have cost a fabulous sum. Lord Argentine was telling me about it; he was there last Sunday evening. He assures me he has never tasted such a wine, and Argentine, as you know, is an expert. By the way, that reminds me, she must be an oddish sort of woman, this Mrs. Beaumont. Argentine asked her how old the wine was, and what do you think she

said? 'About a thousand years, I believe.' Lord
Argentine thought she was chaffing him, you
know, but when he laughed she said she was
speaking quite seriously and offered to show him
the jar. Of course, he couldn't say anything more
after that; but it seems rather antiquated for a
beverage, doesn't it? Why, here we are at my
rooms. Come in, won't you?"

"Thanks, I think I will. I haven't seen the
curiosity-shop for a while."

It was a room furnished richly, yet oddly, where
every jar and bookcase and table, and every rug
and jar and ornament seemed to be a thing apart,
preserving each its own individuality.

"Anything fresh lately?" said Villiers after a
while.

"No; I think not; you saw those queer jugs, didn't
you? I thought so. I don't think I have come across
anything for the last few weeks."

Austin glanced around the room from cupboard
to cupboard, from shelf to shelf, in search of some
new oddity. His eyes fell at last on an odd chest,
pleasantly and quaintly carved, which stood in a
dark corner of the room.

"Ah," he said, "I was forgetting, I have got
something to show you." Austin unlocked the
chest, drew out a thick quarto volume, laid it on the
table, and resumed the cigar he had put down.

"Did you know Arthur Meyrick the painter,
Villiers?"

"A little; I met him two or three times at the
house of a friend of mine. What has become of
him? I haven't heard his name mentioned for some

time."

"He's dead."

"You don't say so! Quite young, wasn't he?"

"Yes; only thirty when he died."

"What did he die of?"

"I don't know. He was an intimate friend of mine, and a thoroughly good fellow. He used to come here and talk to me for hours, and he was one of the best talkers I have met. He could even talk about painting, and that's more than can be said of most painters. About eighteen months ago he was feeling rather overworked, and partly at my suggestion he went off on a sort of roving expedition, with no very definite end or aim about it. I believe New York was to be his first port, but I never heard from him. Three months ago I got this book, with a very civil letter from an English doctor practicing at Buenos Ayres, stating that he had attended the late Mr. Meyrick during his illness, and that the deceased had expressed an earnest wish that the enclosed packet should be sent to me after his death. That was all."

"And haven't you written for further particulars?"

"I have been thinking of doing so. You would advise me to write to the doctor?"

"Certainly. And what about the book?"

"It was sealed up when I got it. I don't think the doctor had seen it."

"It is something very rare? Meyrick was a collector, perhaps?"

"No, I think not, hardly a collector. Now, what do you think of these Ainu jugs?"

"They are peculiar, but I like them. But aren't you going to show me poor Meyrick's legacy?"

"Yes, yes, to be sure. The fact is, it's rather a peculiar sort of thing, and I haven't shown it to any one. I wouldn't say anything about it if I were you. There it is."

Villiers took the book, and opened it at haphazard.

"It isn't a printed volume, then?" he said.

"No. It is a collection of drawings in black and white by my poor friend Meyrick."

Villiers turned to the first page, it was blank; the second bore a brief inscription, which he read:

Silet per diem universus, nec sine horrore secretus est; lucet nocturnis ignibus, chorus Aegipanum undique personatur: audiuntur et cantus tibiarum, et tinnitus cymbalorum per oram maritimam.

On the third page was a design which made Villiers start and look up at Austin; he was gazing abstractedly out of the window. Villiers turned page after page, absorbed, in spite of himself, in the frightful Walpurgis Night of evil, strange monstrous evil, that the dead artist had set forth in hard black and white. The figures of Fauns and Satyrs and Aegipans danced before his eyes, the darkness of the thicket, the dance on the mountain-top, the scenes by lonely shores, in green vineyards, by rocks and desert places, passed before him: a world before which the human soul seemed to shrink back and shudder. Villiers whirled over the remaining pages; he had seen enough, but the picture on the last leaf caught his eye, as he almost closed the book.

"Austin!"

"Well, what is it?"

"Do you know who that is?"

It was a woman's face, alone on the white page.

"Know who it is? No, of course not."

"I do."

"Who is it?"

"It is Mrs. Herbert."

"Are you sure?"

"I am perfectly sure of it. Poor Meyrick! He is one more chapter in her history."

"But what do you think of the designs?"

"They are frightful. Lock the book up again, Austin. If I were you I would burn it; it must be a terrible companion even though it be in a chest."

"Yes, they are singular drawings. But I wonder what connection there could be between Meyrick and Mrs. Herbert, or what link between her and these designs?"

"Ah, who can say? It is possible that the matter may end here, and we shall never know, but in my own opinion this Helen Vaughan, or Mrs. Herbert, is only the beginning. She will come back to London, Austin; depend on it, she will come back, and we shall hear more about her then. I doubt it will be very pleasant news."

VI: The Suicides

L ord Argentine was a great favorite in London Society. At twenty he had been a poor man, decked with the surname of an illustrious family, but forced to earn a livelihood as best he could, and the most speculative of money-lenders would not have entrusted him with fifty pounds on the chance of his ever changing his name for a title, and his poverty for a great fortune. His father had been near enough to the fountain of good things to secure one of the family livings, but the son, even if he had taken orders, would scarcely have obtained so much as this, and moreover felt no vocation for the ecclesiastical estate. Thus he fronted the world with no better amour than the bachelor's gown and the wits of a younger son's grandson, with which equipment he contrived in some way to make a very tolerable fight of it. At twenty-five Mr. Charles Aubernon saw himself still a man of struggles and of warfare with the world, but out of the seven who stood before him and the high places of his family three only remained. These three, however, were "good lives," but yet not proof against the Zulu assegais and typhoid fever, and so one morning Aubernon woke up and found himself Lord Argentine, a man of thirty who had faced the difficulties of existence, and had conquered. The situation amused him immensely, and he resolved that riches should be as pleasant to him as poverty had always been. Argentine, after some little consideration, came to the conclusion that dining, regarded as a fine art, was perhaps the most amusing pursuit open to fallen humanity, and thus his dinners became famous in London, and an invitation to his table a thing covetously desired. After ten years of lordship and dinners Argentine still declined to be jaded, still persisted in enjoying life, and by a kind of infection had become recognized as the cause of joy in others, in short, as the best of company. His sudden and tragical death therefore caused a wide and deep sensation. People could scarcely believe it, even though the newspaper was before their eyes, and the cry of "Mysterious Death of a Nobleman" came ringing up from the street. But there stood the brief paragraph: "Lord Argentine was found dead this morning by his valet under distressing circumstances. It is stated that there can be no doubt that his lordship committed suicide, though no motive can be assigned for the act. The deceased nobleman was widely known in society, and much liked for his genial manner and sumptuous hospitality. He is succeeded by," etc., etc.

By slow degrees the details came to light, but the case still remained a mystery. The chief witness at the inquest was the deceased's valet, who said that the night before his death Lord Argentine had dined with a lady of good position, whose named was suppressed in the newspaper reports. At about eleven o'clock Lord Argentine had returned, and informed his man that he should not require his services till the next morning. A little later the valet had occasion to cross the hall and was somewhat astonished to see his master quietly letting himself out at the front door. He had taken off his evening clothes, and was dressed in a Norfolk coat and knickerbockers, and wore a low brown hat. The valet had no reason to suppose that Lord Argentine had seen him, and though his master rarely kept late hours, thought little of the occurrence till the next morning, when he knocked at the bedroom door at a quarter to nine as usual. He received no answer, and, after knocking two or three times, entered the room, and saw Lord Argentine's body leaning forward at an angle from the bottom of the bed. He found that his master had tied a cord securely to one of the short bedposts, and, after making a running noose and slipping it round his neck, the unfortunate man must have resolutely fallen forward, to die by slow strangulation. He was dressed in the light suit in which the valet had seen him go out, and the doctor who was summoned pronounced that life had been extinct for more than four hours. All papers, letters, and so forth seemed in perfect order, and nothing was discovered which pointed in the most remote way to any scandal either great or small. Here the evidence ended; nothing more could be discovered. Several persons had been present at the dinner-party at which Lord Augustine had assisted, and to all these he seemed in his usual genial spirits. The valet, indeed, said he thought his master appeared a little excited when he came home, but confessed that the alteration in his manner was very slight, hardly noticeable, indeed. It seemed hopeless to seek for any clue, and the suggestion that Lord Argentine had been suddenly attacked by acute suicidal mania was generally accepted.

It was otherwise, however, when within three weeks, three more gentlemen, one of them a nobleman, and the two others men of good position and ample means, perished miserably in the almost precisely the same manner. Lord Swanleigh was found one morning in his dressing-room, hanging from a peg affixed to the wall, and Mr. Collier-Stuart and Mr. Herries had chosen to die as Lord Argentine. There was no explanation in either case; a few bald facts; a living man in the evening, and a body with a black swollen face in the morning. The police had been forced to confess themselves powerless to arrest or to explain the sordid murders of Whitechapel; but before the horrible suicides of Piccadilly and Mayfair they were dumbfounded, for not even the mere ferocity which did duty as an explanation of the crimes of the East End, could be of service in the West. Each of these men who had resolved to die a tortured shameful death was rich, prosperous, and to all appearances in love with the world, and not the acutest research should ferret out any shadow of a lurking motive in either case. There was a horror in the air, and men looked at one another's faces when they met, each wondering whether the other was to be the victim of the fifth nameless tragedy. Journalists sought in vain for their scrapbooks for materials whereof to concoct reminiscent articles; and the morning paper was unfolded in many a house with a feeling of awe; no man knew when or where the next blow would light.

A short while after the last of these terrible

events, Austin came to see Mr. Villiers. He was curious to know whether Villiers had succeeded in discovering any fresh traces of Mrs. Herbert, either through Clarke or by other sources, and he asked the question soon after he had sat down.

"No," said Villiers, "I wrote to Clarke, but he remains obdurate, and I have tried other channels, but without any result. I can't find out what became of Helen Vaughan after she left Paul Street, but I think she must have gone abroad. But to tell the truth, Austin, I haven't paid much attention to the matter for the last few weeks; I knew poor Herries intimately, and his terrible death has been a great shock to me, a great shock."

"I can well believe it," answered Austin gravely, "you know Argentine was a friend of mine. If I remember rightly, we were speaking of him that day you came to my rooms."

"Yes; it was in connection with that house in Ashley Street, Mrs. Beaumont's house. You said something about Argentine's dining there."

"Quite so. Of course you know it was there Argentine dined the night before—before his death."

"No, I had not heard that."

"Oh, yes; the name was kept out of the papers to spare Mrs. Beaumont. Argentine was a great favorite of hers, and it is said she was in a terrible state for sometime after."

A curious look came over Villiers' face; he seemed undecided whether to speak or not. Austin began again.

"I never experienced such a feeling of horror as

when I read the account of Argentine's death. I didn't understand it at the time, and I don't now. I knew him well, and it completely passes my understanding for what possible cause he—or any of the others for the matter of that—could have resolved in cold blood to die in such an awful manner. You know how men babble away each other's characters in London, you may be sure any buried scandal or hidden skeleton would have been brought to light in such a case as this; but nothing of the sort has taken place. As for the theory of mania, that is very well, of course, for the coroner's jury, but everybody knows that it's all nonsense. Suicidal mania is not smallpox."

Austin relapsed into gloomy silence. Villiers sat silent, also, watching his friend. The expression of indecision still fleeted across his face; he seemed as if weighing his thoughts in the balance, and the considerations he was resolving left him still silent. Austin tried to shake off the remembrance of tragedies as hopeless and perplexed as the labyrinth of Daedalus, and began to talk in an indifferent voice of the more pleasant incidents and adventures of the season.

"That Mrs. Beaumont," he said, "of whom we were speaking, is a great success; she has taken London almost by storm. I met her the other night at Fulmar's; she is really a remarkable woman."

"You have met Mrs. Beaumont?"

"Yes; she had quite a court around her. She would be called very handsome, I suppose, and yet there is something about her face which I didn't like. The features are exquisite, but the expression

71

is strange. And all the time I was looking at her, and afterwards, when I was going home, I had a curious feeling that very expression was in some way or another familiar to me."

"You must have seen her in the Row."

"No, I am sure I never set eyes on the woman before; it is that which makes it puzzling. And to the best of my belief I have never seen anyone like her; what I felt was a kind of dim far-off memory, vague but persistent. The only sensation I can compare it to, is that odd feeling one sometimes has in a dream, when fantastic cities and wondrous lands and phantom personages appear familiar and accustomed."

Villiers nodded and glanced aimlessly round the room, possibly in search of something on which to turn the conversation. His eyes fell on an old chest somewhat like that in which the artist's strange legacy lay hid beneath a Gothic scutcheon.

"Have you written to the doctor about poor Meyrick?" he asked.

"Yes; I wrote asking for full particulars as to his illness and death. I don't expect to have an answer for another three weeks or a month. I thought I might as well inquire whether Meyrick knew an Englishwoman named Herbert, and if so, whether the doctor could give me any information about her. But it's very possible that Meyrick fell in with her at New York, or Mexico, or San Francisco; I have no idea as to the extent or direction of his travels."

"Yes, and it's very possible that the woman may have more than one name."

"Exactly. I wish I had thought of asking you to lend me the portrait of her which you possess. I might have enclosed it in my letter to Dr. Matthews."

"So you might; that never occurred to me. We might send it now. Hark! what are those boys calling?"

While the two men had been talking together a confused noise of shouting had been gradually growing louder. The noise rose from the eastward and swelled down Piccadilly, drawing nearer and nearer, a very torrent of sound; surging up streets usually quiet, and making every window a frame for a face, curious or excited. The cries and voices came echoing up the silent street where Villiers lived, growing more distinct as they advanced, and, as Villiers spoke, an answer rang up from the pavement:

"The West End Horrors; Another Awful Suicide; Full Details!"

Austin rushed down the stairs and bought a paper and read out the paragraph to Villiers as the uproar in the street rose and fell. The window was open and the air seemed full of noise and terror.

"Another gentleman has fallen a victim to the terrible epidemic of suicide which for the last month has prevailed in the West End. Mr. Sidney Crashaw, of Stoke House, Fulham, and King's Pomeroy, Devon, was found, after a prolonged search, hanging dead from the branch of a tree in his garden at one o'clock today. The deceased gentleman dined last night at the Carlton Club and seemed in his usual health and spirits. He left the club at about ten o'clock, and was seen walking lei-surely up St. James's Street a little later. Subsequent to this his movements cannot be traced. On the discovery of the body medical aid was at once summoned, but life had evidently been long extinct. So far as is known, Mr. Crashaw had no trouble or anxiety of any kind. This painful suicide, it will be remembered, is the fifth of the kind in the last month. The authorities at Scotland Yard are unable to suggest any explanation of these terrible occurrences."

Austin put down the paper in mute horror.

"I shall leave London tomorrow," he said, "it is a city of nightmares. How awful this is, Villiers!"

Mr. Villiers was sitting by the window quietly looking out into the street. He had listened to the newspaper report attentively, and the hint of indecision was no longer on his face.

"Wait a moment, Austin," he replied, "I have made up my mind to mention a little matter that occurred last night. It stated, I think, that Crashaw was last seen alive in St. James's Street shortly after ten?"

"Yes, I think so. I will look again. Yes, you are quite right."

"Quite so. Well, I am in a position to contradict that statement at all events. Crashaw was seen after that; considerably later indeed."

"How do you know?"

"Because I happened to see Crashaw myself at about two o'clock this morning."

"You saw Crashaw? You, Villiers?"

"Yes, I saw him quite distinctly; indeed, there

were but a few feet between us."

"Where, in Heaven's name, did you see him?"

"Not far from here. I saw him in Ashley Street. He was just leaving a house."

"Did you notice what house it was?"

"Yes. It was Mrs. Beaumont's."

"Villiers! Think what you are saying; there must be some mistake. How could Crashaw be in Mrs. Beaumont's house at two o'clock in the morning? Surely, surely, you must have been dreaming, Villiers; you were always rather fanciful."

"No; I was wide awake enough. Even if I had been dreaming as you say, what I saw would have roused me effectually."

"What you saw? What did you see? Was there anything strange about Crashaw? But I can't believe it; it is impossible."

"Well, if you like I will tell you what I saw, or if you please, what I think I saw, and you can judge for yourself."

"Very good, Villiers."

The noise and clamor of the street had died away, though now and then the sound of shouting still came from the distance, and the dull, leaden silence seemed like the quiet after an earthquake or a storm. Villiers turned from the window and began speaking.

"I was at a house near Regent's Park last night, and when I came away the fancy took me to walk home instead of taking a hansom. It was a clear pleasant night enough, and after a few minutes I had the streets pretty much to myself. It's a curious thing, Austin, to be alone in London at night, the

75

gas-lamps stretching away in perspective, and the dead silence, and then perhaps the rush and clatter of a hansom on the stones, and the fire starting up under the horse's hoofs. I walked along pretty briskly, for I was feeling a little tired of being out in the night, and as the clocks were striking two I turned down Ashley Street, which, you know, is on my way. It was quieter than ever there, and the lamps were fewer; altogether, it looked as dark and gloomy as a forest in winter. I had done about half the length of the street when I heard a door closed very softly, and naturally I looked up to see who was abroad like myself at such an hour. As it happens, there is a street lamp close to the house in question, and I saw a man standing on the step. He had just shut the door and his face was towards me, and I recognized Crashaw directly. I never knew him to speak to, but I had often seen him, and I am positive that I was not mistaken in my man. I looked into his face for a moment, and then—I will confess the truth—I set off at a good run, and kept it up till I was within my own door."

"Why?"

"Why? Because it made my blood run cold to see that man's face. I could never have supposed that such an infernal medley of passions could have glared out of any human eyes; I almost fainted as I looked. I knew I had looked into the eyes of a lost soul, Austin, the man's outward form remained, but all hell was within it. Furious lust, and hate that was like fire, and the loss of all hope and horror that seemed to shriek aloud to the night, though his teeth were shut; and the utter blackness of despair. I am sure that he did not see me; he saw nothing that you or I can see, but what he saw I hope we never shall. I do not know when he died; I suppose in an hour, or perhaps two, but when I passed down Ashley Street and heard the closing door, that man no longer belonged to this world; it was a devil's face I looked upon."

There was an interval of silence in the room when Villiers ceased speaking. The light was failing, and all the tumult of an hour ago was quite hushed. Austin had bent his head at the close of the story, and his hand covered his eyes.

"What can it mean?" he said at length.

"Who knows, Austin, who knows? It's a black business, but I think we had better keep it to ourselves, for the present at any rate. I will see if I cannot learn anything about that house through private channels of information, and if I do light upon anything I will let you know."

VII: The Encounter in Soho

T hree weeks later Austin received a note from Villiers, asking him to call either that afternoon or the next. He chose the nearer date, and found Villiers sitting as usual by the window, apparently lost in meditation on the drowsy traffic of the street. There was a bamboo table by his side, a fantastic thing, enriched with gilding and queer painted scenes, and on it lay a little pile of papers arranged and docketed as neatly as anything in Mr. Clarke's office.

"Well, Villiers, have you made any discoveries in the last three weeks?"

"I think so; I have here one or two memoranda which struck me as singular, and there is a statement to which I shall call your attention."

"And these documents relate to Mrs. Beaumont? It was really Crashaw whom you saw that night standing on the doorstep of the house in Ashley Street?"

"As to that matter my belief remains unchanged, but neither my inquiries nor their results have any special relation to Crashaw. But my investigations have had a strange issue. I have found out who Mrs. Beaumont is!"

"Who is she? In what way do you mean?"

"I mean that you and I know her better under another name."

"What name is that?"

"Herbert."

"Herbert!" Austin repeated the word, dazed

with astonishment.

"Yes, Mrs. Herbert of Paul Street, Helen Vaughan of earlier adventures unknown to me. You had reason to recognize the expression of her face; when you go home look at the face in Meyrick's book of horrors, and you will know the sources of your recollection."

"And you have proof of this?"

"Yes, the best of proof; I have seen Mrs. Beaumont, or shall we say Mrs. Herbert?"

"Where did you see her?"

"Hardly in a place where you would expect to see a lady who lives in Ashley Street, Piccadilly. I saw her entering a house in one of the meanest and most disreputable streets in Soho. In fact, I had made an appointment, though not with her, and she was precise to both time and place."

"All this seems very wonderful, but I cannot call it incredible. You must remember, Villiers, that I have seen this woman, in the ordinary adventure of London society, talking and laughing, and sipping her coffee in a commonplace drawing room with commonplace people. But you know what you are saying."

"I do; I have not allowed myself to be led by surmises or fancies. It was with no thought of finding Helen Vaughan that I searched for Mrs. Beaumont in the dark waters of the life of London, but such has been the issue."

"You must have been in strange places, Villiers."

"Yes, I have been in very strange places. It would have been useless, you know, to go to Ashley Street, and ask Mrs. Beaumont to give me a short sketch of her previous history. No; assuming, as I had to assume, that her record was not of the cleanest, it would be pretty certain that at some previous time she must have moved in circles not quite so refined as her present ones. If you see mud at the top of a stream, you may be sure that it was once at the bottom. I went to the bottom. I have always been fond of diving into Queer Street for my amusement, and I found my knowledge of that locality and its inhabitants very useful. It is, perhaps, needless to say that my friends had never heard the name of Beaumont, and as I had never seen the lady, and was quite unable to describe her, I had to set to work in an indirect way. The people there know me; I have been able to do some of them a service now and again, so they made no difficulty about giving their information; they were aware I had no communication direct or indirect with Scotland Yard. I had to cast out a good many lines, though, before I got what I wanted, and when I landed the fish I did not for a moment suppose it was my fish. But I listened to what I was told out of a constitutional liking for useless information, and I found myself in possession of a very curious story, though, as I imagined, not the story I was looking for. It was to this effect. Some five or six years ago, a woman named Raymond suddenly made her appearance in the neighborhood to which I am referring. She was described to me as being quite young, probably not more than seventeen or eighteen, very handsome, and looking as if she came from the country. I should be wrong in saying that she found her level in going to this particular quarter, or associating with these people, for from what I was told, I should think the worst den in London far too good for her. The person from whom I got my information, as you may suppose, no great Puritan, shuddered and grew sick in telling me of the nameless infamies which were laid to her charge. After living there for a year, or perhaps a little more, she disappeared as suddenly as she came, and they saw nothing of her till about the time of the Paul Street case. At first she came to her old haunts only occasionally, then more frequently, and finally took up her abode there as before, and remained for six or eight months. It's of no use my going into details as to the life that woman led; if you want particulars you can look at Meyrick's legacy. Those designs were not drawn from his imagination. She again disappeared, and the people of the place saw nothing of her till a few months ago. My informant told me that she had taken some rooms in a house which he pointed out, and these rooms she was in the habit of visiting two or three times a week and always at ten in the morning. I was led to expect that one of these visits would be paid on a certain day about a week ago, and I accordingly managed to be on the lookout in company with my cicerone at a quarter to ten, and the hour and the lady came with equal punctuality. My friend and I were standing under an archway, a little way back from the street, but she saw us, and gave me a glance that I shall be long in forgetting. That look was quite enough for me; I knew Miss Raymond to be Mrs. Herbert; as for Mrs. Beaumont she had quite gone out of my head. She went into the house, and I watched it till four o'clock, when she came out, and then I followed her. It was a long chase, and I had to be very careful to keep a long way in the background, and yet not lose sight of the woman. She took me down to the Strand, and then to Westminster, and then up St. James's Street, and along Piccadilly. I felt queerish when I saw her turn up Ashley Street; the thought that Mrs. Herbert was Mrs. Beaumont came into my mind, but it seemed too impossible to be true. I waited at the corner, keeping my eye on her all the time, and I took particular care to note the house at which she stopped. It was the house with the gay curtains, the home of flowers, the house out of which Crashaw came the night he hanged himself in his garden. I was just going away with my discovery, when I saw an empty carriage come round and draw up in front of the house, and I came to the conclusion that Mrs. Herbert was going out for a drive, and I was right. There, as it happened, I met a man I know, and we stood talking together a little distance from the carriageway, to which I had my back. We had not been there for ten minutes when my friend took off his hat, and I glanced round and saw the lady I had been following all day. 'Who is that?' I said, and his answer was 'Mrs. Beaumont; lives in Ashley Street.' Of course there could be no doubt after that. I don't know whether she saw me, but I don't think she did. I went home at once, and, on consideration, I thought that I had a sufficiently good case with which to go to Clarke."

"Why to Clarke?"

"Because I am sure that Clarke is in possession of

facts about this woman, facts of which I know nothing."

"Well, what then?"

Mr. Villiers leaned back in his chair and looked reflectively at Austin for a moment before he answered:

"My idea was that Clarke and I should call on Mrs. Beaumont."

"You would never go into such a house as that? No, no, Villiers, you cannot do it. Besides, consider; what result—"

"I will tell you soon. But I was going to say that my information does not end here; it has been completed in an extraordinary manner.

"Look at this neat little packet of manuscript; it is paginated, you see, and I have indulged in the civil coquetry of a ribbon of red tape. It has almost a legal air, hasn't it? Run your eye over it, Austin. It is an account of the entertainment Mrs. Beaumont provided for her choicer guests. The man who wrote this escaped with his life, but I do not think he will live many years. The doctors tell him he must have sustained some severe shock to the nerves."

Austin took the manuscript, but never read it. Opening the neat pages at haphazard his eye was caught by a word and a phrase that followed it; and, sick at heart, with white lips and a cold sweat pouring like water from his temples, he flung the paper down.

"Take it away, Villiers, never speak of this again. Are you made of stone, man? Why, the dread and horror of death itself, the thoughts of the man who

stands in the keen morning air on the black plat-
form, bound, the bell tolling in his ears, and waits
for the harsh rattle of the bolt, are as nothing
compared to this. I will not read it; I should never
sleep again."

"Very good. I can fancy what you saw. Yes; it is
horrible enough; but after all, it is an old story, an
old mystery played in our day, and in dim London
streets instead of amidst the vineyards and the olive
gardens. We know what happened to those who
chanced to meet the Great God Pan, and those who
are wise know that all symbols are symbols of
something, not of nothing. It was, indeed, an
exquisite symbol beneath which men long ago
veiled their knowledge of the most awful, most
secret forces which lie at the heart of all things;
forces before which the souls of men must wither
and die and blacken, as their bodies blacken under
the electric current. Such forces cannot be named,
cannot be spoken, cannot be imagined except under
a veil and a symbol, a symbol to the most of us
appearing a quaint, poetic fancy, to some a foolish
tale. But you and I, at all events, have known
something of the terror that may dwell in the secret
place of life, manifested under human flesh; that
which is without form taking to itself a form. Oh,
Austin, how can it be? How is it that the very
sunlight does not turn to blackness before this
thing, the hard earth melt and boil beneath such a
burden?"

Villiers was pacing up and down the room, and
the beads of sweat stood out on his forehead.
Austin sat silent for a while, but Villiers saw him

make a sign upon his breast.

"I say again, Villiers, you will surely never enter such a house as that? You would never pass out alive."

"Yes, Austin, I shall go out alive—I, and Clarke with me."

What do you mean? You cannot, you would not dare—"

"Wait a moment. The air was very pleasant and fresh this morning; there was a breeze blowing, even through this dull street, and I thought I would take a walk. Piccadilly stretched before me a clear, bright vista, and the sun flashed on the carriages and on the quivering leaves in the park. It was a joyous morning, and men and women looked at the sky and smiled as they went about their work or their pleasure, and the wind blew as blithely as upon the meadows and the scented gorse. But somehow or other I got out of the bustle and the gaiety, and found myself walking slowly along a quiet, dull street, where there seemed to be no sunshine and no air, and where the few foot-passengers loitered as they walked, and hung indecisively about corners and archways. I walked along, hardly knowing where I was going or what I did there, but feeling impelled, as one sometimes is, to explore still further, with a vague idea of reaching some unknown goal. Thus I forged up the street, noting the small traffic of the milk-shop, and wondering at the incongruous medley of penny pipes, black tobacco, sweets, newspapers, and comic songs which here and there jostled one another in the short compass of a single window. I think it was a cold shudder that suddenly passed through me that first told me that I had found what I wanted. I looked up from the pavement and stopped before a dusty shop, above which the lettering had faded, where the red bricks of two hundred years ago had grimed to black; where the windows had gathered to themselves the dust of winters innumerable. I saw what I required; but I think it was five minutes before I had steadied myself and could walk in and ask for it in a cool voice and with a calm face. I think there must even then have been a tremor in my words, for the old man who came out of the back parlor, and fumbled slowly amongst his goods, looked oddly at me as he tied the parcel. I paid what he asked, and stood leaning by the counter, with a strange reluctance to take up my goods and go. I asked about the business, and learnt that trade was bad and the profits cut down sadly; but then the street was not what it was before traffic had been diverted, but that was done forty years ago, 'just before my father died,' he said. I got away at last, and walked along sharply; it was a dismal street indeed, and I was glad to return to the bustle and the noise. Would you like to see my purchase?"

Austin said nothing, but nodded his head slightly; he still looked white and sick. Villiers pulled out a drawer in the bamboo table, and showed Austin a long coil of cord, hard and new; and at one end was a running noose.

"It is the best hempen cord," said Villiers, "just as it used to be made for the old trade, the man told me. Not an inch of jute from end to end."

Austin set his teeth hard, and stared at Villiers, growing whiter as he looked.

"You would not do it," he murmured at last. "You would not have blood on your hands. My God!" he exclaimed, with sudden vehemence, "you cannot mean this, Villiers, that you will make yourself a hangman?"

"No. I shall offer a choice, and leave Helen Vaughan alone with this cord in a locked room for fifteen minutes. If when we go in it is not done, I shall call the nearest policeman. That is all."

"I must go now. I cannot stay here any longer; I cannot bear this. Goodnight."

"Goodnight, Austin."

The door shut, but in a moment it was open again, and Austin stood, white and ghastly, in the entrance.

"I was forgetting," he said, "that I too have something to tell. I have received a letter from Dr. Harding of Buenos Ayres. He says that he attended Meyrick for three weeks before his death."

"And does he say what carried him off in the prime of life? It was not fever?"

"No, it was not fever. According to the doctor, it was an utter collapse of the whole system, probably caused by some severe shock. But he states that the patient would tell him nothing, and that he was consequently at some disadvantage in treating the case."

"Is there anything more?"

"Yes. Dr. Harding ends his letter by saying: 'I think this is all the information I can give you about your poor friend. He had not been long in Buenos

Ayres, and knew scarcely any one, with the exception of a person who did not bear the best of characters, and has since left—a Mrs. Vaughan.'"

VIII: The Fragments

Amongst the papers of the well-known physician, Dr. Robert Matheson, of Ashley Street, Piccadilly, who died suddenly, of apoplectic seizure, at the beginning of 1892, a leaf of manuscript paper was found, covered with pencil jottings. These notes were in Latin, much abbreviated, and had evidently been made in great haste. The MS. was only deciphered with difficulty, and some words have up to the present time evaded all the efforts of the expert employed. The date, "XXV Jul. 1888," is written on the right-hand corner of the MS. The following is a translation of Dr. Matheson's manuscript.

*

"Whether science would benefit by these brief notes if they could be published, I do not know, but rather doubt. But certainly I shall never take the responsibility of publishing or divulging one word of what is here written, not only on account of my oath given freely to those two persons who were present, but also because the details are too abominable. It is probably that, upon mature consideration, and after weighting the good and evil, I shall one day destroy this paper, or at least leave it under seal to my friend D., trusting in his discretion, to use it or to burn it, as he may think fit.

"As was befitting, I did all that my knowledge suggested to make sure that I was suffering under no delusion. At first astounded, I could hardly think, but in a minute's time I was sure that my pulse was steady and regular, and that I was in my real and true senses. I then fixed my eyes quietly on what was before me.

"Though horror and revolting nausea rose up within me, and an odor of corruption choked my breath, I remained firm. I was then privileged or accursed, I dare not say which, to see that which was on the bed, lying there black like ink, transformed before my eyes. The skin, and the flesh, and the muscles, and the bones, and the firm structure of the human body that I had thought to be unchangeable, and permanent as adamant, began to melt and dissolve.

"I know that the body may be separated into its elements by external agencies, but I should have refused to believe what I saw. For here there was some internal force, of which I knew nothing, that caused dissolution and change.

"Here too was all the work by which man had been made repeated before my eyes. I saw the form waver from sex to sex, dividing itself from itself, and then again reunited. Then I saw the body descend to the beasts whence it ascended, and that which was on the heights go down to the depths, even to the abyss of all being. The principle of life, which makes organism, always remained, while the outward form changed.

"The light within the room had turned to blackness, not the darkness of night, in which objects are seen dimly, for I could see clearly and without difficulty. But it was the negation of light; objects were presented to my eyes, if I may say so, without any medium, in such a manner that if there had been a prism in the room I should have seen no colors represented in it.

"I watched, and at last I saw nothing but a substance as jelly. Then the ladder was ascended again—[here the MS. is illegible]—for one instance I saw a Form, shaped in dimness before me, which I will not farther describe. But the symbol of this form may be seen in ancient sculptures, and in paintings which survived beneath the lava, too foul to be spoken of—as a horrible and unspeakable shape, neither man nor beast, was changed into human form, there came finally death.

"I who saw all this, not without great horror and loathing of soul, here write my name, declaring all that I have set on this paper to be true.

"Robert Matheson, Med. Dr."

*

Such, Raymond, is the story of what I know and what I have seen. The burden of it was too heavy for me to bear alone, and yet I could tell it to none but you. Villiers, who was with me at the last, knows nothing of that awful secret of the wood, of how what we both saw die, lay upon the smooth, sweet turf amidst the summer flowers, half in sun and half in shadow, and holding the girl Rachel's hand, called and summoned those companions, and shaped in solid form, upon the earth we tread upon, the horror which we can but hint at, which we can only name under a figure. I would not tell

Villiers of this, nor of that resemblance, which struck me as with a blow upon my heart, when I saw the portrait, which filled the cup of terror at the end. What this can mean I dare not guess. I know that what I saw perish was not Mary, and yet in the last agony Mary's eyes looked into mine. Whether there can be any one who can show the last link in this chain of awful mystery, I do not know, but if there be any one who can do this, you, Raymond, are the man. And if you know the secret, it rests with you to tell it or not, as you please.

I am writing this letter to you immediately on my getting back to town. I have been in the country for the last few days; perhaps you may be able to guess in which part. While the horror and wonder of London was at its height—for "Mrs. Beaumont," as I have told you, was well known in society—I wrote to my friend Dr. Phillips, giving some brief outline, or rather hint, of what happened, and asking him to tell me the name of the village where the events he had related to me occurred. He gave me the name, as he said with the less hesitation, because Rachel's father and mother were dead, and the rest of the family had gone to a relative in the State of Washington six months before. The parents, he said, had undoubtedly died of grief and horror caused by the terrible death of their daughter, and by what had gone before that death. On the evening of the day which I received Phillips' letter I was at Caermaen, and standing beneath the moldering Roman walls, white with the winters of seventeen hundred years, I looked over the meadow where once had stood the older temple of the "God of the Deeps," and saw a house gleaming in the sunlight. It was the house where Helen had lived. I stayed at Caermaen for several days. The people of the place, I found, knew little and had guessed less. Those whom I spoke to on the matter seemed surprised that an antiquarian (as I professed myself to be) should trouble about a village tragedy, of which they gave a very commonplace version, and, as you may imagine, I told nothing of what I knew. Most of my time was spent in the great wood that rises just above the village and climbs the hillside, and goes down to the river in the valley; such another long lovely valley, Raymond, as that on which we looked one summer night, walking to and fro before your house. For many an hour I strayed through the maze of the forest, turning now to right and now to left, pacing slowly down long alleys of under-growth, shadowy and chill, even under the midday sun, and halting beneath great oaks; lying on the short turf of a clearing where the faint sweet scent of wild roses came to me on the wind and mixed with the heavy perfume of the elder, whose mingled odor is like the odor of the room of the dead, a vapor of incense and corruption. I stood at the edges of the wood, gazing at all the pomp and procession of the foxgloves towering amidst the bracken and shining red in the broad sunshine, and beyond them into deep thickets of close under-growth where springs boil up from the rock and nourish the water-weeds, dank and evil. But in all my wanderings I avoided one part of the wood; it was not till yesterday that I climbed to the summit of the hill, and stood upon the ancient Roman road that threads the highest ridge of the wood. Here they had walked, Helen and Rachel, along this quiet causeway, upon the pavement of green turf, shut in on either side by high banks of red earth, and tall hedges of shining beech, and here I followed in their steps, looking out, now and again, through partings in the boughs, and seeing on one side the sweep of the wood stretching far to right and left, and sinking into the broad level, and beyond, the yellow sea, and the land over the sea. On the other side was the valley and the river and hill following hill as wave on wave, and wood and meadow, and cornfield, and white houses gleaming, and a great wall of mountain, and far blue peaks in the north. And so at least I came to the place. The track went up a gentle slope, and widened out into an open space with a wall of thick undergrowth around it, and then, narrowing again, passed on into the distance and the faint blue mist of summer heat. And into this pleasant summer glade Rachel passed a girl, and left it, who shall say what? I did not stay long there.

In a small town near Caermaen there is a museum, containing for the most part Roman remains which have been found in the neighborhood at various times. On the day after my arrival in Caermaen I walked over to the town in question, and took the opportunity of inspecting the museum. After I had seen most of the sculptured stones, the coffins, rings, coins, and fragments of tessellated pavement which the place contains, I was shown a small square pillar of white stone, which had been recently discovered in the wood of which I have been speaking, and, as I found on inquiry, in that open space where the Roman road broadens out. On one side of the pillar was an inscription, of which I took a note. Some of the letters have been defaced, but I do not think there can be any doubt as to those which I supply. The inscription is as follows:

DEVOMNODENTi
FLAvIVSSENILISPOSSvit
PROPTERNVPtias

QuaSVIDITSVBVMra

"To the great god Nodens (the god of the Great Deep or Abyss) Flavius Senilis has erected this pillar on account of the marriage which he saw beneath the shade."

The custodian of the museum informed me that local antiquaries were much puzzled, not by the inscription, or by any difficulty in translating it, but as to the circumstance or rite to which allusion is made.

*

And now, my dear Clarke, as to what you tell me about Helen Vaughan, whom you say you saw die under circumstances of the utmost and almost incredible horror. I was interested in your account, but a good deal, nay all, of what you told me I knew already. I can understand the strange likeness you remarked in both the portrait and in the actual face; you have seen Helen's mother. You remember that still summer night so many years ago, when I talked to you of the world beyond the shadows, and of the god Pan. You remember Mary. She was the mother of Helen Vaughan, who was born nine months after that night.

Mary never recovered her reason. She lay, as you saw her, all the while upon her bed, and a few days after the child was born she died. I fancy that just at the last she knew me; I was standing by the bed, and the old look came into her eyes for a second, and then she shuddered and groaned and died. It was an ill work I did that night when you were present; I broke open the door of the house of life, without knowing or caring what might pass forth or enter in. I recollect your telling me at the time, sharply enough, and rightly too, in one sense, that I had ruined the reason of a human being by a foolish experiment, based on an absurd theory. You did well to blame me, but my theory was not all absurdity. What I said Mary would see she saw, but I forgot that no human eyes can look on such a sight with impunity. And I forgot, as I have just said, that when the house of life is thus thrown open, there may enter in that for which we have no name, and human flesh may become the veil of a horror one dare not express. I played with energies which I did not understand, you have seen the ending of it. Helen Vaughan did well to bind the cord about her neck and die, though the death was horrible. The blackened face, the hideous form upon the bed, changing and melting before your eyes from woman to man, from man to beast, and from beast to worse than beast, all the strange horror that you witness, surprises me but little. What you say the doctor whom you sent for saw and shuddered at I noticed long ago; I knew what I had done the moment the child was born, and when it was scarcely five years old I surprised it, not once or twice but several times with a playmate, you may guess of what kind. It was for me a constant, an incarnate horror, and after a few years I felt I could bear it no more, and I sent Helen Vaughan away. You know now what frightened the boy in the wood. The rest of the strange story, and all else that you tell me, as discovered by your friend, I have contrived to learn from time to time, almost to the last chapter. And now Helen is with her companions.

The Hill of Dreams

Arthur Machen

I

There was a glow in the sky as if great furnace doors were opened.

But all the afternoon his eyes had looked on glamour; he had strayed in fairyland. The holidays were nearly done, and Lucian Taylor had gone out resolved to lose himself, to discover strange hills and prospects that he had never seen before. The air was still, breathless, exhausted after heavy rain, and the clouds looked as if they had been molded of lead. No breeze blew upon the hill, and down in the well of the valley not a dry leaf stirred, not a bough shook in all the dark January woods.

About a mile from the rectory he had diverged from the main road by an opening that promised mystery and adventure. It was an old neglected lane, little more than a ditch, worn ten feet deep by its winter waters, and shadowed by great untrimmed hedges, densely woven together. On each side were turbid streams, and here and there a torrent of water gushed down the banks, flooding the lane. It was so deep and dark that he could not get a glimpse of the country through which he was passing, but the way went down and down to some unconjectured hollow.

Perhaps he walked two miles between the high walls of the lane before its descent ceased, but he thrilled with the sense of having journeyed very far, all the long way from the known to the unknown. He had come as it were into the bottom of a bowl amongst the hills, and black woods shut out the world. From the road behind him, from the road before him, from the unseen wells beneath the trees, rivulets of waters swelled and streamed down towards the center to the brook that crossed the lane. Amid the dead and wearied silence of the air, beneath leaden and motionless clouds, it was strange to hear such a tumult of gurgling and rushing water, and he stood for a while on the quivering footbridge and watched the rush of dead wood and torn branches and wisps of straw, all hurrying madly past him, to plunge into the heaped spume, the barmy froth that had gathered against a fallen tree.

Then he climbed again, and went up between limestone rocks, higher and higher, till the noise of waters became indistinct, a faint humming of swarming hives in summer. He walked some distance on level ground, till there was a break in the banks and a stile on which he could lean and look out. He found himself, as he had hoped, afar and forlorn; he had strayed into outland and occult territory. From the eminence of the lane, skirting the brow of a hill, he looked down into deep valleys and dingles, and beyond, across the trees, to remoter country, wild bare hills and dark wooded lands meeting the gray still sky. Immediately beneath his feet the ground sloped steep down to the valley, a hillside of close grass patched with dead bracken, and dotted here and there with stunted thorns, and below there were deep oak woods, all still and silent, and lonely as if no one ever passed that way. The grass and bracken and thorns and woods, all were brown and gray beneath the leaden sky, and as Lucian looked he was amazed, as though he were reading a wonderful story, the meaning of which was a little greater than his understanding. Then, like the hero of a fairy-book, he went on and on, catching now and again glimpses of the amazing country into which he had penetrated, and perceiving rather than seeing that as the day waned everything grew more gray and somber. As he advanced he heard the evening sounds of the farms, the low of the cattle, and the barking of the sheepdogs; a faint thin noise from far away. It was growing late, and as the shadows blackened he walked faster, till once more the lane began to descend, there was a sharp turn, and he found himself, with a good deal of relief, and a little disappointment, on familiar ground. He had nearly described a circle, and knew this end of the lane very well; it was not much more than a mile from home. He walked smartly down the hill; the air was all glimmering and indistinct, transmuting trees and hedges into ghostly shapes, and the walls of the White House Farm flickered on the hillside, as if they were moving towards him. Then a change came. First, a little breath of wind brushed with a dry whispering sound through the hedges, the few leaves left on the boughs began to stir, and one or two danced madly, and as the wind freshened and came up from a new quarter, the sapless branches above rattled against one another like bones. The growing breeze seemed to clear the air and lighten it. He was passing the stile where a path led to old Mrs. Gibbon's desolate little cottage, in the middle of the fields, at some distance even from the lane, and he saw the light blue smoke of her chimney rise distinct above the gaunt greengage trees, against a pale band that was broadening along the horizon. As he passed the stile with his head bent, and his eyes on the ground, something white started out from the black shadow of the hedge, and in the strange twilight, now tinged with a flush from the west, a figure seemed to swim past him and disappear. For a moment he wondered who it could be, the light was so flickering and unsteady, so unlike the real atmosphere of the day, when he recollected it was only Annie Morgan, old Morgan's daughter at the White House. She was three years older than he, and it annoyed him to find that though she was only fifteen, there had been a dreadful increase in her height since the summer holidays. He had got to the bottom of the hill, and, lifting up his eyes, saw the strange changes of the sky. The pale band had broadened into a clear vast space of light, and above, the heavy leaden clouds were breaking apart and driving across the heaven before the wind. He stopped to watch, and looked up at the great mound that jutted out from the hills into mid-valley. It was a natural formation, and always it must have had something of the form of a fort, but its steepness had been increased by Roman art, and there were high banks on the summit which Lucian's father had told him were the *vallum* of the camp, and a deep ditch had been dug to the north to sever it from the hillside. On this summit oaks had grown, queer stunted-looking trees with twisted and contorted trunks, and writhing branches; and these now stood out black against the lighted sky. And then the air changed once more; the flush increased, and a spot like blood appeared in the pond by the gate, and all the clouds were touched with fiery spots and dapples of flame; here and there it looked as if awful furnace doors were being opened.

The wind blew wildly, and it came up through the woods with a noise like a scream, and a great oak by the roadside ground its boughs together with a dismal grating jar. As the red gained in the sky, the earth and all upon it glowed, even the gray winter fields and the bare hillsides crimsoned, the water pools were cisterns of molten brass, and the very road glittered. He was wonder-struck, almost aghast, before the scarlet magic of the afterglow. The old Roman fort was invested with fire; flames from heaven were smitten about its walls, and above there was a dark floating cloud, like fume of smoke, and every haggard writhing tree showed as black as midnight against the black of the furnace.

When he got home he heard his mother's voice calling: "Here's Lucian at last. Mary, Master Lucian has come, you can get the tea ready." He told a long tale of his adventures, and felt somewhat mortified when his father seemed perfectly acquainted with the whole course of the lane, and knew the names of the wild woods through which he had passed in awe.

"You must have gone by the Darren, I suppose"—that was all he said. "Yes, I noticed the sunset; we shall have some stormy weather. I don't expect to see many in church tomorrow."

There was buttered toast for tea "because it was holidays." The red curtains were drawn, and a bright fire was burning, and there was the old familiar furniture, a little shabby, but charming from association. It was much pleasanter than the cold and squalid schoolroom; and much better to be reading *Chamber's Journal* than learning Euclid; and better to talk to his father and mother than to be answering such remarks as: "I say, Taylor, I've torn my trousers; how much to do you charge for mending?" "Lucy, dear, come quick and sew this button on my shirt."

That night the storm woke him, and he groped with his hands amongst the bedclothes, and sat up, shuddering, not knowing where he was. He had seen himself, in a dream, within the Roman fort, working some dark horror, and the furnace doors were opened and a blast of flame from heaven was smitten upon him.

Lucian went slowly, but not discreditably, up the school, gaining prizes now and again, and falling in love more and more with useless reading and unlikely knowledge. He did his elegiacs and iambics well enough, but he preferred exercising himself in the rhymed Latin of the middle ages. He like history, but he loved to meditate on a land laid waste, Britain deserted by the legions, the rare pavements riven by frost, Celtic magic still brooding on the wild hills and in the black depths of the forest, the rosy marbles stained with rain, and the walls growing gray. The masters did not encourage these researches; a pure enthusiasm, they felt, should be for cricket and football, the *dilettanti* might even play fives and read Shakespeare without blame, but healthy English boys should have nothing to do with decadent periods. He was once found guilty of recommending Villon to a schoolfellow named Barnes. Barnes tried to extract unpleasantness from the text during preparation, and rioted in his place, owing to his incapacity for the language. The matter was a serious one; the headmaster had never heard of Villon, and the culprit gave up the name of his literary admirer without remorse. Hence, sorrow for Lucian, and complete immunity for the miserable illiterate Barnes, who resolved to confine his researches to the Old Testament, a book which the headmaster knew well. As for Lucian, he plodded on, learning his work decently, and sometimes doing very creditable Latin and Greek prose. His schoolfellows thought him quite mad, and tolerated him, and indeed were very kind to him in their barbarous manner. He often remembered in after life acts of generosity and good nature done by wretches like Barnes, who had no care for old French nor for curious meters, and such recollections always moved him to emotion. Travelers tell such tales; cast upon cruel shores amongst savage races, they have found no little kindness and warmth of hospitality.

He looked forward to the holidays as joyfully as the rest of them. Barnes and his friend Duscot used to tell him their plans and anticipation; they were going home to brothers and sisters, and to cricket, more cricket, or to football, more football, and in the winter there were parties and jollities of all sorts. In return he would announce his intention of studying the Hebrew language, or perhaps Provençal, with a walk up a bare and desolate mountain by way of open-air amusement, and on a rainy day for choice. Whereupon Barnes would impart to Duscot his confident belief that old Taylor was quite cracked. It was a queer, funny life that of school, and so very unlike anything in *Tom Brown*. He once saw the headmaster patting the head of the bishop's little boy, while he called him "my little man," and smiled hideously. He told the tale grotesquely in the lower fifth room the same day, and earned much applause, but forfeited all liking directly by proposing a voluntary course of scholastic logic. One barbarian threw him to the ground and another jumped on him, but it was done very pleasantly. There were, indeed, some few of a worse class in the school, solemn sycophants, prigs perfected from tender years, who thought life already "serious," and yet, as the headmaster said, were "joyous, manly young fellows." Some of these dressed for dinner at home, and talked of dances when they came back in January. But this virulent sort was comparatively infrequent, and achieved great success in after life. Taking his school days as a whole, he always spoke up for the system, and years afterward he described with enthusiasm the strong beer at a roadside tavern, some way out of the town. But he always maintained that the taste for tobacco, acquired in early life, was the great life, was the great note of the English Public School.

Three years after Lucian's discovery of the

narrow lane and the vision of the flaming fort, the August holidays brought him home at a time of great heat. It was one of those memorable years of English weather, when some Provençal spell seems wreathed round the island in the northern sea, and the grasshoppers chirp loudly as the cicadas, the hills smell of rosemary, and white walls of the old farmhouses blaze in the sunlight as if they stood in Arles or Avignon or famed Tarascon by Rhone.

Lucian's father was late at the station, and consequently Lucian bought the *Confessions of an English Opium Eater* which he saw on the bookstall. When his father did drive up, Lucian noticed that the old trap had had a new coat of dark paint, and that the pony looked advanced in years.

"I was afraid that I should be late, Lucian," said his father, "though I made old Polly go like anything. I was just going to tell George to put her into the trap when young Philip Harris came to me in a terrible state. He said his father fell down 'all of a sudden like' in the middle of the field, and they couldn't make him speak, and would I please to come and see him. So I had to go, though I couldn't do anything for the poor fellow. They had sent for Dr. Burrows, and I am afraid he will find it a bad case of sunstroke. The old people say they never remember such a heat before."

The pony jogged steadily along the burning turnpike road, taking revenge for the hurrying on the way to the station. The hedges were white with the limestone dust, and the vapor of heat palpitated over the fields. Lucian showed his *Confessions* to his father, and began to talk of the beautiful bits he had already found. Mr. Taylor knew the book well —had read it many years before. Indeed he was almost as difficult to surprise as that character in Daudet, who had one formula for all the chances of life, and when he saw the drowned Academician dragged out of the river, merely observed *"J'ai vu tout ça."* Mr. Taylor the parson, as his parishioners called him, had read the fine books and loved the hills and woods, and now knew no more of pleasant or sensational surprises. Indeed the living was much depreciated in value, and his own private means were reduced almost to vanishing point, and under such circumstances the great style loses many of its finer savors. He was very fond of Lucian, and cheered by his return, but in the evening he would be a sad man again, with his head resting on one hand, and eyes reproaching sorry fortune.

Nobody called out "Here's your master with Master Lucian; you can get tea ready," when the pony jogged up to the front door. His mother had been dead a year, and a cousin kept house. She was a respectable person called Deacon, of middle age, and ordinary standards; and, consequently, there was cold mutton on the table. There was a cake, but nothing of flour, baked in ovens, would rise at Miss Deacon's evocation. Still, the meal was laid in the beloved "parlor," with the view of hills and valleys and climbing woods from the open window, and the old furniture was still pleasant to see, and the old books in the shelves had many memories. One of the most respected of the armchairs had become weak in the castors and had to be artfully propped up, but Lucian found it very comfortable after the hard forms. When tea was over he went out and strolled in the garden and orchards, and looked over the stile down into the brake, where foxgloves and bracken and broom mingled with the hazel undergrowth, where he knew of secret glades and untracked recesses, deep in the woven green, the cabinets for many years of his lonely meditations. Every path about his home, every field and hedgerow had dear and friendly memories for him; and the odor of the meadowsweet was better than the incense steaming in the sunshine. He loitered, and hung over the stile till the far-off woods began to turn purple, till the white mists were wreathing in the valley.

Day after day, through all that August, morning and evening were wrapped in haze; day after day the earth shimmered in the heat, and the air was strange, unfamiliar. As he wandered in the lanes and sauntered by the cool sweet verge of the woods, he saw and felt that nothing was common or accustomed, for the sunlight transfigured the meadows and changed all the form of the earth. Under the violent Provençal sun, the elms and beeches looked exotic trees, and in the early morning, when the mists were thick, the hills had put on an unearthly shape.

The one adventure of the holidays was the visit to the Roman fort, to that fantastic hill about whose steep bastions and haggard oaks he had seen the flames of sunset writhing nearly three years before. Ever since that Saturday evening in January, the lonely valley had been a desirable place to him; he

111

had watched the green battlements in summer and winter weather, had seen the heaped mounds rising dimly amidst the drifting rain, had marked the violent height swim up from the ice-white bulwarks glimmer and vanish in hovering April twilight. In the hedge of the lane there was a gate on which he used to lean and look down south to where the hill surged up so suddenly, its summit defined on summer evenings not only by the rounded ramparts but by the ring of dense green foliage that marked the circle of oak trees. Higher up the lane, on the way he had come that Saturday afternoon, one could see the white walls of Morgan's farm on the hillside to the north, and on the south there was the stile with the view of old Mrs. Gibbon's cottage smoke; but down in the hollow, looking over the gate, there was no hint of human work, except those green and antique battlements, on which the oaks stood in circle, guarding the inner wood.

The ring of the fort drew him with stronger fascination during that hot August weather. Standing, or as his headmaster would have said, "mooning" by the gate, and looking into that enclosed and secret valley, it seemed to his fancy as if there were a halo about the hill, an aureole that played like flame around it. One afternoon as he gazed from his station by the gate the sheer sides and the swelling bulwarks were more than ever things of enchantment; the green oak ring stood out against the sky as still and bright as in a picture, and Lucian, in spite of his respect for the law of trespass, slid over the gate. The farmers and their men were busy on the uplands with the harvest, and the adventure was irresistible. At first he stole along by the brook in the shadow of the alders, where the grass and the flowers of wet meadows grew richly; but as he drew nearer to the fort, and its height now rose sheer above him, he left all shelter, and began desperately to mount. There was not a breath of wind; the sunlight shone down on the bare hillside; the loud chirp of the grasshoppers was the only sound. It was a steep ascent and grew steeper as the valley sank away. He turned for a moment, and looked down towards the stream which now seemed to wind remote between the alders; above the valley there were small dark figures moving in the cornfield, and now and again there came the faint echo of a high-pitched voice singing through the air as on a wire. He was wet with heat; the sweat streamed off his face, and he could feel it trickling all over his body. But above him the green bastions rose defiant, and the dark ring of oaks promised coolness. He pressed on, and higher, and at last began to crawl up the *vallum*, on hands and knees, grasping the turf and here and there the roots that had burst through the red earth. And then he lay, panting with deep breaths, on the summit.

Within the fort it was all dusky and cool and hollow; it was as if one stood at the bottom of a great cup. Within, the wall seemed higher than without, and the ring of oaks curved up like a dark green vault. There were nettles growing thick and rank in the foss; they looked different from the common nettles in the lanes, and Lucian, letting his hand touch a leaf by accident, felt the sting burn like fire. Beyond the ditch there was an undergrowth, a dense thicket of trees, stunted and old, crooked and withered by the winds into awkward and ugly forms; beech and oak and hazel and ash and yew twisted and so shortened and deformed that each seemed, like the nettle, of no common kind. He began to fight his way through the ugly growth, stumbling and getting hard knocks from the rebound of twisted boughs. His foot struck once or twice against something harder than wood, and looking down he saw stones white with the leprosy of age, but still showing the work of the axe. And farther, the roots of the stunted trees gripped the foot-high relics of a wall; and a round heap of fallen stones nourished rank, unknown herbs, that smelt poisonous. The earth was black and unctuous, and bubbling under the feet, left no track behind. From it, in the darkest places where the shadow was thickest, swelled the growth of an abominable fungus, making the still air sick with its corrupt odor, and he shuddered as he felt the horrible thing pulped beneath his feet. Then there was a gleam of sunlight, and as he thrust the last boughs apart, he stumbled into the open space in the heart of the camp. It was a lawn of sweet close turf in the center of the matted brake, of clean firm earth from which no shameful growth sprouted, and near the middle of the glade was a stump of a felled yew-tree, left untrimmed by the woodman. Lucian thought it must have been made for a seat; a crooked bough through which a little sap still ran was a support for the back, and he sat down and rested after his toil. It was not really so comfortable a seat as one of the school forms, but the satisfaction was to find anything at all that would serve for a chair. He sat there, still panting after the climb and his struggle through the dank and jungle-like thicket, and he felt as if he were growing hotter and hotter; the sting of the nettle was burning his hand, and the tingling fire seemed to spread all over his body.

Suddenly, he knew that he was alone. Not merely solitary; that he had often been amongst the woods and deep in the lanes; but now it was a wholly different and a very strange sensation. He thought of the valley winding far below him, all its fields by the brook green and peaceful and still, without path or track. Then he had climbed the abrupt surge of the hill, and passing the green and swelling battlements, the ring of oaks, and the matted thicket, had come to the central space. And behind there were, he knew, many desolate fields, wild as common, untrodden, unvisited. He was utterly alone. He still grew hotter as he sat on the stump, and at last lay down at full length on the soft grass, and more at his ease felt the waves of heat pass over his body.

And then he began to dream, to let his fancies stray over half-imagined, delicious things, indulging a virgin mind in its wanderings. The hot air seemed to beat upon him in palpable waves, and the nettle sting tingled and itched intolerably; and he was alone upon the fairy hill, within the great mounds, within the ring of oaks, deep in the heart of the matted thicket. Slowly and timidly he began to untie his boots, fumbling with the laces, and glancing all the while on every side at the ugly misshapen trees that hedged the lawn. Not a branch was straight, not one was free, but all were interlaced and grew one about another; and just above ground, where the cankered stems joined the protuberant roots, there were forms that imitated the human shape, and faces and twining limbs that amazed him. Green mosses were hair, and tresses were stark in gray lichen; a twisted root swelled into a limb; in the hollows of the rotted bark he saw the masks of men. His eyes were fixed and fascinated by the simulacra of the wood, and could not see his hands, and so at last, and suddenly, it seemed, he lay in the sunlight, beautiful with his olive skin, dark haired, dark eyed, the gleaming bodily vision of a strayed faun.

Quick flames now quivered in the substance of his nerves, hints of mysteries, secrets of life passed trembling through his brain, unknown desires stung him. As he gazed across the turf and into the thicket, the sunshine seemed really to become green, and the contrast between the bright glow poured on the lawn and the black shadow of the brake made an odd flickering light, in which all the grotesque postures of stem and root began to stir; the wood was alive. The turf beneath him heaved and sank as with the deep swell of the sea. He fell asleep, and lay still on the grass, in the midst of the thicket.

He found out afterwards that he must have slept for nearly an hour. The shadows had changed when he awoke; his senses came to him with a sudden shock, and he sat up and stared at his bare limbs in stupid amazement. He huddled on his clothes and laced his boots, wondering what folly had beset him. Then, while he stood indecisive, hesitating, his brain a whirl of puzzled thought, his body trembling, his hands shaking; as with electric heat, sudden remembrance possessed him. A flaming blush shone red on his cheeks, and glowed and thrilled through his limbs. As he awoke, a brief and slight breeze had stirred in a nook of the matted boughs, and there was a glinting that might have been the flash of sudden sunlight across shadow, and the branches rustled and murmured for a moment, perhaps at the wind's passage.

He stretched out his hands, and cried to his visitant to return; he entreated the dark eyes that had shone over him, and the scarlet lips that had kissed him. And then panic fear rushed into his heart, and he ran blindly, dashing through the wood. He climbed the *vallum*, and looked out, crouching, lest anybody should see him. Only the shadows were changed, and a breath of cooler air mounted from the brook; the fields were still and peaceful, the black figures moved, far away, amidst the corn, and the faint echo of the high-pitched voices sang thin and distant on the evening wind. Across the stream, in the cleft on the hill, opposite to the fort, the blue wood smoke stole up a spiral pillar from the chimney of old Mrs. Gibbon's cottage. He began to run full tilt down the steep surge of the hill, and never stopped till he was over the gate and in the lane again. As he looked back, down the valley to the south, and saw the violent ascent, the green swelling bulwarks, and the dark ring of oaks; the sunlight seemed to play about the fort with an aureole of flame.

"Where on earth have you been all this time, Lucian?" said his cousin when he got home. "Why, you look quite ill. It is really madness of you to go walking in such weather as this. I wonder you haven't got a sunstroke. And the tea must be nearly cold. I couldn't keep your father waiting, you know."

He muttered something about being rather tired, and sat down to his tea. It was not cold, for the "cozy" had been put over the pot, but it was black and bitter strong, as his cousin expressed it. The draught was unpalatable, but it did him good, and the thought came with great consolation that he had only been asleep and dreaming queer, nightmarish dreams. He shook off all his fancies with resolution, and thought the loneliness of the camp, and the burning sunlight, and possibly the nettle sting, which still tingled most abominably, must have been the only factors in his farrago of impossible recollections. He remembered that when he had felt the sting, he had seized a nettle with thick folds of his handkerchief, and having twisted off a good length, and put it in his pocket to show his father. Mr. Taylor was almost interested when he came in from his evening stroll about the garden and saw the specimen.

"Where did you manage to come across that, Lucian?" he said. "You haven't been to Caermaen, have you?"

"No. I got it in the Roman fort by the common."

"Oh, the twyn. You must have been trespassing then. Do you know what it is?"

"No. I thought it looked different from the common nettles."

"Yes; it's a Roman nettle—*arctic pilulifera*. It's a rare plant. Burrows says it's to be found at Caermaen, but I was never able to come across it. I must add it to the *flora* of the parish."

Mr. Taylor had begun to compile a *flora* accompanied by a *hortus siccus*, but both stayed on high shelves dusty and fragmentary. He put the specimen on his desk, intending to fasten it in the book, but the maid swept it away, dry and withered, in a day or two.

Lucian tossed and cried out in his sleep that night, and the awakening in the morning was, in a measure, a renewal of the awakening in the fort. But the impression was not so strong, and in a plain room it seemed all delirium, a phantasmagoria. He had to go down to Caermaen in the afternoon, for Mrs. Dixon, the vicar's wife, had "commanded" his presence at tea. Mr. Dixon, though fat and short and clean-shaven, ruddy of face, was a safe man, with no extreme views on anything. He "deplored" all extreme party convictions, and thought the great needs of our beloved Church were conciliation, moderation, and above all "amolgamation"—so he pronounced the word. Mrs. Dixon was tall, imposing, splendid, well fitted for the Episcopal order, with gifts that would have shone at the palace. There were daughters, who studied German Literature, and thought Miss Frances Ridley Havergal wrote poetry, but Lucian had no fear of them; he dreaded the boys. Everybody said they were such fine, manly fellows, such gentlemanly boys, with such a good manner, sure to get on in the world. Lucian had said "Bother!" in a very violent manner when the gracious invitation was conveyed to him, but there was no getting out of it. Miss Deacon did her best to make him look smart; his ties were all so disgraceful that she had to supply the want with a narrow ribbon of a sky-blue tint; and she brushed him so long and so violently that he quite understood why a horse sometimes bites and sometimes kicks the groom. He set out between two and three in a gloomy frame of mind; he knew too well what spending the afternoon with honest manly boys meant. He found the reality more lurid than his anticipation. The boys were in the field, and the first remark he heard when he got in sight of the group was:

"Hullo, Lucian, how much for the tie?" "Fine tie," another, a stranger, observed. "You bagged it from the kitten, didn't you?"

Then they made up a game of cricket, and he was put in first. He was l.b.w. in his second over, so they all said, and had to field for the rest of the afternoon. Arthur Dixon, who was about his own age, forgetting all the laws of hospitality, told him he was a beastly muff when he missed a catch, rather a difficult catch. He missed several catches, and it seemed as if he were always panting after balls, which, as Edward Dixon said, any fool, even a baby, could have stopped. At last the game broke up, solely from Lucian's lack of skill, as everybody declared. Edward Dixon, who was thirteen, and had a swollen red face and a projecting eye, wanted to fight him for spoiling the game, and the others agreed that he funked the fight in a rather dirty manner. The strange boy, who was called De Carti, and was understood to be faintly related to Lord De Carti of M'Carthytown, said openly that the fellows at his place wouldn't stand such a sneak for five minutes. So the afternoon passed off very pleasantly indeed, till it was time to go into the vicarage for weak tea, homemade cake, and unripe plums. He got away at last. As he went out at the gate, he heard De Carti's final observation:

"We like to dress well at our place. His governor must be beastly poor to let him go about like that. D'y' see his trousers are all ragged at heel? Is old Taylor a gentleman?"

It had been a very gentlemanly afternoon, but there was a certain relief when the vicarage was far behind, and the evening smoke of the little town, once the glorious capital of Siluria, hung haze-like over the ragged roofs and mingled with the river mist. He looked down from the height of the road on the huddled houses, saw the points of light start out suddenly from the cottages on the hillside beyond, and gazed at the long lovely valley fading in the twilight, till the darkness came and all that remained was the somber ridge of the forest. The way was pleasant through the solemn scented lane, with glimpses of dim country, the vague mystery of night overshadowing the woods and meadows. A warm wind blew gusts of odor from the meadow-sweet by the brook, now and then bee and beetle span homeward through the air, booming a deep note as from a great organ far away, and from the verge of the wood came the "who-oo, who-oo, who-oo" of the owls, a wild strange sound that mingled with the whirr and rattle of the night-jar, deep in the bracken. The moon swam up through the films of misty cloud, and hung, a golden glorious lantern, in mid-air; and, set in the dusky hedge, the little green fires of the glowworms appeared. He sauntered slowly up the lane, drinking in the religion of the scene, and thinking the country by night as mystic and wonderful as a dimly lit cathedral. He had quite forgotten the "manly young fellows" and their sports, and only wished as the land began to shimmer and gleam in the moonlight that he knew by some medium of words or color how to represent the loveliness about his way.

"Had a pleasant evening, Lucian?" said his father when he came in.

"Yes, I had a nice walk home. Oh, in the afternoon we played cricket. I didn't care for it much. There was a boy named De Carti there; he is staying with the Dixons. Mrs. Dixon whispered to me when we were going in to tea, 'He's a second cousin of Lord De Carti's,' and she looked quite grave as if she were in church."

The parson grinned grimly and lit his old pipe.

"Baron De Carti's great-grandfather was a Dublin attorney," he remarked. "Which his name was Jeremiah M'Carthy. His prejudiced fellow-citizens called him the Unjust Steward, also the Bloody Attorney, and I believe that 'to hell with M'Carthy' was quite a popular cry about the time of the

Union."

Mr. Taylor was a man of very wide and irregular reading and a tenacious memory; he often used to wonder why he had not risen in the Church. He had once told Mr. Dixon a singular and *drolatique* anecdote concerning the bishop's college days, and he never discovered why the prelate did not bow according to his custom when the name of Taylor was called at the next visitation. Some people said the reason was lighted candles, but that was impossible, as the Reverend and Honorable Smallwood Stafford, Lord Beamys's son, who had a cure of souls in the cathedral city, was well known to burn no end of candles, and with him the bishop was on the best of terms. Indeed the bishop often stayed at Coplesey (pronounced "Copsey") Hall, Lord Beamys's place in the west.

Lucian had mentioned the name of De Carti with intention, and had perhaps exaggerated a little Mrs. Dixon's respectful manner. He knew such incidents cheered his father, who could never look at these subjects from a proper point of view, and, as people said, sometimes made the strangest remarks for a clergyman. This irreverent way of treating serious things was one of the great bonds between father and son, but it tended to increase their isolation. People said they would often have liked to asked Mr. Taylor to garden-parties, and tea-parties, and other cheap entertainments, if only he had not been such an *extreme* man and so *queer*. Indeed, a year before, Mr. Taylor had gone to a garden-party at the Castle, Caermaen, and had made such fun of the bishop's recent address on missions to the Portuguese, that the Gervases and Dixons and all who heard him were quite shocked and annoyed. And, as Mrs. Meyrick of Lanyravon observed, his black coat was perfectly *green* with age; so on the whole the Gervases did not like to invite Mr. Taylor again. As for the son, nobody cared to have him; Mrs. Dixon, as she said to her husband, really asked him out of charity.

"I am afraid he seldom gets a real meal at home," she remarked, "so I thought he would enjoy a good wholesome tea for once in a way. But he is such an *unsatisfactory* boy, he would only have one slice of that nice plain cake, and I couldn't get him to take more than two plums. They were really quite ripe too, and boys are usually so fond of fruit."

Thus Lucian was forced to spend his holidays chiefly in his own company, and make the best he could of the ripe peaches on the south wall of the rectory garden. There was a certain corner where the heat of that hot August seemed concentrated, reverberated from one wall to the other, and here he liked to linger of mornings, when the mists were still thick in the valleys, "mooning," meditating, extending his walk from the quince to the medlar and back again, beside the moldering walls of mellowed brick. He was full of a certain wonder and awe, not unmixed with a swell of strange exultation, and wished more and more to be alone, to think over that wonderful afternoon within the fort. In spite of himself the impression was fading; he could not understand that feeling of mad panic terror that drove him through the thicket and down the steep hillside; yet, he had experienced so clearly the physical shame and reluctance of the flesh; he recollected that for a few seconds after his awakening the sight of his own body had made him shudder and writhe as if it had suffered some profoundest degradation. He saw before him a vision of two forms; a faun with tingling and prickling flesh lay expectant in the sunlight, and there was also the likeness of a miserable shamed boy, standing with trembling body and shaking, unsteady hands. It was all confused, a procession of blurred images, now of rapture and ecstasy, and now of terror and shame, floating in a light that was altogether phantasmal and unreal. He dared not approach the fort again; he lingered in the road to Caermaen that passed behind it, but a mile away, and separated by the wild land and a strip of wood from the towering battlements. Here he was looking over a gate one day, doubtful and wondering, when he heard a heavy step behind him, and glancing round quickly saw it was old Morgan of the White House.

"Good afternoon, Master Lucian," he began. "Mr. Taylor pretty well, I suppose? I be goin' to the house a minute; the men in the fields are wantin' some more cider. Would you come and taste a drop of cider, Master Lucian? It's very good, sir, indeed."

Lucian did not want any cider, but he thought it would please old Morgan if he took some, so he said he should like to taste the cider very much indeed. Morgan was a sturdy, thickset old man of the ancient stock; a stiff churchman, who breakfasted regularly on fat broth and Caerphilly cheese in the fashion of his ancestors; hot, spiced elder wine was for winter nights, and gin for festal seasons. The farm had always been the freehold of the family, and when Lucian, in the wake of the yeoman, passed through the deep porch by the oaken door, down into the long dark kitchen, he felt as though the seventeenth century still lingered on. One mullioned window, set deep in the sloping wall, gave all the light there was through quarries of thick glass in which there were whorls and circles, so that the lapping rose-branch and the garden and the fields beyond were distorted to the sight. Two heavy beams, oaken but whitewashed, ran across the ceiling; a little glow of fire sparkled in the great fireplace, and a curl of blue smoke fled up the cavern of the chimney. Here was the genuine chimney corner of our fathers; there were seats on each side of the fireplace where one could sit snug and sheltered on December nights, warm and merry in the blazing light, and listen to the battle of the storm, and hear the flame spit and hiss at the falling snowflakes. At the back of the fire were great blackened tiles with raised initials and a date, "I.M., 1684."

"Sit down, Master Lucian, sit down, sir," said Morgan.

"Annie," he called through one of the numerous doors, "here's Master Lucian, the parson, would like a drop of cider. Fetch a jug, will you, directly?"

"Very well, father," came the voice from the dairy and presently the girl entered, wiping the jug she held. In his boyish way Lucian had been a good deal disturbed by Annie Morgan; he could see her on Sundays from his seat in church, and her skin, curiously pale, her lips that seemed as though they were stained with some brilliant pigment, her black hair, and the quivering black eyes, gave him odd fancies which he had hardly shaped to himself. Annie had grown into a woman in three years, and he was still a boy. She came into the kitchen, curtsying and smiling.

"Good-day, Master Lucian, and how is Mr. Taylor, sir?"

"Pretty well, thank you. I hope you are well."

"Nicely, sir, thank you. How nice your voice do sound in church, Master Lucian, to be sure. I was telling father about it last Sunday."

Lucian grinned and felt uncomfortable, and the girl set down the jug on the round table and brought a glass from the dresser. She bent close over him as she poured out the green oily cider, fragrant of the orchard; her hand touched his shoulder for a moment, and she said, "I beg your pardon, sir," very prettily. He looked up eagerly at her face; the black eyes, a little oval in shape, were shining, and the lips smiled. Annie wore a plain dress of some black stuff, open at the throat; her skin was beautiful. For a moment the ghost of a fancy hovered unsubstantial in his mind; and then Annie curtsied as she handed him the cider, and replied to his thanks with, "And welcome kindly, sir."

The drink was really good; not thin, nor sweet, but round and full and generous, with a fine yellow flame twinkling through the green when one held it up to the light. It was like a stray sunbeam

127

hovering on the grass in a deep orchard, and he swallowed the glassful with relish, and had some more, warmly commending it. Mr. Morgan was touched.

"I see you do know a good thing, sir," he said. "Is, indeed, now, its good stuff, though it's my own makin'. My old grandfather he planted the trees in the time of the wars, and he was a very good judge of an apple in his day and generation. And a famous grafter he was, to be sure. You will never see no swelling in the trees he grafted at all whatever. Now there's James Morris, Penyrhaul, he's a famous grafter, too, and yet them Redstreaks he grafted for me five year ago, they be all swollen-like below the graft already. Would you like to taste a Blemmin pippin, now, Master Lucian? There be a few left in the loft, I believe."

Lucian said he should like an apple very much, and the farmer went out by another door, and Annie stayed in the kitchen talking. She said Mrs. Trevor, her married sister, was coming to them soon to spend a few days.

"She's got such a beautiful baby," said Annie, "and he's quite sensible-like already, though he's only nine months old. Mary would like to see you, sir, if you would be so kind as to step in; that is, if it's not troubling you at all, Master Lucian. I suppose you must be getting a fine scholar now, sir?"

"I am doing pretty well, thank you," said the boy. "I was first in my form last term."

"Fancy! To think of that! D'ye hear, father, what a scholar Master Lucian be getting?"

"He be a rare grammarian, I'm sure," said the farmer. "You do take after your father, sir; I always do say that nobody have got such a good deliverance in the pulpit."

Lucian did not find the Blenheim Orange as good as the cider, but he ate it with all the appearance of relish, and put another, with thanks, in his pocket. He thanked the farmer again when he got up to go; and Annie curtsied and smiled, and wished him good day, and welcome, kindly.

Lucian heard her saying to her father as he went out what a nice-mannered young gentleman he was getting, to be sure; and he went on his way, thinking that Annie was really very pretty, and speculating as to whether he would have the courage to kiss her, if they met in a dark lane. He was quite sure she would only laugh, and say, "Oh, Master Lucian!"

For many months he had occasional fits of recollection, both cold and hot; but the bridge of time, gradually lengthening, made those dreadful and delicious images grow more and more indistinct, till at last they all passed into that wonderland which a youth looks back upon in amazement, not knowing why this used to be a symbol of terror or that of joy. At the end of each term he would come home and find his father a little more despondent, and harder to cheer even for a moment; and the wallpaper and the furniture grew more and more dingy and shabby. The two cats, loved and ancient beasts, that he remembered when he was quite a little boy, before he went to school, died miserably, one after the other. Old

Polly, the pony, at last fell down in the stable from the weakness of old age, and had to be killed there; the battered old trap ran no longer along the well-remembered lanes. There was long meadow grass on the lawn, and the trained fruit trees on the wall had got quite out of hand. At last, when Lucian was seventeen, his father was obliged to take him from school; he could no longer afford the fees. This was the sorry ending of many hopes, and dreams of a double-first, a fellowship, distinction and glory that the poor parson had long entertained for his son, and the two moped together, in the shabby room, one on each side of the sulky fire, thinking of dead days and finished plans, and seeing a gray future in the years that advanced towards them. At one time there seemed some chance of a distant relative coming forward to Lucian's assistance; and indeed it was quite settled that he should go up to London with certain definite aims. Mr. Taylor told the good news to his acquaintances—his coat was too green now for any pretence of friendship; and Lucian himself spoke of his plans to Burrows the doctor and Mr. Dixon, and one or two others. Then the whole scheme fell through, and the parson and his son suffered much sympathy. People, of course, had to say they were sorry, but in reality the news was received with high spirits, with the joy with which one sees a stone, as it rolls down a steep place, give yet another bounding leap towards the pool beneath. Mrs. Dixon heard the pleasant tidings from Mrs. Colley, who came in to talk about the Mothers' Meeting and the Band of Hope. Mrs. Dixon was nursing little Athelwig, or some such name, at the time, and made many affecting observations on the general righteousness with which the world was governed. Indeed, poor Lucian's disappointment seemed distinctly to increase her faith in the Divine Order, as if it had been some example in Butler's *Analogy*.

"Aren't Mr. Taylor's views very *extreme*?" she said to her husband the same evening.

"I am afraid they are," he replied. "I was quite *grieved* at the last Diocesan Conference at the way in which he spoke. The dear old bishop had given an address on Auricular Confession; he was *forced* to do so, you know, after what had happened, and I must say that I never felt prouder of our beloved Church."

Mr. Dixon told all the Homeric story of the conference, reciting the achievements of the champions, "deploring" this and applauding that. It seemed that Mr. Taylor had had the audacity to quote authorities which the bishop could not very well repudiate, though they were directly opposed to the "safe" Episcopal pronouncement.

Mrs. Dixon of course was grieved; it was "sad" to think of a clergyman behaving so shamefully.

"But you know, dear," she proceeded, "I have been thinking about that unfortunate Taylor boy and his disappointments, and after what you've just told me, I am sure it's some kind of judgment on them both. Has Mr. Taylor forgotten the vows he took at his ordination? But don't you think, dear, I am right, and that he has been punished: 'The sins of the fathers'?"

Somehow or other Lucian divined the atmosphere of threatenings and judgments, and shrank more and more from the small society of the countryside. For his part, when he was not "mooning" in the beloved fields and woods of happy memory, he shut himself up with books, reading whatever could be found on the shelves, and amassing a store of incongruous and obsolete knowledge. Long did he linger with the men of the seventeenth century; delaying the gay sunlit streets with Pepys, and listening to the charmed sound of the Restoration Revel; roaming by peaceful streams with Izaak Walton, and the great Catholic divines; enchanted with the portrait of Herber the loving ascetic; awed by the mystic breath of Crashaw. Then the cavalier poets sang their gallant songs; and Herrick made Dean Prior magic ground by the holy incantation of a verse. And in the old proverbs and homely sayings of the time he found the good and beautiful English life, a time full of grace and dignity and rich merriment. He dived deeper and deeper into his books; he had taken all obsolescence to be his province; in his disgust at the stupid usual questions, "Will it pay?" "What good is it?" and so forth, he would only read what was uncouth and useless. The strange pomp and symbolism of the Cabala, with its hint of more terrible things; the Rosicrucian mysteries of Fludd, the enigmas of Vaughan, dreams of alchemists—all these were his delight. Such were his companions, with the hills and hanging woods, the brooks and lonely water pools; books, the thoughts of books, the stirrings of imagination, all fused into one fantasy by the magic of the outland country. He held himself aloof from the walls of the fort; he was content to see the heaped mounds, the violent height with faerie bulwarks, from the gate in the lane, and to leave all within the ring of oaks in the mystery of his boyhood's vision. He professed to laugh at himself and at his fancies of that hot August afternoon, when sleep came to him within the thicket, but in his heart of hearts there was something that never faded—something that glowed like the red glint of a gypsy's fire seen from afar across the hills and mists of the night, and known to be burning in a wild land. Sometimes, when he was sunken in his books, the flame of delight shot up, and showed him a whole province and continent of his nature, all shining and aglow; and in the midst of the exultation and triumph he would draw back, a little afraid. He had become ascetic in his studious and melancholy isolation, and the vision of such ecstasies frightened him. He began to write a little; at first very tentatively and feebly, and then with more confidence. He showed some of his verses to his father, who told him with a sigh that he had once hoped to write—in the old days at Oxford, he added.

"They are very nicely done," said the parson; "but I'm afraid you won't find anybody to print them, my boy."

So he pottered on; reading everything, imitating what struck his fancy, attempting the effect of the classic meters in English verse, trying his hand at a masque, a Restoration comedy, forming impossible plans for books which rarely got beyond half a dozen lines on a sheet of paper; beset with splendid fancies which refused to abide before the pen. But the vain joy of conception was not altogether vain, for it gave him some armor about his heart.

The months went by, monotonous, and sometimes blotted with despair. He wrote and planned and filled the wastepaper basket with hopeless efforts. Now and then he sent verses or prose articles to magazines, in pathetic ignorance of the trade. He felt the immense difficulty of the career of literature without clearly understanding it; the battle was happily in a mist, so that the host of the enemy, terribly arrayed, was to some extent hidden. Yet there was enough of difficulty to appall; from following the intricate course of little nameless brooks, from hushed twilight woods, from the vision of the mountains, and the breath of the great wind, passing from deep to deep, he would come home filled with thoughts and emotions, mystic fancies which he yearned to translate into the written word. And the result of the effort seemed always to be bathos! Wooden sentences, a portentous stilted style, obscurity, and awkwardness clogged the pen; it seemed impossible to win the great secret of language; the stars glittered only in the darkness, and vanished away in clearer light. The periods of despair were often long and heavy, the victories very few and trifling; night after night he sat writing after his father had knocked out his last pipe, filling a page with difficulty in an hour, and usually forced to thrust the stuff away in despair, and go unhappily to bed, conscious that after all his labor he had done nothing. And these were moments when the accustomed vision of the land alarmed him, and the wild domed hills and darkling woods seemed symbols of some terrible secret in the inner life of that stranger—himself. Sometimes when he was deep in his books and papers, sometimes on a lonely walk, sometimes amidst the tiresome chatter of Caermaen "society," he would thrill with a sudden sense of awful hidden things, and there ran that quivering flame through his nerves that brought back the recollection of the matted thicket, and that earlier appearance of the bare black boughs enwrapped with flames. Indeed, though he avoided the solitary lane, and the sight of the sheer height, with its ring of oaks and molded mounds, the image of it grew more intense as the symbol of certain hints and suggestions. The exultant and insurgent flesh seemed to have its temple and castle within those olden walls, and he longed with all his heart to escape, to set himself free in the wilderness of London, and to be secure amidst the murmur of modern streets.

II

Lucian was growing really anxious about his manuscript. He had gained enough experience at twenty-three to know that editors and publishers must not be hurried; but his book had been lying at Messrs Beit's office for more than three months. For six weeks he had not dared to expect an answer, but afterwards life had become agonizing. Every morning, at post-time, the poor wretch nearly choked with anxiety to know whether his sentence had arrived, and the rest of the day was racked with alternate pangs of hope and despair. Now and then he was almost assured of success; conning over these painful and eager pages in memory, he found parts that were admirable, while again, his inexperience reproached him, and he feared he had written a raw and awkward book, wholly unfit for print. Then he would compare what he remembered of it with notable magazine articles and books praised by reviewers, and fancy that after all there might be good points in the thing; he could not help liking the first chapter for instance. Perhaps the letter might come tomorrow. So it went on; week after week of sick torture made more exquisite by such gleams of hope; it was as if he were stretched in anguish on the rack, and the pain relaxed and kind words spoken now and again by the tormentors, and then once more the grinding pang and burning agony. At last he could bear suspense no longer, and he wrote to Messrs Beit, inquiring in a humble manner whether the manuscript had arrived in safety. The firm replied in a very polite letter, expressing regret that their reader had been suffering from a cold in the head, and had therefore been unable to send in his report. A final decision was promised in a week's time, and the letter ended with apologies for the delay and a hope that he had suffered no inconvenience. Of course the "final decision" did not come at the end of the week, but the book was returned at the end of three weeks, with a circular thanking the author for his kindness in submitting the manuscript, and regretting that the firm did not see their way to producing it. He felt relieved; the operation that he had dreaded and deprecated for so long was at last over, and he would no longer grow sick of mornings when the letters were brought in. He took his parcel to the sunny corner of the garden, where the old wooden seat stood sheltered from the biting March winds. Messrs Beit had put in with the circular one of their short lists, a neat booklet, headed: *Messrs Beit & Co.'s Recent Publications*.

He settled himself comfortably on the seat, lit his pipe, and began to read: "*A Bad Un to Beat*: a Novel of Sporting Life, by the Honorable Mrs. Scudamore Runnymede, author of *Yoicks, With the Mudshire Pack, The Sportleigh Stables*, etc., etc., 3 vols. At all Libraries." The *Press*, it seemed, pronounced this to be a "charming book. Mrs. Runnymede has wit and humor enough to furnish forth half-a-dozen ordinary sporting novels." "Told with the sparkle and vivacity of a past-mistress in the art of novel writing," said the *Review*; while Miranda, of *Smart*

Society, positively bubbled with enthusiasm. "You must forgive me, Aminta," wrote this young person, "if I have not sent the description I promised of Madame Lulu's new creations and others of that ilk. I must a tale unfold; Tom came in yesterday and began to rave about the Honorable Mrs. Scudamore Runnymede's last novel, *A Bad Un to Beat*. He says all the Smart Set are talking of it, and it seems the police have to regulate the crowd at Mudie's. You know I read everything Mrs. Runnymede writes, so I set out Miggs directly to beg, borrow or steal a copy, and I confess I burnt the midnight oil before I laid it down. Now, mind you get it, you will find it so awfully *chic*." Nearly all the novelists on Messrs Beit's list were ladies, their works all ran to three volumes, and all of them pleased the *Press*, the *Review*, and Miranda of *Smart Society*. One of these books, *Millicent's Marriage*, by Sarah Pocklington Sanders, was pronounced fit to lie on the school-room table, on the drawing-room bookshelf, or beneath the pillow of the most gently nurtured of our daughters. "This," the reviewer went on, "is high praise, especially in these days when we are deafened by the loud-voiced clamor of self-styled 'artists.' We would warn the young men who prate so persistently of style and literature, construction and prose harmonies, that we believe the English reading public will have none of them. Harmless amusement, a gentle flow of domestic interest, a faithful reproduction of the open and manly life of the hunting field, pictures of innocent and healthy English girlhood such as Miss Sanders here affords us; these are the topics that will always find a welcome in our homes, which remain bolted and barred against the abandoned artist and the scrofulous stylist."

He turned over the pages of the little book and chuckled in high relish; he discovered an honest enthusiasm, a determination to strike a blow for the good and true that refreshed and exhilarated. A beaming face, spectacled and whiskered probably, an expansive waistcoat, and a tender heart, seemed to shine through the words which Messrs Beit had quoted; and the alliteration of the final sentence; that was good too; there was style for you if you wanted it. The champion of the blushing cheek and the gushing eye showed that he too could handle the weapons of the enemy if he cared to trouble himself with such things. Lucian leant back and roared with indecent laughter till the tabby tom-cat who had succeeded to the poor dead beasts looked up reproachfully from his sunny corner, with a face like the reviewer's, innocent and round and whiskered. At last he turned to his parcel and drew out some half-dozen sheets of manuscript, and began to read in a rather desponding spirit; it was pretty obvious, he thought, that the stuff was poor and beneath the standard of publication. The book had taken a year and a half in the making; it was a pious attempt to translate into English prose the form and mystery of the domed hills, the magic of occult valleys, the sound of the red swollen brook swirling through leafless woods. Day-dreams and toil at nights had gone into the eager pages, he had labored hard to do his very best, writing and re-writing, weighing his cadences, beginning over and over again, grudging no patience, no trouble if only it might be pretty good; good enough to print and sell to a reading public which had become critical. He glanced through the manuscript in his hand, and to his astonishment, he could not help thinking that in its measure it was decent work. After three months his prose seemed fresh and strange as if it had been wrought by another man, and in spite of himself he found charming things, and impressions that were not commonplace. He knew how weak it all was compared with his own conceptions; he had seen an enchanted city, awful, glorious, with flame smitten about its battlements, like the cities of the Sangraal, and he had molded his copy in such poor clay as came to his hand; yet, in spite of the gulf that yawned between the idea and the work, he knew as he read that the thing accomplished was very far from a failure. He put back the leaves carefully, and glanced again at Messrs Beit's list. It had escaped his notice that *A Bad Un to Beat* was in its third three-volume edition. It was a great thing, at all events, to know in what direction to aim, if he wished to succeed. If he worked hard, he thought, he might some day win the approval of the coy and retiring Miranda of *Smart Society*; that modest maiden might in his praise interrupt her task of disinterested advertisement, her philanthropic counsels to "go to Jumper's, and mind you ask for Mr. C. Jumper, who will show you the lovely blue paper with the yellow spots at ten shillings the piece." He put down the pamphlet, and laughed again at the books and the reviewers: so that he might not weep. This then was English fiction, this was English criticism, and farce, after all, was but an ill-played tragedy.

The rejected manuscript was hidden away, and his father quoted Horace's maxim as to the benefit of keeping literary works for some time "in the wood." There was nothing to grumble at, though Lucian was inclined to think the duration of the reader's catarrh a little exaggerated. But this was a trifle; he did not arrogate to himself the position of a small commercial traveler, who expects prompt civility as a matter of course, and not at all as a favor. He simply forgot his old book, and resolved that he would make a better one if he could. With the hot fit of resolution, the determination not to be snuffed out by one refusal upon him, he began to beat about in his mind for some new scheme. At first it seemed that he had hit upon a promising subject; he began to plot out chapters and scribble hints for the curious story that had entered his mind, arranging his circumstances and noting the effects to be produced with all the enthusiasm of the artist. But after the first breath the aspect of the work changed; page after page was tossed aside as hopeless, the beautiful sentences he had dreamed of refused to be written, and his puppets remained stiff and wooden, devoid of life or motion. Then all the old despairs came back, the agonies of the artificer who strives and perseveres in vain; the scheme that seemed of amorous fire turned to cold hard ice in his hands. He let the pen drop from his fingers, and wondered how he could have ever dreamed of writing books. Again, the thought occurred that he might do something if he could only get away, and join the sad procession in the murmuring London streets, far from the shadow of those awful hills. But it was quite impossible; the relative who had once promised assistance was appealed to, and wrote expressing his regret that Lucian had turned out a "loafer," wasting his time in scribbling, instead of trying to earn his living. Lucian felt rather hurt at this letter, but the parson only grinned grimly as usual. He was thinking of how he signed a check many years before, in the days of his prosperity, and the check was payable to this didactic relative, then in but a poor way, and of a thankful turn of mind.

The old rejected manuscript had almost passed out of his recollection. It was recalled oddly enough. He was looking over the *Reader*, and enjoying the admirable literary criticisms, some three months after the return of his book, when his eye was attracted by a quoted passage in one of the notices. The thought and style both wakened memory, the cadences were familiar and beloved. He read through the review from the beginning; it was a very favorable one, and pronounced the volume an immense advance on Mr. Ritson's previous work. "Here, undoubtedly, the author has discovered a vein of pure metal," the reviewer added, "and we predict that he will go far." Lucian had not yet reached his father's stage, he was unable to grin in the manner of that irreverent parson. The passage selected for high praise was taken almost word for word from the manuscript now resting in his room, the work that had not reached the high standard of Messrs Beit & Co., who, curiously enough, were the publishers of the book reviewed in the *Reader*. He had a few shillings in his possession, and wrote at once to a bookseller in London for a copy of *The Chorus in Green*, as the author had oddly named the book. He wrote on June 21st and thought he might fairly expect to receive the interesting volume by the 24th; but the postman, true to his tradition, brought nothing for him, and in the afternoon he resolved to walk down to Caermaen, in case it might have come by a second post; or it might have been mislaid at the office; they forgot parcels sometimes, especially when the bag was heavy and the weather hot. This 24th was a sultry and oppressive day; a gray veil of cloud obscured the sky, and a vaporous mist hung heavily over the land, and fumed up from the valleys. But at five o'clock, when he started, the clouds began to break, and the sunlight suddenly streamed down through the misty air, making ways and channels of rich glory, and bright islands in the gloom. It was a pleasant and shining evening when, passing by devious back streets to avoid the barbarians (as he very rudely called the respectable inhabitants of the town), he reached the post office; which was also the general shop.

"Yes, Mr. Taylor, there is something for you, sir," said the man. "Williams the postman forgot to take it up this morning," and he handed over the packet. Lucian took it under his arm and went slowly through the ragged winding lanes till he came into the country. He got over the first stile on the road, and sitting down in the shelter of a hedge, cut the strings and opened the parcel. *The Chorus in Green* was got up in what reviewers call a dainty manner: a bronze-green cloth, well-cut gold lettering, wide margins and black "old-face" type, all witnessed to the good taste of Messrs Beit & Co. He cut the pages hastily and began to read. He soon found that he had wronged Mr. Rison—that old literary hand had by no means stolen his book wholesale, as he had expected. There were about two hundred pages in the pretty little volume, and of these about ninety were Lucian's, dovetailed into a rather different scheme with skill that was nothing short of exquisite. And Mr. Ritson's own work was often very good; spoilt here and there for some tastes by the "cataloging" method, a somewhat materialistic way of taking an inventory of the holy country things; but, for that very reason, contrasting to a great advantage with Lucian's hints and dreams and note of haunting. And here and there Mr. Ritson had made little alterations in the style of the passages he had conveyed, and most of these alterations were amendments, as Lucian was obliged to confess, though he would have liked to argue one or two points with his collaborator and corrector. He lit his pipe and leant back comfortably in the hedge, thinking things over, weighing very coolly his experience of humanity, his contact with the "society" of the countryside, the affair of the *The Chorus in Green*, and even some little incidents that had struck him as he was walking through the streets of Caermaen that evening. At the post office, when he was inquiring for his parcel, he had heard two old women grumbling in the street; it seemed, so far as he could make out, that both had been disappointed in much the same way. One was a Roman Catholic, hardened, and beyond the reach of conversion; she had been advised to ask alms of the priests, "who are always creeping and crawling about." The other old sinner was a Dissenter, and, "Mr. Dixon has quite enough to do to relieve good Church people."

Mrs. Dixon, assisted by Henrietta, was, it seemed, the lady high almoner, who dispensed these charities. As she said to Mrs. Colley, they would end by keeping all the beggars in the county, and they really couldn't afford it. A large family was an expensive thing, and the girls *must* have new frocks. "Mr. Dixon is always telling me and the girls that we must not *demoralize* the people by indiscriminate charity." Lucian had heard of these sage counsels, and through it them as he listened to the bitter complaints of the gaunt, hungry old women. In the back street by which he passed out of the town he saw a large "healthy" boy kicking a sick cat; the poor creature had just strength enough to crawl under an outhouse door; probably to die in torments. He did not find much satisfaction in thrashing the boy, but he did it with hearty good will. Further on, at the corner where the turnpike used to be, was a big notice, announcing a meeting at the schoolroom in aid of the missions to the Portuguese. "Under the Patronage of the Lord Bishop of the Diocese," was the imposing headline; the Reverend Merivale Dixon, vicar of Caermaen, was to be in the chair, supported by Stanley Gervase, Esq., J.P., and by many of the clergy and gentry of the neighborhood. Senhor Diabo, "formerly a Romanist priest, now an evangelist in Lisbon," would address the meeting. "Funds are urgently needed to carry on this good work," concluded the notice. So he lay well back in the shade of the hedge, and thought whether some sort of an article could not be made by vindicating the terrible Yahoos; one might point out that they were in many respects a simple and unsophisticated race, whose faults were the result of their enslaved position, while such virtues as they had were all their own. They might be compared, he thought, much to their advantage, with more complex civilizations. There was no hint of anything like the Beit system of publishing in existence amongst them; the great Yahoo nation would surely never feed and encourage a scabby Houyhnhnm, expelled for his foulness from the horse-community, and the witty dean, in all his minuteness, had said nothing of "safe" Yahoos. On reflection, however, he did not feel quite secure of this part of his defense; he remembered that the leading brutes had favorites, who were employed in certain simple domestic offices about their masters, and it seemed doubtful whether the contemplated vindication would not break down on this point. He smiled queerly to himself as he thought of these comparisons, but his heart burned with a dully fury. Throwing back his unhappy memory, he recalled all the contempt and scorn he had suffered; as a boy he had heard the masters murmuring their disdain of him and of his desire to learn other than ordinary school work. As a young man he had suffered the insolence of these wretched people about him; their cackling laughter at his poverty jarred and grated in his ears; he saw the acrid grin of some miserable idiot woman, some creature beneath the swine in intelligence and manners, merciless, as he went by with his eyes on the dust, in his ragged clothes. He and his father seemed to pass down an avenue of jeers and contempt, and contempt from such animals as these! This putrid filth, molded into human shape, made only to fawn on the rich and beslaver them, thinking no foulness too foul if it were done in honor of those in power and authority; and no refined cruelty of contempt too cruel if it were contempt of the poor and humble and oppressed; it was to this obscene and ghastly throng that he was something to be pointed at. And these men and women spoke of sacred things, and knelt before the awful altar of God, before the altar of tremendous fire, surrounded as they professed by Angels and Archangels and all the Company of Heaven; and in their very church they had one aisle for the rich and another for the poor. And the species was not peculiar to Caermaen; the rich business men in London and the successful brother author were probably amusing themselves at the expense of the poor struggling creature they had injured and wounded; just as the "healthy" boy had burst into a great laugh when the miserable sick cat cried out in bitter agony, and trailed its limbs slowly, as it crept away to die. Lucian looked into his own life and his own will; he saw that in spite of his follies, and his want of success, he had not been consciously malignant, he had never deliberately aided in oppression, or looked on it with enjoyment and approval, and he felt that when he lay dead beneath the earth, eaten by swarming worms, he would be in a purer company than now, when he lived amongst human creatures. And he was to call this loathsome beast, all sting and filth, brother! "I had rather call the devils my brothers," he said in his heart, "I would fare better in hell." Blood was in his eyes, and as he looked up the sky seemed of blood, and the earth burned with fire.

The sun was sinking low on the mountain when he set out on the way again. Burrows, the doctor, coming home in his trap, met him a little lower on the road, and gave him a friendly goodnight.

"A long way round on this road, isn't it?" said the doctor. "As you have come so far, why don't you try the short cut across the fields? You will find it easily enough; second stile on the left hand, and then go straight ahead."

He thanked Dr. Burrows and said he would try the short cut, and Burrows span on homeward. He was a gruff and honest bachelor, and often felt very sorry for the lad, and wished he could help him. As he drove on, it suddenly occurred to him that Lucian had an awful look on his face, and he was sorry he had not asked him to jump in, and to come to supper. A hearty slice of beef, with strong ale, whisky and soda afterwards, a good pipe, and certain Rabelaisian tales which the doctor had treasured for many years, would have done the poor fellow a lot of good, he was certain. He half turned round on his seat, and looked to see if Lucian were still in sight, but he had passed the corner, and the doctor drove on, shivering a little;

the mists were beginning to rise from the wet banks of the river.

Lucian trailed slowly along the road, keeping a look out for the stile the doctor had mentioned. It would be a little of an adventure, he thought, to find his way by an unknown track; he knew the direction in which his home lay, and he imagined he would not have much difficulty in crossing from one stile to another. The path led him up a steep bare field, and when he was at the top, the town and the valley winding up to the north stretched before him. The river was stilled at the flood, and the yellow water, reflecting the sunset, glowed in its deep pools like dull brass. These burning pools, the level meadows fringed with shuddering reeds, the long dark sweep of the forest on the hill, were all clear and distinct, yet the light seemed to have clothed them with a new garment, even as voices from the streets of Caermaen sounded strangely, mounting up thin with the smoke. There beneath him lay the huddled cluster of Caermaen, the ragged and uneven roofs that marked the winding and sordid streets, here and there a pointed gable rising above its meaner fellows; beyond he recognized the piled mounds that marked the circle of the amphitheatre, and the dark edge of trees that grew where the Roman wall whitened and waxed old beneath the frosts and rains of eighteen hundred years. Thin and strange, mingled together, the voices came up to him on the hill; it was as if an outland race inhabited the ruined city and talked in a strange language of strange and terrible things. The sun had slid down the sky, and hung quivering over the huge dark dome of the mountain like a burnt sacrifice, and then suddenly vanished. In the afterglow the clouds began to writhe and turn scarlet, and shone so strangely reflected in the pools of the snake-like river, that one would have said the still waters stirred, the fleeting and changing of the clouds seeming to quicken the stream, as if it bubbled and sent up gouts of blood. But already about the town the darkness was forming; fast, fast the shadows crept upon it from the forest, and from all sides banks and wreaths of curling mist were gathering, as if a ghostly leaguer were being built up against the city, and the strange race who lived in its streets. Suddenly there burst out from the stillness the clear and piercing music of the *réveillé*, calling, recalling, iterated, reiterated, and ending with one long high fierce shrill note with which the steep hills rang. Perhaps a boy in the school band was practicing on his bugle, but for Lucian it was magic. For him it was the note of the Roman trumpet, *tuba mirum spargens sonum*, filling all the hollow valley with its command, reverberated in dark places in the far forest, and resonant in the old graveyards without the walls. In his imagination he saw the earthen gates of the tombs broken open, and the serried legion swarming to the eagles. Century by century they passed by; they rose, dripping, from the river bed, they rose from the level, their armor shone in the quiet orchard, they gathered in ranks and companies from the cemetery, and as the trumpet sounded, the hill fort above the town gave up its dead. By hundreds and thousands the ghostly battle surged about the standard, behind the quaking mist, ready to march against the moldering walls they had built so many years before.

He turned sharply; it was growing very dark, and he was afraid of missing his way. At first the path led him by the verge of a wood; there was a noise of rustling and murmuring from the trees as if they were taking evil counsel together. A high hedge shut out the sight of the darkening valley, and he stumbled on mechanically, without taking much note of the turnings of the track, and when he came out from the wood shadow to the open country, he stood for a moment quite bewildered and uncertain. A dark wild twilight country lay before him, confused dim shapes of trees near at hand, and a hollow below his feet, and the further hills and woods were dimmer, and all the air was very still. Suddenly the darkness about him glowed; a furnace fire had shot up on the mountain, and for a moment the little world of the woodside and the steep hill shone in a pale light, and he thought he saw his path beaten out in the turf before him. The great flame sank down to a red glint of fire, and it led him on down the ragged slope, his feet striking against ridges of ground, and falling from beneath him at a sudden dip. The bramble bushes shot out long prickly vines, amongst which he was entangled, and lower he was held back by wet bubbling earth. He had descended into a dark and shady valley, beset and tapestried with gloomy thickets; the weird wood noises were the only sounds, strange, unutterable mutterings, dismal, inarticulate. He pushed on in what he hoped was the right direction, stumbling from stile to gate, peering through mist and shadow, and still vainly seeking for any known landmark. Presently another sound broke upon the grim air, the murmur of water poured over stones, gurgling against the old misshapen roots of trees, and running clear in a deep channel. He passed into the chill breath of the brook, and almost fancied he heard two voices speaking in its murmur; there seemed a ceaseless utterance of words, an endless argument. With a mood of horror pressing on him, he listened to the noise of waters, and the wild fancy seized him that he was not deceived, that two unknown beings stood together there in the darkness and tried the balances of his life, and spoke his doom. The hour in the matted thicket rushed over the great bridge of years to his thought; he had sinned against the earth, and the earth trembled and shook for vengeance. He stayed still for a moment, quivering with fear, and at last went on blindly, no longer caring for the path, if only he might escape from the toils of that dismal shuddering hollow. As he plunged through the hedges the bristling thorns tore his face and hands; he fell amongst stinging nettles and was pricked as he beat out his way amidst the gorse. He raced headlong, his head over his shoulder, through a windy wood, bare of undergrowth; there lay about the ground moldering stumps, the relics of trees that had thundered to their fall, crashing and tearing to earth, long ago; and from these remains there flowed out a pale thin radiance, filling the spaces of the sounding wood with a dream of light. He had lost all count of the track; he felt he had fled for hours, climbing and descending, and yet not advancing; it was as if he stood still and the shadows of the land went by, in a vision. But at last a hedge, high and straggling, rose before him, and as he broke through it, his feet slipped, and he fell headlong down a steep bank into a lane. He lay still, half-stunned, for a moment, and then rising unsteadily, he looked desperately into the darkness before him, uncertain and bewildered. In front it was black as a midnight cellar, and he turned about, and saw a glint in the distance, as if a candle were flickering in a farmhouse window. He began to walk with trembling feet towards the light, when suddenly something pale started out from the shadows before him, and seemed to swim and float down the air. He was going down hill, and he hastened onwards, and he could see the bars of a stile framed dimly against the sky, and the figure still advanced with that gliding motion. Then, as the road declined to the valley, the landmark he had been seeking appeared. To his right there surged up in the darkness the darker summit of the Roman fort, and the streaming fire of the great full moon glowed through the bars of the wizard oaks, and made a halo shine about the hill. He was now quite close to the white appearance, and saw that it was only a woman walking swiftly down the lane; the floating movement was an effect due to the somber air and the moon's glamour. At the gate, where he had spent so many hours gazing at the fort, they walked foot to foot, and he saw it was Annie

Morgan.

"Good evening, Master Lucian," said the girl, "it's very dark, sir, indeed."

"Good evening, Annie," he answered, calling her by her name for the first time, and he saw that she smiled with pleasure. "You are out late, aren't you?"

"Yes, sir; but I've been taking a bit of supper to old Mrs. Gibbon. She's been very poorly the last few days, and there's nobody to do anything for her."

Then there were really people who helped one another; kindness and pity were not mere myths, fictions of "society," as useful as Doe and Roe, and as non-existent. The thought struck Lucian with a shock; the evening's passion and delirium, the wild walk and physical fatigue had almost shattered him in body and mind. He was "degenerate," *decadent*, and the rough rains and blustering winds of life, which a stronger man would have laughed at and enjoyed, were to him "hail-storms and fire-showers." After all, Messrs Beit, the publishers, were only sharp men of business, and these terrible Dixons and Gervases and Colleys merely the ordinary limited clergy and gentry of a quiet country town; sturdier sense would have dismissed Dixon as an old humbug, Stanley Gervase, Esquire, J.P., as a "bit of a bounder," and the ladies as "rather a shoddy lot." But he was walking slowly now in painful silence, his heavy, lagging feet striking against the loose stones. He was not thinking of the girl beside him; only something seemed to swell and grow and swell within his heart; it was all the torture of his days, weary hopes and weary disappointment, scorn rankling and throbbing, and the thought "I had rather call the devils my brothers and live with them in hell." He choked and gasped for breath, and felt involuntary muscles working in his face, and the impulses of a madman stirring him; he himself was in truth the realization of the vision of Caermaen that night, a city with moldering walls beset by the ghostly legion. Life and the world and the laws of the sunlight had passed away, and the resurrection and kingdom of the dead began. The Celt assailed him, becoming from the weird wood he called the world, and his far-off ancestors, the "little people," crept out of their caves, muttering charms and incantations in hissing inhuman speech; he was beleaguered by desires that had slept in his race for ages.

"I am afraid you are very tired, Master Lucian. Would you like me to give you my hand over this rough bit?"

He had stumbled against a great round stone and had nearly fallen. The woman's hand sought his in the darkness; as he felt the touch of the soft warm flesh he moaned, and a pang shot through his arm to his heart. He looked up and found he had only walked a few paces since Annie had spoken; he had thought they had wandered for hours together. The moon was just mounting above the oaks, and the halo round the dark hill brightened. He stopped short, and keeping his hold of Annie's hand, looked into her face. A hazy glory of moonlight shone around them and lit up their eyes.

He had not greatly altered since his boyhood; his face was pale olive in color, thin and oval; marks of pain had gathered about the eyes, and his black hair was already stricken with gray. But the eager, curious gaze still remained, and what he saw before him lit up his sadness with a new fire. She stopped too, and did not offer to draw away, but looked back with all her heart. They were alike in many ways; her skin was also of that olive color, but her face was sweet as a beautiful summer night, and her black eyes showed no dimness, and the smile on the scarlet lips was like a flame when it brightens a dark and lonely land.

"You are sorely tired, Master Lucian, let us sit down here by the gate."

It was Lucian who spoke next: "My dear, my dear." And their lips were together again, and their arms locked together, each holding the other fast. And then the poor lad let his head sink down on his sweethearts' breast, and burst into a passion of weeping. The tears streamed down his face, and he shook with sobbing, in the happiest moment that he had ever lived. The woman bent over him and tried to comfort him, but his tears were his consolation and his triumph. Annie was whispering to him, her hand laid on his heart; she was whispering beautiful, wonderful words, that soothed him as a song. He did not know what they meant.

"Annie, dear, dear Annie, what are you saying to me? I have never heard such beautiful words. Tell me, Annie, what do they mean?"

She laughed, and said it was only nonsense that

the nurses sang to the children.

"No, no, you are not to call me Master Lucian any more," he said, when they parted, "you must call me Lucian; and I, I worship you, my dear Annie."

He fell down before her, embracing her knees, and adored, and she allowed him, and confirmed his worship. He followed slowly after her, passing the path which led to her home with a longing glance. Nobody saw any difference in Lucian when he reached the rectory. He came in with his usual dreamy indifference, and told how he had lost his way by trying the short cut. He said he had met Dr. Burrows on the road, and that he had recommended the path by the fields. Then, as dully as if he had been reading some story out of a newspaper, he gave his father the outlines of the Beit case, producing the pretty little book called *The Chorus in Green*. The parson listened in amazement.

"You mean to tell me that *you* wrote this book?" he said. He was quite roused.

"No; not all of it. Look; that bit is mine, and that; and the beginning of this chapter. Nearly the whole of the third chapter is by me."

He closed the book without interest, and indeed he felt astonished at his father's excitement. The incident seemed to him unimportant.

"And you say that eighty or ninety pages of this book are yours, and these scoundrels have stolen your work?"

"Well, I suppose they have. I'll fetch the manuscript, if you would like to look at it."

The manuscript was duly produced, wrapped in

brown paper, with Messrs Beit's address label on it, and the post-office dated stamps.

"And the other book has been out a month." The parson, forgetting the sacerdotal office, and his good habit of grinning, swore at Messrs Beit and Mr. Ritson, calling them damned thieves, and then began to read the manuscript, and to compare it with the printed book.

"Why, it's splendid work. My poor fellow," he said after a while, "I had no notion you could write so well. I used to think of such things in the old days at Oxford; 'old Bill,' the tutor, used to praise my essays, but I never wrote anything like this. And this infernal ruffian of a Ritson has taken all your best things and mixed them up with his own rot to make it go down. Of course you'll expose the gang?"

Lucian was mildly amused; he couldn't enter into his father's feelings at all. He sat smoking in one of the old easy chairs, taking the rare relish of a hot grog with his pipe, and gazing out of his dreamy eyes at the violent old parson. He was pleased that his father liked his book, because he knew him to be a deep and sober scholar and a cool judge of good letters; but he laughed to himself when he saw the magic of print. The parson had expressed no wish to read the manuscript when it came back in disgrace; he had merely grinned, said something about boomerangs, and quoted Horace with relish. Whereas now, before the book in its neat case, lettered with another man's name, his approbation of the writing and his disapproval of the "scoundrels," as he called them, were loudly expressed, and, though a good smoker, he blew and puffed vehemently at his pipe.

"You'll expose the rascals, of course, won't you?" he said again.

"Oh no, I think not. It really doesn't matter much, does it? After all, there are some very weak things in the book; doesn't it strike you as 'young?' I have been thinking of another plan, but I haven't done much with it lately. But I believe I've got hold of a really good idea this time, and if I can manage to see the heart of it I hope to turn out a manuscript worth stealing. But it's so hard to get at the core of an idea—the heart, as I call it," he went on after a pause. "It's like having a box you can't open, though you know there's something wonderful inside. But I do believe I've a fine thing in my hands, and I mean to try my best to work it."

Lucian talked with enthusiasm now, but his father, on his side, could not share these ardors. It was his part to be astonished at excitement over a book that was not even begun, the mere ghost of a book flitting elusive in the world of unborn masterpieces and failures. He had loved good letters, but he shared unconsciously in the general belief that literary attempt is always pitiful, though he did not subscribe to the other half of the popular faith—that literary success is a matter of very little importance. He thought well of books, but only of printed books; in manuscripts he put no faith, and the *paulo-post-futurum* tense he could not in any manner conjugate. He returned once more to the topic of palpable interest.

"But about this dirty trick these fellows have

played on you. You won't sit quietly and bear it, surely? It's only a question of writing to the papers."

"They wouldn't put the letter in. And if they did, I should only get laughed at. Some time ago a man wrote to the *Reader*, complaining of his play being stolen. He said that he had sent a little one-act comedy to Burleigh, the great dramatist, asking for his advice. Burleigh gave his advice and took the idea for his own very successful play. So the man said, and I daresay it was true enough. But the victim got nothing by his complaint. 'A pretty state of things,' everybody said. 'Here's a Mr. Tomson, that no one has ever heard of, bothers Burleigh with his rubbish, and then accuses him of petty larceny. Is it likely that a man of Burleigh's position, a playwright who can make his five thousand a year easily, would borrow from an unknown Tomson?' I should think it very likely, indeed," Lucian went on, chuckling, "but that was their verdict. No; I don't think I'll write to the papers."

"Well, well, my boy, I suppose you know your own business best. I think you are mistaken, but you must do as you like."

"It's all so unimportant," said Lucian, and he really thought so. He had sweeter things to dream of, and desired no communion of feeling with that madman who had left Caermaen some few hours before. He felt he had made a fool of himself, he was ashamed to think of the fatuity of which he had been guilty, such boiling hatred was not only wicked, but absurd. A man could do no good who put himself into a position of such violent antagonism against his fellow-creatures; so Lucian rebuked his heart, saying that he was old enough to know better. But he remembered that he had sweeter things to dream of; there was a secret ecstasy that he treasured and locked tight away, as a joy too exquisite even for thought till he was quite alone; and then there was that scheme for a new book that he had laid down hopelessly some time ago; it seemed to have arisen into life again within the last hour; he understood that he had started on a false tack, he had taken the wrong aspect of his idea. Of course the thing couldn't be written in that way; it was like trying to read a page turned upside down; and he saw those characters he had vainly sought suddenly disambushed, and a splendid inevitable sequence of events unrolled before him.

It was a true resurrection; the dry plot he had constructed revealed itself as a living thing, stirring and mysterious, and warm as life itself. The parson was smoking stolidly to all appearance, but in reality he was full of amazement at his own son, and now and again he slipped sly furtive glances towards the tranquil young man in the armchair by the empty hearth. In the first place, Mr. Taylor was genuinely impressed by what he had read of Lucian's work; he had so long been accustomed to look upon all effort as futile that success amazed him. In the abstract, of course, he was prepared to admit that some people did write well and got published and made money, just as other persons successfully backed an outsider at heavy odds; but it had seemed as improbable that Lucian should show even the beginnings of achievement in one direction as in the other. Then the boy evidently cared so little about it; he did not appear to be proud of being worth robbing, nor was he angry with the robbers.

He sat back luxuriously in the disreputable old chair, drawing long slow wreaths of smoke, tasting his whisky from time to time, evidently well at ease with himself. The father saw him smile, and it suddenly dawned upon him that his son was very handsome; he had such kind gentle eyes and a kind mouth, and his pale cheeks were flushed like a girl's. Mr. Taylor felt moved. What a harmless young fellow Lucian had been; no doubt a little queer and different from others, but wholly inoffensive and patient under disappointment. And Miss Deacon, her contribution to the evening's discussion had been characteristic; she had remark-ed, firstly, that writing was a very unsettling occupation, and secondly, that it was extremely foolish to entrust one's property to people of whom one knew nothing. Father and son had smiled together at these observations, which were probably true enough. Mr. Taylor at last left Lucian along; he shook hands with a good deal of respect, and said, almost deferentially:

"You mustn't work too hard, old fellow. I wouldn't stay up too late, if I were you, after that long walk. You must have gone miles out of your way."

"I'm not tired now, though. I feel as if I could write my new book on the spot"; and the young man laughed a gay sweet laugh that struck the father as a new note in his son's life.

He sat still a moment after his father had left the room. He cherished his chief treasure of thought in its secret place; he would not enjoy it yet. He drew up a chair to the table at which he wrote or tried to write, and began taking pens and paper from the drawer. There was a great pile of ruled paper there; all of it used, on one side, and signifying many hours of desperate scribbling, of heart-searching and rack of his brain; an array of poor, eager lines written by a waning fire with waning hope; all useless and abandoned. He took up the sheets cheerfully, and began in delicious idleness to look over these fruitless efforts. A page caught his attention; he remembered how he wrote it while a November storm was dashing against the panes; and there was another, with a queer blot in one corner; he had got up from his chair and looked out, and all the earth was white fairyland, and the snowflakes whirled round and round in the wind. Then he saw the chapter begun of a night in March: a great gale blew that night and rooted up one of the ancient yews in the churchyard. He had heard the trees shrieking in the woods, and the long wail of the wind, and across the heaven a white moon fled awfully before the streaming clouds. And all these poor abandoned pages now seemed sweet, and past unhappiness was transmuted into happiness, and the nights of toil were holy. He turned over half a dozen leaves and began to sketch out the outlines of the new book on the unused pages; running out a skeleton plan on one page, and dotting fancies, suggestions, hints on others. He wrote rapidly, overjoyed to find that loving phrases grew under his pen; a particular scene he had imagined filled him with desire; he gave his hand free course, and saw the written work glowing; and action and all the heat of existence quickened and beat on the wet page. Happy fancies took shape in happier words, and when at last he leant back in his chair he felt the stir and rush of the story as if it had been some portion of his own life. He read over what he had done with a renewed pleasure in the nimble and flowing workmanship, and as he put the little pile of manuscript tenderly in the drawer he paused to enjoy the anticipation of tomorrow's labor.

And then—but the rest of the night was given to tender and delicious things, and when he went up to bed a scarlet dawn was streaming from the east.

III

F or days Lucian lay in a swoon of pleasure, smiling when he was addressed, sauntering happily in the sunlight, hugging recollection warm to his heart. Annie had told him that she was going on a visit to her married sister, and said, with a caress, that he must be patient. He protested against her absence, but she fondled him, whispering her charms in his ear till he gave in and then they said good-bye, Lucian adoring on his knees. The parting was as strange as the meeting, and that night when he laid his work aside, and let himself sink deep into the joys of memory, all the encounter seemed as wonderful and impossible as magic.

"And you really don't mean to do anything about those rascals?" said his father.

"Rascals? Which rascals? Oh, you mean Beit. I had forgotten all about it. No; I don't think I shall trouble. They're not worth powder and shot."

And he returned to his dream, pacing slowly from the medlar to the quince and back again. It seemed trivial to be interrupted by such questions; he had not even time to think of the book he had recommenced so eagerly, much less of this labor of long ago. He recollected without interest that it cost him many pains, that it was pretty good here and there, and that it had been stolen, and it seemed that there was nothing more to be said on the matter. He wished to think of the darkness in the lane, of the kind voice that spoke to him, of the kind hand that sought his own, as he stumbled on the rough way. So far, it was wonderful. Since he had left school and lost the company of the worthy barbarians who had befriended him there, he had almost lost the sense of kinship with humanity; he had come to dread the human form as men dread the hood of the cobra. To Lucian a man or a woman meant something that stung, that spoke words that rankled, and poisoned his life with scorn. At first such malignity shocked him: he would ponder over words and glances and wonder if he were not mistaken, and he still sought now an then for sympathy. The poor boy had romantic ideas about women; he believed they were merciful and pitiful, very kind to the unlucky and helpless. Men perhaps had to be different; after all, the duty of a man was to get on in the world, or, in plain language, to make money, to be successful; to cheat rather than to be cheated, but always to be successful; and he could understand that one who fell below this high standard must expect to be severely judged by his fellows. For example, there was young Bennett, Miss Spurry's nephew. Lucian had met him once or twice when he was spending his holidays with Miss Spurry, and the two young fellows compared literary notes together. Bennett showed some beautiful things he had written, over which Lucian had grown both sad and enthusiastic. It was such exquisite magic verse, and so much better than anything he ever hoped to write, that there was a touch of anguish in his congratulations. But when Bennett, after many vain prayers to his aunt, threw up a safe position in the bank, and betook himself to a London garret, Lucian was not surprised at the general verdict.

Mr. Dixon, as a clergyman, viewed the question from a high standpoint and found it all deplorable, but the general opinion was that Bennett was a hopeless young lunatic. Old Mr. Gervase went purple when his name was mentioned, and the young Dixons sneered very merrily over the adventure.

"I always thought he was a beastly young ass," said Edward Dixon, "but I didn't think he'd chuck away his chances like that. Said he couldn't stand a bank! I hope he'll be able to stand bread and water. That's all those littery fellows get, I believe, except Tennyson and Mark Twain and those sort of people."

Lucian of course sympathized with the unfortunate Bennett, but such judgments were after all only natural. The young man might have stayed in the bank and succeeded to his aunt's thousand a year, and everybody would have called him a very nice young fellow—"clever, too." But he had deliberately chosen, as Edward Dixon had said, to chuck his chances away for the sake of literature; piety and a sense of the main chance had alike pointed the way to a delicate course of wheedling, to a little harmless practicing on Miss Spurry's infirmities, to frequent compliances of a soothing nature, and the "young ass" had been blind to the direction of one and the other. It seemed almost right that the vicar should moralize, that Edward Dixon should sneer, and that Mr. Gervase should grow purple with contempt. Men, Lucian thought, were like judges, who may pity the criminal in their hearts, but are forced to vindicate the outraged majesty of the law by a severe sentence. He felt the same considerations applied to his own case; he knew that his father should have had more money, that his clothes should be newer and of a better cut, that he should have gone to the university and made good friends. If such had been his fortune he could have looked his fellow men proudly in the face, upright and unashamed. Having put on the whole armor of a first-rate West End tailor, with money in his purse, having taken anxious thought for the morrow, and having some useful friends and good prospects; in such a case he might have held his head high in a gentlemanly and Christian community. As it was he had usually avoided the reproachful glance of his fellows, feeling that he deserved their condemnation. But he had cherished for a long time his romantic sentimentalities about women; literary conventions borrowed from the minor poets and pseudo-medievalists, or so he thought afterwards. But, fresh from school, wearied a little with the perpetual society of barbarian though worthy boys, he had in his soul a charming image of womanhood, before which he worshipped with mingled passion and devotion. It was a nude figure, perhaps, but the shining arms were to be wound about the neck of a vanquished knight; there was rest for the head of a wounded lover; the hands were stretched forth to do works of pity, and the smiling lips were to murmur not love alone, but consolation in defeat. Here was the refuge for a broken heart; here the scorn of men would but make tenderness increase; here was all pity and all charity with loving-kindness. It was a delightful picture, conceived in the "come rest on this bosom," and "a ministering angel thou" manner, with touches of allurement that made devotion all the sweeter. He soon found that he had idealized a little; in the affair of young Bennett, while the men were contemptuous the women were virulent. He had been rather fond of Agatha Gervase, and she, so other ladies said, had "set her cap" at him. Now, when he rebelled, and lost the goodwill of his aunt, dear Miss Spurry, Agatha insulted him with all conceivable rapidity. "After all, Mr. Bennett," she said, "you will be nothing better than a beggar; now, will you? You mustn't think me cruel, but I can't help speaking the truth. *Write books!*" Her expression filled up the incomplete sentence; she waggled with indignant emotion. These passages came to Lucian's ears, and indeed the Gervases boasted of "how well poor Agatha had behaved."

"Never mind, Gathy," old Gervase had observed. "If the impudent young puppy comes here again, we'll see what Thomas can do with the horse-whip."

"Poor dear child," Mrs. Gervase added in telling the tale, "and she was so fond of him too. But of course it couldn't go on after his shameful behavior."

But Lucian was troubled; he sought vainly for the ideal womanly, the tender note of "come rest on this bosom." Ministering angels, he felt convinced, do not rub red pepper and sulfuric acid into the wounds of suffering mortals.

Then there was the case of Mr. Vaughan, a squire in the neighborhood, at whose board all the aristocracy of Caermaen had feasted for years. Mr. Vaughan had a first-rate cook, and his cellar was rare, and he was never so happy as when he shared his good things with his friends. His mother kept his house, and they delighted all the girls with frequent dances, while the men sighed over the amazing champagne. Investments proved disastrous, and Mr. Vaughan had to sell the gray manor house by the river. He and his mother took a little modern stucco villa in Caermaen, wishing to be near their dear friends. But the men were "very sorry; rough on you, Vaughan. Always thought those Patagonians were risky, but you wouldn't hear of it. Hope we shall see you before very long; you and Mrs. Vaughan must come to tea some day after Christmas."

"Of course we are all very sorry for them," said Henrietta Dixon. "No, we haven't called on Mrs. Vaughan yet. They have no regular servant, you know; only a woman in the morning. I hear old mother Vaughan, as Edward will call her, does nearly everything. And their house is absurdly small; it's little more than a cottage. One really can't call it a gentleman's house."

Then Mr. Vaughn, his heart in the dust, went to the Gervases and tried to borrow five pounds of Mr. Gervase. He had to be ordered out of the house, and, as Edith Gervase said, it was all very painful; "he went out in such a funny way," she added, "just like the dog when he's had a whipping. Of course it's sad, even if it is all his own fault, as everybody says, but he looked so ridiculous as he was going down the steps that I couldn't help laughing." Mr. Vaughan heard the ringing, youthful laughter as he crossed the lawn.

Young girls like Henrietta Dixon and Edith Gervase naturally viewed the Vaughans' comical position with all the high spirits of their age, but the elder ladies could not look at matters in this frivolous light.

"Hush, dear, hush," said Mrs. Gervase, "it's all too shocking to be a laughing matter. Don't you agree with me, Mrs. Dixon? The sinful extravagance that went on at Pentre always *frightened* me. You remember that ball they gave last year? Mr. Gervase assured me that the champagne must have cost *at least* a hundred and fifty shillings the dozen."

"It's dreadful, isn't it," said Mrs. Dixon, "when one thinks of how many poor people there are who would be thankful for a crust of bread?"

"Yes, Mrs. Dixon," Agatha joined in, "and you know how absurdly the Vaughans spoilt the cottagers. Oh, it was really wicked; one would think Mr. Vaughan wished to make them above their station. Edith and I went for a walk one day nearly as far as Pentre, and we begged a glass of water of old Mrs. Jones who lives in that pretty cottage near the brook. She began praising the Vaughans in the most fulsome manner, and showed us some flannel things they had given her at Christmas. I assure you, my dear Mrs. Dixon, the flannel was the very best quality; no lady could wish for better. It couldn't have cost less than half-a-crown a yard."

"I know, my dear, I know. Mr. Dixon always said it couldn't last. How often I have heard him say that the Vaughans were pauperizing all the common people about Pentre, and putting every one else in a most unpleasant position. Even from a worldly point of view it was very poor taste on their part. So different from the *true* charity that Paul speaks of."

"I only wish they had given away nothing worse than flannel," said Miss Colley, a young lady of very strict views. "But I assure you there was a perfect orgy, I can call it nothing else, every Christmas. Great joints of prime beef, and barrels of strong beer, and snuff and tobacco distributed wholesale; as if the poor wanted to be encouraged in their disgusting habits. It was really impossible to go through the village for weeks after; the whole place was poisoned with the fumes of horrid tobacco pipes."

"Well, we see how that sort of thing ends," said Mrs. Dixon, summing up judicially. "We had intended to call, but I really think it would be impossible after what Mrs. Gervase has told us. The idea of Mr. Vaughan trying to sponge on poor Mr. Gervase in that shabby way! I think meanness of that kind is so hateful."

It was the practical side of all this that astonished Lucian. He saw that in reality there was no high-flown quixotism in a woman's nature; the smooth arms, made he had thought for caressing, seemed muscular; the hands meant for the doing of works of pity in his system, appeared dexterous in the giving of "stingers," as Barnes might say, and the smiling lips could sneer with great ease. Nor was he more fortunate in his personal experiences. As has been told, Mrs. Dixon spoke of him in connection with "judgments," and the younger ladies did not exactly cultivate his acquaintance. Theoretically they "adored" books and thought poetry "too sweet," but in practice they preferred talking about mares and fox terriers and their neighbors.

They were nice girls enough, very like other young ladies in other country towns, content with the teaching of their parents, reading the Bible every morning in their bedrooms, and sitting every Sunday in church amongst the well-dressed "sheep" on the right hand. It was not their fault if they failed to satisfy the ideal of an enthusiastic dreamy boy, and indeed, they would have thought his feigned woman immodest, absurdly sentimental, a fright ("never wears stays, my dear") and *horrid*.

At first he was a good deal grieved at the loss of that charming tender woman, the work of his brain. When the Miss Dixons went haughtily by with a scornful waggle, when the Miss Gervases passed in the wagonette laughing as the mud splashed him, the poor fellow would look up with a face of grief that must have been very comic; "like a dying duck," as Edith Gervase said. Edith was really very pretty, and he would have liked to talk to her, even about fox terriers, if she would have listened. One afternoon at the Dixons' he really forced himself upon her, and with all the obtuseness of an enthusiastic boy tried to discuss the *Lotus Eaters* of Tennyson. It was too absurd. Captain Kempton was making signals to Edith all the time, and Lieutenant Gatwick had gone off in disgust, and he had promised to bring her a puppy "by Vick out of Wasp." At last the poor girl could bear it no longer:

"Yes, it's very sweet," she said at last. "When did you say you were going to London, Mr. Taylor?"

It was about the time that his disappointment became known to everybody, and the shot told. He gave her a piteous look and slunk off, "just like the dog when he's had a whipping," to use Edith's own expression. Two or three lessons of this description produced their due effect; and when he saw a male Dixon or Gervase approaching him he bit his lip and summoned up his courage. But when he descried a "ministering angel" he made haste and hid behind a hedge or took to the woods. In course of time the desire to escape became an instinct, to be followed as a matter of course; in the same way he avoided the adders on the mountain. His old ideals were almost if not quite forgotten; he knew that the female of the *bête humaine*, like the adder, would in all probability sting, and he therefore shrank from its trail, but without any feeling of special resentment. The one had a poisoned tongue as the other had a poisoned fang, and it was well to leave them both alone. Then had come that sudden fury of rage against all humanity, as he went out of Caermaen carrying the book that had been stolen from him by the enterprising Beit. He shuddered as he though of how nearly he had approached the verge of madness, when his eyes filled with blood and the earth seemed to burn with fire. He remembered how he had looked up to the horizon and the sky was blotched with scarlet; and the earth was deep red, with red woods and red fields. There was something of horror in the memory, and in the vision of that wild night walk through dim country, when every shadow seemed a symbol of some terrible impending doom. The murmur of the brook, the wind shrilling through the wood, the pale light flowing from the moldered trunks, and the picture of his own figure fleeing and fleeting through the shades; all these seemed unhappy things that told a story in fatal hieroglyphics. And then the life and laws of the sunlight had passed away, and the resurrection and kingdom of the dead began. Though his limbs were weary, he had felt his muscles grow strong as steel; a woman, one of the hated race, was beside him in the darkness, and the wild beast woke within him, ravening for blood and brutal lust; all the raging desires of the dim race from which he came assailed his heart. The ghosts issued out from the weird wood and from the caves in the hills, besieging him, as he had imagined the spiritual legion besieging Caermaen, beckoning him to a hideous battle and a victory that he had never imagined in his wildest dreams. And then out of the darkness the kind voice spoke again, and the kind hand was stretched out to draw him up from the pit. It was sweet to think of that which he had found at last; the boy's picture incarnate, all the passion and compassion of his longing, all the pity and love and consolation. She, that beautiful passionate woman offering up her beauty in sacrifice to him, she was worthy indeed of his worship. He remembered how his tears had fallen upon her breast, and how tenderly she had soothed him, whispering those wonderful unknown words that sang to his heart. And she had made herself defenseless before him, caressing and fondling the body that had been so despised. He exulted in the happy thought that he had knelt down on the ground before her, and had embraced her knees and worshipped. The woman's body had become his religion; he lay awake at night looking into the darkness with hungry eyes; wishing for a miracle, that the appearance of the so-desired form might be shaped before him. And when he was alone in quiet places in the wood, he fell down again on his knees, and even on his face, stretching out vain hands in the air, as if they would feel her flesh. His father noticed in those days that the inner pocket of his coat was stuffed with papers; he would see Lucian walking up and down in a secret shady place at the bottom of the orchard, reading from his sheaf of manuscript, replacing the leaves, and again drawing them out. He would walk a few quick steps, and pause as if enraptured, gazing in the air as if he looked through the shadows of the world into some sphere of glory, feigned by his thought. Mr. Taylor was almost alarmed at the sight; he concluded of course that Lucian was writing a book. In the first place, there seemed something immodest in seeing the operation performed under one's eyes; it was as if the "make-up" of a beautiful actress were done on the stage, in full audience; as if one saw the rounded calves fixed in position, the fleshings drawn on, the voluptuous outlines of the figure produced by means purely mechanical, blushes mantling from the paint-pot, and the golden tresses well secured by the wigmaker. Books, Mr. Taylor thought, should swim into one's ken mysteriously; they should appear all printed and bound, without apparent genesis; just as children are suddenly told that they have a little sister, found by mamma in the garden. But Lucian was not only engaged in composition; he was plainly rapturous, enthusiastic; Mr. Taylor saw him throw up his hands, and bow his head with strange gesture. The parson began to fear that his son was like some of those mad Frenchmen of whom he had read, young fellows who had a sort of fury of literature, and gave their whole lives to it, spending days over a page, and years over a book, pursuing art as Englishmen pursue money, building up a romance as if it were a business. Now Mr. Taylor held firmly by the "walking-stick" theory; he believed that a man of letters should have a real profession, some solid employment in life. "Get something to do," he would have liked to say, "and then you can write as much as you please. Look at Scott, look at Dickens and Trollope." And then there was the social point of view; it might be right, or it might be wrong, but there could be no doubt that the literary man, as such, was not thought much of in English society. Mr. Taylor knew his Thackeray, and he remembered that old Major Pendennis, society personified, did not exactly boast of his nephew's occupation. Even

Warrington was rather ashamed to own his connection with journalism, and Pendennis himself laughed openly at his novel writing as an agreeable way of making money, a useful appendage to the cultivation of dukes, his true business in life. This was the plain English view, and Mr. Taylor was no doubt right enough in thinking it good, practical common sense. Therefore when he saw Lucian loitering and sauntering, musing amorously over his manuscript, exhibiting manifest signs of that fine fury which Britons have ever found absurd, he felt grieved at heart, and more than ever sorry that he had not been able to send the boy to Oxford.

"B.N.C. would have knocked all this nonsense out of him," he thought. "He would have taken a double First like my poor father and made something of a figure in the world. However, it can't be helped." The poor man sighed, and lit his pipe, and walked in another part of the garden.

But he was mistaken in his diagnosis of the symptoms. The book that Lucian had begun lay unheeded in the drawer; it was a secret work that he was engaged on, and the manuscripts that he took out of that inner pocket never left him day or night. He slept with them next to his heart, and he would kiss them when he was quite alone, and pay them such devotion as he would have paid to her whom they symbolized. He wrote on these leaves a wonderful ritual of praise and devotion; it was the liturgy of his religion. Again and again he copied and recopied this madness of a lover; dallying all days over the choice of a word, searching for more exquisite phrases. No common words, no such phrases as he might use in a tale would suffice; the sentences of worship must stir and be quickened, they must glow and burn, and be decked out as with rare work of jewelry. Every part of that holy and beautiful body must be adored; he sought for terms of extravagant praise, he bent his soul and mind low before her, licking the dust under her feet, abased and yet rejoicing as a Templar before the image of Baphomet. He exulted more especially in the knowledge that there was nothing of the conventional or common in his ecstasy; he was not the fervent, adoring lover of Tennyson's poems, who loves with passion and yet with a proud respect, with the love always of a gentleman for a lady. Annie was not a lady; the Morgans had farmed their land for hundreds of years; they were what Miss Gervase and Miss Colley and the rest of them called common people. Tennyson's noble gentleman thought of their ladies with something of reticence; they imagined them dressed in flowing and courtly robes, walking with slow dignity; they dreamed of them as always stately, the future mistresses of their houses, mothers of their heirs. Such lovers bowed, but not too low, remembering their own honor, before those who were to be equal companions and friends as well as wives. It was not such conceptions as these that he embodied in the amazing emblems of his ritual; he was not, he told himself, a young officer, "something in the city," or a rising barrister engaged to a Miss Dixon or a Miss Gervase. He had not thought of looking out for a nice little house in a good residential suburb where they would have pleasant society;

there were to be no consultations about wallpapers, or jocose whispers from friends as to the necessity of having a room that would do for a nursery. No glad young thing had leant on his arm while they chose the suite in white enamel, and china for "our bedroom," the modest salesman doing his best to spare their blushes. When Edith Gervase married she would get mamma to look out for two really good servants, "as we must begin quietly," and mamma would make sure that the drains and everything were right. Then her "girl friends" would come on a certain solemn day to see all her "lovely things." "Two dozen of everything!" "Look, Ethel, did you ever see such ducky frills?" "And that insertion, isn't it quite too sweet?" "My dear Edith, you are a lucky girl." "All the under-linen specially made by Madame Lulu!" "What delicious things!" "I hope he knows what a prize he is winning." "Oh! do look at those lovely ribbon-bows!" "You darling, how happy you must be." "Real Valenciennes!" Then a whisper in the lady's ear, and her reply, "Oh, don't, Nelly!" So they would chirp over their treasures, as in Rabelais they chirped over their cups; and every thing would be done in due order till the wedding-day, when mamma, who had strained her sinews and the commandments to bring the match about, would weep and look indignantly at the unhappy bride-groom. "I *hope* you'll be kind to her, Robert." Then in a rapid whisper to the bride: "Mind, you *insist* on Wyman's flushing the drains when you come back; servants are so careless and dirty too. Don't let him go about by himself in Paris. Men are

so *queer*, one never knows. You *have* got the pills?"
And aloud, after these *secreta*, "God bless you, my
dear; good-bye! *cluck, cluck*, good-bye!"

There were stranger things written in the
manuscript pages that Lucian cherished, sentences
that burnt and glowed like "coals of fire which hath
a most vehement flame." There were phrases that
stung and tingled as he wrote them, and sonorous
words poured out in ecstasy and rapture, as in
some of the old litanies. He hugged the thought
that a great part of what he had invented was in the
true sense of the word occult: page after page might
have been read aloud to the uninitiated without
betraying the inner meaning. He dreamed night
and day over these symbols, he copied and
recopied the manuscript nine times before he wrote
it out fairly in a little book which he made himself
of a skin of creamy vellum. In his mania for
acquirements that should be entirely useless he had
gained some skill in illumination, or limning as he
preferred to call it, always choosing the obscurer
word as the obscurer arts. First he set himself to the
sever practice of the text; he spent many hours and
days of toil in struggling to fashion the serried
columns of black letter, writing and rewriting till he
could shape the massive character with firm true
hand. He cut his quills with the patience of a monk
in the scriptorium, shaving and altering the nib,
lightening and increasing the pressure and
flexibility of the points, till the pen satisfied him,
and gave a stroke both broad and even. Then he
made experiments in inks, searching for some
medium that would rival the glossy black letter of

the old manuscripts; and not till he could produce a fair page of text did he turn to the more entrancing labor of the capitals and borders and ornaments. He mused long over the Lombardic letters, as glorious in their way as a cathedral, and trained his hand to execute the bold and flowing lines; and then there was the art of the border, blossoming in fretted splendor all about the page. His cousin, Miss Deacon, called it all a great waste of time, and his father thought he would have done much better in trying to improve his ordinary handwriting, which was both ugly and illegible. Indeed, there seemed but a poor demand for the limner's art. He sent some specimens of his skill to an "artistic firm" in London; a verse of the "Maud," curiously emblazoned, and a Latin hymn with the notes priced on a red stave. The firm wrote civilly, telling him that his work, though good, was not what they wanted, and enclosing an illuminated text. "We have great demand for this sort of thing," they concluded, "and if you care to attempt something in this style we should be pleased to look at it." The said text was "Thou, God, seest me." The letter was of a degraded form, bearing much the same relation to the true character as a "churchwarden gothic" building does to Canterbury Cathedral; the colors were varied. The initial was pale gold, the *h* pink, the *o* black, the *u* blue, and the first letter was somehow connected with a bird's nest containing the young of the pigeon, who were waited on by the female bird.

"What a pretty text," said Miss Deacon. "I should like to nail it up in my room. Why don't you try to do something like that, Lucian? You might make something by it."

"I sent them these," said Lucian, "but they don't like them much."

"My dear boy! I should think not! Like them! What were you thinking of to draw those queer stiff flowers all round the border? Roses? They don't look like roses at all events. Where do you get such ideas from?"

"But the design is appropriate; look at the words."

"My dear Lucian, I can't read the words; it's such a queer old-fashioned writing. Look how plain that text is; one can see what it's about. And this other one; I can't make it out at all."

"It's a Latin hymn."

"A Latin hymn? Is it a Protestant hymn? I may be old-fashioned, but *Hymns Ancient and Modern* is quite good enough for me. This is the music, I suppose? But, my dear boy, there are only four lines, and who ever heard of notes shaped like that: you have made some square and some diamond-shape? Why didn't you look in your poor mother's old music? It's in the ottoman in the drawing room. I could have shown you how to make the notes; there are crotchets, you know, and quavers."

Miss Deacon laid down the illuminated *Urbs Beata* in despair; she felt convinced that her cousin was "next door to an idiot."

And he went out into the garden and raged behind a hedge. He broke two flowerpots and hit an apple tree very hard with his stick, and then, feeling more calm, wondered what was the use in trying to do anything. He would not have put the thought into words, but in his heart he was aggrieved that his cousin liked the pigeons and the text, and did not like his emblematical roses and the Latin hymn. He knew he had taken great pains over the work, and that it was well done, and being still a young man he expected praise. He found that in this hard world there was a lack of appreciation; a critical spirit seemed abroad. If he could have been scientifically observed as he writhed and smarted under the strictures of "the old fool," as he rudely called his cousin, the spectacle would have been extremely diverting. Little boys sometimes enjoy a very similar entertainment; either with their tiny fingers or with mamma's nail scissors they gradually deprive a fly of its wings and legs. The odd gyrations and queer thin buzzing of the creature as it spins comically round and round never fail to provide a fund of harmless amusement. Lucian, indeed, fancied himself a very ill used individual; but he should have tried to imitate the nervous organization of the flies, which, as mamma says, "can't really feel."

But now, as he prepared the vellum leaves, he remembered his art with joy; he had not labored to do beautiful work in vain. He read over his manuscript once more, and thought of the designing of the pages. He made sketches on furtive sheets of paper, and hunted up books in his father's library for suggestions. There were books about architecture, and medieval iron work, and brasses which contributed hints for adornment; and not content with mere pictures he sought in the woods and hedges, scanning the strange forms of trees, and the poisonous growth of great water-plants, and the parasite twining of honeysuckle and bryony. In one of these rambles he discovered a red earth which he made into a pigment, and he found in the unctuous juice of a certain fern an ingredient which he thought made his black ink still more glossy. His book was written all in symbols, and in the same spirit of symbolism he decorated it, causing wonderful foliage to creep about the text, and showing the blossom of certain mystical flowers, with emblems of strange creatures, caught and bound in rose thickets. All was dedicated to love and a lover's madness, and there were songs in it which haunted him with their lilt and refrain. When the book was finished it replaced the loose leaves as his constant companion by day and night. Three times a day he repeated his ritual to himself, seeking out the loneliest places in the woods, or going up to his room; and from the fixed intentness and rapture of his gaze, the father thought him still severely employed in the questionable process of composition. At night he contrived to wake for his strange courtship; and he had a peculiar ceremony when he got up in the dark and lit his candle. From a steep and wild hillside, not far form the house, he had cut from time to time five large boughs of spiked and prickly gorse. He had brought them into the house, one by one, and had hidden them in the big box that stood beside his bed. Often he woke up weeping and murmuring to himself the words of one of his songs, and then when he had lit the candle, he would draw out the gorse-boughs, and place them on the floor, and taking off his nightgown, gently lay himself down on the bed of thorns and spines. Lying on his face, with the candle and the book before him, he would softly and tenderly repeat the praises of his dear, dear Annie, and as he turned over page after page, and saw the raised gold of the majuscules glow and flame in the candle-light, he pressed the thorns into his flesh. At such moments he tasted in all its acute savor the joy of physical pain; and after two or three experiences of such delights he altered his book, making a curious sign in vermilion on the margin of the passages where he was to inflict on himself this sweet torture. Never did he fail to wake at the appointed hour, a strong effort of will broke through all the heaviness of sleep, and he would rise up, joyful though weeping, and reverently set his thorny bed upon the floor, offering his pain with his praise. When he had whispered the last word, and had risen from the ground, his body would be all freckled with drops of blood; he used to view the marks with pride. Here and there a spine would be left deep in the flesh, and he would pull these out roughly, tearing through the skin. On some nights when he had pressed with more fervor on the thorns his thighs would stream with blood, red beads standing out on the flesh, and trickling down to his feet. He had some difficulty in washing away the bloodstains so as not to leave any traces to attract the attention of the servant; and after a time he returned no more to his bed when his duty had been accomplished. For a coverlet he had a dark rug, a good deal worn, and in this he would wrap his naked bleeding body, and lie down on the hard floor, well content to add an aching rest to the account of his pleasures. He was covered with scars, and those that healed during the day were torn open afresh at night; the pale olive skin was red with the angry marks of blood, and the graceful form of the young man appeared like the body of a tortured martyr. He grew thinner and thinner every day, for he ate but little; the skin was stretched on the bones of his face, and the black eyes burnt in dark purple hollows. His relations noticed that he was not looking well.

"Now, Lucian, it's perfect madness of you to go on like this," said Miss Deacon, one morning at breakfast. "Look how your hand shakes; some people would say that you have been taking brandy. And all that you want is a little medicine, and yet you won't be advised. You know it's not my fault; I have asked you to try Dr. Jelly's Cooling Powders again and again."

He remembered the forcible exhibition of the powders when he was a boy, and felt thankful that those days were over. He only grinned at his cousin and swallowed a great cup of strong tea to steady his nerves, which were shaky enough. Mrs. Dixon saw him one day in Caermaen; it was very hot, and he had been walking rather fast. The scars on his body burnt and tingled, and he tottered as he raised his hat to the vicar's wife. She decided without further investigation that he must have been drinking in public houses.

"It seems a mercy that poor Mrs. Taylor was

taken," she said to her husband. "She has certainly been spared a great deal. That wretched young man passed me this afternoon; he was quite intoxicated."

"How very said," said Mr. Dixon. "A little port, my dear?"

"Thank you, Merivale, I will have another glass of sherry. Dr. Burrows is always scolding me and saying I *must* take something to keep up my energy, and this sherry is so weak."

The Dixons were not teetotalers. They regretted it deeply, and blamed the doctor, who "insisted on some stimulant." However, there was some consolation in trying to convert the parish to total abstinence, or, as they curiously called it, temperance. Old women were warned of the sin of taking a glass of beer for supper; aged laborers were urged to try Cork-ho, the new temperance drink; an uncouth beverage, styled coffee, was dispensed at the reading-room. Mr. Dixon preached an eloquent "temperance" sermon, soon after the above conversation, taking as his text: *Beware of the leaven of the Pharisees*. In his discourse he showed that fermented liquor and leaven had much in common, that beer was at the present day "put away" during Passover by the strict Jews; and in a moving peroration he urged his dear brethren, "and more especially those amongst us who are poor in this world's goods," to beware indeed of that evil leaven which was sapping the manhood of our nation. Mrs. Dixon cried after church:

"Oh, Merivale, what a beautiful sermon! How earnest you were. I hope it will do good."

Mr. Dixon swallowed his port with great decorum, but his wife fuddled herself every evening with cheap sherry. She was quite unaware of the fact, and sometimes wondered in a dim way why she always had to scold the children after dinner. And so strange things sometimes happened in the nursery, and now and then the children looked queerly at one another after a red-faced woman had gone out, panting.

Lucian knew nothing of his accuser's trials, but he was not long in hearing of his own intoxication. The next time he went down to Caermaen he was hailed by the doctor.

"Been drinking again today?"

"No," said Lucian in a puzzled voice. "What do you mean?"

"Oh, well, if you haven't, that's all right, as you'll be able to take a drop with me. Come along in?"

Over the whisky and pipes Lucian heard of the evil rumors affecting his character.

"Mrs. Dixon assured me you were staggering from one side of the street to the other. You quite frightened her, she said. Then she asked me if I recommended her to take one or two ounces of spirit at bedtime for the palpitation; and of course I told her two would be better. I have my living to make here, you know. And upon my word, I think she wants it; she's always gurgling inside like waterworks. I wonder how old Dixon can stand it."

"I like 'ounces of spirit,'" said Lucian. "That's taking it medicinally, I suppose. I've often heard of ladies who have to 'take it medicinally'; and that's how it's done?"

"That's it. ' Dr Burrows won't *listen* to me': 'I tell him how I dislike the taste of spirits, but he says they are absolutely *necessary* for my constitution': 'my medical man *insists* on something at bedtime'; that's the style."

Lucian laughed gently; all these people had become indifferent to him; he could no longer feel savage indignation at their little hypocrisies and malignancies. Their voices uttering calumny, and morality, and futility had become like the thin shrill angry note of a gnat on a summer evening; he had his own thoughts and his own life, and he passed on without heeding.

"You come down to Caermaen pretty often, don't you?" said the doctor. "I've seen you two or three times in the last fortnight."

"Yes, I enjoy the walk."

"Well, look me up whenever you like, you know. I am often in just at this time, and a chat with a human being isn't bad, now and then. It's a change for me; I'm often afraid I shall lose my patients."

The doctor had the weakness of these terrible puns, dragged headlong into the conversation. He sometimes exhibited them before Mrs. Gervase, who would smile in a faint and dignified manner, and say:

"Ah, I see. Very amusing indeed. We had an old coachmen once who was very clever, I believe, at that sort of thing, but Mr. Gervase was obliged to send him away, the laughter of the other domestics was so very boisterous."

Lucian laughed, not boisterously, but good-humouredly, at the doctor's joke. He liked Burrows, feeling that he was a man and not an automatic gabbling machine.

"You look a little pulled down," said the doctor, when Lucian rose to go. "No, you don't want my medicine. Plenty of beef and beer will do you more good than drugs. I daresay it's the hot weather that has thinned you a bit. Oh, you'll be all right again in a month."

As Lucian strolled out of the town on his way home, he passed a small crowd of urchins assembled at the corner of an orchard. They were enjoying themselves immensely. The "healthy" boy, the same whom he had seen some weeks ago operating on a cat, seemed to have recognized his selfishness in keeping his amusements to himself. He had found a poor lost puppy, a little creature with bright pitiful eyes, almost human in their fond, friendly gaze. It was not a well-bred little dog; it was certainly not that famous puppy "by Vick out of Wasp"; it had rough hair and a foolish long tail which it wagged beseechingly, at once deprecating severity and asking kindness. The poor animal had evidently been used to gentle treatment; it would look up in a boy's face, and give a leap, fawning on him, and then bark in a small doubtful voice, and cower a moment on the ground, astonished perhaps at the strangeness, the bustle and animation. The boys were beside themselves with eagerness; there was quite a babble of voices, arguing, discussing, suggesting. Each one had a plan of his own which he brought before the leader, a stout and sturdy youth.

"Drown him! What be you thinkin' of, mum?"

he was saying. "'Tain't no sport at all. You shut your mouth, gwaes. Be you goin' to ask your mother for the boiling-water? Is, Bob Williams, I do know all that: but where be you a-going to get the fire from? Be quiet, mun, can't you? Thomas Trevor, be this dog yourn or mine? Now, look you, if you don't all of you shut your bloody mouths, I'll take the dog 'ome and keep him. There now!"

He was a born leader of men. A singular depression and lowness of spirit showed itself on the boys' faces. They recognized that the threat might very possibly be executed, and their countenances were at once composed to humble attention. The puppy was still cowering on the ground in the midst of them: one or two tried to relieve the tension of their feelings by kicking him in the belly with their hobnail boots. It cried out with the pain and writhed a little, but the poor little beast did not attempt to bite or even snarl. It looked up with those beseeching friendly eyes at its persecutors, and fawned on them again, and tried to wag its tail and be merry, pretending to play with a straw on the road, hoping perhaps to win a little favor in that way.

The leader saw the moment for his masterstroke. He slowly drew a piece of rope from his pocket.

"What do you say to that, mun? Now, Thomas Trevor! We'll hang him over that there bough. Will that suit you, Bobby Williams?"

There was a great shriek of approval and delight. All was again bustle and animation. "I'll tie it round his neck?" "Get out, mum, you don't know how it be done." "Is, I do, Charley." "Now, let me, gwaes, now do let me." "You be sure he won't bite?" "He hain't mad, be he?" "Suppose we were to tie up his mouth first?"

The puppy still fawned and curried favor, and wagged that sorry tail, and lay down crouching on one side on the ground, sad and sorry in his heart, but still with a little gleam of hope; for now and again he tried to play, and put up his face, praying with those fond, friendly eyes. And then at last his gambols and poor efforts for mercy ceased, and he lifted up his wretched voice in one long dismal whine of despair. But he licked the hand of the boy that tied the noose.

He was slowly and gently swung into the air as Lucian went by unheeded; he struggled, and his legs twisted and writhed. The "healthy" boy pulled the rope, and his friends danced and shouted with glee. As Lucian turned the corner, the poor dangling body was swinging to and fro, the puppy was dying, but he still kicked a little.

Lucian went on his way hastily, and shuddering with disgust. The young of the human creature were really too horrible; they defiled the earth, and made existence unpleasant, as the pulpy growth of a noxious and obscene fungus spoils an agreeable walk. The sight of those malignant little animals with mouths that uttered cruelty and filthy, with hands dexterous in torture, and feet swift to run all evil errands, had given him a shock and broken up the world of strange thoughts in which he had been dwelling. Yet it was no good being angry with them: it was their nature to be very loathsome. Only he wished they would go about their hideous amusements in their own back gardens where nobody could see them at work; it was too bad that he should be interrupted and offended in a quiet country road. He tried to put the incident out of his mind, as if the whole thing had been a disagreeable story, and the visions amongst which he wished to move were beginning to return, when he was again rudely disturbed. A little girl, a pretty child of eight or nine, was coming along the lane to meet him. She was crying bitterly and looking to left and right, and calling out some word all the time.

"Jack, Jack, Jack! Little Jackie! Jack!"

Then she burst into tears afresh, and peered into the hedge, and tried to peep through a gate into a field.

"Jackie, Jackie, Jackie!"

She came up to Lucian, sobbing as if her heart would break, and dropped him an old-fashioned curtsy.

"Oh, please sir, have you seen my little Jackie?"

"What do you mean?" said Lucian. "What is it you've lost?"

"A little dog, please sir. A little terrier dog with white hair. Father gave me him a month ago, and said I might keep him. Someone did leave the garden gate open this afternoon, and he must 'a got away, sir, and I was so fond of him sir, he was so playful and loving, and I be afraid he be lost."

She began to call again, without waiting for an answer.

"Jack, Jack, Jack!"

"I'm afraid some boys have got your little dog," said Lucian. "They've killed him. You'd better go back home."

He went on, walking as fast as he could in his endeavor to get beyond the noise of the child's crying. It distressed him, and he wished to think of other things. He stamped his foot angrily on the ground as he recalled the annoyances of the afternoon, and longed for some hermitage on the mountains, far above the stench and the sound of humanity.

A little farther, and he came to Croeswen, where the road branched off to right and left. There was a triangular plot of grass between the two roads; there the cross had once stood, "the goodly and famous roode" of the old local chronicle. The words echoed in Lucian's ears as he went by on the right hand. "There were five steps that did go up to the first pace, and seven steps to the second pace, all of clene hewn ashler. And all above it was most curiously and gloriously wrought with thorowgh carved work; in the highest place was the Holy Roode with Christ upon the Cross having Marie on the one syde and John on the other. And below were six splendent and glisteringe archaungels tha bore up the roode, and beneath them in their stories were the most fair and noble images of the xii Apostles and of divers other Saints and Martirs. And in the lowest storie there was a marvelous imagerie of divers Beasts, such as oxen and horses and swine, and little dogs and peacocks, all done in the finest and most curious wise, so that they all seemed as they were caught in a Wood of Thorns, the which is their torment of this life. And here once in the year was a marvelous solemn service, when the parson of Caermaen came out with the singers and all the people, singing the psalm *Benedicite omnia opera* as they passed along the road in their procession. And when they stood at the roode the priest did there his service, making certain prayers for the beasts, and then he went up to the first pace and preached a sermon to the people, shewing them that as our lord Jhu dyed upon the Tree of his deare mercy for us, so we too owe mercy to the beasts his Creatures, for that they are all his poor lieges and silly servants. And that like as the Holy Aungells do atheir suit to him on high, and the Blessed xii Apostles and the Martirs, and all the Blissful Saints served him aforetime on earth and now praise him in heaven, so also do the beasts serve him, though they be in torment of life and below men. For their spirit goeth downward, as Holy Writ teacheth us."

It was a quaint old record, a curious relic of what the modern inhabitants of Caermaen called the Dark Ages. A few of the stones that had formed the base of the cross still remained in position, gray with age, blotched with black lichen and green moss. The remainder of the famous rood had been used to mend the roads, to built pigsties and domestic offices; it had turned Protestant, in fact. Indeed, if it had remained, the parson of Caermaen would have had no time for the service; the coffee-stall, the Portuguese Missions, the Society for the Conversion of the Jews, and important social duties took up all his leisure. Besides, he thought the whole ceremony unscriptural.

Lucian passed on his way, wondering at the

strange contrasts of the middle Ages. How was it that people who could devise so beautiful a service believed in witchcraft, demoniacal possession and obsession, in the incubus and succubus, and in the Sabbath an in many other horrible absurdities? It seemed astonishing that anybody could even pretend to credit such monstrous tales, but there could be no doubt that the dread of old women who rode on broomsticks and liked black cats was once a very genuine terror.

A cold wind blew up from the river at sunset, and the scars on his body began to burn and tingle. The pain recalled his ritual to him, and he began to recite it as he walked along. He had cut a branch of thorn from the hedge and placed it next to his skin, pressing the spikes into the flesh with his hand till the warm blood ran down. He felt it was an exquisite and sweet observance for her sake; and then he thought of the secret golden palace he was building for her, the rare and wonderful city rising in his imagination. As the solemn night began to close about the earth, and the last glimmer of the sun faded from the hills, he gave himself anew to the woman, his body and his mind, all that he was, and all that he had.

IV

I n the course of the week Lucian again visited Caermaen. He wished to view the amphitheatre more precisely, to note the exact position of the ancient walls, to gaze up the valley from certain points within the town, to imprint minutely and clearly on his mind the surge of the hills about the city, and the dark tapestry of the hanging woods. And he lingered in the museum where the relics of the Roman occupation had been stored; he was interested in the fragments of tessellated floors, in the glowing gold of drinking cups, the curious beads of fused and colored glass, the carved amber-work, the scent-flagons that still retained the memory of unctuous odors, the necklaces, brooches, hair-pins of gold and silver, and other intimate objects which had once belonged to Roman ladies. One of the glass flagons, buried in damp earth for many hundred years, had gathered in its dark grave all the splendors of the light, and now shone like an opal with a moonlight glamour and gleams of gold and pale sunset green, and imperial purple. Then there were the wine jars of red earthenware, the memorial stones from graves, and the heads of broken gods, with fragments of occult things used in the secret rites of Mithras. Lucian read on the labels where all these objects were found: in the churchyard, beneath the turf of the meadow, and in the old cemetery near the forest; and whenever it was possible he would make his way to the spot of discovery, and imagine the long darkness that had hidden gold and stone and amber. All these investigations were necessary for the scheme he had in view, so he became for some time quite a familiar figure in the dusty deserted streets and in the meadows by the river. His continual visits to Caermaen were a tortuous puzzle to the inhabitants, who flew to their windows at the sound of a step on the uneven pavements. They were at a loss in their conjectures; his motive for coming down three times a week must of course be bad, but it seemed undiscoverable. And Lucian on his side was at first a good deal put out by occasional encounters with members of the Gervase or Dixon or Colley tribes; he had often to stop and exchange a few conventional expressions, and such meetings, casual as they were, annoyed and distracted him. He was no longer infuriated or wounded by sneers of contempt or by the cackling laughter of the young people when they passed him on the road (his hat was a shocking one and his untidiness terrible), but such incidents were unpleasant just as the smell of a drain was unpleasant, and threw the strange mechanism of his thoughts out of fear for the time. Then he had been disgusted by the affair of the boys and the little dog; the loathsomeness of it had quite broken up his fancies. He had read books of modern occultism, and remembered some of the experiments described. The adept, it was alleged, could transfer the sense of consciousness from his brain to the foot or hand, he could annihilate the world around him and pass into another sphere. Lucian wondered whether he could not perform some such operation for his own benefit. Human beings were constantly annoying him and getting in his way, was it not possible to annihilate the race, or at all events to reduce them to wholly insignificant forms? A certain process suggested itself to his mind, a work partly mental and partly physical, and after two or three experiments he found to his astonishment and delight that it was successful. Here, he thought, he had discovered one of the secrets of true magic; this was the key to the symbolic transmutations of the Eastern tales. The adept could, in truth, change those who were obnoxious to him into harmless and unimportant shapes, not as in the letter of the old stories, by transforming the enemy, but by transforming himself. The magician puts men below him by going up higher, as one looks down on a mountain city from a loftier crag. The stones on the road and such petty obstacles do not trouble the wise man on the great journey, and so Lucian, when obliged to stop and converse with his fellow-creatures, to listen to their poor pretences and inanities, was no more inconvenienced than when he had to climb an awkward stile in the course of a walk. As for the more unpleasant manifestations of humanity; after all they no longer concerned him. Men intent on the great purpose did not suffer the current of their thoughts to be broken by the buzzing of a fly caught in a spider's web, so why should he be perturbed by the misery of a puppy in the hands of village boys? The fly, no doubt, endured its tortures; lying helpless and bound in those slimy bands, it cried out in its thin voice when the claws of the horrible monster fastened on it; but its dying agonies had never vexed the reverie of a lover. Lucian saw no reason why the boys should offend him more than the spider, or why he should pity the dog more than he pitied the fly. The talk of the men and women might be wearisome and inept and often malignant; but he could not imagine an alchemist at the moment of success, a general in the hour of victory, or a financier with a gigantic scheme of swindling well on the market being annoyed by the buzz of insects. The spider is, no doubt, a very terrible brute with a hideous mouth and hairy tiger-like claws when seen through the microscope; but Lucian had taken away the microscope from his eyes. He could now walk the streets of Caermaen confident and secure, without any dread of interruption, for at a moment's notice the transformation could be effected. Once Dr. Burrows caught him and made him promise to attend a bazaar that was to be held in aid of the Hungarian Protestants; Lucian assented the more willingly as he wished to pay a visit to certain curious mounds on a hill a little way out of the town, and he calculated on slinking off from the bazaar early in the afternoon. Lord Beamys was visiting Sir Vivian Ponsonby, a local magnate, and had kindly promised to drive over and declare the bazaar open. It was a solemn moment when the carriage drew up and the great man alighted. He was rather an evil-looking old nobleman, but the clergy and gentry, their wives and sons and daughters welcomed him with great and unctuous joy. Conversations were broken off in mid-sentence, slow people gaped, not realizing why their friends had so suddenly left them, the Meyricks came up hot and perspiring in fear lest they should be too late, Miss Colley, a yellow virgin of austere regard, smiled largely, Mrs. Dixon beckoned wildly with her parasol to the "girls" who were idly strolling in a distant part of the field, and the archdeacon ran at full speed. The air grew dark with bows, and resonant with the genial laugh of the archdeacon, the cackle of the younger ladies, and the shrill parrot-like voices of the matrons; those smiled who had never smiled before, and on some maiden faces there hovered that look of adoring ecstasy with which the old maidens graced their angels. Then, when all the due rites had been performed, the company turned and began to walk towards the booths of their small Vanity Fair. Lord Beamys led the way with Mrs. Gervase, Mrs. Dixon followed with Sir Vivian Ponsonby, and the multitudes that followed cried, saying, "What a dear old man!" "Isn't it *kind* of him to come all this way?" "What a sweet expression, isn't it?" "I think he's an old love." "One of the good old sort." "Real English nobleman." "Oh most correct, I assure you; if a girl gets into trouble, notice to quit at once." "Always stands by the Church." "Twenty livings in his gift." "Voted for the Public Worship Regulation Act." "Ten thousand acres strictly preserved." The old lord was leering pleasantly and muttering to himself: "Some fine gals here. Like the looks of that filly with the pink hat. Ought to see more of her. She'd give Lotty points."

The pomp swept slowly across the grass: the archdeacon had got hold of Mr. Dixon, and they were discussing the misdeeds of some clergyman in the rural deanery.

"I can scarce credit it," said Mr. Dixon.

"Oh, I assure you, there can be no doubt. We have witnesses. There can be no question that there was a procession at Llanfihangel on the Sunday before Easter; the choir and minister went round the church, carrying palm branches in their hands."

"Very shocking."

"It has distressed the bishop. Martin is a hard-working man enough, and all that, but those sort of things can't be tolerated. The bishop told me that he had set his face against processions."

"Quite right: the bishop is perfectly right. Processions are unscriptural."

"It's the thin end of the wedge, you know, Dixon."

"Exactly. I have always resisted anything of the kind here."

"Right. *Principiis obsta*, you know. Martin is so *imprudent*. There's a *way* of doing things."

The "scriptural" procession led by Lord Beamys broke up when the stalls were reached, and gathered round the nobleman as he declared the bazaar open.

Lucian was sitting on a garden-seat, a little distance off, looking dreamily before him. And all that he saw was a swarm of flies clustering and buzzing about a lump of tainted meat that lay on the grass. The spectacle in no way interrupted the harmony of his thoughts, and soon after the opening of the bazaar he went quietly away, walking across the fields in the direction of the ancient mounds he desired to inspect.

All these journeys of his to Caermaen and its neighborhood had a peculiar object; he was gradually leveling to the dust the squalid kraals of modern times, and rebuilding the splendid and golden city of Siluria. All this mystic town was for the delight of his sweetheart and himself; for her the wonderful villas, the shady courts, the magic of tessellated pavements, and the hangings of rich stuffs with their intricate and glowing patterns. Lucian wandered all day through the shining streets, taking shelter sometimes in the gardens beneath the dense and gloomy ilex trees, and listening to the plash and trickle of the fountains. Sometimes he would look out of a window and watch the crowd and color of the market place, and now and again a ship came up the river bringing exquisite silks and the merchandise of unknown lands in the Far East. He had made a curious and accurate map of the town he proposed to inhabit, in which every villa was set down and named. He drew his lines to scale with the gravity of a surveyor, and studied the plan till he was able to find his way from house to house on the darkest summer night. On the southern slopes about the town there were vineyards, always under a glowing sun, and sometimes he ventured to the furthest ridge of the forest, where the wild people still lingered, that he might catch the golden gleam of the city far away, as the light quivered and scintillated on the glittering tiles. And there were gardens outside the city gates where strange and brilliant flowers grew, filling the hot air with their odor, and scenting the breeze that blew along the streets. The dull modern life was far away, and people who saw him at this period wondered what was amiss; the abstraction of his glance was obvious, even to eyes not over-sharp. But men and women had lost all their power of annoyance and vexation; they could no longer even interrupt his thought for a moment. He could listen to Mr. Dixon with apparent attention, while he was in reality enraptured by the entreating music of the double flute, played by a girl in the garden of Avallaunius, for that was the name he had taken. Mr. Dixon was innocently discoursing archeology, giving a brief *résumé* of the view expressed by Mr. Wyndham at the last meeting of the antiquarian society.

"There can be no doubt that the temple of Diana stood there in pagan times," he concluded, and Lucian assented to the opinion, and asked a few questions which seemed pertinent enough. But all the time the flute notes were sounding in his ears, and the ilex threw a purple shadow on the white pavement before his villa. A boy came forward from the garden; he had been walking amongst the vines and plucking the ripe grapes, and the juice had trickled down over his breast. Standing beside the girl, unashamed in the sunlight, he began to sing one of Sappho's love songs. His voice was as full and rich as a woman's, but purged of all emotion; he was an instrument of music in the flesh. Lucian looked at him steadily; the white perfect body shone against the roses and the blue of the sky, clear and gleaming as marble in the glare of the sun. The words he sang burned and flamed with passion, and he was as unconscious of their meaning as the twin pipes of the flute. And the girl was smiling. The vicar shook hands and went on, well pleased with his remarks on the temple of Diana, and also with Lucian's polite interest.

"He is by no means wanting in intelligence," he said to his family. "A little curious in manner, perhaps, but not stupid."

"Oh, papa," said Henrietta, "don't you think he is rather silly? He can't talk about anything — anything interesting, I mean. And he pretends to know a lot about books, but I heard him say the other day he had never read *The Prince of the House of David* or *Ben-Hur*. Fancy!"

The vicar had not interrupted Lucian. The sun still beat upon the roses, and a little breeze bore the scent of them to his nostrils together with the smell of grapes and vine leaves. He had become curious in sensation, and as he leant back upon the cushions covered with glistening yellow silk, he was trying to analyze a strange ingredient in the perfume of the air. He had penetrated far beyond the crude distinctions of modern times, beyond the rough: "there's a smell of roses," "there must be sweetbriar somewhere." Modern perceptions of odor were, he knew, far below those of the savage in delicacy. The degraded black fellow of Australia could distinguish odors in a way that made the consumer of "damper" stare in amazement, but the savage's sensations were all strictly utilitarian. To

Lucian as he sat in the cool porch, his feet on the marble, the air came laden with scents as subtly and wonderfully interwoven and contrasted as the harmonica of a great master. The stained marble of the pavement gave a cool reminiscence of the Italian mountain, the blood-red roses palpitating in the sunlight sent out an odor mystical as passion itself, and there was the hint of inebriation in the perfume of the trellised vines. Besides these, the girl's desire and the unripe innocence of the boy were as distinct as benzoin and myrrh, both delicious and exquisite, and exhaled as freely as the scent of the roses. But there was another element that puzzled him, an aromatic suggestion of the forest. He understood it at last; it was the vapor of the great red pines that grew beyond the garden; their spicy needles were burning in the sun, and the smell was as fragrant as the fume of incense blown from far. The soft entreaty of the flute and the swelling rapture of the boy's voice beat on the air together, and Lucian wondered whether there were in the nature of things any true distinction between the impressions of sound and scent and color. The violent blue of the sky, the one mystery than distinct entities. He could almost imagine that the boy's innocence was indeed a perfume, and that the palpitating roses had become a sonorous chant.

In the curious silence which followed the last notes, when the boy and girl had passed under the purple ilex shadow, he fell into a reverie. The fancy that sensations are symbols and not realities hovered in his mind, and led him to speculate as to whether they could not actually be transmuted one into another. It was possible, he thought, that a whole continent of knowledge had been undiscovered; the energies of men having been expended in unimportant and foolish directions. Modern ingenuity had been employed on such trifles as locomotive engines, electric cables, and cantilever bridges; on elaborate devices for bringing uninteresting people nearer together; the ancients had been almost as foolish, because they had mistaken the symbol for the thing signified. It was not the material banquet which really mattered, but the thought of it; it was almost as futile to eat and take emetics and eat again as to invent telephones and high-pressure boilers. As for some other ancient methods of enjoying life, one might as well set one-self to improve calico printing at once.

"Only in the garden of Avallaunius," said Lucian to himself, "is the true and exquisite science to be found."

He could imagine a man who was able to live in one sense while he pleased; to whom, for example, every impression of touch, taste, hearing, or seeing should be translated into odor; who at the desired kiss should be ravished with the scent of dark violets, to whom music should be the perfume of a rose-garden at dawn.

When, now and again, he voluntarily resumed the experience of common life, it was that he might return with greater delight to the garden in the city of refuge. In the actual world the talk was of Non-conformists, the lodger franchise, and the Stock Exchange; people were constantly reading news-papers, drinking Australian Burgundy, and doing other things equally absurd. They either looked shocked when the fine art of pleasure was mentioned, or confused it with going to musical comedies, drinking bad whisky, and keeping late hours in disreputable and vulgar company. He found to his amusement that the profligate were by many degrees duller than the pious, but that the most tedious of all were the persons who preached promiscuity, and called their system of "pigging" the "New Morality."

He went back to the city lovingly, because it was built and adorned for his love. As the metaphysicians insist on the consciousness of the ego as the implied basis of all thought, so he knew that it was she in whom he had found himself, and through whom and for whom all the true life existed. He felt that Annie had taught him the rare magic which had created the garden of Avallaunius. It was for her that he sought strange secrets and tried to penetrate the mysteries of sensation, for he could only give her wonderful thoughts and a wonderful life, and a poor body stained with the scars of his worship.

It was with this object, that of making the offering of himself a worthy one, that he continually searched for new and exquisite experiences. He made lovers come before him and confess their secrets; he pried into the inmost mysteries of innocence and shame, noting how passion and reluctance strive together for the mastery. In the amphitheatre he sometimes witnessed strange entertainments in which such tales as *Daphnis and Chloe* and *The Golden Ass* were performed before him. These shows were always given at nighttime; a circle of torchbearers surrounded the stage in the center, and above, all the tiers of seats were dark. He would look up at the soft blue of the summer sky, and at the vast dim mountain hovering like a cloud in the west, and then at the scene illumined by a flaring light, and contrasted with violent shadows. The subdued mutter of conversation in a strange language rising from bench after bench, swift hissing whispers of explanation, now and then a shout or a cry as the interest deepened, the restless tossing of the people as the end drew near, an arm lifted, a cloak thrown back, the sudden blaze of a torch lighting up purple or white or the gleam of gold in the black serried ranks; these were impressions that seemed always amazing. And above, the dusky light of the stars, around, the sweet-scented meadows, and the twinkle of lamps from the still city, the cry of the sentries about the walls, the wash of the tide filling the river, and the salt savor of the sea. With such a scenic ornament he saw the tale of Apuleius represented, heard the names of Fotis and Byrrhaena and Lucius proclaimed, and the deep intonation of such sentences as *Ecce Veneris hortator et armiger Liber advenit ultro.* The tale went on through all its marvelous adventures, and Lucian left the amphitheatre and walked beside the river where he could hear indistinctly the noise of voices and the singing Latin, and note how the rumor of the stage mingled with the murmur of the shuddering reeds and the cool lapping of the tide. Then came the farewell of the cantor, the thunder of applause, the crash of cymbals, the calling of the flutes, and the surge of the wind in the great dark wood.

At other times it was his chief pleasure to spend a whole day in a vineyard planted on the steep slope beyond the bridge. A gray stone seat had been placed beneath a shady laurel, and here he often sat without motion or gesture for many hours. Below him the tawny river swept round the town in a half circle; he could see the swirl of the yellow water, its eddies and miniature whirlpools, as the tide poured up from the south. And beyond the river the strong circuit of the walls, and within, the city glittered like a charming piece of mosaic. He freed himself from the obtuse modern view of towns as places where human beings live and make money and rejoice or suffer, for from the standpoint of the moment such facts were wholly impertinent. He knew perfectly well that for his present purpose the tawny sheen and shimmer of the tide was the only fact of importance about the river, and so he regarded the city as a curious work in jewelry. Its radiant marble porticoes, the white walls of the villas, a dome of burning copper, the flash and scintillation of tiled roofs, the quiet red of brickwork, dark groves of ilex, and cypress, and laurel, glowing rose-gardens, and here and there the silver of a fountain, seemed arranged and contrasted with a wonderful art, and the town appeared a delicious ornament, every cube of color owing its place to the thought and inspiration of the artificer. Lucian, as he gazed from his arbor amongst the trellised vines, lost none of the subtle pleasures of the sight; noting every *nuance* of color, he let his eyes dwell for a moment on the scarlet flash of poppies, and then on a glazed roof which in the glance of the sun seemed to spout white fire. A square of vines was like some rare green stone; the grapes were massed so richly amongst the vivid leaves, that even from far off there was a sense of irregular flecks and stains of purple running through the green. The laurel garths were like cool jade; the gardens, where red, yellow, blue and white gleamed together in a mist of heat, had the radiance of opal; the river was a band of dull gold. On every side, as if to enhance the preciousness of the city, the woods hung dark on the hills; above, the sky was violet, specked with minute feathery clouds, white as snowflakes. It reminded him of a beautiful bowl in his villa; the ground was of that same brilliant blue, and the artist had fused into the work, when it was hot, particles of pure white glass.

For Lucian this was a spectacle that enchanted many hours; leaning on one hand, he would gaze at the city glowing in the sunlight till the purple shadows grew down the slopes and the long melodious trumpet sounded for the evening watch. Then, as he strolled beneath the trellises, he would see all the radiant facets glimmering out, and the city faded into haze, a white wall shining here and there, and the gardens veiled in a dim glow of color. On such an evening he would go home with the sense that he had truly lived a day, having received for many hours the most acute impressions of beautiful color.

Often he spent the night in the cool court of his villa, lying amidst soft cushions heaped upon the marble bench. A lamp stood on the table at his elbow, its light making the water in the cistern twinkle. There was no sound in the court except the soft continual plashing of the fountain. Throughout these still hours he would meditate, and he became more than ever convinced that man could, if he pleased, become lord of his own sensations. This, surely, was the true meaning concealed under the beautiful symbolism of alchemy. Some years before he had read many of the wonderful alchemical books of the later Middle Ages, and had suspected that something other than the turning of lead into gold was intended. This impression was deepened when he looked into *Lumen de Lumine* by Vaughan, the brother of the Silurist, and he had long puzzled himself in the endeavor to find a reasonable interpretation of the hermetic mystery, and of the red powder, "glistening and glorious in the sun." And the solution shone out at last, bright and amazing, as he lay quiet in the court of Avallaunius. He knew that he himself had solved the riddle, that he held in his hand the powder of projection, the philosopher's stone transmuting all it touched to fine gold; the gold of exquisite impressions. He understood now something of the alchemical symbolism; the crucible and the furnace, the "Green Dragon," and the "Son Blessed of the Fire" had, he saw, a peculiar meaning. He understood, too, why the uninitiated were warned of the terror and danger through which they must pass; and the vehemence with which the adepts disclaimed all desire for material riches no longer struck him as singular. The wise man does not endure the torture of the furnace in order that he may be able to compete with operators in pork and company promoters; neither a steam yacht, nor a grouse-moor, nor three liveried footmen would add at all to his gratifications. Again Lucian said to himself:

"Only in the court of Avallaunius is the true science of the exquisite to be found."

He saw the true gold into which the beggarly matter of existence may be transmuted by spagyric art; a succession of delicious moments, all the rare flavors of life concentrated, purged of their lees, and preserved in a beautiful vessel. The moonlight fell green on the fountain and on the curious pavements, and in the long sweet silence of the night he lay still and felt that thought itself was an acute pleasure, to be expressed perhaps in terms of odor or color by the true artist.

And he gave himself other and even stranger gratifications. Outside the city walls, between the baths and the amphitheatre, was a tavern, a place where wonderful people met to drink wonderful wine. There he saw priests of Mithras and Isis and of more occult rites from the East, men who wore robes of bright colors, and grotesque ornaments, symbolizing secret things. They spoke amongst themselves in a rich jargon of colored words, full of hidden meanings and the sense of matters unintelligible to the uninitiated, alluding to what was concealed beneath roses, and calling each other by strange names. And there were actors who gave the shows in the amphitheatre, officers of the legion who had served in wild places, singers, and dancing girls, and heroes of strange adventure.

The walls of the tavern were covered with pictures painted in violent hues; blues and reds and greens jarring against one another and lighting up the gloom of the place. The stone benches were always crowded, the sunlight came in through the door in a long bright beam, casting a dancing shadow of vine leaves on the further wall. There a painter had made a joyous figure of the young Bacchus driving the leopards before him with his ivy-staff, and the quivering shadow seemed a part of the picture. The room was cool and dark and cavernous, but the scent and heat of the summer gushed in through the open door. There was ever a full sound, with noise and vehemence, there, and the rolling music of the Latin tongue never ceased.

"The wine of the siege, the wine that we saved," cried one.

"Look for the jar marked *Faunus*; you will be glad."

"Bring me the wine of the Owl's Face."

"Let us have the wine of Saturn's Bridge."

The boys who served brought the wine in dull red jars that struck a charming note against their white robes. They poured out the violet and purple and golden wine with calm sweet faces as if they were assisting in the mysteries, without any sign that they heard the strange words that flashed from side to side. The cups were all of glass; some were of deep green, of the color of the sea near the land, flawed and specked with the bubbles of the furnace. Others were of brilliant scarlet, streaked with irregular bands of white, and having the appearance of white globules in the molded stem. There were cups of dark glowing blue, deeper and more shining than the blue of the sky, and running through the substance of the glass were veins of rich gamboge yellow, twining from the brim to the foot. Some cups were of a troubled and clotted red, with alternating blotches of dark and light, some were variegated with white and yellow stains, some wore a film of rainbow colors, some glittered, shot with gold threads through the clear crystal, some were as if sapphires hung suspended in running water, some sparkled with the glint of stars, some were black and golden like tortoiseshell.

A strange feature was the constant and fluttering motion of hands and arms. Gesture made a constant commentary on speech; white fingers, whiter arms, and sleeves of all colors, hovered restlessly, appeared and disappeared with an effect of threads crossing and re-crossing on the loom. And the odor of the place was both curious and memorable; something of the damp cold breath of the cave meeting the hot blast of summer, the strangely mingled aromas of rare wines as they fell plashing and ringing into the cups, the drugged vapor of the East that the priests of Mithras and Isis bore from their steaming temples; these were always strong and dominant. And the women were scented, sometimes with unctuous and overpowering perfumes, and to the artist the experiences of those present were hinted in subtle and delicate *nuances* of odor.

They drank their wine and caressed all day in the tavern. The women threw their round white arms about their lover's necks, they intoxicated them with the scent of their hair, the priests muttered their fantastic jargon of Theurgy. And through the sonorous clash of voices there always seemed the ring of the cry:

"Look for the jar marked *Faunus*; you will be glad."

Outside, the vine tendrils shook on the white walls glaring in the sunshine; the breeze swept up from the yellow river, pungent with the salt sea savor.

These tavern scenes were often the subject of Lucian's meditation as he sat amongst the cushions on the marble seat. The rich sound of the voices impressed him above all things, and he saw that words have a far higher reason than the utilitarian office of imparting a man's thought. The common notion that language and linked words are important only as a means of expression he found a little ridiculous; as if electricity were to be studied solely with the view of "wiring" to people, and all its other properties left unexplored, neglected. Language, he understood, was chiefly important for the beauty of its sounds, by its possession of words resonant, glorious to the ear, by its capacity, when exquisitely arranged, of suggesting wonderful and indefinable impressions, perhaps more ravishing and farther removed from the domain of strict thought than the impressions excited by music itself. Here lay hidden the secret of the sensuous art of literature; it was the secret of suggestion, the art of causing delicious sensation by the use of words. In a way, therefore, literature was independent of thought; the mere English listener, if he had an ear attuned, could recognize the beauty of a splendid Latin phrase.

Here was the explanation of the magic of *Lycidas*. From the standpoint of the formal understanding it was an affected lament over some wholly uninteresting and unimportant Mr. King; it was full of nonsense about "shepherds" and "flocks" and "muses" and such stale stock of poetry; the introduction of St Peter on a stage thronged with nymphs and river gods was blasphemous, absurd, and, in the worst taste; there were touches of greasy Puritanism, the twang of the conventicle was only too apparent. And *Lycidas* was probably the most perfect piece of pure literature in existence; because every word and phrase and line were sonorous, ringing and echoing with music.

"Literature," he re-enunciated in his mind, "is the sensuous art of causing exquisite impressions by means of words."

And yet there was something more; besides the logical thought, which was often a hindrance, a troublesome though inseparable accident, besides the sensation, always a pleasure and a delight, besides these there were the indefinable inexpressible images which all fine literature summons to the mind. As the chemist in his experiments is sometimes astonished to find unknown, unexpected elements in the crucible or the receiver, as the world of material things is considered by some a thin veil of the immaterial universe, so he who reads wonderful prose or verse is conscious of suggestions that cannot be put into words, which do not rise from the logical sense, which are rather parallel to than connected with the sensuous delight. The world so disclosed is rather the world of dreams, rather the world in which children sometimes live, instantly appearing, and instantly vanishing away, a world beyond all expression or analysis, neither of the intellect nor of the senses. He called these fancies of his "Meditations of a Tavern," and was amused to think that a theory of letters should have risen from the eloquent noise that rang all day about the violet and golden wine.

"Let us seek for more exquisite things," said Lucian to himself. He could almost imagine the magic transmutation of the senses accomplished, the strong sunlight was an odor in his nostrils; it poured down in the white marble and the palpitating roses like a flood. The sky was a glorious blue, making the heart joyous, and the eyes could rest in the dark green leaves and purple shadow of the ilex. The earth seemed to burn and leap beneath the sun, he fancied he could see the vine tendrils stir and quiver in the heat, and the faint fume of the scorching pine needles was blown across the gleaming garden to the seat beneath the porch. Wine was before him in a cup of carved amber; a wine of the color of a dark rose, with a glint as of a star or of a jet of flame deep beneath the brim; and the cup was twined about with a delicate wreath of ivy. He was often loath to turn away from the still contemplation of such things, from the mere joy of the violent sun, and the responsive earth. He loved his garden and the view of the tessellated city from the vineyard on the hill, the strange clamor of the tavern, and white Fotis appearing on the torch-lit stage. And there were shops in the town in which he delighted, the shops of the perfume makers, and jewelers, and dealers in curious ware. He loved to see all things made for ladies' use, to touch the gossamer silks that were to touch their bodies, to finger the beads of amber and the gold chains which would stir above their hearts, to handle the carved hairpins and brooches, to smell odors which were already dedicated to love.

But though these were sweet and delicious gratifications, he knew that there were more exquisite things of which he might be a spectator. He had seen the folly of regarding fine literature from the standpoint of the logical intellect, and he now began to question the wisdom of looking at life as if it were a moral representation. Literature, he knew, could not exist without some meaning, and considerations of right and wrong were to a certain extent inseparable from the conception of life, but to insist on ethics as the chief interest of the human pageant was surely absurd. One might as well read *Lycidas* for the sake of its denunciation of "our corrupted Clergy," or Homer for "manners and customs." An artist entranced by a beautiful landscape did not greatly concern himself with the geological formation of the hills, nor did the lover of a wild sea inquire as to the chemical analysis of the water. Lucian saw a colored and complex life displayed before him, and he sat enraptured at the spectacle, not concerned to know whether actions were good or bad, but content if they were curious.

In this spirit he made a singular study of corruption. Beneath his feet, as he sat in the garden porch, was a block of marble through which there ran a scarlet stain. It began with a faint line, thin as a hair, and grew as it advanced, sending out offshoots to right and left, and broadening to a pool of brilliant red. There were strange lives into which he looked that were like the block of marble; women with grave sweet faces told him the astounding tale of their adventures, and how, they said, they had met the faun when they were little children. They told him how they had played and watched by the vines and the fountains, and dallied with the nymphs, and gazed at images reflected in the water pools, till the authentic face appeared from the wood. He heard others tell how they had loved the satyrs for many years before they knew their race; and there were strange stories of those who had longed to speak but knew not the word of the enigma, and searched in all strange paths and ways before they found it.

He heard the history of the woman who fell in love with her slave boy, and tempted him for three years in vain. He heard the tale from the woman's full red lips, and watched her face, full of the ineffable sadness of lust, as she described her curious stratagems in mellow phrases. She was drinking a sweet yellow wine from a gold cup as she spoke, and the odor in her hair and the aroma of the precious wine seemed to mingle with the soft strange words that flowed like an unguent from a carven jar. She told how she bought the boy in the market of an Asian city, and had him carried to her house in the grove of fig trees. "Then," she went on, "he was led into my presence as I sat between the columns of my court. A blue veil was spread above to shut out the heat of the sun, and rather twilight than light shone on the painted walls, and the wonderful colors of the pavement, and the images of Love and the Mother of Love. The men who brought the boy gave him over to my girls, who undressed him before me, one drawing gently away his robe, another stroking his brown and flowing hair, another praising the whiteness of his limbs, and another caressing him, and speaking loving words in his ear. But the boy looked sullenly at them all, striking away their hands, and pouting with his lovely and splendid lips, and I saw a blush, like the rosy veil of dawn, reddening his body and his cheeks. Then I made them bathe him, and anoint him with scented oils from head to foot, till his limbs shone and glistened with the gentle and mellow glow of an ivory statue. Then I said: 'You are bashful, because you shine alone amongst us all; see, we too will be your fellows.' The girls began first of all, fondling and kissing one another, and doing for each other the offices of waiting-maids. They drew out the pins and loosened the bands of their hair, and I never knew before that they were so lovely. The soft and shining tresses flowed down, rippling like sea-waves; some had hair golden and radiant as this wine in my cup, the faces of others appeared amidst the blackness of ebony; there were locks that seemed of burnished and scintillating copper, some glowed with hair of tawny splendor, and others were crowned with the brightness of the sardonyx. Then, laughing, and without the appearance of shame, they unfastened the brooches and bands which sustained their robes, and so allowed silk and linen to flow swiftly to the stained floor, so that one would have said there was a sudden apparition of the fairest nymphs. With many festive and jocose words they began to incite each other to mirth, praising the beauties that shone on every side, and calling the boy by a girl's name, they invited him to be their playmate. But he refused, shaking his head, and still standing dumb-founded and abashed, as if he saw a forbidden and terrible spectacle. Then I ordered the women to undo my hair and my clothes, making them caress me with the tenderness of the fondest lover, but without avail, for the foolish boy still scowled and pouted out his lips, stained with an imperial and glorious scarlet."

She poured out more of the topaz-colored wine in her cup, and Lucian saw it glitter as it rose to the brim and mirrored the gleam of the lamps. The tale went on, recounting a hundred strange devices. The woman told how she had tempted the boy by idleness and ease, giving him long hours of sleep, and allowing him to recline all day on soft cushions, that swelled about him, enclosing his body. She tried the experiment of curious odors: causing him to smell always about him the oil of roses, and burning in his presence rare gums from the East. He was allured by soft dresses, being clothed in silks that caressed the skin with the sense of a fondling touch. Three times a day they spread before him a delicious banquet, full of savor and odor and color; three times a day they endeavored to intoxicate him with delicate wine.

"And so," the lady continued, "I spared nothing to catch him in the glistening nets of love; taking only sour and contemptuous glances in return. And at last in an incredible shape I won the victory, and then, having gained a green crown, fighting in agony against his green and crude immaturity, I devoted him to the theatre, where he amused the people by the splendor of his death."

On another evening he heard the history of the man who dwelt alone, refusing all allurements, and was at last discovered to be the lover of a black statue. And there were tales of strange cruelties, of men taken by mountain robbers, and curiously maimed and disfigured, so that when they escaped and returned to the town, they were thought to be monsters and killed at their own doors. Lucian left no dark or secret nook of life unvisited; he sat down, as he said, at the banquet, resolved to taste all the savors, and to leave no flagon unvisited.

His relations grew seriously alarmed about him at this period. While he heard with some inner ear the suave and eloquent phrases of singular tales, and watched the lamp-light in amber and purple wine, his father saw a lean pale boy, with black eyes that burnt in hollows, and sad and sunken cheeks.

"You ought to try and eat more, Lucian," said the parson; "and why don't you have some beer?"

He was looking feebly at the roast mutton and sipping a little water; but he would not have eaten or drunk with more relish if the choicest meat and drink had been before him.

His bones seemed, as Miss Deacon said, to be growing through his skin; he had all the appearance of an ascetic whose body has been reduced to misery by long and grievous penance. People who chanced to see him could not help saying to one another: "How ill and wretched that Lucian Taylor looks!" They were of course quite unaware of the joy and luxury in which his real life was spent, and some of them began to pity him, and to speak to him kindly.

It was too late for that. The friendly words had as much lost their meaning as the words of contempt. Edward Dixon hailed him cheerfully in the street one day:

"Come in to my den, won't you, old fellow?" he said. "You won't see the pater. I've managed to bag a bottle of his old port. I know you smoke like a furnace, and I've got some ripping cigars. You will come, won't you! I can tell you the pater's booze is first-rate."

He gently declined and went on. Kindness and unkindness, pity and contempt had become for him mere phrases; he could not have distinguished one from the other. Hebrew and Chinese, Hungarian and Pushtu would be pretty much alike to an agricultural laborer; if he cared to listen he might detect some general differences in sound, but all four tongues would be equally devoid of significance.

To Lucian, entranced in the garden of Avallaunius, it seemed very strange that he had once been so ignorant of all the exquisite meanings of life. Now, beneath the violet sky, looking through the brilliant trellis of the vines, he saw the picture; before, he had gazed in sad astonishment at the squalid rag which was wrapped about it.

V

And he was at last in the city of the unending murmuring streets, a part of the stirring shadow, of the amber-lighted gloom.

It seemed a long time since he had knelt before his sweetheart in the lane, the moon-fire streaming upon them from the dark circle of the fort, the air and the light and his soul full of haunting, the touch of the unimaginable thrilling his heart; and now he sat in a terrible "bed-sitting-room" in a western suburb, confronted by a heap and litter of papers on the desk of a battered old bureau.

He had put his breakfast tray out on the landing, and was thinking of the morning's work, and of some very dubious pages that he had blackened the night before. But when he had lit his disreputable briar, he remembered there was an unopened letter waiting for him on the table; he had recognized the vague, staggering script of Miss Deacon, his cousin. There was not much news; his father was "just the same as usual," there had been a good deal of rain, the farmers expected to make a lot of cider, and so forth. But at the close of the letter Miss Deacon became useful for reproof and admonition.

"I was at Caermaen on Tuesday," she said, "and called on the Gervases and the Dixons. Mr. Gervase smiled when I told him you were a literary man, living in London, and said he was afraid you wouldn't find it a very practical career. Mrs. Gervase was very proud of Henry's success; he passed fifth for some examination, and will begin with nearly four hundred a year. I don't wonder the

Gervases are delighted. Then I went to the Dixons, and had tea. Mrs. Dixon wanted to know if you had published anything yet, and I said I thought not. She showed me a book everybody is talking about, called the *Dog and the Doctor*. She says it's selling by thousands, and that one can't take up a paper without seeing the author's name. She told me to tell you that you ought to try to write something like it. Then Mr. Dixon came in from the study, and your name was mentioned again. He said he was afraid you had made rather a mistake in trying to take up literature as if it were a profession, and seemed to think that a place in a house of business would be more *suitable* and more practical. He pointed out that you had not had the advantages of a university training, and said that you would find men who had made good friends, and had the *tone* of the university, would be before you at every step. He said Edward was doing very well at Oxford. He writes to them that he knows several noblemen, and that young Philip Bullingham (son of Sir John Bullingham) is his most intimate friend; of course this is *very* satisfactory for the Dixons. I am afraid, my dear Lucian, you have rather overrated your powers. Wouldn't it be better, even now, to look out for some *real work* to do, instead of wasting your time over those silly old books? I know quite well how the Gervases and the Dixons feel; they think idleness so injurious for a young man, and likely to lead to *bad habits*. You know, my dear Lucian, I am only writing like this because of my affection for you, so I am sure, my dear boy, you won't be offended."

Lucian pigeon-holed the letter solemnly in the receptacle lettered "Barbarians." He felt that he ought to ask himself some serious questions: "Why haven't I passed fifth? Why isn't Philip (son of Sir John) my most intimate friend? Why am I an idler, liable to fall into bad habits?" but he was eager to get to his work, a curious and intricate piece of analysis. So the battered bureau, the litter of papers, and the thick fume of his pipe, engulfed him and absorbed him for the rest of the morning. Outside were the dim October mists, the dreary and languid life of a side street, and beyond, on the main road, the hum and jangle of the gliding trains. But he heard none of the uneasy noises of the quarter, not even the shriek of the garden gates nor the yelp of the butcher on his round, for delight in his great task made him unconscious of the world outside.

He had come by curious paths to this calm hermitage between Shepherd's Bush and Acton Vale. The golden weeks of the summer passed on in their enchanted procession, and Annie had not returned, neither had she written. Lucian, on his side, sat apart, wondering why his longing for her were not shaper. As he though of his raptures he would smile faintly to himself, and wonder whether he had not lost the world and Annie with it. In the garden of Avallaunius his sense of external things had grown dim and indistinct; the actual, material life seemed every day to become a show, a fleeting of shadows across a great white light. At last the news came that Annie Morgan had been married from her sister's house to a young farmer, to whom it appeared, she had been long engaged, and Lucian was ashamed to find himself only conscious of amusement, mingled with gratitude. She had been the key that opened the shut palace, and he was now secure on the throne of ivory and gold. A few days after he had heard the news he repeated the adventure of his boyhood; for the second time he scaled the steep hillside, and penetrated the matted brake. He expected violent disillusion, but his feeling was rather astonishment at the activity of boyish imagination. There was no terror nor amazement now in the green bulwarks, and the stunted undergrowth did not seem in any way extraordinary. Yet he did not laugh at the memory of his sensations, he was not angry at the cheat. Certainly it had been all illusion, all the heats and chills of boyhood, its thoughts of terror were without significance. But he recognized that the illusions of the child only differed from those of the man in that they were more picturesque; belief in fairies and belief in the Stock Exchange as bestowers of happiness were equally vain, but the latter form of faith was ugly as well as inept. It was better, he knew, and wiser, to wish for a fairy coach than to cherish longings for a well-appointed brougham and liveried servants.

He turned his back on the green walls and the dark oaks without any feeling of regret or resentment. After a little while he began to think of his adventures with pleasure; the ladder by which he had mounted had disappeared, but he was safe on the height. By the chance fancy of a beautiful girl he had been redeemed from a world of misery and torture, the world of external things into which he had come a stranger by which he had been tormented. He looked back at a kind of vision of himself seen as he was a year before, a pitiable creature burning and twisting on the hot coals of the pit, crying lamentably to the laughing bystanders for but one drop of cold water wherewith to cool his tongue. He confessed to himself, with some contempt, that he had been a social being, depending for his happiness on the goodwill of others; he had tried hard to write, chiefly, it was true, from love of the art, but a little from a social motive. He had imagined that a written book and the praise of responsible journals would ensure him the respect of the county people. It was a quaint idea, and he saw the lamentable fallacies naked; in the first place, a painstaking artist in words was not respected by the respectable; secondly, books should not be written with the object of gaining the goodwill of the landed and commercial interests; thirdly and chiefly, no man should in any way depend on another.

From this utter darkness, from danger of madness, the ever dear and sweet Annie had rescued him. Very beautifully and fitly, as Lucian thought, she had done her work without any desire to benefit him, she had simply willed to gratify her own passion, and in doing this had handed to him the priceless secret. And he, on his side, had reversed the process; merely to make himself a splendid offering for the acceptance of his sweetheart, he had cast aside the vain world, and had found the truth, which now remained with him, precious and enduring.

And since the news of the marriage he found that his worship of her had by no means vanished; rather in his heart was the eternal treasure of a happy love, untarnished and spotless; it would be like a mirror of gold without alloy, bright and lustrous for ever. For Lucian, it was no defect in the woman that she was desirous and faithless; he had not conceived an affection for certain moral or intellectual accidents, but for the very woman. Guided by the self-evident axiom that humanity is to be judged by literature, and not literature by humanity, he detected the analogy between *Lycidas* and Annie. Only the dullard would object to the nauseous cant of the one, or to the indiscretions of the other. A sober critic might say that the man who could generalize Herbert and Laud, Donne and Herrick, Sanderson and Juxon, Hammond and Lancelot Andrewes into "our corrupted Clergy" must be either an imbecile or a scoundrel, or probably both. The judgment would be perfectly true, but as a criticism of *Lycidas* it would be a piece of folly. In the case of the woman one could imagine the attitude of the conventional lover; of the chevalier who, with his tongue in his cheek, "reverences and respects" all women, and coming home early in the morning writes a leading article on St. English Girl. Lucian, on the other hand, felt profoundly grateful to the delicious Annie, because she had at precisely the right moment voluntarily removed her image from his way. He confessed to himself that, latterly, he had a little dreaded her return as an interruption; he had shivered at the thought that their relations would become what was so terribly called an "intrigue" or "affair." There would be all the threadbare and common stratagems, the vulgarity of secret assignations, and an atmosphere suggesting the period of Mr. Thomas Moore and Lord Byron and "segars." Lucian had been afraid of all this; he had feared lest love itself should destroy love.

He considered that now, freed from the torment of the body, leaving untasted the green water that makes thirst more burning, he was perfectly initiated in the true knowledge of the splendid and glorious love. There seemed to him a monstrous paradox in the assertion that there could be no true love without a corporal presence of the beloved; even the popular sayings of "Absence makes the heart grow fonder," and "familiarity breeds contempt," witnessed to the contrary. He thought, sighing, and with compassion, of the manner in which men are continually led astray by the cheat of the senses. In order that the unborn might still be added to the born, nature had inspired men with the wild delusion that the bodily companionship of the lover and the beloved was desirable above all things, and so, by the false show of pleasure, the human race was chained to vanity, and doomed to an eternal thirst for the nonexistent.

Again and again he gave thanks for his own escape; he had been set free from a life of vice and sin and folly, from all the dangers and illusions that are most dreaded by the wise. He laughed as he remembered what would be the common view of the situation. An ordinary lover would suffer all the sting of sorrow and contempt; there would be grief for a lost mistress, and rage at her faithlessness, and hate in the heart; one foolish passion driving on another, and driving the man to ruin. For what would be commonly called the real woman he now cared nothing; if he had heard that she had died in her farm in Utter Gwent, he would have experienced only a passing sorrow, such as he might feel at the death of any one he had once known. But he did not think of the young farmer's wife as the real Annie; he did not think of the frost-bitten leaves in winter as the real rose. Indeed, the life of many reminded him of the flowers; perhaps more especially of those flowers which to all appearance are for many years but dull and dusty clumps of green, and suddenly, in one night, burst into the flame of blossom, and fill all the misty lawns with odor; till the morning. It was in that night that the flower lived, not through the long unprofitable years; and, in like manner, many human lives, he thought, were born in the evening and dead before the coming of day. But he had preserved the precious flower in all its glory, not suffering it to wither in the hard light, but keeping it in a secret place, where it could never be destroyed. Truly now, and for the first time, he possessed Annie, as a man possesses the gold which he has dug from the rock and purged of its baseness.

He was musing over these things when a piece of news, very strange and unexpected, arrived at the rectory. A distant, almost a mythical relative, known from childhood as "Cousin Edward in the Isle of Wight," had died, and by some strange freak had left Lucian two thousand pounds. It was a pleasure to give his father five hundred pounds, and the rector on his side forgot for a couple of days to lean his head on his hand. From the rest of the capital, which was well invested, Lucian found he would derive something between sixty and seventy pounds a year, and hid old desires for literature and a refuge in the murmuring streets returned to him. He longed to be free from the incantations that surrounded him in the country, to work and live in a new atmosphere; and so, with many good wishes from his father, he came to the retreat in the waste places of London.

He was in high spirits when he found the square, clean room, horribly furnished, in the bystreet that branched from the main road, and advanced in an unlovely sweep to the mud pits and the desolation that was neither town nor country. On every side monotonous gray streets, each house the replica of its neighbor, to the east an unexplored wilderness, north and west and south the brickfields and market gardens, everywhere the ruins of the country, the tracks where sweet lanes had been, gangrened stumps of trees, the relics of hedges, here and there an oak stripped of its bark, white and haggard and leprous, like a corpse. And the air seemed always gray, and the smoke from the brickfields was gray.

At first he scarcely realized the quarter into which chance had led him. His only thought was of the great adventure of letters in which he proposed to engage, and his first glance round his "bed-sitting-room" showed him that there was no piece of furniture suitable for his purpose. The table, like the rest of the suite, was of bird's-eye maple; but the maker seemed to have penetrated the druidic secret of the rocking-stone, the thing was in a state of unstable equilibrium perpetually. For some days he wandered through the streets, inspecting the second-hand furniture shops, and at last, in a forlorn byway, found an old Japanese bureau, dishonored and forlorn, standing amongst rusty bedsteads, sorry china, and all the refuse of homes dead and desolate. The bureau pleased him in spite of its grime and grease and dirt. Inlaid mother-of-pearl, the gleam of lacquer dragons in red gold, and hits of curious design shone through the film of neglect and ill-usage, and when the woman of the shop showed him the drawers and well and pigeon-holes, he saw that it would be an apt instrument for his studies.

The bureau was carried to his room and replaced the "bird's-eye" table under the gas jet. As Lucian arranged what papers he had accumulated: the sketches of hopeless experiments, shreds and tatters of stories begun but never completed, outlines of plots, two or three notebooks scribbled through and through with impressions of the abandoned hills, he felt a thrill of exaltation at the prospect of work to be accomplished, of a new world all open before him.

He set out on the adventure with a fury of enthusiasm; his last thought at night when all the maze of streets was empty and silent was of the problem, and his dreams ran on phrases, and when he awoke in the morning he was eager to get back to his desk. He immersed himself in a minute, almost a microscopic analysis of fine literature. It was no longer enough, as in the old days, to feel the charm and incantation of a line or a word; he wished to penetrate the secret, to understand something of the wonderful suggestion, all apart from the sense, that seemed to him the *differentia* of literature, as distinguished from the long follies of "character-drawing," "psychological analysis," and all the stuff that went to make the three-volume novel of commerce.

He found himself curiously strengthened by the change from the hills to the streets. There could be no doubt, he thought, that living a lonely life, interested only in himself and his own thoughts, he had become in a measure inhuman. The form of external things, black depths in woods, pools in lonely places, those still valleys curtained by hills on every side, sounding always with the ripple of their brooks, had become to him an influence like that of a drug, giving a certain peculiar color and outline to his thoughts. And from early boyhood there had been another strange flavor in his life, the dream of the old Roman world, those curious impressions that he had gathered from the white walls of Caermaen, and from the looming bastions of the fort. It was in reality the subconscious fancies of many years that had rebuilt the golden city, and had shown him the vine-trellis and the marbles and the sunlight in the garden of Avallaunius. And the rapture of love had made it all so vivid and warm with life, that even now, when he let his pen drop, the rich noise of the tavern and the chant of the theatre sounded above the murmur of the streets. Looking back, it was as much a part of his life as his schooldays, and the tessellated pavements were as real as the square of faded carpet beneath his feet.

But he felt that he had escaped. He could now survey those splendid and lovely visions from without, as if he read of opium dreams, and he no longer dreaded a weird suggestion that had once beset him, that his very soul was being molded into the hills, and passing into the black mirror of still water pools. He had taken refuge in the streets, in the harbor of a modern suburb, from the vague, dreaded magic that had charmed his life. Whenever he felt inclined to listen to the old wood-whisper or to the singing of the fauns he bent more earnestly to his work, turning a deaf ear to the incantations.

In the curious labor of the bureau he found refreshment that was continually renewed. He experienced again, and with a far more violent impulse, the enthusiasm that had attended the writing of his book a year or two before, and so, perhaps, passed from one drug to another. It was, indeed, with something of rapture that he imagined the great procession of years all to be devoted to the intimate analysis of words, to the construction of the sentence, as if it were a piece of jewelry or mosaic.

Sometimes, in the pauses of the work, he would pace up and down his cell, looking out of the window now and again and gazing for an instant into the melancholy street. As the year advanced the days grew more and more misty, and he found himself the inhabitant of a little island wreathed about with the waves of a white and solemn sea. In the afternoon the fog would grow denser, shutting out not only sight but sound; the shriek of the garden gates, the jangling of the tram-bell echoed as if from a far way. Then there were days of heavy incessant rain; he could see a gray drifting sky and the drops plashing in the street, and the houses all dripping and saddened with wet.

He cured himself of one great aversion. He was no longer nauseated at the sight of a story begun and left unfinished. Formerly, even when an idea rose in his mind bright and wonderful, he had always approached the paper with a feeling of sickness and dislike, remembering all the hopeless beginnings he had made. But now he understood that to begin a romance was almost a separate and special art, a thing apart from the story, to be practiced with sedulous care. Whenever an opening scene occurred to him he noted it roughly in a book, and he devoted many long winter evenings to the elaboration of these beginnings. Sometimes the first impression would yield only a paragraph or a sentence, and once or twice but a splendid and sonorous word, which seemed to Lucian all dim and rich with unsurmised adventure. But often he was able to write three or four vivid pages, studying above all things the hint and significance of the words and actions, striving to work into the lines the atmosphere of expectation and promise, and the murmur of wonderful events to come.

In this one department of his task the labor seemed almost endless. He would finish a few pages and then rewrite them, using the same incident and nearly the same words, but altering that indefinite something which is scarcely so much style as manner, or atmosphere. He was astonished at the enormous change that was thus effected, and often, though he himself had done the work, he could scarcely describe in words how it was done. But it was clear that in this art of manner, or suggestion, lay all the chief secrets of literature, that by it all the great miracles were performed. Clearly it was not style, for style in itself was untranslatable, but it was that high theurgic magic that made the English *Don Quixote*, roughly traduced by some Jervas, perhaps the best of all English books. And it was the same element that made the journey of Roderick Random to London, so ostensibly a narrative of coarse jokes and common experiences and burlesque manners, told in no very choice diction, essentially a wonderful vision of the eighteenth century, carrying to one's very nostrils the aroma of the Great North Road, iron-bound under black frost, darkened beneath shuddering woods, haunted by highwaymen, with an adventure waiting beyond every turn, and great old echoing inns in the midst of lonely winter lands.

It was this magic that Lucian sought for his opening chapters; he tried to find that quality that gives to words something beyond their sound and beyond their meaning, that in the first lines of a book should whisper things unintelligible but all significant. Often he worked for many hours without success, and the grim wet dawn once found him still searching for hieroglyphic sentences, for words mystical, symbolic. On the shelves, in the upper part of his bureau, he had placed the books which, however various as to matter, seemed to have a part in this curious quality of suggestion, and in that sphere which might almost be called supernatural. To these books he often had recourse, when further effort appeared altogether hopeless, and certain pages in Coleridge and Edgar Allan Poe had the power of holding him in a trance of delight, subject to emotions and impressions which he knew to transcend altogether the realm of the formal understanding. Such lines as:

Bottomless vales and boundless floods,
And chasms, and caves, and Titan woods,
With forms that no man can discover
For the dews that drip all over.

These had for Lucian more than the potency of a drug, lulling him into a splendid waking-sleep, every word being a supreme incantation. And it was not only his mind that was charmed by such passages, for he felt at the same time a strange and delicious bodily languor that held him motionless, without the desire or power to stir from his seat. And there were certain phrases in *Kubla Khan* that had such a magic that he would sometimes wake up, as it were, to the consciousness that he had been lying on the bed or sitting in the chair by the bureau, repeating a single line over and over again for two or three hours. Yet he knew perfectly well that he had not been really asleep; a little effort recalled a constant impression of the wallpaper, with its pink flowers on a buff ground, and of the muslin-curtained window, letting in the gray winter light. He had been some seven months in London when this odd experience first occurred to him. The day opened dreary and cold and clear, with a gusty and restless wind whirling round the corner of the street, and lifting the dead leaves and scraps of paper that littered the roadway into eddying mounting circles, as if a storm of black rain were to come. Lucian had sat late the night before, and rose in the morning feeling weary and listless and heavy-headed. While he dressed, his legs dragged him as with weights, and he staggered and nearly fell in bending down to the mat outside for his tea tray. He lit the spirit lamp on the hearth with shaking, unsteady hands, and could scarcely pour out the tea when it was ready. A delicate cup of tea was one of his few luxuries; he was fond of the strange flavor of the green leaf, and this morning he drank the straw-colored liquid eagerly, hoping it would disperse the cloud of languor. He tried his best to coerce himself into the sense of vigor and enjoyment with which he usually began the day, walking briskly up and down and arranging his papers in order. But he could not free himself from depression; even as he opened the dear bureau a wave of melancholy came upon him, and he began to ask himself whether he were not pursuing a vain dream, searching for treasures that had no existence. He drew out his cousin's letter and read it again, sadly enough. After all there was a good deal of truth in what she said; he had "overrated" his powers, he had no friends, no real education. He began to count up the months since he had come to London; he had received his two thousand pounds in March, and in May he had said good-bye to the woods and to the dear and friendly paths. May, June, July, August, September, October, November, and half of December had gone by; and what had he to show? Nothing but the experiment, the attempt, futile scribblings which had no end nor shining purpose. There was nothing in his desk that he could produce as evidence of his capacity, no fragment even of accomplishment. It was a thought of intense bitterness, but it seemed as if the barbarians were in the right—a place in a house of business would have been more suitable. He leaned his head on his desk overwhelmed with the severity of his own judgment. He tried to comfort himself again by the thought of all the hours of happy enthusiasm he had spent amongst his papers, working for a great idea with infinite patience. He recalled to mind something that he had always tried to keep in the background of his hopes, the foundation-stone of his life, which he had hidden out of sight. Deep in his heart was the hope that he might one day write a valiant book; he scarcely dared to entertain the aspiration, he felt his incapacity too deeply, but yet this longing was the foundation of all his painful and patient effort. This he had proposed in secret to himself, that if he labored without ceasing, without tiring, he might produce something which would at all events be art, which would stand wholly apart from the objects shaped like books, printed with printers' ink, and called by the name of books that he had read. Giotto, he knew, was a painter, and the man who imitated walnut-wood on the deal doors opposite was a painter, and he had wished to be a very humble pupil in the class of the former. It was better, he thought, to fail in attempting exquisite things than to succeed in the department of the utterly contemptible; he had vowed he would be the dunce of Cervantes's school rather than top-boy in the academy of *A Bad Un to Beat* and *Millicent's Marriage*. And with this purpose he had devoted himself to laborious and joyous years, so that how-ever mean his capacity, the pains should not be wanting. He tried now to rouse himself from a growing misery by the recollection of this high aim, but it all seemed hopeless vanity. He looked out into the gray street, and it stood a symbol of his life, chill and dreary and gray and vexed with a horrible wind. There were the dull inhabitants of the quarter going about their common business; a man was crying "mackerel" in a doleful voice, slowly passing up the street, and staring into the white-curtained "parlors," searching for the face of a purchaser behind the India-rubble plants, stuffed birds, and piles of gaudy gilt books that adorned the windows. One of the blistered doors over the way banged, and a woman came scurrying out on some errand, and the garden gate shrieked two melancholy notes as she opened it and let it swing back after her. The little patches called gardens were mostly untilled, uncared for, squares of slimy moss, dotted with clumps of coarse ugly grass, but here and there were the blackened and rotting remains of sunflowers and marigolds. And beyond, he knew, stretched the labyrinth of streets more or less squalid, but all gray and dull, and behind were the mud pits and the steaming heaps of yellowish bricks, and to the north was a great wide cold waste, treeless, desolate, swept by bitter wind. It was all like his own life, he said again to himself, a maze of unprofitable dreariness and desolation, and his mind grew as black and hopeless as the winter sky. The morning went thus dismally till twelve o'clock, and he put on his hat and greatcoat. He always went out for an hour every day between twelve and one; the exercise was a necessity, and the landlady made his bed in the interval. The wind blew the smoke from the chimneys into his face as he shut the door, and with the acrid smoke came the prevailing odor of the street, a blend of cabbage water and burnt bones and the faint sickly vapor from the brickfields. Lucian walked mechanically for the hour, going eastward, along the main road. The wind pierced him, and the dust was blinding, and the dreariness of the street increased his misery. The row of common shops, full of common things, the blatant public-houses, the Independent chapel, a horrible stucco parody of a Greek temple with a façade of hideous columns that was a nightmare, villas like smug Pharisees, shops again, a church in cheap Gothic, an old garden blasted and riven by the builder, these were the pictures of the way. When he got home again he flung himself on the bed, and lay there stupidly till sheer hunger roused him. He ate a hunch of bread and drank some water, and began to pace up and down the room, wondering whether there were no escape from despair. Writing seemed quite impossible, and hardly knowing what he did he opened his bureau and took out a book from the shelves. As his eyes fell on the page the air grew dark and heavy as night, and the wind wailed suddenly, loudly, terribly.

"By woman wailing for her Demon lover." The words were on his lips when he raised his eyes again. A broad band of pale clear light was shining into the room, and when he looked out of the window he saw the road all brightened by glittering pools of water, and as the last drops of the rainstorm starred these mirrors the sun sank into the wrack. Lucian gazed about him, perplexed, till his eyes fell on the clock above his empty hearth. He had been sitting, motionless, for nearly two hours without any sense of the passage of time, and without ceasing he had murmured those words as he dreamed an endless wonderful story. He experienced somewhat the sensations of Coleridge himself; strange, amazing, ineffable things seemed to have been presented to him, not in the form of the idea, but actually and materially, but he was less fortunate than Coleridge in that he could not, even vaguely, image to himself what he had seen.

Yet when he searched his mind he knew that the consciousness of the room in which he sat had never left him; he had seen the thick darkness gather, and had heard the whirl of rain hissing through the air. Windows had been shut down with a crash, he had noted the pattering footsteps of people running to shelter, the landlady's voice crying to some one to look at the rain coming in under the door. It was like peering into some old bituminous picture, one could see at last that the mere blackness resolved itself into the likeness of trees and rocks and travelers. And against this background of his room, and the storm, and the noises of the street, his vision stood out illuminated, he felt he had descended to the very depths, into the caverns that are hollowed beneath the soul. He tried vainly to record the history of his impressions; the symbols remained in his memory, but the meaning was all conjecture.

The next morning, when he awoke, he could scarcely understand or realize the bitter depression of the preceding day. He found it had all vanished away and had been succeeded by an intense exaltation. Afterwards, when at rare intervals he experienced the same strange possession of the consciousness, he found this to be the invariable result, the hour of vision was always succeeded by a feeling of delight, by sensations of brightened and intensified powers. On that bright December day after the storm he rose joyously, and set about the labor of the bureau with the assurance of success, almost with the hope of formidable difficulties to be overcome. He had long busied himself with those

curious researches which Poe had indicated in the
Philosophy of Composition, and many hours had been
spent in analyzing the singular effects which may
be produced by the sound and resonance of words.
But he had been struck by the thought that in the
finest literature there were more subtle tones than
the loud and insistent music of "nevermore," and
he endeavored to find the secret of those pages and
sentences which spoke, less directly, and less
obviously, to the soul rather than to the ear, being
filled with a certain grave melody and the sensation
of singing voices. It was admirable, no doubt, to
write phrases that showed at a glance their design-
ed rhythm, and rang with sonorous words, but he
dreamed of a prose in which the music should be
less explicit, of names rather than notes. He was
astonished that morning at his own fortune and
facility; he succeeded in covering a page of ruled
paper wholly to his satisfaction, and the sentences,
when he read them out, appeared to suggest a
weird elusive chanting, exquisite but almost
imperceptible, like the echo of the plainsong
reverberated from the vault of a monastic church.

He thought that such happy mornings well
repaid him for the anguish of depression which he
sometimes had to suffer, and for the strange
experience of "possession" recurring at rare
intervals, and usually after many weeks of severe
diet. His income, he found, amounted to sixty-five
pounds a year, and he lived for weeks at a time on
fifteen shillings a week. During these austere
periods his only food was bread, at the rate of a loaf
a day; but he drank huge draughts of green tea, and

smoked a black tobacco, which seemed to him a more potent mother of thought than any drug from the scented East. "I hope you go to some nice place for dinner," wrote his cousin; "there used to be some excellent eating-houses in London where one could get a good cut from the joint, *with plenty of gravy*, and a boiled potato, for a shilling. Aunt Mary writes that you should try Mr. Jones's in Water Street, Islington, whose father came from near Caermaen, and was always most comfortable in her day. I daresay the walk there would do you good. It is such a pity you smoke that horrid tobacco. I had a letter from Mrs. Dolly (Jane Diggs, who married your cousin John Dolly) the other day, and she said they would have been delighted to take you for only twenty-five shillings a week for the sake of the family if you had not been a smoker. She told me to ask you if you had ever seen a horse or a dog smoking tobacco. They are such nice, comfortable people, and the children would have been company for you. Johnnie, who used to be such a dear little fellow, has just gone into an office in the City, and seems to have excellent prospects. How I wish, my dear Lucian, that you could do something in the same way. Don't forget Mr. Jones's in Water Street, and you might mention your name to him."

Lucian never troubled Mr. Jones; but these letters of his cousin's always refreshed him by the force of contrast. He tried to imagine himself a part of the Dolly family, going dutifully every morning to the City on the bus, and returning in the evening for high tea. He could conceive the fine odor of hot roast beef hanging about the decorous house on Sunday afternoons, papa asleep in the dining-room, mamma lying down, and the children quite good and happy with their "Sunday books." In the evening, after supper, one read the *Quiver* till bed-time. Such pictures as these were to Lucian a comfort and a help, a remedy against despair. Often when he felt overwhelmed by the difficulty of the work he had undertaken, he thought of the alternative career, and was strengthened.

He returned again and again to that desire of a prose which should sound faintly, not so much with an audible music, but with the memory and echo of it. In the night, when the last tram had gone jangling by, and he had looked out and seen the street all wrapped about in heavy folds of the mist, he conducted some of his most delicate experiments. In that white and solitary midnight of the suburban street he experienced the curious sense of being on a tower, remote and apart and high above all the troubles of the earth. The gas lamp, which was nearly opposite, shone in a pale halo of light, and the houses themselves were merely indistinct marks and shadows amidst that palpable whiteness, shutting out the world and its noises. The knowledge of the swarming life that was so still, though it surrounded him, made the silence seem deeper than that of the mountains before the dawn; it was as if he alone stirred and looked out amidst a host sleeping at his feet. The fog came in by the open window in freezing puffs, and as Lucian watched he noticed that it shook and wavered like the sea, tossing up wreaths and drifts across the pale halo of the lamp, and, these vanishing, others succeeded. It was as if the mist passed by from the river to the north, as if it still passed by in the silence.

He would shut his window gently, and sit down in his lighted room with all the consciousness of the white advancing shroud upon him. It was then that he found himself in the mood for curious labors, and able to handle with some touch of confidence the more exquisite instruments of the craft. He sought for that magic by which all the glory and glamour of mystic chivalry were made to shine through the burlesque and gross adventures of Don Quixote, by which Hawthorne had lit his infernal Sabbath fires, and fashioned a burning aureole about the village tragedy of *The Scarlet Letter*. In Hawthorne the story and the suggestion, though quite distinct and of different worlds, were rather parallel than opposed to one another; but Cervantes had done a stranger thing. One read of Don Quixote, beaten, dirty, and ridiculous, mistaking windmills for giants, sheep for an army; but the impression was of the enchanted forest, of Avalon, of the San Graal, "far in the spiritual city." And Rabelais showed him, beneath the letter, the Tourainian sun shining on the hot rock above Chinon, on the maze of narrow, climbing streets, on the high-pitched, gabled roofs, on the gray-blue *tourelles*, pricking upward from the fantastic labyrinth of walls. He heard the sound of sonorous plainsong from the monastic choir, of gross exuberant gaiety from the rich vineyards; he listened to the eternal mystic mirth of those that halted in the purple shadow of the *sorbier* by the white, steep road. The gracious and ornate *châteaux* on the Loire and the Vienne rose fair and shining to confront the incredible secrets of vast, dim, far-lifted Gothic naves, that seemed ready to take the great deep, and float away from the mist and dust of earthly streets to anchor in the haven of the clear city that hath foundations. The rank tale of the *garderobe*, of the farm kitchen, mingled with the reasoned, endless legend of the schools, with luminous Platonic argument; the old pomp of the Middle Ages put on the robe of a fresh life. There was a smell of wine and of incense, of June meadows and of ancient books, and through it all he hearkened, intent, to the exultation of chiming bells ringing for a new feast in a new land. He would cover pages with the analysis of these marvels, tracking the suggestion concealed beneath the words, and yet glowing like the golden threads in a robe of samite, or like that device of the old binders by which a vivid picture appeared on the shut edges of a book. He tried to imitate this art, to summon even the faint shadow of the great effect, rewriting a page of Hawthorne, experimenting and changing an epithet here and there, noting how sometimes the alteration of a trifling word would plunge a whole scene into darkness, as if one of those blood-red fires had instantly been extinguished. Sometimes, for severe practice, he attempted to construct short tales in the manner of this or that master. He sighed over these desperate attempts, over the clattering pieces of mechanism which would not even simulate life; but he urged himself to an infinite perseverance. Through the white hours he worked on amidst the heap and litter of papers; books and manuscripts overflowed from the bureau to the floor; and if he looked out he saw the mist still pass by, still passing from the river to the north.

It was not till the winter was well advanced that he began at all to explore the region in which he lived. Soon after his arrival in the gray street he had taken one or two vague walks, hardly noticing where he went or what he saw; but for all the summer he had shut himself in his room, beholding nothing but the form and color of words. For his morning walk he almost invariably chose the one direction, going along the Uxbridge Road towards Notting Hill, and returning by the same monotonous thoroughfare. Now, however, when the new year was beginning its dull days, he began to diverge occasionally to right and left, sometimes eating his luncheon in odd corners, in the bulging parlors of eighteenth-century taverns, that still fronted the surging sea of modern streets, or perhaps in brand new "publics" on the broken borders of the brickfields, smelling of the clay from which they had swollen. He found waste by-places behind railway embankments where he could smoke his pipe sheltered from the wind; sometimes there was a wooden fence by an old pear-orchard where he sat and gazed at the wet desolation of the market gardens, munching a few currant biscuits by way of dinner. As he went farther afield a sense of immensity slowly grew upon him; it was as if, from the little island of his room, that one friendly place, he pushed out into the gray unknown, into a city that for him was uninhabited as the desert.

He came back to his cell after these purposeless wanderings always with a sense of relief, with the thought of taking refuge from gray. As he lit the gas and opened the desk of his bureau and saw the pile of papers awaiting him, it was as if he had passed from the black skies and the stinging wind and the dull maze of the suburb into all the warmth and sunlight and violent color of the south.

VI

I t was in this winter after his coming to the gray street that Lucian first experienced the pains of desolation. He had all his life known the delights of solitude, and had acquired that habit of mind which makes a man find rich company on the bare hillside and leads him into the heart of the wood to meditate by the dark water pools. But now in the blank interval when he was forced to shut up his desk, the sense of loneliness overwhelmed him and filled him with unutterable melancholy. On such days he carried about with him an unceasing gnawing torment in his breast; the anguish of the empty page awaiting him in his bureau, and the knowledge that it was worse than useless to attempt the work. He had fallen into the habit of always using this phrase "the work" to denote the adventure of literature; it had grown in his mind to all the austere and grave significance of "the great work" on the lips of the alchemists; it included every trifling and laborious page and the vague magnificent fancies that sometimes hovered below him. All else had become mere by-play, unimportant, trivial; the work was the end, and the means and the food of his life—it raised him up in the morning to renew the struggle, it was the symbol which charmed him as he lay down at night. All through the hours of toil at the bureau he was enchanted, and when he went out and explored the unknown coasts, the one thought allured him, and was the colored glass between his eyes and the world. Then as he drew nearer home his steps would quicken, and the more weary and gray the walk, the more he rejoiced as he thought of his hermitage and of the curious difficulties that awaited him there. But when, suddenly and without warning, the faculty disappeared, when his mind seemed a hopeless waste from which nothing could arise, then he became subject to a misery so piteous that the barbarians themselves would have been sorry for him. He had known some foretaste of these bitter and inexpressible griefs in the old country days, but then he had immediately taken refuge in the hills, he had rushed to the dark woods as to an anodyne, letting his heart drink in all the wonder and magic of the wild land. Now in these days of January, in the suburban street, there was no such refuge.

He had been working steadily for some weeks, well enough satisfied on the whole with the daily progress, glad to awake in the morning, and to read over what he had written on the night before. The new year opened with faint and heavy weather and a breathless silence in the air, but in a few days the great frost set in. Soon the streets began to suggest the appearance of a beleaguered city, the silence that had preceded the frost deepened, and the mist hung over the earth like a dense white smoke. Night after night the cold increased, and people seemed unwilling to go abroad, till even the main thoroughfares were empty and deserted, as if the inhabitants were lying close in hiding. It was at this dismal time that Lucian found himself reduced to impotence. There was a sudden break in his thought, and when he wrote on valiantly, hoping against hope, he only grew more aghast on the discovery of the imbecilities he had committed to paper. He ground his teeth together and persevered, sick at heart, feeling as if all the world were fallen from under his feet, driving his pen on mechanically, till he was overwhelmed. He saw the stuff he had done without veil or possible concealment, a lamentable and wretched sheaf of verbiage, worse, it seemed, than the efforts of his boyhood. He was not longer tautological, he avoided tautology with the infernal art of a leader-writer, filling his wind bags and mincing words as if he had been a trained journalist on the staff of the *Daily Post.* There seemed all the matter of an insufferable tragedy in these thoughts; that his patient and enduring toil was in vain, that practice went for nothing, and that he had wasted the labor of Milton to accomplish the tenth-rate. Unhappily he could not "give in"; the longing, the fury for the work burnt within him like a burning fire; he lifted up his eyes in despair.

It was then, while he knew that no one could help him, that he languished for help, and then, though he was aware that no comfort was possible, he fervently wished to be comforted. The only friend he had was his father, and he knew that his father would not even understand his distress. For him, always, the printed book was the beginning and end of literature; the agony of the maker, his despair and sickness, were as accursed as the pains of labor. He was ready to read and admire the work of the great Smith, but he did not wish to hear of the period when the great Smith had writhed and twisted like a scorched worm, only hoping to be put out of his misery, to go mad or die, to escape somehow from the bitter pains. And Lucian knew no one else. Now and then he read in the paper the fame of the great *littérateurs*; the Gypsies were entertaining the Prince of Wales, the Jolly Beggars were dining with the Lord Mayor, the Old Mumpers were mingling amicably and gorgeously with the leading members of the Stock Exchange. He was so unfortunate as to know none of these gentlemen, but it hardly seemed likely that they could have done much for him in any case. Indeed, in his heart, he was certain that help and comfort from without were in the nature of things utterly impossible, his ruin and grief were within, and only his own assistance could avail. He tried to reassure himself, to believe that his torments were a proof of his vocation, that the facility of the novelist who stood six years deep in contracts to produce romances was a thing wholly undesirable, but all the while he longed for but a drop of that inexhaustible fluency which he professed to despise.

He drove himself out from that dreary contemplation of the white paper and the idle pen. He went into the frozen and deserted streets, hoping that he might pluck the burning coal from his heart, but the fire was not quenched. As he walked furiously along the grim iron roads he fancied that those persons who passed him cheerfully on their way to friends and friendly hearths shrank from him into the mists as they went by.

Lucian imagined that the fire of his torment and anguish must in some way glow visibly about him; he moved, perhaps, in a nimbus that proclaimed the blackness and the flames within. He knew, of course, that in misery he had grown delirious, that the well-coated, smooth-hatted personages who loomed out of the fog upon him were in reality shuddering only with cold, but in spite of common sense he still conceived that he saw on their faces an evident horror and disgust, and something of the repugnance that one feels at the sight of a venomous snake, half-killed, trailing its bleeding vileness out of sight. By design Lucian tried to make for remote and desolate places, and yet when he had succeeded in touching on the open country, and knew that the icy shadow hovering through the mist was a field, he longed for some sound and murmur of life, and turned again to roads where pale lamps were glimmering, and the dancing flame of firelight shone across the frozen shrubs. And the sight of these homely fires, the thought of affection and consolation waiting by them, stung him the more sharply perhaps because of the contrast with his own chills and weariness and helpless sickness, and chiefly because he knew that he had long closed an everlasting door between his heart and such felicities. If those within had come out and had called him by his name to enter and be comforted, it would have been quite unavailing, since between them and him there was a great gulf fixed. Perhaps for the first time he realized that he had lost the art of humanity forever. He had thought when he closed his ears to the wood whisper and changed the fauns' singing for the murmur of the streets, the black pools for the shadows and amber light of London, that he had put off the old life, and had turned his soul to healthy activities, but the truth was that he had merely exchanged one drug for another. He could not be human, and he wondered whether there were some drop of the fairy blood in his body that made him foreign and a stranger in the world.

He did not surrender to desolation without repeated struggles. He strove to allure himself to his desk by the promise of some easy task; he would not attempt invention, but he had memoranda and rough jottings of ideas in his note-books, and he would merely amplify the suggestions ready to his hand. But it was hopeless, again and again it was hopeless. As he read over his notes, trusting that he would find some hint that might light up the dead fires, and kindle again that pure flame of enthusiasm, he found how desperately his fortune had fallen. He could see no light, no color in the lines he had scribbled with eager trembling fingers; he remembered how splendid all these things had been when he wrote them down, but now they were meaningless, faded into gray. The few words he had dashed on to the paper, enraptured at the thought of the happy hours they promised, had become mere jargon, and when he understood the idea it seemed foolish, dull, unoriginal. He discovered something at last that appeared to have a grain of promise, and determined to do his best to put it into shape, but the first paragraph appalled him; it might have been written by an unintelligent schoolboy. He tore the paper in pieces, and shut and locked his desk, heavy despair sinking like lead into his heart. For the rest of that day he lay motionless on the bed, smoking pipe after pipe in the hope of stupefying himself with tobacco fumes. The air in the room became blue and thick with smoke; it was bitterly cold, and he wrapped himself up in his greatcoat and drew the counterpane over him. The night came on and the window darkened, and at last he fell asleep.

He renewed the effort at intervals, only to plunge deeper into misery. He felt the approaches of madness, and knew that his only hope was to walk till he was physically exhausted, so that he might come home almost fainting with fatigue, but ready to fall asleep the moment he got into bed. He passed the mornings in a kind of torpor, endeavoring to avoid thought, to occupy his mind with the pattern of the paper, with the advertisements at the end of a book, with the curious grayness of the light that glimmered through the mist into his room, with the muffled voices that rumbled now and then from the street. He tried to make out the design that had once colored the faded carpet on the floor, and wondered about the dead artist in Japan, the adorner of his bureau. He speculated as to what his thoughts had been as he inserted the rainbow mother-of-pearl and made that great flight of shining birds, dipping their wings as they rose from the reeds, or how he had conceived the lacquer dragons in red gold, and the fantastic houses in the garden of peach-trees. But sooner or later the oppression of his grief returned, the loud shriek and clang of the garden-gate, the warning bell of some passing bicyclist steering through the fog, the noise of his pipe falling to the floor, would suddenly awaken him to the sense of misery. He knew that it was time to go out; he could not bear to sit still and suffer. Sometimes he cut a slice of bread and put it in his pocket, sometimes he trusted to the chance of finding a public house, where he could have a sandwich and a glass of beer. He turned always from the main streets and lost himself in the intricate suburban byways, willing to be engulfed in the infinite whiteness of the mist.

The roads had stiffened into iron ridges, the fences and trees were glittering with frost crystals, everything was of strange and altered aspect. Lucian walked on and on through the maze, now in a circle of shadowy villas, awful as the buried streets of Herculaneum, now in lanes dipping onto open country, that led him past great elm trees whose white boughs were all still, and past the bitter lonely fields where the mist seemed to fade away into gray darkness. As he wandered along these unfamiliar and ghastly paths he became the more convinced of his utter remoteness from all humanity, he allowed that grotesque suggestion of there being something visibly amiss in his outward appearance to grow upon him, and often he looked with a horrible expectation into the faces of those who passed by, afraid lest his own senses gave him false intelligence, and that he had really assumed some frightful and revolting shape. It was curious that, partly by his own fault, and largely, no doubt, through the operation of mere coincidence, he was once or twice strongly confirmed in this fantastic delusion. He came one day into a lonely and unfrequented byway, a country lane falling into ruin, but still fringed with elms that had formed an avenue leading to the old manor-house. It was now the road of communication between two far outlying suburbs, and on these winter nights lay as black, dreary, and desolate as a mountain track. Soon after the frost began, a gentleman had been set upon in this lane as he picked his way between the corner where the bus had set him down, and his home where the fire was blazing, and his wife watched the clock. He was stumbling uncertainly through the gloom, growing a little nervous because the walk seemed so long, and peering anxiously for the lamp at the end of his street, when the two footpads rushed at him out of the fog. One caught him from behind, the other struck him with a heavy bludgeon, and as he lay senseless they robbed him of his watch and money, and vanished across the fields. The next morning all the suburb rang with the story; the unfortunate merchant had been grievously hurt, and wives watched their husbands go out in the morning with sickening apprehension, not knowing what might happen at night. Lucian of course was ignorant of all these rumors, and struck into the gloomy by-road without caring where he was or whither the way would lead him.

He had been driven out that day as with whips, another hopeless attempt to return to the work had agonized him, and existence seemed an intolerable pain. As he entered the deeper gloom, where the fog hung heavily, he began, half consciously, to gesticulate; he felt convulsed with torment and shame, and it was a sorry relief to clench his nails into his palm and strike the air as he stumbled heavily along, bruising his feet against the frozen ruts and ridges. His impotence was hideous, he said to himself, and he cursed himself and his life, breaking out into a loud oath, and stamping on the ground. Suddenly he was shocked at a scream of terror, it seemed in his very ear, and looking up he saw for a moment a woman gazing at him out of the mist, her features distorted and stiff with fear. A momentary convulsion twitched her arms into the ugly mimicry of a beckoning gesture, and she turned and ran for dear life, howling like a beast.

Lucian stood still in the road while the woman's cries grew faint and died away. His heart was chilled within him as the significance of this strange incident became clear. He remembered nothing of his violent gestures; he had not known at the time that he had sworn out loud, or that he was grinding his teeth with impotent rage. He only thought of that ringing scream, of the horrible fear on the white face that had looked upon him, of the woman's headlong flight from his presence. He stood trembling and shuddering, and in a little while he was feeling his face, searching for some loathsome mark, for the stigmata of evil branding his forehead. He staggered homewards like a drunken man, and when he came into the Uxbridge Road some children saw him and called after him as he swayed and caught at the lamppost. When he got to his room he sat down at first in the dark. He did not dare to light the gas. Everything in the room was indistinct, but he shut his eyes as he passed the dressing table, and sat in a corner, his face turned to the wall. And when at last he gathered courage and the flame leapt hissing from the jet, he crept piteously towards the glass, and ducked his head, crouching miserably, and struggling with his terrors before he could look at his own image.

To the best of his power he tried to deliver himself from these more grotesque fantasies; he assured himself that there was nothing terrific in his countenance but sadness, that his face was like the face of other men. Yet he could not forget that reflection he had seen in the woman's eyes, how the surest mirrors had shown him a horrible dread, her soul itself quailing and shuddering at an awful sight. Her scream rang and rang in his ears; she had fled away from him as if he offered some fate darker than death.

He looked again and again into the glass, tortured by a hideous uncertainty. His senses told him there was nothing amiss, yet he had had a proof, and yet, as he peered most earnestly, there was, it seemed, something strange and not altogether usual in the expression of the eyes. Perhaps it might be the unsteady flare of the gas, or perhaps a flaw in the cheap looking glass, that gave some slight distortion to the image. He walked briskly up and down the room and tried to gaze steadily, indifferently, into his own face. He would not allow himself to be misguided by a word.

When he had pronounced himself incapable of humanity, he had only meant that he could not enjoy the simple things of common life. A man was not necessarily monstrous, merely because he did not appreciate high tea, a quiet chat about the neighbors, and a happy noisy evening with the children. But with what message, then, did he appear charged that the woman's mouth grew so stark? Her hands had jerked up as if they had been pulled with frantic wires; she seemed for the instant like a horrible puppet. Her scream was a thing from the nocturnal Sabbath.

He lit a candle and held it close up to the glass so that his own face glared white at him, and the reflection of the room became an indistinct darkness. He saw nothing but the candle flame and his own shining eyes, and surely they were not as the eyes of common men. As he put down the light, a sudden suggestion entered his mind, and he drew a quick breath, amazed at the thought. He hardly knew whether to rejoice or to shudder. For the thought he conceived was this: that he had mistaken all the circumstances of the adventure, and had perhaps repulsed a sister who would have welcomed him to the Sabbath.

He lay awake all night, turning from one dreary and frightful thought to the other, scarcely dozing for a few hours when the dawn came. He tried for a moment to argue with himself when he got up; knowing that his true life was locked up in the bureau, he made a desperate attempt to drive the phantoms and hideous shapes from his mind. He was assured that his salvation was in the work, and he drew the key from his pocket, and made as if he would have opened the desk. But the nausea, the remembrances of repeated and utter failure, were too powerful. For many days he hung about the Manor Lane, half dreading, half desiring another meeting, and he swore he would not again mistake the cry of rapture, nor repulse the arms extended in a frenzy of delight. In those days he dreamed of some dark place where they might celebrate and make the marriage of the Sabbath, with such rites as he had dared to imagine.

It was perhaps only the shock of a letter from his father that rescued him from these evident approaches to madness. Mr. Taylor wrote how they had missed him at Christmas, how the farmers had inquired after him, of the homely familiar things that recalled his boyhood, his mother's voice, the friendly fireside, and the good old fashions that had nurtured him. He remembered that he had once been a boy, loving the cake and puddings and the radiant holly, and all the seventeenth-century mirth that lingered on in the ancient farmhouses. And there came to him the more holy memory of Mass on Christmas morning. How sweet the dark and frosty earth had smelt as he walked beside his mother down the winding lane, and from the stile near the church they had seen the world glimmering to the dawn, and the wandering lanthorns advancing across the fields. Then he had come into the church and seen it shining with candles and holly, and his father in pure vestments of white linen sang the longing music of the liturgy at the altar, and the people answered him, till the sun rose with the grave notes of the Paternoster, and a red beam stole through the chancel window.

The worst horror left him as he recalled the memory of these dear and holy things. He cast away the frightful fancy that the scream he had heard was a shriek of joy, that the arms, rigidly jerked out, invited him to an embrace. Indeed, the thought that he had longed for such an obscene illusion, that he had gloated over the recollection of that stark mouth, filled him with disgust. He resolved that his senses were deceived, that he had neither seen nor heard, but had for a moment externalized his own slumbering and morbid dreams. It was perhaps necessary that he should be wretched, that his efforts should be discouraged, but he would not yield utterly to madness.

Yet when he went abroad with such good resolutions, it was hard to resist an influence that seemed to come from without and within. He did not know it, but people were everywhere talking of the great frost, of the fog that lay heavy on London, making the streets dark and terrible, of strange birds that came fluttering about the windows in the silent squares. The Thames rolled out duskily, bearing down the jarring ice blocks, and as one looked on the black water from the bridges it was like a river in a northern tale. To Lucian it all seemed mythical, of the same substance as his own fantastic thoughts. He rarely saw a newspaper, and did not follow from day to day the systematic readings of the thermometer, the reports of ice-fairs, of coaches driven across the river at Hampton, of the skating on the fens; and hence the iron roads, the beleaguered silence and the heavy folds of mist appeared as amazing as a picture, significant, appalling. He could not look out and see a common suburban street foggy and dull, nor think of the inhabitants as at work or sitting cheerfully eating nuts about their fires; he saw a vision of a gray road vanishing, of dim houses all empty and deserted, and the silence seemed eternal. And when he went out and passed through street after street, all void, by the vague shapes of houses that appeared for a moment and were then instantly swallowed up, it seemed to him as if he had strayed into a city that had suffered some inconceivable doom, that he alone wandered where myriads had once dwelt. It was a town as great as Babylon, terrible as Rome, marvelous as Lost Atlantis, set in the midst of a white wilderness surrounded by waste places. It was impossible to escape from it; if he skulked between hedges, and crept away beyond the frozen pools, presently the serried stony lines confronted him like an army, and far and far they swept away into the night, as some fabled wall that guards an empire in the vast dim East. Or in that distorting medium of the mist, changing all things, he imagined that he trod an infinite desolate plain, abandoned from ages, but circled and encircled with dolmen and menhir that loomed out at him, gigantic, terrible. All London was one gray temple of an awful rite, ring within ring of wizard stones circled about some central place, every circle was an initiation, every initiation eternal loss. Or perhaps he was astray forever in a land of gray rocks. He had seen the light of home, the flicker of the fire on the walls; close at hand, it seemed, was the open door, and he had heard dear voices calling to him across the gloom, but he had just missed the path. The lamps vanished, the voices sounded thin and died away, and yet he knew that those within were waiting, that they could not bear to close the door, but waited, calling his name, while he had missed the way, and wandered in the pathless desert of the gray rocks. Fantastic, hideous, they beset him wherever he turned, piled up into strange shapes, pricked with sharp peaks, assuming the appearance of goblin towers, swelling into a vague dome like a fairy rath, huge and terrible. And as one dream faded into another, so these last fancies were perhaps the most tormenting and persistent; the rocky avenues became the camp and fortalice of some half-human, malignant race who swarmed in hiding, ready to bear him away into the heart of their horrible hills. It was awful to think that all his goings were surrounded, that in the darkness he was watched and surveyed, that every step but led him deeper and deeper into the labyrinth.

When, of an evening, he was secure in his room, the blind drawn down and the gas flaring, he made vigorous efforts toward sanity. It was not of his free will that he allowed terror to overmaster him, and he desired nothing better than a placid and harmless life, full of work and clear thinking. He knew that he deluded himself with imagination, that he had been walking through London suburbs and not through Pandemonium, and that if he could but unlock his bureau all those ugly forms would be resolved into the mist. But it was hard to say if he consoled himself effectually with such reflections, for the return to common sense meant also the return to the sharp pangs of defeat. It recalled him to the bitter theme of his own inefficiency, to the thought that he only desired one thing of life, and that this was denied him. He was willing to endure the austerities of a monk in a severe cloister, to suffer cold, to be hungry, to be lonely and friendless, to forbear all the consolation of friendly speech, and to be glad of all these things, if only he might be allowed to illuminate the manuscript in quietness. It seemed a hideous insufferable cruelty that he should so fervently desire that which he could never gain.

He was led back to the old conclusion; he had lost the sense of humanity, he was wretched because he was an alien and a stranger amongst citizens. It seemed probable that the enthusiasm of literature, as he understood it, the fervent desire for the fine art, had in it something of the inhuman, and dissevered the enthusiast from his fellow-creatures. It was possible that the barbarian suspected as much, that by some slow process of rumination he had arrived at his fixed and inveterate impression, by no means a clear reasoned conviction; the average Philistine, if pressed for the reasons of his dislike, would either become inarticulate, ejaculating "faugh" and "pah" like an old-fashioned Scots Magazine, or else he would give some imaginary and absurd reason, alleging that all "littery men" were poor, that composers never cut their hair, that painters were rarely public-school men, that sculptors couldn't

271

ride straight to hounds to save their lives, but clearly these imbecilities were mere afterthoughts; the average man hated the artist from a deep instinctive dread of all that was strange, uncanny, alien to his nature; he gibbered, uttered his harsh, semi-bestial "faugh," and dismissed Keats to his gallipots from much the same motives as usually impelled the black savages to dismiss the white man on an even longer journey.

Lucian was not especially interested in this hatred of the barbarian for the maker, except from this point, that it confirmed him in his belief that the love of art dissociated the man from the race. One touch of art made the whole world alien, but surely miseries of the civilized man cast amongst savages were not so much caused by dread of their ferocity as by the terror of his own thoughts; he would perhaps in his last despair leave his retreat and go forth to perish at their hands, so that he might at least die in company, and hear the sound of speech before death. And Lucian felt most keenly that in his case there was a double curse; he was as isolated as Keats, and as inarticulate as his reviewers. The consolation of the work had failed him, and he was suspended in the void between two worlds.

It was no doubt the composite effect of his failures, his loneliness of soul, and solitude of life, that had made him invest those common streets with such grim and persistent terrors. He had perhaps yielded to a temptation without knowing that he had been tempted, and, in the manner of De Quincey, had chosen the subtle in exchange for the more tangible pains. Unconsciously, but still of free will, he had preferred the splendor and the gloom of a malignant vision before his corporal pains, before the hard reality of his own impotence. It was better to dwell in vague melancholy, to stray in the forsaken streets of a city doomed from ages, to wander amidst forlorn and desperate rocks than to awake to a gnawing and ignoble torment, to confess that a house of business would have been more suitable and more practical, that he had promised what he could never perform. Even as he struggled to beat back the phantasmagoria of the mist, and resolved that he would no longer make all the streets a stage of apparitions, he hardly realized what he had done, or that the ghosts he had called might depart and return again.

He continued his long walks, always with the object of producing a physical weariness and exhaustion that would enable him to sleep of nights. But even when he saw the foggy and deserted avenues in their proper shape, and allowed his eyes to catch the pale glimmer of the lamps, and the dancing flame of the firelight, he could not rid himself of the impression that he stood afar off, that between those hearths and himself there was a great gulf fixed. As he paced down the footpath he could often see plainly across the frozen shrubs into the homely and cheerful rooms. Sometimes, late in the evening, he caught a passing glimpse of the family at tea, father, mother, and children laughing and talking together, well pleased with each other's company. Sometimes a wife or a child was standing by the garden gate peering anxiously through the fog, and the sight of it all, all the little details, the hideous but comfortable armchairs turned ready to the fire, maroon-red curtains being drawn close to shut out the ugly night, the sudden blaze and illumination as the fire was poked up so that it might be cheerful for father; these trivial and common things were acutely significant. They brought back to him the image of a dead boy—himself. They recalled the shabby old "parlor" in the country, with its shabby old furniture and fading carpet, and renewed a whole atmosphere of affection and homely comfort. His mother would walk to the end of the drive and look out for him when he was late (wandering then about the dark woodlands); on winter evenings she would make the fire blaze, and have his slippers warming by the hearth, and there was probably buttered toast "as a treat." He dwelt on all these insignificant petty circumstances, on the genial glow and light after the muddy winter lanes, on the relish of the buttered toast and the smell of the hot tea, on the two old cats curled fast asleep before the fender, and made them instruments of exquisite pain and regret. Each of these strange houses that he passed was identified in his mind with his own vanished home; all was prepared and ready as in the old days, but he was shut out, judged and condemned to wander in the frozen mist, with weary feet, anguished and forlorn, and they that would pass from within to help him could not, neither could he pass to them. Again, for the hundredth time, he came back to the sentence: he could not gain the art of letters and he had lost the art of humanity. He saw the vanity of all his thoughts; he was an ascetic caring nothing for warmth and cheerfulness and the small comforts of life, and yet he allowed his mind to dwell on such things. If one of those passers-by, who walked briskly, eager for home, should have pitied him by some miracle and asked him to come in, it would have been worse than useless, yet he longed for pleasures that he could not have enjoyed. It was as if he were come to a place of torment, where they who could not drink longed for water, where they who could feel no warmth shuddered in the eternal cold. He was oppressed by the grim conceit that he himself still slept within the matted thicket, imprisoned by the green bastions of the Roman fort. He had never come out, but a changeling had gone down the hill, and now stirred about the earth.

Beset by such ingenious terrors, it was not wonderful that outward events and common incidents should abet his fancies. He had succeeded one day in escaping from the mesh of the streets, and fell on a rough and narrow lane that stole into a little valley. For the moment he was in a somewhat happier mood; the afternoon sun glowed through the rolling mist, and the air grew clearer. He saw quiet and peaceful fields, and a wood descending in a gentle slope from an old farmstead of warm red brick. The farmer was driving the slow cattle home from the hill, and his loud halloo to his dog came across the land a cheerful mellow note. From another side a cart was approaching the clustered barns, hesitating, pausing while the great horses rested, and then starting again into lazy motion. In the well of the valley a wandering line of bushes showed where a brook crept in and out amongst the meadows, and, as Lucian stood, lingering, on the bridge, a soft and idle breath ruffled through the boughs of a great elm. He felt soothed, as by calm music, and wondered whether it would not be better for him to live in some such quiet place, within reach of the streets and yet remote from them. It seemed a refuge for still thoughts; he could imagine himself sitting at rest beneath the black yew tree in the farm garden, at the close of a summer day. He had almost determined that he would knock at the door and ask if they would take him as a lodger, when he saw a child running towards him down the lane. It was a little girl, with bright curls tossing about her head, and, as she came on, the sunlight glowed upon her, illuminating her brick-red frock and the yellow king-cups in her hat. She had run with her eyes on the ground, chirping and laughing to herself, and did not see Lucian till she was quite near him. She started and glanced into his eyes for a moment, and began to cry; he stretched out his hand, and she ran from him screaming, frightened no doubt by what was to her a sudden and strange apparition. He turned back towards London, and the mist folded him in its thick darkness, for on that evening it was tinged with black. It was only by the intensest strain of resolution that he did not yield utterly to the poisonous anodyne which was always at hand. It had been a difficult struggle to escape from the mesh of the hills, from the music of the fauns, and even now he was drawn by the memory of these old allurements. But he felt that here, in his lonely-ness, he was in greater danger, and beset by a blacker magic. Horrible fancies rushed wantonly into his mind; he was not only ready to believe that something in his soul sent a shudder through all that was simple and innocent, but he came trembling home one Saturday night, believing, or half-believing, that he was in communion with evil. He had passed through the clamorous and blatant crowd of the "high street," where, as one climbed the hill, the shops seemed all aflame, and the black night air glowed with the flaring gas-jets and the naphtha-lamps, hissing and wavering before the February wind. Voices, raucous, clamant, abominable, were belched out of the blazing public-houses as the doors swung to and fro, and above these doors were hideous brassy lamps, very slowly swinging in a violent blast of air, so that they might have been infernal thuribles, censing the people. Some man was calling his wares in one long continuous shriek that never stopped or paused, and, as a respond, a deeper, louder voice roared to him from across the road. An Italian whirled the handle of his piano-organ in a fury, and a ring of imps danced mad figures around him, danced and flung up their legs till the rags dropped from some of them, and they still danced on. A flare of naphtha, burning with a rushing noise, threw a light on one point of the circle, and Lucian watched a lank girl of fifteen as she came round and round to the flash. She was quite drunk, and had kicked her petticoats away, and the crowd howled laughter and applause at her. Her black hair poured down and leapt on her scarlet bodice; she sprang and leapt round the ring, laughing in Bacchic frenzy, and led the orgy to triumph. People were crossing to and fro, jostling against each other, swarming about certain shops and stalls in a dense dark mass that quivered and sent out feelers as if it were one writhing organism. A little farther a group of young men, arm in arm, were marching down the roadway chanting some music-hall verse in full chorus, so that it sounded like plainsong. An impossible hubbub, a hum of voices angry as swarming bees, the squeals of five or six girls who ran in and out, and dived up dark passages and darted back into the crowd; all these mingled together till his ears quivered. A young fellow was playing the concertina, and he touched the keys with such slow fingers that the tune wailed solemn into a dirge; but there was nothing so strange as the burst of sound that swelled out when the public-house doors were opened.

He walked amongst these people, looked at their faces, and looked at the children amongst them. He had come out thinking that he would see the English working class, "the best-behaved and the best-tempered crowd in the world," enjoying the simple pleasure of the Saturday night's shopping. Mother bought the joint for Sunday's dinner, and perhaps a pair of boots for father; father had an honest glass of beer, and the children were given bags of sweets, and then all these worthy people went decently home to their well-earned rest. De Quincey had enjoyed the sight in his day, and had studied the rise and fall of onions and potatoes.

Lucian, indeed, had desired to take these simple emotions as an opiate, to forget the fine fret and fantastic trouble of his own existence in plain things and the palpable joy of rest after labor. He was only afraid lest he should be too sharply reproached by the sight of these men who fought bravely year after year against starvation, who knew nothing of intricate and imagined grief, but only the weariness of relentless labor, of the long battle for their wives and children. It would be pathetic, he thought, to see them content with so little, brightened by the expectation of a day's rest and a good dinner, forced, even then, to reckon every penny, and to make their children laugh with halfpence. Either he would be ashamed before so much content, or else he would be again touched by the sense of his inhumanity which could take no interest in the common things of life. But still he went to be at least taken out of himself, to be forced to look at another side of the world, so that he might perhaps forget a little while his own sorrows.

He was fascinated by what he saw and heard. He wondered whether De Quincey also had seen the same spectacle, and had concealed his impressions out of reverence for the average reader. Here there were no simple joys of honest toilers, but wonderful orgies, that drew out his heart to horrible music. At first the violence of sound and sight had overwhelmed him; the lights flaring in the night wind, the array of naphtha lamps, the black shadows, the roar of voices. The dance about the piano-organ had been the first sign of an inner meaning, and the face of the dark girl as she came

round and round to the flame had been amazing in
its utter furious abandon. And what songs they
were singing all around him, and what terrible
words rang out, only to excite peals of laughter. In
the public-houses the workmen's wives, the wives
of small tradesmen, decently dressed in black, were
drinking their faces to a flaming red, and urging
their husbands to drink more. Beautiful young
women, flushed and laughing, put their arms
round the men's necks and kissed them, and then
held up the glass to their lips. In the dark corners,
at the openings of side streets, the children were
talking together, instructing each other, whispering
what they had seen; a boy of fifteen was plying a
girl of twelve with whisky, and presently they crept
away. Lucian passed them as they turned to go,
and both looked at him. The boy laughed, and the
girl smiled quietly. It was above all in the faces
around him that he saw the most astounding
things, the Bacchic fury unveiled and unashamed.
To his eyes it seemed as if these revelers recognized
him as a fellow, and smiled up in his face, aware
that he was in the secret. Every instinct of religion,
of civilization even, was swept away; they gazed at
one another and at him, absolved of all scruples,
children of the earth and nothing more. Now and
then a couple detached themselves from the swarm,
and went away into the darkness, answering the
jeers and laughter of their friends as they vanished.

On the edge of the pavement, not far from where
he was standing, Lucian noticed a tall and lovely
young woman who seemed to be alone. She was in
the full light of a naphtha flame, and her bronze

hair and flushed cheeks shone illuminate as she viewed the orgy. She had dark brown eyes, and a strange look as of an old picture in her face; and her eyes brightened with an urgent gleam. He saw the revelers nudging each other and glancing at her, and two or three young men went up and asked her to come for a walk. She shook her head and said "No thank you" again and again, and seemed as if she were looking for somebody in the crowd.

"I'm expecting a friend," she said at last to a man who proposed a drink and a walk afterwards; and Lucian wondered what kind of friend would ultimately appear. Suddenly she turned to him as he was about to pass on, and said in a low voice:

"I'll go for a walk with you if you like; you just go on, and I'll follow in a minute."

For a moment he looked steadily at her. He saw that the first glance has misled him; her face was not flushed with drink as he had supposed, but it was radiant with the most exquisite color, a red flame glowed and died on her cheek, and seemed to palpitate as she spoke. The head was set on the neck nobly, as in a statue, and about the ears the bronze hair strayed into little curls. She was smiling and waiting for his answer.

He muttered something about being very sorry, and fled down the hill out of the orgy, from the noise of roaring voices and the glitter of the great lamps very slowly swinging in the blast of wind. He knew that he had touched the brink of utter desolation; there was death in the woman's face, and she had indeed summoned him to the Sabbath. Somehow he had been able to refuse on the instant, but if he had delayed he knew he would have abandoned himself to her, body and soul. He locked himself in his room and lay trembling on the bed, wondering if some subtle sympathy had shown the woman her perfect companion. He looked in the glass, not expecting now to see certain visible and outward signs, but searching for the meaning of that strange glance that lit up his eyes. He had grown even thinner than before in the last few months, and his cheeks were wasted with hunger and sorrow, but there were still about his features the suggestion of a curious classic grace, and the look as of a faun who has strayed from the vineyards and olive gardens. He had broken away, but now he felt the mesh of her net about him, a desire for her that was a madness, as if she held every nerve in his body and drew him to her, to her mystic world, to the rosebush where every flower was a flame.

He dreamed all night of the perilous things he had refused, and it was loss to awake in the morning, pain to return to the world. The frost had broken and the fog had rolled away, and the gray street was filled with a clear gray light. Again he looked out on the long dull sweep of the monotonous houses, hidden for the past weeks by a curtain of mist. Heavy rain had fallen in the night, and the garden rails were still dripping, the roofs still dark with wet, all down the line the dingy white blinds were drawn in the upper windows. Not a soul walked the street; every one was asleep after the exertions of the night before; even on the main road it was only at intervals that some straggler paddled by. Presently a woman in a brown Ulster shuffled off on some errand, then a man in shirtsleeves poked out his head, holding the door half-open, and stared up at a window opposite. After a few minutes he slunk in again, and three loafers came slouching down the street, eager for mischief or beastliness of some sort. They chose a house that seemed rather smarter than the rest, and, irritated by the neat curtains, the little grass plot with its dwarf shrub, one of the ruffians drew out a piece of chalk and wrote some words on the front door. His friends kept watch for him, and the adventure achieved, all three bolted, bellowing yahoo laughter. Then a bell began, tang, tang, tang, and here and there children appeared on their way to Sunday School, and the chapel "teachers" went by with verjuice eyes and lips, scowling at the little boy who cried "Piper, piper!" On the main road many respectable people, the men shining and ill-fitted, the women hideously bedizened, passed in the direction of the Independent nightmare, the stuccoed thing with Doric columns, but on the whole life was stagnant. Presently Lucian smelt the horrid fumes of roast beef and cabbage; the early risers were preparing the one-o'clock meal, but many lay in bed and put off dinner till three, with the effect of prolonging the cabbage atmosphere into the late afternoon. A drizzly rain began as the people were coming out of church, and the mothers of little boys in velvet and little girls in foolishness of every kind were impelled to slap their offspring, and to threaten them with father. Then the torpor of beef and beer and cabbage settled down on the street; in some houses they snorted and read the Parish Magazine, in some they snored and read the murders and collected filth of the week; but the only movement of the afternoon was a second procession of children, now bloated and distended with food, again answering the summons of tang, tang, tang. On the main road the trams, laden with impossible people, went humming to and fro, and young men who wore bright blue ties cheerfully haw-hawed and smoked penny cigars. They annoyed the shiny and respectable and verjuice-lipped, not by the frightful stench of the cigars, but because they were cheerful on Sunday. By and by the children, having heard about Moses in the Bulrushes and Daniel in the Lion's Den, came straggling home in an evil humor. And all the day it was as if one a gray sheet gray shadows flickered, passing by.

And in the rose garden every flower was a flame! He thought in symbols, using the Persian imagery of a dusky court, surrounded by white cloisters, gilded by gates of bronze. The stars came out, the sky glowed a darker violet, but the cloistered wall, the fantastic trellises in stone, shone whiter. It was like a hedge of may-blossom, like a lily within a cup of lapis-lazuli, like sea-foam tossed on the heaving sea at dawn. Always those white cloisters trembled with the lute music, always the garden sang with the clear fountain, rising and falling in the mysterious dusk. And there was a singing voice stealing through the white lattices and the bronze gates, a soft voice chanting of the Lover and the Beloved, of the Vineyard, of the Gate and the Way.

Oh! the language was unknown; but the music of the refrain returned again and again, swelling and trembling through the white nets of the latticed cloisters. And every rose in the dusky air was a flame.

He had seen the life which he expressed by these symbols offered to him, and he had refused it; and he was alone in the gray street, with its lamps just twinkling through the dreary twilight, the blast of a ribald chorus sounding from the main road, a doggerel hymn whining from some parlor, to the accompaniment of the harmonium. He wondered why he had turned away from that woman who knew all secrets, in whose eyes were all the mysteries. He opened the desk of his bureau, and was confronted by the heap and litter of papers, lying in confusion as he had left them. He knew that there was the motive of his refusal; he had been unwilling to abandon all hope of the work. The glory and the torment of his ambition glowed upon him as he looked at the manuscript; it seemed so pitiful that such a single desire should be thwarted. He was aware that if he chose to sit down now before the desk he could, in a manner, write easily enough—he could produce a tale which would be formally well constructed and certain of favorable reception. And it would not be the utterly commonplace, entirely hopeless favorite of the circulating library; it would stand in those ranks where the real thing is skillfully counterfeited, amongst the books which give the reader his orgy of emotions, and yet contrive to be superior, and "art," in his opinion. Lucian had often observed this species of triumph, and had noted the acclamation that never failed the clever sham. *Romola*, for example, had made the great host of the serious, the portentous, shout for joy, while the real book, *The Cloister and the Hearth*, was a comparative failure.

He knew that he could write a *Romola*; but he thought the art of counterfeiting half-crowns less detestable than this shabby trick of imitating literature. He had refused definitely to enter the atelier of the gentleman who pleased his clients by ingeniously simulating the grain of walnut; and though he had seen the old oaken ambry kicked out contemptuously into the farmyard, serving perhaps the necessities of hens or pigs, he would not apprentice himself to the masters of veneer. He paced up and down the room, glancing now and again at his papers, and wondering if there were not hope for him. A great thing he could never do, but he had longed to do a true thing, to imagine sincere and genuine pages.

He was stirred again to this fury for the work by the event of the evening before, by all that had passed through his mind since the melancholy dawn. The lurid picture of that fiery street, the flaming shops and flaming glances, all its wonders and horrors, lit by the naphtha flares and by the burning souls, had possessed him; and the noises, the shriek and the whisper, the jangling rattle of the piano-organ, the long-continued scream of the butcher as he dabbled in the blood, the lewd litany of the singers, these seemed to be resolved into an infernal overture, loud with the expectation of lust and death. And how the spectacle was set in the cloud of dark night, a phantom play acted on that fiery stage, beneath those hideous brassy lamps, very slowly swinging in a violent blast. As all the medley of outrageous sights and sounds now fused themselves within his brain into one clear impression, it seemed that he had indeed witnessed and acted in a drama, that all the scene had been prepared and vested for him, and that the choric songs he had heard were but preludes to a greater act. For in that woman was the consummation and catastrophe of it all, and the whole stage waited for their meeting. He fancied that after this the voices and the lights died away, that the crowd sank swiftly into the darkness, and that the street was at once denuded of the great lamps and of all its awful scenic apparatus.

Again, he thought, the same mystery would be represented before him; suddenly on some dark and gloomy night, as he wandered lonely on a deserted road, the wind hurrying before him, suddenly a turn would bring him again upon the fiery stage, and the antique drama would be re-enacted. He would be drawn to the same place, to find that woman still standing there; again he would watch the rose radiant and palpitating upon her cheek, the argent gleam in her brown eyes, the bronze curls gilding the white splendor of her neck. And for the second time she would freely offer herself. He could hear the wail of the singers swelling to a shriek, and see the dusky dancers whirling round in a faster frenzy, and the naphtha flares tinged with red, as the woman and he went away into the dark, into the cloistered court where every flower was a flame, whence he would never come out.

His only escape was in the desk; he might find salvation if he could again hide his heart in the heap and litter of papers, and again be rapt by the cadence of a phrase. He threw open his window and looked out on the dim world and the glimmering amber lights. He resolved that he would rise early in the morning, and seek once more for his true life in the work.

But there was a strange thing. There was a little bottle on the mantelpiece, a bottle of dark blue glass, and he trembled and shuddered before it, as if it were a fetish.

VII

It was very dark in the room. He seemed by slow degrees to awake from a long and heavy torpor, from an utter forgetfulness, and as he raised his eyes he could scarcely discern the pale whiteness of the paper on the desk before him. He remembered something of a gloomy winter afternoon, of driving rain, of gusty wind: he had fallen asleep over his work, no doubt, and the night had come down.

He lay back in his chair, wondering whether it were late; his eyes were half closed, and he did not make the effort and rouse himself. He could hear the stormy noise of the wind, and the sound reminded him of the half-forgotten days. He thought of his boyhood, and the old rectory, and the great elms that surrounded it. There was something pleasant in the consciousness that he was still half dreaming; he knew he could wake up whenever he pleased, but for the moment he amused himself by the pretence that he was a little boy again, tired with his rambles and the keen air of the hills. He remembered how he would sometimes wake up in the dark at midnight, and listen sleepily for a moment to the rush of the wind straining and crying amongst the trees, and hear it beat upon the walls, and then he would fall to dreams again, happy in his warm, snug bed.

The wind grew louder, and the windows rattled. He half opened his eyes and shut them again, determined to cherish that sensation of long ago. He felt tired and heavy with sleep; he imagined that he was exhausted by some effort; he had, perhaps, been writing furiously without rest. He could not recollect at the instant what the work had been; it would be delightful to read the pages when he had made up his mind to bestir himself.

Surely that was the noise of boughs, swaying and grinding in the wind. He remembered one night at home when such a sound had roused him suddenly from a deep sweet sleep. There was a rushing and beating as of wings upon the air, and a heavy dreary noise, like thunder far away upon the mountain. He had got out of bed and looked from behind the blind to see what was abroad. He remembered the strange sight he had seen, and he pretended it would be just the same if he cared to look out now. There were clouds flying awfully from before the moon, and a pale light that made the familiar land look strange and terrible. The blast of wind came with a great shriek, and the trees tossed and bowed and quivered; the wood was scourged and horrible, and the night air was ghastly with a confused tumult, and voices as of a host. A huge black cloud rolled across the heaven from the west and covered up the moon, and there came a torrent of bitter hissing rain.

It was all a vivid picture to him as he sat in his chair, unwilling to wake. Even as he let his mind stray back to that night of the past years, the rain beat sharply on the window-panes, and though there were no trees in the gray suburban street, he heard distinctly the crash of boughs. He wandered vaguely from thought to thought, groping indistinctly amongst memories, like a man trying to cross from door to door in a darkened unfamiliar room. But, no doubt, if he were to look out, by some magic the whole scene would be displayed before him. He would not see the curve of monotonous two-storied houses, with here and there a white blind, a patch of light, and shadows appearing and vanishing, not the rain plashing in the muddy road, not the amber of the gas-lamp opposite, but the wild moonlight poured on the dearly loved country; far away the dim circle of the hills and woods, and beneath him the tossing trees about the lawn, and the wood heaving under the fury of the wind.

He smiled to himself, amidst his lazy meditations, to think how real it seemed, and yet it was all far away, the scenery of an old play long ended and forgotten. It was strange that after all these years of trouble and work and change he should be in any sense the same person as that little boy peeping out, half frightened, from the rectory window. It was as if looking in the glass one should see a stranger, and yet know that the image was a true reflection.

The memory of the old home recalled his father and mother to him, and he wondered whether his mother would come if he were to cry out suddenly. One night, on just such a night as this, when a great storm blew from the mountain, a tree had fallen with a crash and a bough had struck the roof, and he awoke in a fright, calling for his mother. She had come and had comforted him, soothing him to sleep, and now he shut his eyes, seeing her face shining in the uncertain flickering candle light, as she bent over his bed. He could not think she had died; the memory was but a part of the evil dreams that had come afterwards.

He said to himself that he had fallen asleep and dreamed sorrow and agony, and he wished to forget all the things of trouble. He would return to happy days, to the beloved land, to the dear and friendly paths across the fields. There was the paper, white before him, and when he chose to stir, he would have the pleasure of reading his work. He could not quite recollect what he had been about, but he was somehow conscious that the had been successful and had brought some long labor to a worthy ending. Presently he would light the gas, and enjoy the satisfaction that only the work could give him, but for the time he preferred to linger in the darkness, and to think of himself as straying from stile to stile through the scented meadows, and listening to the bright brook that sang to the alders.

It was winter now, for he heard the rain and the wind, and the swaying of the trees, but in those old days how sweet the summer had been. The great hawthorn bush in blossom, like a white cloud upon the earth, had appeared to him in twilight, he had lingered in the enclosed valley to hear the nightingale, a voice swelling out from the rich gloom, from the trees that grew around the well. The scent of the meadowsweet was blown to him across the bridge of years, and with it came the dream and the hope and the longing, and the afterglow red in the sky, and the marvel of the earth. There was a quiet walk that he knew so well; one went up from a little green byroad, following an unnamed brooklet scarce a foot wide, but yet wandering like a river, gurgling over its pebbles, with its dwarf bushes shading the pouring water. One went through the meadow grass, and came to the larch wood that grew from hill to hill across the stream, and shone a brilliant tender green, and sent vague sweet spires to the flushing sky. Through the wood the path wound, turning and dipping, and beneath, the brown fallen needles of last year were soft and thick, and the resinous cones gave out their odor as the warm night advanced, and the shadows darkened. It was quite still; but he stayed, and the faint song of the brooklet sounded like the echo of a river beyond the mountains. How strange it was to look into the wood, to see the tall straight stems rising, pillar-like, and then the dusk, uncertain, and then the blackness. So he came out from the larch wood, from the green cloud and the vague shadow, into the dearest of all hollows, shut in on one side by the larches and before him by high violent walls of turf, like the slopes of a fort, with a clear line dark against the twilight sky, and a weird thorn bush that grew large, mysterious, on the summit, beneath the gleam of the evening star.

And he retraced his wanderings in those deep old lanes that began from the common road and went away towards the unknown, climbing steep hills, and piercing the woods of shadows, and dipping down into valleys that seemed virgin, unexplored, secret for the foot of man. He entered such a lane not knowing where it might bring him, hoping he had found the way to fairyland, to the woods beyond the world, to that vague territory that haunts all the dreams of a boy. He could not tell where he might be, for the high banks rose steep, and the great hedges made a green vault above. Marvelous ferns grew rich and thick in the dark red earth, fastening their roots about the roots of hazel and beech and maple, clustering like the carven capitals of a cathedral pillar. Down, like a dark shaft, the lane dipped to the well of the hills, and came amongst the limestone rocks. He climbed the bank at last, and looked out into a country that seemed for a moment the land he sought, a mysterious realm with unfamiliar hills and valleys and fair plains all golden, and white houses radiant in the sunset light.

And he thought of the steep hillsides where the bracken was like a wood, and of bare places where the west wind sang over the golden gorse, of still circles in mid-lake, of the poisonous yew-tree in the middle of the wood, shedding its crimson cups on the dank earth. How he lingered by certain black water pools hedged on every side by drooping wych elms and black-stemmed alders, watching the faint waves widening to the banks as a leaf or a twig dropped from the trees.

And the whole air and wonder of the ancient forest came back to him. He had found his way to the river valley, to the long lovely hollow between the hills, and went up and up beneath the leaves in the warm hush of midsummer, glancing back now and again through the green alleys, to the river winding in mystic esses beneath, passing hidden glens receiving the streams that rushed down the hillside, ice cold from the rock, passing the immemorial tumulus, the graves where the legionaries waited for the trumpet, the gray farmhouses sending the blue wreaths of wood smoke into the still air. He went higher and higher, till at last he entered the long passage of the Roman road, and from this, the ridge and summit of the wood, he saw the waves of green swell and dip and sink towards the marshy level and the gleaming yellow sea. He looked on the surging forest, and thought of the strange deserted city moldering into a petty village on its verge, of its encircling walls melting into the turf, of vestiges of an older temple which the earth had buried utterly.

It was winter now, for he heard the wail of the wind, and a sudden gust drove the rain against the panes, but he thought of the bee's song in the clover, of the foxgloves in full blossom, of the wild roses, delicate, enchanting, swaying on a long stem above the hedge. He had been in strange places, he had known sorrow and desolation, and had grown gray and weary in the work of letters, but he lived again in the sweetness, in the clear bright air of early morning, when the sky was blue in June, and the mist rolled like a white sea in the valley. He laughed when he recollected that he had sometimes fancied himself unhappy in those days; in those days when he could be glad because the sun shone, because the wind blew fresh on the mountain. On those bright days he had been glad, looking at the fleeting and passing of the clouds upon the hills, and had gone up higher to the broad dome of the mountain, feeling that joy went up before him.

He remembered how, a boy, he had dreamed of love of an adorable and ineffable mystery which transcended all longing and desire. The time had come when all the wonder of the earth seemed to prefigure this alone, when he found the symbol of the Beloved in hill and wood and stream, and every flower and every dark pool discoursed a pure ecstasy. It was the longing for longing, the love of love, that had come to him when he awoke one morning just before the dawn, and for the first time felt the sharp thrill of passion.

He tried in vain to express to himself the exquisite joys of innocent desire. Even now, after troubled years, in spite of some dark cloud that overshadowed the background of his thought, the sweetness of the boy's imagined pleasure came like a perfume into his reverie. It was no love of a woman but the desire of womanhood, the Eros of the unknown, that made the heart tremble. He hardly dreamed that such a love could ever be satisfied, that the thirst of beauty could be slaked. He shrank from all contact of actuality, not venturing so much as to imagine the inner place and sanctuary of the mysteries. It was enough for him to adore in the outer court, to know that within, in the sweet gloom, were the vision and the rapture, the altar and the sacrifice.

He remembered, dimly, the passage of many heavy years since that time of hope and passion, but, perhaps, the vague shadow would pass away, and he could renew the boy's thoughts, the unformed fancies that were part of the bright day, of the wild roses in the hedgerow. All other things should be laid aside, he would let them trouble him no more after this winter night. He saw now that from the first he had allowed his imagination to bewilder him, to create a fantastic world in which he suffered, molding innocent forms into terror and dismay. Vividly, he saw again the black circle of oaks, growing in a haggard ring upon the bastions of the Roman fort. The noise of the storm without grew louder, and he thought how the wind had come up the valley with the sound of a scream, how a great tree had ground its boughs together, shuddering before the violent blast. Clear and distinct, as if he were standing now in the lane, he saw the steep slopes surging from the valley, and the black crown of the oaks set against the flaming sky, against a blaze and glow of light as if great furnace doors were opened. He saw the fire, as it were, smitten about the bastions, about the heaped mounds that guarded the fort, and the crooked evil boughs seemed to writhe in the blast of flame that beat from heaven. Strangely with the sight of the burning fort mingled the impression of a dim white shape floating up the dusk of the lane towards him, and he saw across the valley of years a girl's face, a momentary apparition that shone and vanished away.

Then there was a memory of another day, of violent summer, of white farmhouse walls blazing in the sun, and a far call from the reapers in the cornfields. He had climbed the steep slope and penetrated the matted thicket and lay in the heat, alone on the soft short grass that grew within the fort. There was a cloud of madness, and confusion of broken dreams that had no meaning or clue but only an indefinable horror and defilement. He had fallen asleep as he gazed at the knotted fantastic boughs of the stunted brake about him, and when he woke he was ashamed, and fled away fearing that "they" would pursue him. He did not know who "they" were, but it seemed as if a woman's face watched him from between the matted boughs, and that she summoned to her side awful companions who had never grown old through all the ages.

He looked up, it seemed, at a smiling face that bent over him, as he sat in the cool dark kitchen of the old farmhouse, and wondered why the sweetness of those red lips and the kindness of the eyes mingled with the nightmare in the fort, with the horrible Sabbath he had imagined as he lay sleeping on the hot soft turf. He had allowed these disturbed fancies, all this mad wreck of terror and shame that he had gathered in his mind, to trouble him for too long a time; presently he would light up the room, and leave all the old darkness of his life behind him, and from henceforth he would walk in the day.

He could still distinguish, though very vaguely, the pile of papers beside him, and he remembered, now, that he had finished a long task that afternoon, before he fell asleep. He could not trouble himself to recollect the exact nature of the work, but he was sure that he had done well; in a few minutes, perhaps, he would strike a match, and read the title, and amuse himself with his own forgetfulness. But the sight of the papers lying there in order made him think of his beginnings, of those first unhappy efforts which were so impossible and so hopeless. He saw himself bending over the table in the old familiar room, desperately scribbling, and then laying down his pen dismayed at the sad results on the page. It was late at night, his father had been long in bed, and the house was still. The fire was almost out, with only a dim glow here and there amongst the cinders, and the room was growing chilly. He rose at last from his work and looked out on a dim earth and a dark and cloudy sky.

Night after night he had labored on, persevering in his effort, even through the cold sickness of despair, when every line was doomed as it was made. Now, with the consciousness that he knew at least the conditions of literature, and that many years of thought and practice had given him some sense of language, he found these early struggles both pathetic and astonishing. He could not understand how he had persevered so stubbornly, how he had had the heart to begin a fresh page when so many folios of blotted, painful effort lay torn, derided, impossible in their utter failure. It seemed to him that it must have been a miracle or an infernal possession, a species of madness, that had driven him on, every day disappointed, and every day hopeful.

And yet there was a joyous side to the illusion. In these dry days that he lived in, when he had bought, by a long experience and by countless hours of misery, a knowledge of his limitations, of the vast gulf that yawned between the conception and the work, it was pleasant to think of a time when all things were possible, when the most splendid design seemed an affair of a few weeks. Now he had come to a frank acknowledgment; so far as he was concerned, he judged every book wholly impossible till the last line of it was written, and he had learnt patience, the art of sighing and putting the fine scheme away in the pigeonhole of what could never be. But to think of those days! Then one could plot out a book that should be more curious than Rabelais, and jot down the outlines of a romance to surpass Cervantes, and design renaissance tragedies and volumes of *contes*, and comedies of the Restoration; everything was to be done, and the masterpiece was always the rainbow cup, a little way before him.

He touched the manuscript on the desk, and the feeling of the pages seemed to restore all the papers that had been torn so long ago. It was the atmosphere of the silent room that returned, the light of the shaded candle falling on the abandoned leaves. This had been painfully excogitated while the snowstorm whirled about the lawn and filled the lanes, this was of the summer night, this of the harvest moon rising like a fire from the tithebarn on the hill. How well he remembered those half-dozen pages of which he had once been so proud; he had thought out the sentences one evening, while he leaned on the footbridge and watched the brook swim across the road. Every word smelt of the meadowsweet that grew thick upon the banks; now, as he recalled the cadence and the phrase that had seemed so charming, he saw again the ferns beneath the vaulted roots of the beech, and the green light of the glowworm in the hedge.

And in the west the mountains swelled to a great dome, and on the dome was a mound, the memorial of some forgotten race, that grew dark and large against the red sky, when the sun set. He had lingered below it in the solitude, amongst the winds, at evening, far away from home; and oh, the labor and the vain efforts to make the form of it and the awe of it in prose, to write the hush of the vast hill, and the sadness of the world below sinking into the night, and the mystery, the suggestion of the rounded hillock, huge against the magic sky.

He had tried to sing in words the music that the brook sang, and the sound of the October wind rustling through the brown bracken on the hill. How many pages he had covered in the effort to show a white winter world, a sun without warmth in a gray-blue sky, all the fields, all the land white and shining, and one high summit where the dark pines towered, still in the still afternoon, in the pale violet air.

To win the secret of words, to make a phrase that would murmur of summer and the bee, to summon the wind into a sentence, to conjure the odor of the night into the surge and fall and harmony of a line; this was the tale of the long evenings, of the candle flame white upon the paper and the eager pen.

He remembered that in some fantastic book he had seen a bar or two of music, and, beneath, the inscription that here was the musical expression of Westminster Abbey. His boyish effort seemed hardly less ambitious, and he no longer believed that language could present the melody and the awe and the loveliness of the earth. He had long known that he, at all events, would have to be content with a far approach, with a few broken notes that might suggest, perhaps, the magistral everlasting song of the hill and the streams.

But in those far days the impossible was but a part of wonderland that lay before him, of the world beyond the wood and the mountain. All was to be conquered, all was to be achieved; he had but to make the journey and he would find the golden world and the golden word, and hear those songs that the sirens sang. He touched the manuscript; whatever it was, it was the result of painful labor and disappointment, not of the old flush of hope, but it came of weary days, of correction and re-correction. It might be good in its measure; but afterwards he would write no more for a time. He would go back again to the happy world of masterpieces, to the dreams of great and perfect books, written in an ecstasy.

Like a dark cloud from the sea came the memory of the attempt he had made, of the poor piteous history that had once embittered his life. He sighed and said alas, thinking of his folly, of the hours when he was shaken with futile, miserable rage. Some silly person in London had made his manuscript more saleable and had sold it without rendering an account of the profits, and for that he had been ready to curse humanity. Black, horrible, as the memory of a stormy day, the rage of his heart returned to his mind, and he covered his eyes, endeavoring to darken the picture of terror and hate that shone before him. He tried to drive it all out of his thought, it vexed him to remember these foolish trifles; the trick of a publisher, the small pomposities and malignancies of the country folk, the cruelty of a village boy, had inflamed him almost to the pitch of madness. His heart had burnt with fury, and when he looked up the sky was blotched, and scarlet as if it rained blood.

Indeed he had almost believed that blood had rained upon him, and cold blood from a sacrifice in heaven; his face was wet and chill and dripping, and he had passed his hand across his forehead and looked at it. A red cloud had seemed to swell over the hill, and grow great, and come near to him; he was but an ace removed from raging madness.

It had almost come to that; the drift and the breath of the scarlet cloud had well nigh touched him. It was strange that he had been so deeply troubled by such little things, and strange how after all the years he could still recall the anguish and rage and hate that shook his soul as with a spiritual tempest.

The memory of all that evening was wild and troubled; he resolved that it should vex him no more, that now, for the last time, he would let himself be tormented by the past. In a few minutes he would rise to a new life, and forget all the storms that had gone over him.

Curiously, every detail was distinct and clear in his brain. The figure of the doctor driving home, and the sound of the few words he had spoken came to him in the darkness, through the noise of the storm and the pattering of the rain. Then he stood upon the ridge of the hill and saw the smoke drifting up from the ragged roofs of Caermaen, in the evening calm; he listened to the voices mounting thin and clear, in a weird tone, as if some outland folk were speaking in an unknown tongue of awful things.

He saw the gathering darkness, the mystery of twilight changing the huddled squalid village into an unearthly city, into some dreadful Atlantis, inhabited by a ruined race. The mist falling fast, the gloom that seemed to issue from the black depths of the forest, to advance palpably towards the walls, were shaped before him; and beneath, the river wound, snake-like, about the town, swimming to the flood and glowing in its still pools like molten brass. And as the water mirrored the afterglow and sent ripples and gouts of blood against the shuddering reeds, there came suddenly the piercing trumpet call, the loud reiterated summons that rose and fell, that called and recalled, echoing through all the valley, crying to the dead as the last note rang. It summoned the legion from the river and the graves and the battlefield, the host floated up from the sea, the centuries swarmed about the eagles, the array was set for the last great battle, behind the leaguer of the mist.

He could imagine himself still wandering through the dim unknown, terrible country, gazing affrighted at the hills and woods that seemed to have put on an unearthly shape, stumbling amongst the briars that caught his feet. He lost his way in a wild country, and the red light that blazed up from the furnace on the mountains only showed him a mysterious land, in which he strayed aghast, with the sense of doom weighing upon him. The dry mutter of the trees, the sound of an unseen brook, made him afraid as if the earth spoke of his sin, and presently he was fleeing through a desolate shadowy wood, where a pale light flowed from the moldering stumps, a dream of light that shed a ghostly radiance.

And then again the dark summit of the Roman fort, the black sheer height rising above the valley, and the moonfire streaming around the ring of oaks, glowing about the green bastions that guarded the thicket and the inner place.

The room in which he sat appeared the vision, the trouble of the wind and rain without was but illusion, the noise of the waves in the seashell. Passion and tears and adoration and the glories of the summer night returned, and the calm sweet face of the woman appeared, and he thrilled at the soft touch of her hand on his flesh.

She shone as if she had floated down into the lane from the moon that swam between films of cloud above the black circle of the oaks. She led him away from all terror and despair and hate, and gave herself to him with rapture, showing him love, kissing his tears away, pillowing his cheek upon her breast.

His lips dwelt on her lips, his mouth upon the breath of her mouth, her arms were strained about him, and oh! she charmed him with her voice, with sweet kind words, as she offered her sacrifice. How her scented hair fell down, and floated over his eyes, and there was a marvelous fire called the moon, and her lips were aflame, and her eyes shone like a light on the hills.

All beautiful womanhood had come to him in the lane. Love had touched him in the dusk and had flown away, but he had seen the splendor and the glory, and his eyes had seen the enchanted light.

Ave Atque Vale

The old words sounded in his ears like the ending of a chant, and he heard the music's close. Once only in his weary hapless life, once the world had passed away, and he had known her, the dear, dear Annie, the symbol of all mystic womanhood.

The heaviness of languor still oppressed him, holding him back amongst these old memories, so that he could not stir from his place. Oddly, there seemed something unaccustomed about the darkness of the room, as if the shadows he had summoned had changed the aspect of the walls. He was conscious that on this night he was not altogether himself; fatigue, and the weariness of sleep, and the waking vision had perplexed him. He remembered how once or twice when he was a little boy startled by an uneasy dream, and had stared with a frightened gaze into nothingness, not knowing where he was, all trembling, and breathing quick, till he touched the rail of his bed, and the familiar outlines of the looking-glass and the chiffonier began to glimmer out of the gloom. So now he touched the pile of manuscript and the desk at which he had worked so many hours, and felt reassured, though he smiled at himself, and he felt the old childish dread, the longing to cry out for some one to bring a candle, and show him that he really was in his own room. He glanced up for an instant, expecting to see perhaps the glitter of the brass gas jet that was fixed on the wall, just beside his bureau, but it was too dark, and he could not rouse himself and make the effort that would drive the cloud and the muttering thoughts away.

He leant back again, picturing the wet street without, the rain driving like fountain spray about the gas lamp, the shrilling of the wind on those waste places to the north. It was strange how in the brick and stucco desert where no trees were, he all the time imagined the noise of tossing boughs, the grinding of the boughs together. There was a great storm and tumult in this wilderness of London, and for the sound of the rain and the wind he could not hear the hum and jangle of the trams, and the jar and shriek of the garden gates as they opened and shut. But he could imagine his street, the rain-swept desolate curve of it, as it turned northward, and beyond the empty suburban roads, the twinkling villa windows, the ruined field, the broken lane, and then yet another suburb rising, a solitary gas lamp glimmering at a corner, and the plane tree lashing its boughs, and driving great showers against the glass.

It was wonderful to think of. For when these remote roads were ended one dipped down the hill into the open country, into the dim world beyond the glint of friendly fires. Tonight, how waste they were, these wet roads, edged with the red brick houses, with shrubs whipped by the wind against one another, against the paling and the wall. There the wind swayed the great elms scattered on the sidewalk, the remnants of the old stately fields, and beneath each tree was a pool of wet, and a torment of raindrops fell with every gust. And one passed through the red avenues, perhaps by a little settlement of flickering shops, and passed the last sentinel wavering lamp, and the road became a ragged lane, and the storm screamed from hedge to hedge across the open fields. And then, beyond, one touched again upon a still remoter avant-garde of London, an island amidst the darkness, surrounded by its pale of twinkling, starry lights.

He remembered his wanderings amongst these outposts of the town, and thought how desolate all their ways must be tonight. They were solitary in wet and wind, and only at long intervals some one pattered and hurried along them, bending his eyes down to escape the drift of rain. Within the villas, behind the close-drawn curtains, they drew about the fire, and wondered at the violence of the storm, listening for each great gust as it gathered far away, and rocked the trees, and at last rushed with a huge shock against their walls as if it were the coming of the sea. He thought of himself walking, as he had often walked, from lamp to lamp on such a night, treasuring his lonely thoughts, and weighing the hard task awaiting him in his room. Often in the evening, after a long day's labor, he had thrown down his pen in utter listlessness, feeling that he could struggle no more with ideas and words, and he had gone out into driving rain and darkness, seeking the word of the enigma as he tramped on and on beneath these outer battlements of London.

Or on some gray afternoon in March or November he had sickened of the dull monotony and the stagnant life that he saw from his window, and had taken his design with him to the lonely places, halting now and again by a gate, and pausing in the shelter of a hedge through which the austere wind shivered, while, perhaps, he dreamed of Sicily, or of sunlight on the Provençal olives. Often as he strayed solitary from street to field, and passed the Syrian fig tree imprisoned in Britain, nailed to an ungenial wall, the solution of the puzzle became evident, and he laughed and hurried home eager to make the page speak, to note the song he had heard on his way.

Sometimes he had spent many hours treading this edge and brim of London, now lost amidst the dun fields, watching the bushes shaken by the wind, and now looking down from a height whence he could see the dim waves of the town, and a barbaric water tower rising from a hill, and the snuff-colored cloud of smoke that seemed blown up from the streets into the sky.

There were certain ways and places that he had cherished; he loved a great old common that stood on high ground, curtained about with ancient spacious houses of red brick, and their cedarn gardens. And there was on the road that led to this common a space of ragged uneven ground with a pool and a twisted oak, and here he had often stayed in autumn and looked across the mist and the valley at the great theatre of the sunset, where a red cloud like a charging knight shone and conquered a purple dragon shape, and golden lances glittered in a field of faerie green.

Or sometimes, when the unending prospect of trim, monotonous, modern streets had wearied him, he had found an immense refreshment in the discovery of a forgotten hamlet, left in a hollow, while all new London pressed and surged on every side, threatening the rest of the red roofs with its vulgar growth. These little peaceful houses, huddled together beneath the shelter of trees, with their bulging leaded windows and uneven roofs, somehow brought back to him the sense of the country, and soothed him with the thought of the old farmhouses, white or gray, the homes of quiet lives, harbors where, perhaps, no tormenting thoughts ever broke in.

For he had instinctively determined that there was neither rest nor health in all the arid waste of streets about him. It seemed as if in those dull rows of dwellings, in the prim new villas, red and white and staring, there must be a leaven working which transformed all to base vulgarity. Beneath the dull sad slates, behind the blistered doors, love turned to squalid intrigue, mirth to drunken clamor, and the mystery of life became a common thing; religion was sought for in the greasy piety and flatulent oratory of the Independent chapel, the stuccoed nightmare of the Doric columns. Nothing fine, nothing rare, nothing exquisite, it seemed, could exist in the weltering suburban sea, in the habitations which had risen from the stench and slime of the brickfields. It was as if the sickening fumes that steamed from the burning bricks had been sublimed into the shape of houses, and those who lived in these gray places could also claim kinship with the putrid mud.

Hence he had delighted in the few remains of the past that he could find still surviving on the suburb's edge, in the grave old houses that stood apart from the road, in the moldering taverns of the eighteenth century, in the huddled hamlets that had preserved only the glow and the sunlight of all the years that had passed over them. It appeared to him that vulgarity, and greasiness and squalor had come with a flood, that not only the good but also the evil in man's heart had been made common and ugly, that a sordid scum was mingled with all the springs, of death as of life. It would be alike futile to search amongst these mean two-storied houses for a splendid sinner as for a splendid saint; the very vices of these people smelt of cabbage water and a pothouse vomit.

And so he had often fled away from the serried maze that encircled him, seeking for the old and worn and significant as an antiquary looks for the fragments of the Roman temple amidst the modern shops. In some way the gusts of wind and the beating rain of the night reminded him of an old house that had often attracted him with a strange indefinable curiosity. He had found it on a grim gray day in March, when he had gone out under a leaden-molded sky, cowering from a dry freezing wind that brought with it the gloom and the doom of far unhappy Siberian plains. More than ever that day the suburb had oppressed him; insignificant, detestable, repulsive to body and mind, it was the only hell that a vulgar age could conceive or make, an inferno created not by Dante but by the jerry-builder. He had gone out to the north, and when he lifted up his eyes again he found that he had chanced to turn up by one of the little lanes that still strayed across the broken fields. He had never chosen this path before because the lane at its outlet was so wholly degraded and offensive, littered with rusty tins and broken crockery, and hedged in with a paling fashioned out of scraps of wire, rotting timber, and bending worn-out rails. But on this day, by happy chance, he had fled from the high road by the first opening that offered, and he no longer groped his way amongst obscene refuse, sickened by the bloated bodies of dead dogs, and fetid odors from unclean decay, but the malpassage had become a peaceful winding lane, with warm shelter beneath its banks from the dismal wind. For a mile he had walked quietly, and then a turn in the road showed him a little glen or hollow, watered by such a tiny rushing brooklet as his own woods knew, and beyond, alas, the glaring foreguard of a "new neighborhood"; raw red villas, semi-detached, and then a row of lamentable shops.

But as he was about to turn back, in the hope of finding some other outlet, his attention was charmed by a small house that stood back a little from the road on his right hand. There had been a white gate, but the paint had long faded to gray and black, and the wood crumbled under the touch, and only moss marked out the lines of the drive. The iron railing round the lawn had fallen, and the poor flowerbeds were choked with grass and a faded growth of weeds. But here and there a rosebush lingered amidst suckers that had sprung grossly from the root, and on each side of the hall door were box trees, untrimmed, ragged, but still green. The slate roof was all stained and livid, blotched with the drippings of a great elm that stood at one corner of the neglected lawn, and marks of damp and decay were thick on the uneven walls, which had been washed yellow many years before. There was a porch of trelliswork before the door, and Lucian had seen it rock in the wind, swaying as if every gust must drive it down. There were two windows on the ground floor, one on each side of the door, and two above, with a blind space where a central window had been blocked up.

This poor and desolate house had fascinated him. Ancient and poor and fallen, disfigured by the slate roof and the yellow wash that had replaced the old mellow dipping tiles and the warm red walls, and disfigured again by spots and patches of decay; it seemed as if its happy days were for ever ended. To Lucian it appealed with a sense of doom and horror; the black streaks that crept upon the walls, and the green drift upon the roof, appeared not so much the work of foul weather and dripping boughs, as the outward signs of evil working and creeping in the lives of those within.

The stage seemed to him decked for doom, painted with the symbols of tragedy; and he wondered as he looked whether any one were so unhappy as to live there still. There were torn blinds in the windows, but he had asked himself who could be so brave as to sit in that room, darkened by the dreary box, and listen of winter nights to the rain upon the window, and the moaning of wind amongst the tossing boughs that beat against the roof.

He could not imagine that any chamber in such a house was habitable. Here the dead had lain, through the white blind the thin light had filtered on the rigid mouth, and still the floor must be wet with tears and still that great rocking elm echoed the groaning and the sobs of those who watched. No doubt, the damp was rising, and the odor of the earth filled the house, and made such as entered draw back, foreseeing the hour of death.

Often the thought of this strange old house had haunted him; he had imagined the empty rooms where a heavy paper peeled from the walls and hung in dark strips; and he could not believe that a light ever shone from those windows that stared black and glittering on the neglected lawn. But tonight the wet and the storm seemed curiously to bring the image of the place before him, and as the wind sounded he thought how unhappy those must be, if any there were, who sat in the musty chambers by a flickering light, and listened to the elm-tree moaning and beating and weeping on the walls.

And tonight was Saturday night; and there was about that phrase something that muttered of the condemned cell, of the agony of a doomed man.

Ghastly to his eyes was the conception of any one sitting in that room to the right of the door behind the larger box tree, where the wall was cracked above the window and smeared with a black stain in an ugly shape.

He knew how foolish it had been in the first place to trouble his mind with such conceits of a dreary cottage on the outskirts of London. And it was more foolish now to meditate these things, fantasies, feigned forms, the issue of a sad mood and a bleak day of spring. For soon, in a few moments, he was to rise to a new life. He was but reckoning up the account of his past, and when the light came he was to think no more of sorrow and heaviness, of real or imagined terrors. He had stayed too long in London, and the would once more taste the breath of the hills, and see the river winding in the long lovely valley; ah! he would go home.

Something like a thrill, the thrill of fear, passed over him as he remembered that there was no home. It was in the winter, a year and a half after his arrival in town, that he had suffered the loss of his father. He lay for many days prostrate, overwhelmed with sorrow and with the thought that now indeed he was utterly alone in the world. Miss Deacon was to live with another cousin in Yorkshire; the old home was at last ended and done. He felt sorry that he had not written more frequently to his father: there were things in his cousin's letters that had made his heart sore. "Your poor father was always looking for your letters," she wrote, "they used to cheer him so much. He nearly broke down when you sent him that money last Christmas; he got it into his head that you were starving yourself to send it him. He was hoping so much that you would have come down this Christmas, and kept asking me about the plum-puddings months ago."

It was not only his father that had died, but with him the last strong link was broken, and the past life, the days of his boyhood, grew faint as a dream. With his father his mother died again, and the long years died, the time of his innocence, the memory of affection. He was sorry that his letters had gone home so rarely; it hurt him to imagine his father looking out when the post came in the morning, and forced to be sad because there was nothing. But he had never thought that his father valued the few lines that he wrote, and indeed it was often difficult to know what to say. It would have been useless to write of those agonizing nights when the pen seemed an awkward and outlandish instrument, when every effort ended in shameful defeat, or of the happier hours when at last wonder appeared and the line glowed, crowned and exalted. To poor Mr. Taylor such tales would have seemed but trivial histories of some Oriental game, like an odd story from a land where men have time for the infinitely little, and can seriously make a science of arranging blossoms in a jar, and discuss perfumes instead of politics. It would have been useless to write to the rectory of his only interest, and so he wrote seldom.

And then he had been sorry because he could never write again and never see his home. He had wondered whether he would have gone down to the old place at Christmas, if his father had lived. It was curious how common things evoked the bitterest griefs, but his father's anxiety that the plum pudding should be good, and ready for him, had brought the tears into his eyes. He could hear him saying in a nervous voice that attempted to be cheerful: "I suppose you will be thinking of the Christmas puddings soon, Jane; you remember how fond Lucian used to be of plum pudding. I hope we shall see him this December." No doubt poor Miss Deacon paled with rage at the suggestion that she should make Christmas pudding in July; and returned a sharp answer; but it was pathetic. The wind wailed, and the rain dashed and beat again and again upon the window. He imagined that all his thoughts of home, of the old rectory amongst the elms, had conjured into his mind the sound of the storm upon the trees, for, tonight, very clearly he heard the creaking of the boughs, the noise of boughs moaning and beating and weeping on the walls, and even a pattering of wet, on wet earth, as if there were a shrub near the window that shook off the raindrops, before the gust.

That thrill, as it were a shudder of fear, passed over him again, and he knew not what had made him afraid. There were some dark shadow on his mind that saddened him; it seemed as if a vague memory of terrible days hung like a cloud over his thought, but it was all indefinite, perhaps the last grim and ragged edge of the melancholy wrack that had swelled over his life and the bygone years. He shivered and tried to rouse himself and drive away

317

the sense of dread and shame that seemed so real and so awful, and yet he could not grasp it. But the torpor of sleep, the burden of the work that he had ended a few hours before, still weighed down his limb and bound his thoughts. He could scarcely believe that he had been busy at his desk a little while ago, and that just before the winter day closed it and the rain began to fall he had laid down the pen with a sigh of relief, and had slept in his chair. It was rather as if he had slumbered deeply through a long and weary night, as if an awful vision of flame and darkness and the worm that dieth not had come to him sleeping. But he would dwell no more on the darkness; he went back to the early days in London when he had said farewell to the hills and to the water pools, and had set to work in this little room in the dingy street.

How he had toiled and labored at the desk before him! He had put away the old wild hopes of the masterpiece and executed in a fury of inspiration, wrought out in one white heat of creative joy; it was enough if by dint of long perseverance and single-ness of desire he could at last, in pain and agony and despair, after failure and disappointment and effort constantly renewed, fashion something of which he need not be ashamed. He had put himself to school again, and had, with what patience he could command, ground his teeth into the rudiments, resolved that at last he would test out the heart of the mystery. They were good nights to remember, these; he was glad to think of the little ugly room, with its silly wall-paper and its "bird's-eye" furniture, lighted up, while he sat at the bureau and wrote on into the cold stillness of the London morning, when the flickering lamplight and the daystar shone together. It was an interminable labor, and he had always known it to be as hopeless as alchemy. The gold, the great and glowing masterpiece, would never shine amongst the dead ashes and smoking efforts of the crucible, but in the course of the life, in the interval between the failures, he might possibly discover curious things.

These were the good nights that he could look back on without any fear or shame, when he had been happy and content on a diet of bread and tea and tobacco, and could hear of some imbecility passing into its hundredth thousand, and laugh cheerfully—if only that last page had been imagined aright, if the phrases noted in the still hours rang out their music when he read them in the morning. He remembered the drolleries and fantasies that the worthy Miss Deacon used to write to him, and how he had grinned at her words of reproof, admonition, and advice. She had once instigated Dolly *fils* to pay him a visit, and that young prop of respectability had talked about the extraordinary running of Bolter at the Scurragh meeting in Ireland; and then, glancing at Lucian's books, had inquired whether any of them had "warm bits." He had been kind though patronizing, and seemed to have moved freely in the most brilliant society of Stoke Newington. He had not been able to give any information as to the present condition of Edgar Allan Poe's old school. It appeared eventually that his report at home had not been a very favorable one, for no invitation to high tea had followed, as Miss Deacon had hoped. The Dollys knew many nice people, who were well off, and Lucian's cousin, as she afterwards said, had done *her* best to introduce him to the *beau monde* of those northern suburbs.

But after the visit of the young Dolly, with what joy he had returned to the treasures which he had concealed from profane eyes. He had looked out and seen his visitor on board the tram at the street corner, and he laughed out loud, and locked his door. There had been moments when he was lonely, and wished to hear again the sound of friendly speech, but, after such an irruption of suburban futility, it was a keen delight, to feel that he was secure on his tower, that he could absorb himself in his wonderful task as safe and silent as if he were in mid-desert.

But there was one period that he dared not revive; he could no bear to think of those weeks of desolation and terror in the winter after his coming to London. His mind was sluggish, and he could not quite remember how many years had passed since that dismal experience; it sounded all an old story, but yet it was still vivid, a flaming scroll of terror from which he turned his eyes away. One awful scene glowed into his memory, and he could not shut out the sight of an orgy, of dusky figures whirling in a ring, of lurid naphtha flares blazing in the darkness, of great glittering lamps, like infernal thuribles, very slowly swaying in a violent blast of air. And there was something else, something which he could not remember, but it filled him with terror, but it slunk in the dark places of his soul, as a wild beast crouches in the depths of a cave.

Again, and without reason, he began to image to himself that old moldering house in the field. With what a loud incessant noise the wind must be clamoring about on this fearful night, how the great elm swayed and cried in the storm, and the rain dashed and pattered on the windows, and dripped on the sodden earth from the shaking shrubs beside the door. He moved uneasily on his chair, and struggled to put the picture out of his thoughts; but in spite of himself he saw the stained uneven walls, that ugly blot of mildew above the window, and perhaps a feeble gleam of light filtered through the blind, and some one, unhappy above all and for ever lost, sat within the dismal room. Or rather, every window was black, without a glimmer of hope, and he who was shut in thick darkness heard the wind and the rain, and the noise of the elm-tree moaning and beating and weeping on the walls.

For all his effort the impression would not leave him, and as he sat before his desk looking into the vague darkness he could almost see that chamber which he had so often imagined; the low white-washed ceiling held up by a heavy beam, the smears of smoke and long usage, the cracks and fissures of the plaster. Old furniture, shabby, deplorable, battered, stood about the room; there was a horsehair sofa worn and tottering, and a dismal paper, patterned in a livid red, blackened and moldered near the floor, and peeled off and hung in strips from the dank walls. And there was that odor of decay, of the rank soil steaming, of rotting wood, a vapor that choked the breath and made the heart full of fear and heaviness.

Lucian again shivered with a thrill of dread; he was afraid that he had overworked himself and that he was suffering from the first symptoms of grave illness. His mind dwelt on confused and terrible recollections, and with a mad ingenuity gave form and substance to phantoms; and even now he drew a long breath, almost imagining that the air in his room was heavy and noisome, that it entered his nostrils with some taint of the crypt. And his body was still languid, and though he made a half motion to rise he could not find enough energy for the effort, and he sank again into the chair. At all events, he would think no more of that sad house in the field; he would return to those long struggles with letters, to the happy nights when he had gained victories.

He remembered something of his escape from the desolation and the worse than desolation that had obsessed him during that first winter in London. He had gone free one bleak morning in February, and after those dreary terrible weeks the desk and the heap and litter of papers had once more engulfed and absorbed him. And in the succeeding summer, of a night when he lay awake and listened to the birds, shining images came wantonly to him. For an hour, while the dawn brightened, he had felt the presence of an age, the resurrection of the life that the green fields had hidden, and his heart stirred for joy when he knew that the held and possessed all the loveliness that had so long moldered. He could scarcely fall asleep for eager and leaping thoughts, and as soon as his breakfast was over he went out and bought paper and pens of a certain celestial stationer in Notting Hill. The street was not changed as he passed to and fro on his errand. The rattling wagons jostled by at intervals, a rare hansom came spinning down from London, there sounded the same hum and jangle of the gliding trams. The languid life of the pavement was unaltered; a few people, un-classed, without salience or possible description, lounged and walked from east to west, and from west to east, or slowly dropped into the byways to wander in the black waste to the north, or perhaps go astray in the systems that stretched towards the river. He glanced down these byroads as he passed, and was astonished, as always, at their mysterious and desert aspect. Some were utterly empty; lines of neat, appalling residences, trim and garnished as if for occupation, edging the white glaring road; and not a soul was abroad, and not a sound broke their stillness. It was a picture of the desolation of midnight lighted up, but empty and waste as the most profound and solemn hours before the day. Other of these byroads, of older settlement, were furnished with more important houses, standing far back from the pavement, each in a little wood of greenery, and thus one might look down as through a forest vista, and see a way smooth and guarded with low walls and yet intrude, and all a leafy silence. Here and there in some of these echoing roads a figure seemed laxily advancing in the distance, hesitating and delaying, as if lost in the labyrinth. It was difficult to say which were the more dismal, these deserted streets that wandered away to right and left, or the great main thoroughfare with its narcotic and shadowy life. For the latter appeared vast, interminable, gray, and those who traveled by it were scarcely real, the bodies of the living, but rather the uncertain and misty shapes that come and go across the desert in an Eastern tale, when men look up from the sand and see a caravan pass them, all in silence, without a cry or a greeting. So they passed and repassed each other on those pavements, appearing and vanishing, each intent on his own secret, and wrapped in obscurity. One might have sworn that not a man saw his neighbor who met him or jostled him, that here every one was a phantom for the other, though the lines of their paths crossed and recrossed, and their eyes stared like the eyes of live men. When two went by together, they mumbled and cast distrustful glances behind them as though afraid all the world was an enemy, and the pattering of feet was like the noise of a shower of rain. Curious appearances and simulations of life gathered at points in the road, for at intervals the villas ended and shops began in a dismal row, and looked so hopeless that one wondered who could buy. There were women fluttering uneasily about the greengrocers, and shabby things in rusty black touched and retouched the red lumps that an unshaven butcher offered, and already in the corner public there was a confused noise, with a tossing of voices that rose and fell like a Jewish chant, with the senseless stir of marionettes jerked into an imitation of gaiety. Then, in crossing a side street that seemed like gray mid-winter in stone, he trespassed from one world to another, for an old decayed house amidst its garden held the opposite corner. The laurels had grown into black skeletons, patched with green drift, the ilex gloomed over the porch, the deodar had blighted the flower-beds. Dark ivies swarmed over an elm-tree, and a brown clustering fungus sprang in gross masses on the lawn, showing where the roots of dead trees moldered. The blue verandah, the blue balcony over the door, had faced to gray, and the stucco was blotched with ugly marks of weather, and a dank smell of decay, that vapor of black rotten earth in old town gardens, hung heavy about the gates. And then a row of musty villas had pushed out in shops to the pavement, and the things in faded black buzzed and stirred about the limp cabbages, and the red lumps of meat.

It was the same terrible street, whose pavements he had trodden so often, where sunshine seemed but a gaudy light, where the fume of burning bricks always drifted. On black winter nights he had seen the sparse lights glimmering through the rain and drawing close together, as the dreary road vanished in long perspective. Perhaps this was its most appropriate moment, when nothing of its smug villas and skeleton shops remained but the bright patches of their windows, when the old house amongst its moldering shrubs was but a dark cloud, and the streets to the north and south seemed like starry wastes, beyond them the blackness of infinity. Always in the daylight it had been to him abhorred and abominable, and its gray houses and purlieus had been fungus-like sproutings, an efflorescence of horrible decay.

But on that bright morning neither the dreadful street nor those who moved about it appalled him. He returned joyously to his den, and reverently laid out the paper on his desk. The world about him was but a gray shadow hovering on a shining wall; its noises were faint as the rustling of trees in a distant wood. The lovely and exquisite forms of those who served the Amber Venus were his distinct, clear, and manifest visions, and for one amongst them who came to him in a fire of bronze hair his heart stirred with the adoration of love. She it was who stood forth from all the rest and fell down prostrate before the radiant form in amber, drawing out her pins in curious gold, her glowing brooches of enamel, and pouring from a silver box all her treasures of jewels and precious stones, chrysoberyl and sardonyx, opal and diamond, topaz and pearl. And then she stripped from her body her precious robes and stood before the goddess in the glowing mist of her hair, praying that to her who had given all and came naked to the shrine, love might be given, and the grace of Venus. And when at last, after strange adventures, her prayer was granted, then when the sweet light came from the sea, and her lover turned at dawn to that bronze glory, he saw beside him a little statuette of amber. And in the shrine, far in Britain where the black rains stained the marble, they found the splendid and sumptuous statue of the Golden Venus, the last fine robe of silk that the lady had dedicated falling from her fingers, and the jewels lying at her feet. And her face was like the lady's face when the sun had brightened it on that day of her devotion.

The bronze mist glimmered before Lucian's eyes; he felt as though the soft floating hair touched his forehead and his lips and his hands. The fume of burning bricks, the reek of cabbage water, never reached his nostrils that were filled with the perfume of rare unguents, with the breath of the violet sea in Italy. His pleasure was an inebriation, an ecstasy of joy that destroyed all the vile Hottentot kraals and mud avenues as with one white lightning flash, and through the hours of that day he sat enthralled, not contriving a story with patient art, but rapt into another time, and entranced by the urgent gleam in the lady's eyes.

The little tale of *The Amber Statuette* had at last issued from a humble office in the spring after his father's death. The author was utterly unknown; the author's Murray was a wholesale stationer and printer in process of development, so that Lucian was astonished when the book became a moderate success. The reviewers had been sadly irritated, and even now he recollected with cheerfulness an article in an influential daily paper, an article pleasantly headed: "Where are the disinfectants?"

And then—but all the months afterwards seemed doubtful, there were only broken revelations of the laborious hours renewed, and the white nights when he had seen the moonlight fade and the gaslight grow wan at the approach of dawn.

He listened. Surely that was the sound of rain falling on sodden ground, the heavy sound of great swollen drops driven down from wet leaves by the gust of wind, and then again the strain of boughs sang above the tumult of the air; there was a doleful noise as if the storm shook the masts of a ship. He had only to get up and look out of the window and he would see the treeless empty street, and the rain starring the puddles under the gas-lamp, but he would wait a little while.

He tried to think why, in spite of all his resolutions, a dark horror seemed to brood more and more over all his mind. How often he had sat and worked on just such nights as this, contented if the words were in accord though the wind might wail, though the air were black with rain. Even about the little book that he had made there seemed some taint, some shuddering memory that came to him across the gulf of forgetfulness. Somehow the remembrance of the offering to Venus, of the phrases that he had so lovingly invented, brought back again the dusky figures that danced in the orgy, beneath the brassy glittering lamps; and again the naphtha flares showed the way to the sad house in the fields, and the red glare lit up the mildewed walls and the black hopeless windows. He gasped for breath, he seemed to inhale a heavy air that reeked of decay and rottenness, and the odor of the clay was in his nostrils.

That unknown cloud that had darkened his thoughts grew blacker and engulfed him, despair was heavy upon him, his heart fainted with a horrible dread. In a moment, it seemed, a veil would be drawn away and certain awful things would appear.

He strove to rise from his chair, to cry out, but he could not. Deep, deep the darkness closed upon him, and the storm sounded far away. The Roman fort surged up, terrific, and he saw the writhing boughs in a ring, and behind them a glow and heat of fire. There were hideous shapes that swarmed in the thicket of the oaks; they called and beckoned to him, and rose into the air, into the flame that was smitten from heaven about the walls. And amongst them was the form of the beloved, but jets of flame issued from her breasts, and beside her was a horrible old woman, naked; and they, too, summoned him to mount the hill.

He heard Dr. Burrows whispering of the strange things that had been found in old Mrs. Gibbon's cottage, obscene figures, and unknown contrivances. She was a witch, he said, and the mistress of witches.

He fought against the nightmare, against the illusion that bewildered him. All his life, he thought, had been an evil dream, and for the common world he had fashioned an unreal red garment, that burned in his eyes. Truth and the dream were so mingled that now he could not divide one from the other. He had let Annie drink his soul beneath the hill, on the night when the moonfire shone, but he had not surely seen her exalted in the flame, the Queen of the Sabbath. Dimly he remembered Dr. Burrows coming to see him in London, but had he not imagined all the rest?

Again he found himself in the dusky lane, and Annie floated down to him from the moon above the hill. His head sank upon her breast again, but, alas, it was aflame. And he looked down, and he saw that his own flesh was aflame, and he knew that the fire could never be quenched.

There was a heavy weight upon his head, his feet were nailed to the floor, and his arms bound tight beside him. He seemed to himself to rage and struggle with the strength of a madman; but his hand only stirred and quivered a little as it lay upon the desk.

Again he was astray in the mist; wandering through the waste avenues of a city that had been ruined from ages. It had been splendid as Rome, terrible as Babylon, and forever the darkness had covered it, and it lay desolate forever in the ac-cursed plain. And far and far the gray passages stretched into the night, into the icy fields, into the place of eternal gloom.

Ring within ring the awful temple closed around him; unending circles of vast stones, circle within circle, and every circle less throughout all ages. In the center was the sanctuary of the infernal rite, and he was borne thither as in the eddies of a whirlpool, to consummate his ruin, to celebrate the wedding of the Sabbath. He flung up his arms and beat the air, resisting with all his strength, with muscles that could throw down mountains; and this time his little finger stirred for an instant, and his foot twitched upon the floor.

Then suddenly a flaring street shone before him. There was darkness round about him, but it flamed with hissing jets of light and naphtha fires, and great glittering lamps swayed very slowly in a violent blast of air. A horrible music, and the exultation of discordant voices, swelled in his ears, and he saw an uncertain tossing crowd of dusky figures that circled and leapt before him. There was a noise like the chant of the lost, and then there appeared in the midst of the orgy, beneath a red flame, the figure of a woman. Her bronze hair and flushed cheeks were illuminate, and an argent light shone from her eyes, and with a smile that froze his heart her lips opened to speak to him. The tossing crowd faded away, falling into a gulf of darkness, and then she drew out from her hair pins of curious gold, and glowing brooches in enamel, and poured out jewels before him from a silver box, and then she stripped form her body her precious robes, and stood in the glowing mist of her hair, and held out her arms to him. But he raised his eyes and saw the mould and decay gaining on the walls of a dismal room, and a gloomy paper was dropping to the rotting floor. A vapor of the grave entered his nostrils, and he cried out with a loud scream; but there was only an indistinct guttural murmur in his throat.

And presently the woman fled away from him, and he pursued her. She fled away before him through midnight country, and he followed after her, chasing her from thicket to thicket, from valley to valley. And at last he captured her and won her with horrible caresses, and they went up to celebrate and make the marriage of the Sabbath. They were within the matted thicket, and they writhed in the flames, insatiable, forever. They were tortured, and tortured one another, in the sight of thousands who gathered thick about them; and their desire rose up like a black smoke.

Without, the storm swelled to the roaring of an awful sea, the wind grew to a shrill long scream, the elm-tree was riven and split with the crash of a thunderclap. To Lucian the tumult and the shock came as a gentle murmur, as if a brake stirred before a sudden breeze in summer. And then a vast silence overwhelmed him.

A few minutes later there was a shuffling of feet in the passage, and the door was softly opened. A woman came in, holding a light, and she peered curiously at the figure sitting quite still in the chair before the desk. The woman was half dressed, and she had let her splendid bronze hair flow down, her cheeks were flushed, and as she advanced into the shabby room, the lamp she carried cast quaking shadows on the moldering paper, patched with marks of rising damp, and hanging in strips from the wet, dripping wall. The blind had not been drawn, but no light or glimmer of light filtered through the window, for a great straggling box tree that beat the rain upon the panes shut out even the night. The woman came softly, and as she bent down over Lucian an argent gleam shone from her brown eyes, and the little curls upon her neck were like golden work upon marble. She put her hand to his heart, and looked up, and beckoned to some one who was waiting by the door.

"Come in, Joe," she said. "It's just as I thought it would be: 'Death by misadventure'"; and she held up a little empty bottle of dark blue glass that was standing on the desk. "He would take it, and I always knew he would take a drop too much one of these days."

"What's all those papers that he's got there?"

"Didn't I tell you? It was crool to see him. He got it into 'is 'ead he could write a book; he's been at it for the last six months. Look 'ere."

She spread the neat pile of manuscript broadcast over the desk, and took a sheet at haphazard. It was all covered with illegible hopeless scribblings; only here and there it was possible to recognize a word.

"Why, nobody could read it, if they wanted to."

"It's all like that. He thought it was beautiful. I used to 'ear him jabbering to himself about it, dreadful nonsense it was he used to talk. I did my best to tongue him out of it, but it wasn't any good."

"He must have been a bit dotty. He's left you everything."

"Yes."

"You'll have to see about the funeral."

"There'll be the inquest and all that first."

"You've got evidence to show he took the stuff."

"Yes, to be sure I have. The doctor told him he would be certain to do for himself, and he was found two or three times quite silly in the streets. They had to drag him away from a house in Halden Road. He was carrying on dreadful, shaking at the gaite, and calling out it was 'is 'ome and they wouldn't let him in. I heard Dr. Manning myself tell 'im in this very room that he'd kill 'imself one of these days. Joe! Aren't you ashamed of yourself. I declare you're quite rude, and it's almost Sunday too. Bring the light over here, can't you?"

The man took up the blazing paraffin lamp, and set it on the desk, beside the scattered heap of that terrible manuscript. The flaring light shone through the dead eyes into the dying brain, and there was a glow within, as if great furnace doors were opened.

The Angels of Mons

Arthur Machen

Introduction

I have been asked to write an introduction to the story of "The Bowmen," on its publication in book form together with three other tales of similar fashion. And I hesitate. This affair of "The Bowmen" has been such an odd one from first to last, so many queer complications have entered into it, there have been so many and so divers currents and crosscurrents of rumor and speculation concerning it, that I honestly do not know where to begin. I propose, then, to solve the difficulty by apologizing for beginning at all.

For, usually and fitly, the presence of an introduction is held to imply that there is something of consequence and importance to be introduced. If, for example, a man has made an anthology of great poetry, he may well write an introduction justifying his principle of selection, pointing out here and there, as the spirit moves him, high beauties and supreme excellencies, discoursing of the magnates and lords and princes of literature, whom he is merely serving as groom of the chamber. Introductions, that is, belong to the masterpieces and classics of the world, to the great and ancient and accepted things; and I am here introducing a short, small story of my own which appeared in *The Evening News* about ten months ago.

I appreciate the absurdity, nay, the enormity of the position in all its grossness. And my excuse for these pages must be this: that though the story itself is nothing, it has yet had such odd and unforeseen consequences and adventures that the tale of them may possess some interest. And then, again, there are certain psychological morals to be drawn from the whole matter of the tale and its sequel of rumors and discussions that are not, I think, devoid of consequence; and so to begin at the beginning.

This was in last August, to be more precise, on the last Sunday of last August. There were terrible things to be read on that hot Sunday morning between meat and mass. It was in *The Weekly Dispatch* that I saw the awful account of the retreat from Mons. I no longer recollect the details; but I have not forgotten the impression that was then on my mind, I seemed to see a furnace of torment and death and agony and terror seven times heated, and in the midst of the burning was the British Army. In the midst of the flame, consumed by it and yet aureoled in it, scattered like ashes and yet triumphant, martyred and forever glorious. So I saw our men with a shining about them, so I took these thoughts with me to church, and, I am sorry to say, was making up a story in my head while the deacon was singing the Gospel.

This was not the tale of "The Bowmen." It was the first sketch, as it were, of "The Soldiers' Rest." I only wish I had been able to write it as I conceived it. The tale as it stands is, I think, a far better piece of craft than "The Bowmen," but the tale that came to me as the blue incense floated above the Gospel Book on the desk between the tapers: that indeed was a noble story—like all the stories that never get written. I conceived the dead men coming up through the flames and in the flames, and being welcomed in the Eternal Tavern with songs and flowing cups and everlasting mirth. But every man is the child of his age, however much he may hate it; and our popular religion has long determined that jollity is wicked. As far as I can make out modern Protestantism believes that Heaven is something like Evensong in an English cathedral, the service by Stainer and the Dean preaching. For those opposed to dogma of any kind—even the mildest—I suppose it is held that a Course of Ethical Lectures will be arranged.

Well, I have long maintained that on the whole the average church, considered as a house of preaching, is a much more poisonous place than the average tavern; still, as I say, one's age masters one, and clouds and bewilders the intelligence, and the real story of "The Soldiers' Rest," with its *"sonus epulantium in aeterno convivio,"* was ruined at the moment of its birth, and it was some time later that the actual story got written. And in the meantime the plot of "The Bowmen" occurred to me. Now it has been murmured and hinted and suggested and whispered in all sorts of quarters that before I wrote the tale I had heard something. The most decorative of these legends is also the most precise: "I know for a fact that the whole thing was given him in typescript by a lady-in-waiting." This was not the case; and all vaguer reports to the effect that I had heard some rumors or hints of rumors are equally void of any trace of truth.

Again I apologize for entering so pompously into the minutiae of my bit of a story, as if it were the lost poems of Sappho; but it appears that the subject interests the public, and I comply with my instructions. I take it, then, that the origins of "The Bowmen" were composite. First of all, all ages and nations have cherished the thought that spiritual hosts may come to the help of earthly arms, that gods and heroes and saints have descended from their high immortal places to fight for their worshippers and clients. Then Kipling's story of the ghostly Indian regiment got in my head and got mixed with the medievalism that is always there; and so "The Bowmen" was written. I was heartily disappointed with it, I remember, and thought it — as I still think it—an indifferent piece of work. However, I have tried to write for these thirty-five long years, and if I have not become practiced in letters, I am at least a past master in the Lodge of Disappointment. Such as it was, "The Bowmen" appeared in *The Evening News* of September 29th, 1914.

Now the journalist does not, as a rule, dwell much on the prospect of fame; and if he be an evening journalist, his anticipations of immortality are bounded by twelve o'clock at night at the latest; and it may well be that those insects which begin to live in the morning and are dead by sunset deem themselves immortal. Having written my story, having groaned and growled over it and printed it, I certainly never thought to hear another word of it. My colleague "The Londoner" praised it warmly to my face, as his kindly fashion is; entering, very properly, a technical caveat as to the language of the battle cries of the bowmen. "Why should

English archers use French terms?" he said. I replied that the only reason was this—that a "Monseigneur" here and there struck me as picturesque; and I reminded him that, as a matter of cold historical fact, most of the archers of Agincourt were mercenaries from Gwent, my native country, who would appeal to Mihangel and to saints not known to the Saxons—Teilo, Iltyd, Dewi, Cadwaladyr Vendigeid. And I thought that that was the first and last discussion of "The Bowmen". But in a few days from its publication the editor of *The Occult Review* wrote to me. He wanted to know whether the story had any foundation in fact. I told him that it had no foundation in fact of any kind or sort; I forget whether I added that it had no foundation in rumor but I should think not, since to the best of my belief there were no rumors of heavenly interposition in existence at that time. Certainly I had heard of none. Soon afterwards the editor of *Light* wrote asking a like question, and I made him a like reply. It seemed to me that I had stifled any "Bowmen" mythos in the hour of its birth.

A month or two later, I received several requests from editors of parish magazines to reprint the story. I—or, rather, my editor—readily gave permission; and then, after another month or two, the conductor of one of these magazines wrote to me, saying that the February issue containing the story had been sold out, while there was still a great demand for it. Would I allow them to reprint "The Bowmen" as a pamphlet, and would I write a short preface giving the exact authorities for the story? I replied that they might reprint in pamphlet form with all my heart, but that I could not give my authorities, since I had none, the tale being pure invention. The priest wrote again, suggesting—to my amazement—that I must be mistaken, that the main "facts" of "The Bowmen" must be true, that my share in the matter must surely have been confined to the elaboration and decoration of a veridical history. It seemed that my light fiction had been accepted by the congregation of this particular church as the solidest of facts; and it was then that it began to dawn on me that if I had failed in the art of letters, I had succeeded, unwittingly, in the art of deceit. This happened, I should think, some time in April, and the snowball of rumor that was then set rolling has been rolling ever since, growing bigger and bigger, till it is now swollen to a monstrous size.

It was at about this period that variants of my tale began to be told as authentic histories. At first, these tales betrayed their relation to their original. In several of them the vegetarian restaurant appeared, and St. George was the chief character. In one case an officer—name and address missing—said that there was a portrait of St. George in a certain London restaurant, and that a figure, just like the portrait, appeared to him on the battlefield, and was invoked by him, with the happiest results. Another variant—this, I think, never got into print—told how dead Prussians had been found on the battlefield with arrow wounds in their bodies. This notion amused me, as I had imagined a scene, when I was thinking out the story, in which a German general was to appear before the Kaiser to explain his failure to annihilate the English.

"All-Highest," the general was to say, "it is true, it is impossible to deny it. The men were killed by arrows; the shafts were found in their bodies by the burying parties."

I rejected the idea as over-precipitous even for a mere fantasy. I was therefore entertained when I found that what I had refused as too fantastical for fantasy was accepted in certain occult circles as hard fact.

Other versions of the story appeared in which a cloud interposed between the attacking Germans and the defending British. In some examples the cloud served to conceal our men from the advancing enemy; in others, it disclosed shining shapes which frightened the horses of the pursuing German cavalry. St. George, it will he noted, has disappeared—he persisted some time longer in certain Roman Catholic variants—and there are no more bowmen, no more arrows. But so far angels are not mentioned; yet they are ready to appear, and I think that I have detected the machine which brought them into the story.

In "The Bowmen" my imagined soldier saw "a long line of shapes, with a shining about them." And Mr. A. P. Sinnett, writing in the May issue of *The Occult Review*, reporting what he had heard, states that "those who could see said they saw 'a row of shining beings' between the two armies." Now I conjecture that the word "shining" is the link between my tale and the derivative from it. In the popular view shining and benevolent supernatural beings are angels, and so, I believe, the Bowmen of my story have become "the Angels of Mons." In this shape they have been received with respect and credence everywhere, or almost everywhere.

And here, I conjecture, we have the key to the large popularity of the delusion—as I think it. We have long ceased in England to take much interest in saints, and in the recent revival of the *cultus* of St. George, the saint is little more than a patriotic figurehead. And the appeal to the saints to succor us is certainly not a common English practice; it is held Popish by most of our countrymen. But angels, with certain reservations, have retained their popularity, and so, when it was settled that the English army in its dire peril was delivered by angelic aid, the way was clear for general belief, and for the enthusiasms of the religion of the man in the street. And so soon as the legend got the title "The Angels of Mons" it became impossible to avoid it. It permeated the Press: it would not be neglected; it appeared in the most unlikely quarters—in *Truth* and *Town Topics*, *The New Church Weekly* (Swedenborgian) and *John Bull*. The editor of *The Church Times* has exercised a wise reserve: he awaits that evidence which so far is lacking; but in one issue of the paper I noted that the story furnished a text for a sermon, the subject of a letter, and the matter for an article. People send me cuttings from provincial papers containing hot controversy as to the exact nature of the appearances; the "Office Window" of *The Daily Chronicle* suggests scientific explanations of the hallucination; the *Pall Mall* in a note about St. James says he is of the brotherhood of the Bowmen of Mons—this reversion to the bowmen from the angels being possibly due to the strong statements that I have made on the matter. The pulpits both of the Church and of Non-conformity have been busy: Bishop Welldon, Dean Hensley Henson (a disbeliever), Bishop Taylor Smith (the Chaplain-General), and many other clergy have occupied themselves with the matter. Dr. Horton preached about the "angels" at Manchester; Sir Joseph Compton Rickett (President of the National Federation of Free Church Councils) stated that the soldiers at the front had seen visions and dreamed dreams, and had given testimony of powers and principalities fighting for them or against them. Letters come from all the ends of the earth to the Editor of *The Evening News* with theories, beliefs, explanations, suggestions. It is all somewhat wonderful; one can say that the whole affair is a psychological phenomenon of considerable interest, fairly comparable with the great Russian delusion of last August and September.

Now it is possible that some persons, judging by the tone of these remarks of mine, may gather the impression that I am a profound disbeliever in the possibility of any intervention of the super-physical order in the affairs of the physical order. They will be mistaken if they make this inference; they will be mistaken if they suppose that I think miracles in Judea credible but miracles in France or Flanders incredible. I hold no such absurdities. But I confess, very frankly, that I credit none of the

"Angels of Mons" legends, partly because I see, or think I see, their derivation from my own idle fiction, but chiefly because I have, so far, not received one jot or tittle of evidence that should dispose me to belief. It is idle, indeed, and foolish enough for a man to say: "I am sure that story is a lie, because the supernatural element enters into it;" here, indeed, we have the maggot writhing in the midst of corrupted offal denying the existence of the sun. But if this fellow be a fool—as he is— equally foolish is he who says, "If the tale has anything of the supernatural it is true, and the less evidence the better;" and I am afraid this tends to be the attitude of many who call themselves occultists. I hope that I shall never get to that frame of mind. So I say, not that super-normal interventions are impossible, not that they have not happened during this war—I know nothing as to that point, one way or the other—but that there is not one atom of evidence (so far) to support the current stories of the angels of Mons. For, be it remarked, these stories are specific stories. They rest on the second, third, fourth, fifth hand stories told by "a soldier," by "an officer," by "a Catholic correspondent," by "a nurse," by any number of anonymous people. Indeed, names have been mentioned. A lady's name has been drawn, most unwarrantably as it appears to me, into the discussion, and I have no doubt that this lady has been subject to a good deal of pestering and annoyance. She has written to the Editor of *The Evening News* denying all knowledge of the supposed miracle. The Psychical Research Society's expert confesses that no real evidence has been proffered to her Society on the matter. And then, to my amazement, she accepts as fact the proposition that some men on the battlefield have been "hallucinated," and proceeds to give the theory of sensory hallucination. She forgets that, by her own showing, there is no reason to suppose that anybody has been hallucinated at all. Someone (unknown) has met a nurse (unnamed) who has talked to a soldier (anonymous) who has seen angels. But *that* is not evidence; and not even Sam Weller at his gayest would have dared to offer it as such in the Court of Common Pleas. So far, then, nothing remotely approaching proof has been offered as to any supernatural intervention during the Retreat from Mons. Proof may come; if so, it will be interesting and more than interesting.

But, taking the affair as it stands at present, how is it that a nation plunged in materialism of the grossest kind has accepted idle rumors and gossip of the supernatural as certain truth? The answer is contained in the question: it is precisely because our whole atmosphere is materialist that we are ready to credit anything—save the truth. Separate a man from good drink, he will swallow methylated spirit with joy. Man is created to be inebriated; to be "nobly wild, not mad." Suffer the Cocoa Prophets and their company to seduce him in body and spirit, and he will get himself stuff that will make him ignobly wild and mad indeed. It took hard, practical men of affairs, business men, advanced thinkers, Freethinkers, to believe in Madame Blavatsky and Mahatmas and the famous

347

message from the Golden Shore: "Judge's plan is right; follow him and *stick*."

And the main responsibility for this dismal state of affairs undoubtedly lies on the shoulders of the majority of the clergy of the Church of England. Christianity, as Mr. W. L. Courtney has so admirably pointed out, is a great Mystery Religion; it is *the* Mystery Religion. Its priests are called to an awful and tremendous hierurgy; its pontiffs are to be the pathfinders, the bridge-makers between the world of sense and the world of spirit. And, in fact, they pass their time in preaching, not the eternal mysteries, but a two-penny morality, in changing the Wine of Angels and the Bread of Heaven into ginger beer and mixed biscuits: a sorry transubstantiation, a sad alchemy, as it seems to me.

The Bowmen

It was during the Retreat of the Eighty Thousand, and the authority of the Censorship is sufficient excuse for not being more explicit. But it was on the most awful day of that awful time, on the day when ruin and disaster came so near that their shadow fell over London far away; and, without any certain news, the hearts of men failed within them and grew faint; as if the agony of the army in the battlefield had entered into their souls.

On this dreadful day, then, when three hundred thousand men in arms with all their artillery swelled like a flood against the little English company, there was one point above all other points in our battle line that was for a time in awful danger, not merely of defeat, but of utter annihilation. With the permission of the Censorship and of the military expert, this corner may, perhaps, be described as a salient, and if this angle were crushed and broken, then the English force as a whole would be shattered, the Allied left would be turned, and Sedan would inevitably follow.

All the morning the German guns had thundered and shrieked against this corner, and against the thousand or so of men who held it. The men joked at the shells, and found funny names for them, and had bets about them, and greeted them with scraps of music-hall songs. But the shells came on and burst, and tore good Englishmen limb from limb, and tore brother from brother, and as the heat of the day increased so did the fury of that terrific cannonade. There was no help, it seemed. The English artillery was good, but there was not nearly enough of it; it was being steadily battered into scrap iron.

There comes a moment in a storm at sea when people say to one another, "It is at its worst; it can blow no harder," and then there is a blast ten times more fierce than any before it. So it was in these British trenches.

There were no stouter hearts in the whole world than the hearts of these men; but even they were appalled as this seven-times-heated hell of the German cannonade fell upon them and over-whelmed them and destroyed them. And at this very moment they saw from their trenches that a tremendous host was moving against their lines. Five hundred of the thousand remained, and as far as they could see the German infantry was pressing on against them, column upon column, a grey world of men, ten thousand of them, as it appeared afterwards.

There was no hope at all. They shook hands, some of them. One man improvised a new version of the battle song, "Goodbye, goodbye to Tip-perary," ending with "And we shan't get there". And they all went on firing steadily. The officers pointed out that such an opportunity for high-class, fancy shooting might never occur again; the Germans dropped line after line; the Tipperary humorist asked, "What price Sidney Street?" And the few machine guns did their best. But every-body knew it was of no use. The dead grey bodies lay in companies and battalions, as others came on and on and on, and they swarmed and stirred and advanced from beyond and beyond.

"World without end. Amen," said one of the British soldiers with some irrelevance as he took aim and fired. And then he remembered—he says he cannot think why or wherefore—a queer vegetarian restaurant in London where he had once or twice eaten eccentric dishes of cutlets made of lentils and nuts that pretended to be steak. On all the plates in this restaurant there was printed a figure of St. George in blue, with the motto, *Adsit Anglis Sanctus Geogius*—May St. George be a present help to the English. This soldier happened to know Latin and other useless things, and now, as he fired at his man in the grey advancing mass— 300 yards away—he uttered the pious vegetarian motto. He went on firing to the end, and at last Bill on his right had to clout him cheerfully over the head to make him stop, pointing out as he did so that the King's ammunition cost money and was not lightly to be wasted in drilling funny patterns into dead Germans.

For as the Latin scholar uttered his invocation he felt something between a shudder and an electric shock pass through his body. The roar of the battle died down in his ears to a gentle murmur; instead of it, he says, he heard a great voice and a shout louder than a thunder-peal crying, "Array, array, array!"

His heart grew hot as a burning coal, it grew cold as ice within him, as it seemed to him that a tumult of voices answered to his summons. He heard, or seemed to hear, thousands shouting: "St. George! St. George!"

"Ha! messire; ha! Sweet Saint, grant us good deliverance!"

"St. George for merry England!"

"Harow! Harow! Monseigneur St. George, succor us."

"Ha! St. George! Ha! St. George! A long bow and a strong bow."

"Heaven's Knight, aid us!"

And as the soldier heard these voices he saw before him, beyond the trench, a long line of shapes, with a shining about them. They were like men who drew the bow, and with another shout their cloud of arrows flew singing and tingling through the air towards the German hosts.

The other men in the trench were firing all the while. They had no hope; but they aimed just as if they had been shooting at Bisley. Suddenly one of them lifted up his voice in the plainest English, "Gawd help us!" he bellowed to the man next to him, "but we're blooming marvels! Look at those grey—gentlemen, look at them! D'ye see them? They're not going down in dozens, nor in 'undreds; it's thousands, it is. Look! Look! There's a regiment gone while I'm talking to ye."

"Shut it!" the other soldier bellowed, taking aim, "what are ye gassing about!"

But he gulped with astonishment even as he spoke, for, indeed, the grey men were falling by the thousands. The English could hear the guttural scream of the German officers, the crackle of their revolvers as they shot the reluctant; and still line after line crashed to the earth.

All the while the Latin-bred soldier heard the cry: "Harow! Harow! Monseigneur, dear saint, quick to our aid! St. George help us!"

"High Chevalier, defend us!"

The singing arrows fled so swift and thick that they darkened the air; the heathen horde melted from before them.

"More machine guns!" Bill yelled to Tom.

"Don't hear them," Tom yelled back. "But, thank God, anyway; they've got it in the neck."

In fact, there were ten thousand dead German soldiers left before that salient of the English army, and consequently there was no Sedan. In Germany, a country ruled by scientific principles, the Great General Staff decided that the contemptible English must have employed shells containing an unknown gas of a poisonous nature, as no wounds were discernible on the bodies of the dead German soldiers. But the man who knew what nuts tasted like when they called themselves steak knew also that St. George had brought his Agincourt Bowmen to help the English.

The Soldiers' Rest

T he soldier with the ugly wound in the head opened his eyes at last, and looked about him with an air of pleasant satisfaction.

He still felt drowsy and dazed with some fierce experience through which he had passed, but so far he could not recollect much about it. But—an agreeable glow began to steal about his heart—such a glow as comes to people who have been in a tight place and have come through it better than they had expected. In its mildest form this set of emotions may be observed in passengers who have crossed the Channel on a windy day without being sick. They triumph a little internally, and are suffused with vague, kindly feelings.

The wounded soldier was somewhat of this disposition as he opened his eyes, pulled himself together, and looked about him. He felt a sense of delicious ease and repose in bones that had been racked and weary, and deep in the heart that had so lately been tormented there was an assurance of comfort—of the battle won. The thundering, roaring waves were passed; he had entered into the haven of calm waters. After fatigues and terrors that as yet he could not recollect he seemed now to be resting in the easiest of all easy chairs in a dim, low room.

In the hearth there was a glint of fire and a blue, sweet-scented puff of wood smoke; a great black oak beam roughly hewn crossed the ceiling. Through the leaded panes of the windows he saw a rich glow of sunlight, green lawns, and against the deepest and most radiant of all blue skies the wonderful far-lifted towers of a vast, Gothic cathedral—mystic, rich with imagery.

"Good Lord!" he murmured to himself. "I didn't know they had such places in France. It's just like Wells. And it might be the other day when I was going past the Swan, just as it might be past that window, and asked the ostler what time it was, and he says, 'What time? Why, summertime'; and there outside it looks like summer that would last forever. If this was an inn they ought to call it *The Soldiers' Rest*."

He dozed off again, and when he opened his eyes once more a kindly looking man in some sort of black robe was standing by him.

"It's all right now, isn't it?" he said, speaking in good English.

"Yes, thank you, sir, as right as can be. I hope to be back again soon."

"Well, well; but how did you come here? Where did you get that?" He pointed to the wound on the soldier's forehead.

The soldier put his hand up to his brow and looked dazed and puzzled.

"Well, sir," he said at last, "it was like this, to begin at the beginning. You know how we came over in August, and there we were in the thick of it, as you might say, in a day or two. An awful time it was, and I don't know how I got through it alive. My best friend was killed dead beside me as we lay in the trenches. By Cambrai, I think it was.

"Then things got a little quieter for a bit, and I

was quartered in a village for the best part of a week. She was a very nice lady where I was, and she treated me proper with the best of everything. Her husband he was fighting; but she had the nicest little boy I ever knew, a little fellow of five, or six it might be, and we got on splendid. The amount of their lingo that kid taught me—'We, we' and 'Bong swot' and 'Commong voo potty we' and all—and I taught him English. You should have heard that nipper say "Arf a mo', old un!' It was a treat.

"Then one day we got surprised. There was about a dozen of us in the village, and two or three hundred Germans came down on us early one morning. They got us; no help for it. Before we could shoot.

"Well there we were. They tied our hands behind our backs, and smacked our faces and kicked us a bit, and we were lined up opposite the house where I'd been staying.

"And then that poor little chap broke away from his mother, and he run out and saw one of the Boshes, as we call them, fetch me one over the jaw with his clenched fist. Oh dear! Oh dear! He might have done it a dozen times if only that little child hadn't seen him.

"He had a poor bit of a toy I'd bought him at the village shop; a toy gun it was. And out he came running, as I say, crying out something in French like 'Bad man! Bad man! Don't hurt my Anglish or I shoot you'; and he pointed that gun at the German soldier. The German, he took his bayonet, and he drove it right through the poor little chap's throat."

The soldier's face worked and twitched and

twisted itself into a sort of grin, and he sat grinding his teeth and staring at the man in the black robe. He was silent for a little. And then he found his voice, and the oaths rolled terrible, thundering from him, as he cursed that murderous wretch, and bade him go down and burn forever in hell. And the tears were raining down his face, and they choked him at last.

"I beg your pardon, sir, I'm sure," he said, "especially you being a minister of some kind, I suppose; but I can't help it, he was such a dear little man."

The man in black murmured something to himself: *"Pretiosa in conspectu Domini mors innocentium ejus"*—Dear in the sight of the Lord is the death of His innocents. Then he put a hand very gently on the soldier's shoulder.

"Never mind," said he; "I've seen some service in my time, myself. But what about that wound?"

"Oh, that; that's nothing. But I'll tell you how I got it. It was just like this. The Germans had us fair, as I tell you, and they shut us up in a barn in the village; just flung us on the ground and left us to starve seemingly. They barred up the big door of the barn, and put a sentry there, and thought we were all right.

"There were sort of slits like very narrow windows in one of the walls, and on the second day it was, I was looking out of these slits down the street, and I could see those German devils were up to mischief. They were planting their machine-guns everywhere handy where an ordinary man coming up the street would never see them, but I see them, and I see the infantry lining up behind the garden walls. Then I had a sort of a notion of what was coming; and presently, sure enough, I could hear some of our chaps singing 'Hullo, hullo, hullo!' in the distance; and I says to myself, 'Not this time.'

"So I looked about me, and I found a hole under the wall; a kind of a drain I should think it was, and I found I could just squeeze through. And I got out and crept, round, and away I goes running down the street, yelling for all I was worth, just as our chaps were getting round the corner at the bottom. 'Bang, bang!' went the guns, behind me and in front of me, and on each side of me, and then—bash! Something hit me on the head and over I went; and I don't remember anything more till I woke up here just now."

The soldier lay back in his chair and closed his eyes for a moment. When he opened them he saw that there were other people in the room besides the minister in the black robes. One was a man in a big black cloak. He had a grim old face and a great beaky nose. He shook the soldier by the hand.

"By God! sir," he said, "you're a credit to the British Army; you're a damned fine soldier and a good man, and, by God! I'm proud to shake hands with you."

And then someone came out of the shadow, someone in queer clothes such as the soldier had seen worn by the heralds when he had been on duty at the opening of Parliament by the King.

"Now, by *Corpus Domini*," this man said, "of all knights ye be noblest and gentlest, and ye be of fairest report, and now ye be a brother of the noblest brotherhood that ever was since this world's beginning, since ye have yielded dear life for your friends' sake."

The soldier did not understand what the man was saying to him. There were others, too, in strange dresses, who came and spoke to him. Some spoke in what sounded like French. He could not make it out; but he knew that they all spoke kindly and praised him.

"What does it all mean?" he said to the minister. "What are they talking about? They don't think I'd let down my pals?"

"Drink this," said the minister, and he handed the soldier a great silver cup, brimming with wine.

The soldier took a deep draught, and in that moment all his sorrows passed from him.

"What is it?" he asked?

"*Vin nouveau du Royaume,*" said the minister. "New Wine of the Kingdom, you call it." And then he bent down and murmured in the soldier's ear.

"What," said the wounded man, "the place they used to tell us about in Sunday school? With such drink and such joy—"

His voice was hushed. For as he looked at the minister the fashion of his vesture was changed. The black robe seemed to melt away from him. He was all in amour, if amour be made of starlight, of the rose of dawn, and of sunset fires; and he lifted up a great sword of flame.

Full in the midst, his Cross of Red Triumphant, Michael brandished and trampled the Apostate's pride.

The Monstrance

*Then it fell out in the saying of the Mass that right as
the priest heaved up the Host there came a beam redder
than any rose and smote upon it, and then it was
changed bodily into the shape and   fashion of a Child
having his arms stretched forth, as he had been nailed
upon the Tree.*

—Old Romance.

S o far things were going very well indeed.
The night was thick and black and cloudy,
and the German force had come three-quarters of
their way or more without an alarm. There was no
challenge from the English lines; and indeed the
English were being kept busy by a high shellfire on
their front. This had been the German plan; and it
was coming off admirably. Nobody thought that
there was any danger on the left; and so the
Prussians, writhing on their stomachs over the
ploughed field, were drawing nearer and nearer to
the wood. Once there they could establish
themselves comfortably and securely during what
remained of the night; and at dawn the English
left would be hopelessly enfiladed—and there
would be another of those movements which
people who really understand military matters call
"readjustments of our line."

The noise made by the men creeping and
crawling over the fields was drowned by the
cannonade, from the English side as well as the
German. On the English centre and right things

were indeed very brisk; the big guns were thundering and shrieking and roaring, the machine-guns were keeping up the very devil's racket; the flares and illuminating shells were as good as the Crystal Palace in the old days, as the soldiers said to one another. All this had been thought of and thought out on the other side. The German force was beautifully organized. The men who crept nearer and nearer to the wood carried quite a number of machine guns in bits on their backs; others of them had small bags full of sand; yet others big bags that were empty. When the wood was reached the sand from the small bags was to be emptied into the big bags; the machine-gun parts were to be put together, the guns mounted behind the sandbag redoubt, and then, as Major Von und Zu pleasantly observed, "the English pigs shall to gehenna-fire quickly come."

The major was so well pleased with the way things had gone that he permitted himself a very low and guttural chuckle; in another ten minutes success would be assured. He half turned his head round to whisper a caution about some detail of the sandbag business to the big sergeant major, Karl Heinz, who was crawling just behind him. At that instant Karl Heinz leapt into the air with a scream that rent through the night and through all the roaring of the artillery. He cried in a terrible voice, "The Glory of the Lord!" and plunged and pitched forward, stone dead. They said that his face as he stood up there and cried aloud was as if it had been seen through a sheet of flame.

"They" were one or two out of the few who got

back to the German lines. Most of the Prussians stayed in the ploughed field. Karl Heinz's scream had frozen the blood of the English soldiers, but it had also ruined the major's plans. He and his men, caught all unready, clumsy with the burdens that they carried, were shot to pieces; hardly a score of them returned. The rest of the force were attended to by an English burying party. According to custom the dead men were searched before they were buried, and some singular relies of the campaign were found upon them, but nothing so singular as Karl Heinz's diary.

He had been keeping it for some time. It began with entries about bread and sausage and the ordinary incidents of the trenches; here and there Karl wrote about an old grandfather, and a big china pipe, and pinewoods and roast goose. Then the diarist seemed to get fidgety about his health. Thus:

April 17. Annoyed for some days by murmuring sounds in my head. I trust I shall not become deaf, like my departed uncle Christopher.

April 20. The noise in my head grows worse; it is a humming sound. It distracts me; twice I have failed to hear the captain and have been reprimanded.

April 22. So bad is my head that I go to see the doctor. He speaks of tinnitus, and gives me an inhaling apparatus that shall reach, he says, the middle ear.

April 25. The apparatus is of no use. The sound is now become like the booming of a great church bell. It reminds me of the bell at St. Lambart on that terrible day of last August.

April 26. I could swear that it is the bell of St. Lambart that I hear all the time. They rang it as the procession came out of the church.

The man's writing, at first firm enough, begins to straggle unevenly over the page at this point. The entries show that he became convinced that he heard the bell of St. Lambart's Church ringing, though (as he knew better than most men) there had been no bell and no church at St. Lambart's since the summer of 1914. There was no village either—the whole place was a rubbish-heap.

Then the unfortunate Karl Heinz was beset with other troubles.

May 2. I fear I am becoming ill. To-day Joseph Kleist, who is next to me in the trench, asked me why I jerked my head to the right so constantly. I told him to hold his tongue; but this shows that I am noticed. I keep fancying that there is something white just beyond the range of my sight on the right hand.

May 3. This whiteness is now quite clear, and in front of me. All this day it has slowly passed before me. I asked Joseph Kleist if he saw a piece of newspaper just beyond the trench. He stared at me solemnly—he is a stupid fool—and said, "There is no paper."

May 4. It looks like a white robe. There was a strong smell of incense today in the trench. No one seemed to notice it. There is decidedly a white robe, and I think I can see feet, passing very slowly before me at this moment while I write.

There is no space here for continuous extracts from Karl Heinz's diary. But to condense with severity, it would seem that he slowly gathered about himself a complete set of sensory hallucinations. First the auditory hallucination of the sound of a bell, which the doctor called tinnitus. Then a patch of white growing into a white robe, then the smell of incense. At last he lived in two worlds. He saw his trench, and the level before it, and the English lines; he talked with his comrades and obeyed orders, though with a certain difficulty; but he also heard the deep boom of St. Lambart's bell, and saw continually advancing towards him a white procession of little children, led by a boy who was swinging a censer. There is one extraordinary entry: "But in August those children carried no lilies; now they have lilies in their hands. Why should they have lilies?"

It is interesting to note the transition over the borderline. After May 2 there is no reference in the diary to bodily illness, with two notable exceptions. Up to and including that date the sergeant knows that he is suffering from illusions; after that he accepts his hallucinations as actualities. The man who cannot see what he sees and hear what he hears is a fool. So he writes: "I ask who is singing 'Ave Maria Stella.' That blockhead Friedrich Schumacher raises his crest and answers insolently that no one sings, since singing is strictly forbidden for the present."

A few days before the disastrous night expedition the last figure in the procession appeared to those sick eyes.

The old priest now comes in his golden robe, the two boys holding each side of it. He is looking just as he did when he died, save that when he walked in St. Lambart there was no shining round his head. But this is illusion and contrary to reason, since no one has a shining about his head. I must take some medicine.

Note here that Karl Heinz absolutely accepts the appearance of the martyred priest of St. Lambart as actual, while he thinks that the halo must be an illusion; and so he reverts again to his physical condition.

The priest held up both his hands, the diary states, "as if there were something between them. But there is a sort of cloud or dimness over this object, whatever it may be. My poor Aunt Kathie suffered much from her eyes in her old age."

One can guess what the priest of St. Lambart carried in his hands when he and the little children went out into the hot sunlight to implore mercy, while the great resounding bell of St. Lambart boomed over the plain. Karl Heinz knew what happened then; they said that it was he who killed the old priest and helped to crucify the little child against the church door. The baby was only three years old. He died calling piteously for "mummy" and "daddy."

And those who will may guess what Karl Heinz saw when the mist cleared from before the monstrance in the priest's hands. Then he shrieked and died.

The Dazzling Light

The new head covering is made of heavy steel, which has been specialty treated to increase its resisting power. The walls protecting the skull are particularly thick, and the weight of the helmet renders its use in open warfare out of the question. The rim is large, like that of the headpiece of Mambrino, and the soldier can at will either bring the helmet forward and protect his eyes or wear it so as to protect the base of the skull... Military experts admit that continuance of the present trench warfare may lead to those engaged in it, especially bombing parties and barbed-wire cutters, being more heavily armored than the knights, who fought at Bouvines and at Agincourt.

— The Times, July 22, 1915

T he war is already a fruitful mother of legends. Some people think that there are too many war legends, and a Croydon gentleman— or lady, I am not sure which—wrote to me quite recently telling me that a certain particular legend, which I will not specify, had become the "chief horror of the war." There may be something to be said for this point of view, but it strikes me as interesting that the old myth-making faculty has survived into these days, a relic of noble, far-off Homeric battles. And after all, what do we know? It does not do to be too sure that this, that, or the other hasn't happened and couldn't have happened.

What follows, at any rate, has no claim to be

considered either as legend or as myth. It is merely one of the odd circumstances of these times, and I have no doubt it can easily be "explained away." In fact, the rationalistic explanation of the whole thing is patent and on the surface. There is only one little difficulty, and that, I fancy, is by no means insuperable. In any case this one knot or tangle may be put down as a queer coincidence and nothing more.

Here, then, is the curiosity or oddity in question. A young fellow, whom we will call for avoidance of all identification Delamere Smith—he is now Lieutenant Delamere Smith—was spending his holidays on the coast of west South Wales at the beginning of the war. He was something or other not very important in the City, and in his leisure hours he smattered lightly and agreeably a little literature, a little art, a little antiquarianism. He liked the Italian primitives, he knew the difference between first, second, and third pointed, he had looked through Boutell's "Engraved Brasses." He had been heard indeed to speak with enthusiasm of the brasses of Sir Robert de Septvans and Sir Roger de Trumpington.

One morning—he thinks it must have been the morning of August 16, 1914—the sun shone so brightly into his room that he woke early, and the fancy took him that it would be fine to sit on the cliffs in the pure sunlight. So he dressed and went out, and climbed up Giltar Point, and sat there enjoying the sweet air and the radiance of the sea, and the sight of the fringe of creaming foam about the grey foundations of St. Margaret's Island. Then he looked beyond and gazed at the new white monastery on Caldy, and wondered who the architect was, and how he had contrived to make the group of buildings look exactly like the background of a mediaeval picture.

After about an hour of this and a couple of pipes, Smith confesses that he began to feel extremely drowsy. He was just wondering whether it would be pleasant to stretch himself out on the wild thyme that scented the high place and go to sleep till breakfast, when the mounting sun caught one of the monastery windows, and Smith stared sleepily at the darting flashing light till it dazzled him. Then he felt "queer." There was an odd sensation as if the top of his head were dilating and contracting, and then he says he had a sort of shock, something between a mild current of electricity and the sensation of putting one's hand into the ripple of a swift brook.

Now, what happened next Smith cannot describe at all clearly. He knew he was on Giltar, looking across the waves to Caldy; he heard all the while the hollow, booming tide in the caverns of the rocks far below him, And yet he saw, as if in a glass, a very different country—a level fenland cut by slow streams, by long avenues of trimmed trees.

"It looked," he says, "as if it ought to have been a lonely country, but it was swarming with men; they were thick as ants in an anthill. And they were all dressed in amour; that was the strange thing about it.

"I thought I was standing by what looked as if it had been a farmhouse; but it was all battered to bits, just a heap of ruins and rubbish. All that was left was one tall round chimney, shaped very much like the fifteenth-century chimneys in Pembrokeshire. And thousands and tens of thousands went marching by.

"They were all in amour, and in all sorts of amour. Some of them had overlapping tongues of bright metal fastened on their clothes, others were in chain mail from head to foot, others were in heavy plate amour.

"They wore helmets of all shapes and sorts and sizes. One regiment had steel caps with wide rims, something like the old barbers' basins. Another lot had knights' tilting helmets on, closed up so that you couldn't see their faces. Most of them wore metal gauntlets, either of steel rings or plates, and they had steel over their boots. A great many had things like battle-maces swinging by their sides, and all these fellows carried a sort of string of big metal balls round their waist. Then a dozen regiments went by, every man with a steel shield slung over his shoulder. The last to go by were cross-bowmen."

In fact, it appeared to Delamere Smith that he watched the passing of a host of men in medieval amour before him, and yet he knew—by the position of the sun and of a rosy cloud that was passing over the Worm's Head—that this vision, or whatever it was, only lasted a second or two. Then that slight sense of shock returned, and Smith returned to the contemplation of the physical phenomena of the Pembrokeshire coast—blue waves, grey St. Margaret's, and Caldy Abbey white in the sunlight.

It will be said, no doubt, and very likely with truth, that Smith fell asleep on Giltar, and mingled in a dream the thought of the great war just begun with his smatterings of mediaeval battle and arms and amour. The explanation seems tolerable enough.

But there is the one little difficulty. It has been said that Smith is now Lieutenant Smith. He got his commission last autumn, and went out in May. He happens to speak French rather well, and so he has become what is called, I believe, an officer of liaison, or some such term. Anyhow, he is often behind the French lines.

He was home on short leave last week, and said: "Ten days ago I was ordered to ———. I got there early in the morning, and had to wait a bit before I could see the General. I looked about me, and there on the left of us was a farm shelled into a heap of ruins, with one round chimney standing, shaped like the 'Flemish' chimneys in Pembrokeshire. And then the men in amour marched by, just as I had seen them—French regiments. The things like battle maces were bomb-throwers, and the metal balls round the men's waists were the bombs. They told me that the crossbows were used for bomb-shooting.

"The march I saw was part of a big movement; you will hear more of it before long."

The Bowmen And Other Noble Ghosts

By "The Londoner"

T here was a journalist—and the *Evening News* reader well knows the initials of his name—who lately sat down to write a story.

Of course his story had to be about the war; there are no other stories nowadays. And so he wrote of English soldiers who, in the dusk on a field of France, faced the sullen mass of the oncoming Huns. They were few against fearful odds, but, as they sent the breech-bolt home and aimed and fired, they became aware that others fought beside them. Down the air came cries to St. George and twanging of the bowstring; the old bowmen of England had risen at England's need from their graves in that French earth and were fighting for England.

He said that he made up that story by himself, that he sat down and wrote it out of his head. But others knew better. It must really have happened. There was, I remember, a clergyman of good credit who told him that he was clean mistaken; the archers had really and truly risen up to fight for England: the tale was all up and down the front.

For my part I had thought that he wrote out of his head; I had seen him at the detestable job of doing it. I myself have hated this business of writing ever since I found out that it was not so easy as it looks, and I can always spare a little sympathy for a man who is driving a pen to the task of putting words in their right places. Yet the clergyman persuaded me at last. Who am I that I should doubt the faith of a clerk in holy orders? It must have happened. Those archers fought for us, and the grey-goose feather has flown once again in English battle.

Since that day I look eagerly for the ghosts who must be taking their share in this world war. Never since the world began was such a war as this: surely Marlborough and the Duke, Talbot and Harry of Monmouth, and many another shadowy captain must be riding among our horsemen. The old gods of war are wakened by this loud clamor of the guns.

All the lands are astir. It is not enough that Asia should be humming like an angry hive and the far islands in arms, Australia sending her young men and Canada making herself a camp. When we talk over the war news, we call up ancient names: we debate how Rome stands and what is the matter with Greece.

As for Greece, I have ceased to talk of her. If I wanted to say anything about Greece I should get down the Poetry Book and quote Lord Byron's fine old ranting verse. "The mountains look on Marathon—and Marathon looks on the sea." But "standing on the Persians' grave" Greece seems in the same humor that made Lord Byron give her up as a hopelessly flabby country.

"'Tis Greece, but living Greece no more" is as true as ever it was. That last telegram of the Kaiser must have done its soothing work. You remember how it ran: the Kaiser was too busy to make up new phrases. He telegraphed to his sister the familiar Potsdam sentence: "Woe to those who dare to draw the sword against me." I am sure that I have heard that before. And he added—delightful and significant postscript!—"My compliments to Tino."

And Tino—King Constantine of the Hellenes — understood. He is in bed now with a very bad cold, and like to stay in bed until the weather be more settled. But before going to bed he was able to tell a journalist that Greece was going quietly on with her proper business; it was her mission to carry civilization to the world. Truly that was the mission of ancient Greece. What we get from Tino's modern Greece is not civilization but the little black currants for plum cake.

But Rome. Greece may be dead or in the currant trade. Rome is alive and immortal. Do not talk to me about Signor Giolitti, who is quite sure that the only things that matter in this new Italy, which is old Rome, are her commercial relations with Germany. Rome of the legions, our ancient mistress and conqueror, is alive today, and she cannot be for an ignoble peace. Here in my newspaper is the speech of a poet spoken in Rome to a shouting crowd: I will cut out the column and put it in the Poetry Book.

He calls to the living and to the dead: "I saw the fire of Vesta, O Romans, lit yesterday in the great steel works of Liguria, The fountain of Juturna, O Romans, I saw its water run to temper amour, to chill the drills that hollow out the bore of guns." This is poetry of the old Roman sort. I imagine that scene in Rome: the latest poet of Rome calling upon the Romans in the name of Vesta's holy fire, in the name of the springs at which the Great Twin Brethren washed their horses. I still believe in the power and the ancient charm of noble words. I do not think that Giolitti and the stockbrokers will keep old Rome off the old roads where the legions went.

Postscript

While this volume was passing through the press, Mr. Ralph Shirley, the Editor of "The Occult Review" called my attention to an article that is appearing in the August issue of his magazine, and was kind enough to let me see the advance proof sheets.

The article is called "The Angelic Leaders" It is written by Miss Phyllis Campbell. I have read it with great care.

Miss Campbell says that she was in France when the war broke out. She became a nurse, and while she was nursing the wounded she was informed that an English soldier wanted a "holy picture." She went to the man and found him to be a Lancashire Fusilier. He said that he was a Wesleyan Methodist, and asked "for a picture or medal (he didn't care which) of St. George ... because he had seen him on a white horse, leading the British at Vitry-le-Francois, when the Allies turned."

This statement was corroborated by a wounded R.F.A. man who was present. He saw a tall man with yellow hair, in golden amour, on a white horse, holding his sword up, and his mouth open as if he was saying, "Come on, boys! I'll put the kybosh on the devils." This figure was bareheaded —as appeared later from the testimony of other soldiers—and the R.F.A. man and the Fusilier knew that he was St. George, because he was exactly like the figure of St. George on the sovereigns. "Hadn't

they seen him with his sword on every 'quid'
they'd ever had?"

From further evidence it seemed that while the
English had seen the apparition of St. George
coming out of a "yellow mist" or "cloud of light,"
to the French had been vouchsafed visions of St.
Michael the Archangel and Joan of Arc. Miss
Campbell says: "Everybody has seen them who has
fought through from Mons to Ypres; they all agree
on them individually, and have no doubt at all as to
the final issue of their interference."

Such are the main points of the article as it
concerns the great legend of "The Angels of Mons."
I cannot say that the author has shaken my
incredulity—firstly, because the evidence is second-
hand. Miss Campbell is perhaps acquainted with
"Pickwick" and I would remind her of that famous
(and golden) ruling of Stareleigh, J.: to the effect
that you mustn't tell us what the soldier said; it's
not evidence. Miss Campbell has offended against
this rule, and she has not only told us what the
soldier said, but she has omitted to give us the
soldier's name and address.

If Miss Campbell proffered herself as a witness at
the Old Bailey and said, "John Doe is undoubtedly
guilty. A soldier I met told me that he had seen the
prisoner put his hand into an old gentleman's
pocket and take out a purse"—well, she would find
that the stout spirit of Mr. Justice Stareleigh still
survives in our judges.

The soldier must be produced. Before that is
done we are not technically aware that he exists at
all.

Then there are one or two points in the article itself which puzzle me. The Fusilier and the R.F.A. man had seen "St. George leading the British at Vitry-le-Francois, when the Allies turned." Thus the time of the apparition and the place of the apparition were firmly fixed in the two soldiers' minds.

Yet the very next paragraph in the article begins: "'Where was this?' I asked. But neither of them could tell." This is an odd circumstance. They knew, and yet they did not know; or, rather, they had forgotten a piece of information that they had themselves imparted a few seconds before.

Another point. The soldiers knew that the figure on the horse was St. George by his exact likeness to the figure of the saint on the English sovereign.

This, again, is odd. The apparition was of a bareheaded figure in golden amour. The St. George of the coinage is naked, except for a short cape flying from the shoulders, and a helmet. He is not bareheaded, and has no amour—save the piece on his head. I do not quite see how the soldiers were so certain as to the identity of the apparition.

Lastly, Miss Campbell declares that "everybody" who fought from Mons to Ypres saw the apparitions. If that be so, it is again odd that Nobody has come forward to testify at first hand to the most amazing event of his life. Many men have been back on leave from the front, we have many wounded in hospital, many soldiers have written letters home. And they have all combined, this great host, to keep silence as to the most wonderful of occurrences, the most inspiring assurance, the

surest omen of victory.
It may be so, but—

Arthur Machen